THE INNOCENTS

The Innocents

FRANCESCA SEGAL

HarperCollins Publishers Ltd

Published by HarperCollins Publishers Ltd

First Canadian edition

HarperCollins books may be purchased for educational, business, or
sales promotional use through our Special Markets Department.

HarperCollins Publishers Ltd
2 Bloor Street East, 20th Floor
Toronto, Ontario, Canada
M4W 1A8

www.harpercollins.ca

Library and Archives Canada Cataloguing in Publication
Segal, Francesca, 1980–
The innocents / Francesca Segal.

ISBN 978-1-44340-889-9

I. Title.
PS3619.E374I55 2012   813'.6   C2011-905759-X

Typeset in Bell MT by Palimpsest Book Production Limited,
Falkirk, Stirlingshire
Printed and bound in the United States
RRD 9 8 7 6 5 4 3 2 1

For my parents

In the rotation of crops there was a recognised season for wild oats; but they were not to be sown more than once.

– Edith Wharton,
The Age of Innocence

PART ONE

PART ONE

ONE

Adam had, for the occasion, bought a new suit. He had wavered between dandyish black, chalk-striped and double-breasted, and a more traditional two-button jacket in deep navy wool. After some consideration he had chosen the navy. It seemed a more appropriate suit for a man who was newly engaged.

And now he was in the suit and in synagogue, considering the stained-glass windows that painted a dappled light, pale rose and paler sapphire, on to the painted faces in the women's gallery. There were three of these windows – a red-flamed golden candelabra for Chanukah; a rainbow in a cobalt sky with white leaded doves swooping beneath its arch, and a third pane in which acid-green palm trees framed the two rounded silvery tablets of the Decalogue, an orange and lemon sunburst above them. Beneath this one sat Rachel Gilbert between her mother and her grandmother, looking intently at the pulpit. Adam, in turn, lowered his eyes from the windows and looked intently at Rachel.

They had been together since they were sixteen – twelve years last summer. For twelve years she had been his girlfriend and now, for a week, she had been his fiancée. And it all felt different. He could never have anticipated the shift, profound and inarticulable, that had taken place when he had seen the ring over which he had agonised winking on Rachel's slender finger. It was more than possession, more than union, more than love. It was absolute confidence. It was certainty, and a promise of certainty always.

Beside him Jasper Cohen stirred suddenly, shifting his bulk beneath the folds of his white prayer shawl. 'Rachel's cousin's here.' He nudged Adam in the ribs with a heavy elbow and nodded towards the balcony where the Gilbert women were ranged, coiffed and contemplative, in a mahogany pew. Rachel's mother Jaffa Gilbert sat closest to the rabbi, her cropped and hennaed hair hidden beneath a green hat, red-framed glasses on a red plastic chain resting on the broad velvet shelf of her bosom. Beside her sat Rachel herself demure in high-necked charcoal silk, looking down at her hands, her face half obscured by a sheet of tumbling dark hair. Rachel's grandmother Ziva Schneider was on her other side, peering at the text in her lap with a grimace of either concentration or scepticism. And then the cousin, Ellie Schneider.

'So?'

'You didn't tell me she was back from New York.'

'I didn't know you cared.'

'If there's going to be a half-naked model in *shul* then I care.' Jasper leaned over Adam, straining to see. 'God, she's tall. You'd need a stepladder to get up there.'

'Six foot.'

'Too tall for me. You could handle her.' Jasper flipped over a few pages of his prayer book without looking at them. 'When are we going to get hold of that porn film she was in?'

'Art house,' Adam hissed. Long inured to Jasper's indiscretion, he was nonetheless alarmed by it on this occasion. Whatever other rumours might be circulating about her, he did not want the congregation thinking his fiancée's cousin was a porn star.

Jasper snorted, loudly. Jasper did everything loudly. He was not secure enough to believe that anyone would pay him attention unless he made himself unavoidable.

'Arse house, maybe. I've seen clips on YouTube, mate, it's porn. We've got to order it.'

'No.'

'No it's not porn or no we shouldn't order it? Gideon said that they censored half an hour from the final version but you can still get it uncut in the States.'

'Gideon didn't say that, I said that. Rachel was upset about it.'

'Well either way, Columbia kicked her out for doing it so there's got to be something worth seeing.'

'Shh,' said Adam finally, frowning. He was not the only one, he noticed. Whispered conversation among the men in the back pews was in general permissible, encouraged even, if the content was engaging enough for the surrounding eavesdroppers. Football, in particular, was a much beloved topic. Services on the High Holidays were long; it was understood that one had to pass the time. But sustained discussions about porn during Kol Nidre – the beginning of Yom Kippur and a significant, spiritual incantation – was pushing lenience to its limit. The congregation were fasting until sunset tomorrow night; in the meantime they were meant to be atoning. Adam too had seen clips of Ellie Schneider's acting debut on the Internet; in one she was delivering a breathy and hypnotically rhythmic monologue to the camera, wearing only a stained Columbia University T-shirt while the rest of her was exposed and exploited by a menacing co-star. Synagogue was not a place in which he felt comfortable recalling it. Around them the *Al Chet* prayer continued. For the sin we have committed before you by improper thoughts. For the sin we have committed before you through speech. Pardon us, forgive us, atone for us.

Adam rejected the memory with some effort and instead focused on the women's gallery, hoping to catch Rachel's attention. She looked down at him and widened her eyes. From her expression he could see that she had a great deal to say and was desperate to say it – her cousin was embarrassing her; she could not believe that Ellie was in *shul* at all, let alone that the girl had come to Kol Nidre exposing skin from clavicle to navel, wearing a tuxedo jacket with nothing beneath it and black trousers – trousers! – that clung and shimmered as if she'd been dipped in crude oil. Adam needed little more than a glance to understand Rachel's signalling, for the subtle contractions of her lips and the arching of her dark brows were a language long mastered. He knew their vocabulary, and every expression of her lovely face. He did not see the appeal of unpredictable women. Rachel never surprised him and he considered it a testament to their intimacy that he could predict her reactions with complete confidence. Life, he knew, provided enough of the unexpected. Adam had perspective. A steady and loyal co-pilot was more important than whatever passing frisson might come with more spontaneous spirits. He smiled at her.

Outside the synagogue Adam waited for Rachel and her family. For late September it was warm, tenacious leaves still green and living on the oaks that stood like looming sentries along the edge of the empty car park. Tonight, people were leaving slowly, taking their time to fold prayer shawls, gather coats, greet friends. The fast decreed that there would be no supper; nothing at all, in fact, until the same time tomorrow evening when they would all be leaving synagogue once again, but at a more urgent pace. Tonight they would have to be sated with spiritual – or at least social – sustenance. Men and women were now reunited after the service and families reassembled, lingering on the steps and drifting out past Adam, calling goodbyes to one another into the hazy autumn darkness.

'Hi. Here again.'

The voice was American, low and close behind his shoulder. He turned to find Ellie Schneider winding a long grey scarf around her neck, an unlit cigarette already in one hand.

Until now Adam had had a clear image of Rachel's cousin in his mind assembled from magazines and the Internet – limbs of satin; champagne blonde hair; high cheekbones and high, pointed breasts. He knew about her other life beyond the page, of course. In reality the girl was a mess. But in photographs her pale skin was as smooth as poured cream, and the bright green eyes, Disney wide, evoked a fresh-faced innocence entirely at odds with the darkness he knew was behind them. And so the darkness was easy to ignore. She was related to his girlfriend and he had taken a proprietary interest.

For years, in his head, he had been establishing a relationship with Rachel's younger cousin – close, vaguely paternal, faintly flirtatious but always within the bounds of what was appropriate among old friends. She would confide in him about her antics and he would be fond and exasperated and offer her sage, avuncular advice. When he and Rachel married she would treat their home like her own and would turn to them for refuge, would stay with them (visits during which she might sometimes be glimpsed in her underwear – though, in Adam's defence, this was not usually the focal point of the daydream). They would help her turn around her troubled life. In the pub with Jasper and the boys, he discussed her New York life in a confident, possessive manner. Ellie's seedy glamour, such a contrast to her conventional cousin, nonetheless gave Rachel a certain edge. No one else had so notorious or so alluring a relative. The girls had been close in childhood and in the solitude of his own thoughts, Adam had appropriated this closeness. He was a friend and confidant. Now, he was forced to confront the reality that she was almost a perfect stranger.

The private image he'd constructed was now superimposed, ill-fitting, on to the girl who stood before him. Her eyes were the same extraordinary green, bright and clear and fixed on him with an expression of idle curiosity, but beneath the thick lashes were rings of grey and plum and lavender, as if she'd slept many nights in old make-up or perhaps simply never slept. Around her, the exposed heads of the community's departing women were sleek and blow-dried, neat as a pin in order to stand before God's judgement and each other's, but Ellie's hair was in a loose ponytail of over-bleached straw-blonde, and looked unbrushed. Her heavy, pouting lips were chapped. Beneath the gaping collar of her jacket, her gaunt frame seemed as flat-chested as a little boy and when she turned away for a moment, tugging her hair out from under her scarf, her profile revealed a deep shadow beneath a cheekbone that protruded like sharp flint. He hid his surprise and looked instead at the cigarette, hoping to convey to her that lighting it on Yom Kippur – while still in the grounds of the synagogue – would be flagrantly, extravagantly offensive. He did not want Rachel's parents to be embarrassed further.

'Where again?' he asked. Despite his inventions, he had not expected her to remember him.

'I met you here once, a long time ago. Jaffa brought me with her to pick up Rachel from Israel Tour. I was desperate to come, I'd missed her so much. I was playing on the climbing frame when the buses got in. Just there.' She nodded towards the other end of the car park and his eyes followed hers to the smooth, empty tarmac where years ago had stood a curved rack of low monkey bars and a shallow plastic slide. 'I worshipped her and I was just insanely jealous that summer. I just thought – anyway. You and Rachel got off the coach together, you were carrying her bag. I remember, it was the first time I'd noticed a boy doing that. And then she brought you over and introduced you to Jaffa and Lawrence. So I met you.'

'You were very little then.'

'Ten.'

'Good memory.'

She shrugged. 'You all seemed happy. That's rare enough to make an impression.'

At that moment Rachel's parents appeared behind her and he lost the chance to reply, though Ellie's comment had bothered him. He knew a lot of happy people here. He remembered the day that Ellie described as clearly as she did, not for the stern blonde ten-year-old who'd shaken his hand with the formality of a politician, but for Rachel – he had first met her on that youth group trip to Israel, and as their coach of sunburned teenagers had drawn into the car park he had asked her to be his girlfriend. And – he knew it seemed anachronistic, or simply unfashionable – but from the moment she'd smiled back, bashful and willing, he'd known that they would get married. She'd had such certainty, such a placid conviction in the essential goodness of the world and what it promised her. To Adam, raised by a mother who prepared with steely determination for the worst to happen immediately if not sooner, Rachel's unwavering, no-nonsense optimism had been an elixir. He hadn't known that he was allowed to expect a calm, happy life until Rachel had shown him that she anticipated nothing else. Her belief was such that there seemed no doubt she would have it; whoever shared that life with her would share that calm and happiness.

He'd loved her since that glorious month of freedom in Israel. The boys had pierced their ears, kneeling on blankets for Arab jewellery traders to shoot ill-advised gold studs through their lobes; Rachel and her friends had sat cross-legged on adjacent rugs while Ethiopian girls worked slim braids into their hair, the plaits then wrapped in bright cotton so that one or two worms of green and red stuck out stiffly from each ponytail. Their teenage rebellions that summer had been innocent and conventional and brief – the earrings had been removed at Heathrow; there had only ever been kissing and maybe, for a precocious couple, one hand in a bra. And Adam and Rachel had done neither of those things but instead had begun tentatively, in the final few days, to sit together on the bus. They were all happy then – Ellie was right. But they were happy now, too.

'Good, good, you found each other.'

Rachel's father Lawrence clapped Adam amiably on the back and then, overcome by emotion at the thought of the engagement as he had been intermittently all week, gripped him by the shoulders and held him at arm's length for a loving appraisal. He then enfolded him in a bear hug. Adam and Lawrence were the same height – six foot two – but Adam was broad-shouldered while Lawrence was thin and always slightly stooping, as if to avoid intimidating anyone with this impressively un-Jewish height. Yet still his bear hugs felt enveloping. The warmth of Lawrence's presence alone was enveloping. Proud to be tall, particularly among Ashkenazi men who tend to halt at around five nine, Adam had nonetheless been content to stop growing where he did. It would have felt wrong to stand taller than Lawrence.

Jaffa, small and wide where her husband was tall and slim, was frowning at Ellie's cigarette. 'Ellie, you can wait for that, no? Show respect.' She had removed the green hat to expose short hair home-dyed a deep wine purple, streaked with lighter aubergine shades where it had begun to fade with washing. It was a colour much favoured, for reasons Adam had never fathomed, by Israeli women of a certain age.

Ziva Schneider joined them in time to hear this remonstrance. 'You think,' she asked her daughter, 'that God finds it more respectful if she smokes on Kol Nidre around the corner?'

Jaffa pursed her lips in irritated silence, as her mother knew full well that it was not God's judgement that concerned her. She wanted to stand exultant in the car park as the crowds flooded from the synagogue, graciously accepting congratulations on the triumph of her daughter's engagement to Adam. She wanted to soak up *naches* like a sponge. Such a large assembly would not come together again until Rosh Hashanah the following year – this Yom Kippur she wanted to fire her news at huge clusters of rival mothers. She adored Adam, God only knew, but there had been other engagements recently, newer couples walking down the aisle; the names of girls younger than her daughter featured on the announcements pages of the *Jewish Chronicle*. There had been some concern that Adam would leave it 'too long'. But now it had happened, and Rachel would not yet be thirty at the wedding if they planned it quickly. Today of all days, Jaffa Gilbert did not want to concern herself with her niece's rebellion. She turned her considerable back to both Ziva and Ellie and caught Adam's face between plump hands.

'Ah, Adam, Adam. Rachel says she'll be just a little

while, *bubele*, she is talking to Brooke Goodman about something. You are breaking the fast with us tomorrow, yes?'

Adam nodded, his face still between Jaffa's palms through the first few motions. An assortment of rings – heavy silver and bright moulded plastic – scratched gently against his cheeks.

'I'll wait for Rachel, please go ahead.'

'I am going nowhere, I have a cab,' said Ziva, sitting down neatly on a low brick wall. 'I am an old lady, I will not walk back and no injunction says I must. I am eighty-eight. I am infirm. *Pikuach nefesh.* This morning I already call Addison Lee, and Ellie will come with me.'

'Infirm? *Eze meshugas? At lo chola, Ima!*'

'*Sha shtil,*' said Ziva, waving away Jaffa dismissively. At that moment a black Volkswagen drew up at the kerb and Ziva hopped lightly to her feet, disappearing into it before Jaffa could intervene. Ellie folded herself into the front seat and the car departed. Adam watched her go with curiosity.

'*Eze meshugas?*' Jaffa asked again, this time to herself, pouting and drawing her face further back into her chins. She made no further comment but the force with which she crossed her arms over her immense, velvet-clad breasts was sufficiently expressive. The engagement cast their family into the spotlight this Yom Kippur – absolute propriety was required beneath its glare. A look of anxiety crossed Lawrence's mild face as they departed, Jaffa muttering an outraged monologue in rapid Hebrew to her partially comprehending but entirely supportive husband. Lawrence was a straightforward man. He lived, exclusively and devotedly, for his wife and daughter. He would be happy again only when Jaffa's equilibrium was restored.

Adam sat down on the wall that Ziva and Ellie had just vacated, nodding greetings to the many familiar faces among the congregation. Mostly, these were the occupants of the crowded outer stratum of his world; people with whom his life had intersected at an earlier stage and who now resurfaced often enough for him to know a little of their lives, though he did nothing to seek out either the information or the subjects of it. Such was the way in Jewish north-west London – no one ever disappeared. Instead his contemporaries circled in its gravity, returning from college to rent houses in Hendon, or buy first flats in West Hampstead, held in orbit by the hot sun of the community. And during brief periods away – a year seconded to a law firm in Shanghai, for example, or a residency at an Edinburgh hospital – their parents were still in place and in contact, so that everyone's coordinates remained logged. It had only been at university that he had understood just how unusual it was that he could list the whereabouts of all of his nursery school classmates. He could say if they were married or fat or employed by the civil service. He knew, for the most part, their sexual histories. Unless from a very small village, his fellow students found it incomprehensible. Even in a small village, in fact, when people leave there is little expectation of return.

But tonight, on the eve of Yom Kippur, everyone was here – Hayley Pearl, who was Jasper's girlfriend's sister; Dan Kirsch, who had been in Adam and Jasper's Scout pack and had twice been on tennis camp with Rachel; Ari

Rosenbaum, whose brother had married a girl who'd gone out with Dan Kirsch. Adam smiled at each of them as they passed, but his eyes always returned to the steps of the synagogue, waiting to catch sight of his future wife.

TWO

'She must.'

'What, do it on purpose?'

'Yes, of course. You can't go to *shul* with your tits hanging out and not realise.'

'Adam, that's my cousin! And please don't use that word.' Rachel swatted at his forearm and then immediately patted it, somewhat anxiously, as if to undo the simulated violence of her rebuke. It made her unhappy to disapprove of him. 'Maybe in New York people are just less conservative at synagogue.'

'It's New York, Pumpkin, it's not the moon. How different can it be?'

'Well then I don't know. Everything about her's different from me.'

'That's true,' Adam said. 'Thank goodness.'

They were parking outside Ziva's house in Islington; as he turned to reverse into a space he squeezed her shoulder fondly. She was right, of course. Absolutely everything about her was different from her younger cousin. Ellie seemed restless and too worldly. Rachel liked what she knew and was content for everything to remain precisely as it was, though it would be unfair to say she was ignorant. That there were worlds and lives beyond theirs had not escaped her, but she was certain enough of her own place to be resolutely incurious about the knowledge that those worlds might offer. At sixteen, Adam had been able to see in her eyes the home she would make for him at fifty. Rachel knew who she was.

Their exteriors were equally at odds. Rachel was polished and pink with health, her dark hair sleek, her nails neat and Chanel-varnished. Ellie had looked slightly worn, he'd thought outside the synagogue, though she was only twenty-two; he'd noted the bitten nails and the angry red skin around them, had seen the shadows beneath her eyes. It had been months since Ellie had officially been expelled from the Creative Writing programme at Columbia University – if she had sleepless nights, it wasn't because she was studying.

An evening rain had begun, light and silent, insistent enough to pixelate the world through the windscreen until it blurred. Adam jumped out to open Rachel's door, holding his jacket aloft to shield her hair from the drizzle. Since the engagement he had found himself taking a particular pride in these small gestures of gallantry. She looked different to him now, no longer simply his girlfriend but the woman to whom he had promised his future. He felt the weight of his responsibilities towards her, long unspoken, now confirmed. A twenty-eight-year-old matriarch to future generations of Newmans.

He studied her now as she picked her way up the dark path to Ziva's front door, his jacket covering her head and held tightly beneath her chin like a wimple. Entirely unlike Ellie's long bones and sharp angles, Rachel was rounded and soft and had the same pneumatic breasts as her mother, cartoonishly large on her small frame and always strapped and scaffolded as high as she could cantilever them. These breasts had afforded her hours of backache and embarrassment, and afforded Adam just as many hours of pleasure. It was true that unless she was careful to emphasise her waist she could look a little dumpy. Loose clothes gave the misleading impression that her body thrust out equally far in all directions, a barrel all the way down to her bottom. But naked, they were magnificent. They had ripened into their current proportions only in the years after he and Rachel had got together – he could never have imagined that the size-eight floral bikini he'd admired from afar in Israel could have held such potential. But by the time she eventually undressed for him they were there, the first breasts he had ever touched. Even now he could imagine no better. Ellie looked like a boy when compared to her cousin. As he rang the doorbell he wondered, briefly, what get-up she'd be in this evening.

Ziva was alone, she informed them, but she had just made coffee and they were to help themselves to a little something. Many decades in London had not diminished a robust Austrian accent, and a faintly foreign grammar often shaped her speech despite a vocabulary – in what was her fifth language after German, Yiddish, French and Hebrew – wider than that of most native English speakers. Austria to Mandate Palestine; Israel to London – from Ziva to Jaffa to Rachel encompassed three generations, three accents, one typical Jewish family. When Adam and Rachel had children they would be the first born in the same country as their mother for nearly a century.

It had taken several visits before Adam had noticed that there were provisions in every room. As usual Ziva had set out a bowl of whipped cream on the coffee tray, though Adam had never seen anyone make use of it. Cut crystal bowls on paper doilies held sugared almonds; a long boat of dark coconut wood set permanent sail on the coffee table and was heaped with small dry chocolates sealed in individual sachets, of the type that came alongside aeroplane coffees. In a jar painted with green pears lived jellied fruits. Raisins gathered dust in a Waterford sugar bowl next to the telephone and on the dining-room sideboard, beside a tub of pistachios, were decanters filled with caustic plum and cherry brandies. Adam remembered the afternoon when Rachel had told him that her grandmother never fasted on Yom Kippur; instead it was the one day of the year when she baked, badly but doggedly, until stars pricked the sky and the fast was over. He remembered his sixteen-year-old outrage at the disrespect of it all – his sense of pious disapproval. And he remembered his shame years later when Ziva herself had explained with quiet dignity, 'I have fasted enough days in my lifetime.'

They now assembled in her sitting room, Ziva and Rachel perched on an enormous reproduction Chippendale sofa, mahogany-footed and upholstered in stripes of wine and mustard; Adam sat across from them on a black leather Bauhaus daybed entirely at odds with all the rest of the furniture, whose chrome legs had worn small tracks in the Persian rug beneath it.

Ziva reached for her saucer with difficulty but as Adam sat forward to hand it to her she dismissed him with a frown, exhaling through her teeth and trying again. Her granddaughters knew by now that Ziva would accept assistance only if she had first issued an order – unsolicited offers were grave insults and met with disdain. It was nothing, just a little stiffness when she had sat still too long, she insisted, and the cure was to move. Adam nonetheless found it extremely unsettling when he was not allowed to help.

'You think when I am alone I never pick up a teacup? I only sit?' Saucer in hand, she sat back in the deep sofa with satisfaction and looked from one to the other. 'So. Now you will tell me how you have been.'

'It's so lovely, Granny,' Rachel said. 'Everyone's been so lovely since we got engaged. All these people we barely know keep congratulating us, everyone seems to know already. We went to that party at Ethan and Brooke Goodman's house the other night and there must have been about a hundred people there, and it felt like every single one of them asked us over for dinner.'

'It is a pleasure to invite a new couple. There are not so many good things in life that people want to miss them. *Ach*, I forgot. Will you get the Sacher torte? It's on the table in the kitchen. And plates.'

'Oh, no thank you.' Rachel placed a protective hand over her stomach.

'Shh. Not for you, for Adam. You, I know, will

probably not eat again until the wedding. But I would also like a little something.'

Rachel blushed at this, prompting Adam to realise, as he retrieved the torte, how many slices of cake he had seen her refuse since their engagement. He was amused by the uncharacteristic development and intrigued to know the outcome; the many, many diets that she'd begun over the years had never yet resulted in her losing any weight. But he sensed that this one might be different.

'And the wedding will be when?' Ziva asked.

'We were thinking of next August,' Rachel said, looking across at Adam as she said this because, she knew, he had not been thinking of next August – he wanted to get married this December. But Rachel and her mother insisted that it took many months to plan a wedding, and it was hard to care about anything as much as Jaffa Gilbert, perpetually fervent, seemed to care about everything. Even without Jaffa's interference he would have capitulated to Rachel, he suspected, for these days he could refuse her nothing. She had never seemed so sweetly beautiful to him, and there was a new shyness in her dark eyes that stopped his heart. He looked up sometimes to see her regarding him with a mixture of strange fear and hope, and despite their many years together there was a freshness between them that came, he felt, from the sheer immensity of the vista on which they looked out together. Compared to the long lives that lay ahead, they had barely met. He felt very young at the thought of it yet this, he knew, was the true start of adult life. He smiled back, despite her rebellion.

'I will by August be dead. *Danke*,' Ziva added, accepting a plate from Adam.

'Granny!'

'But it could be true. Why so long?'

'Hear, hear,' said Adam, gratified to have found an ally.

'Weddings take ages. We need to find a hotel, I need a dress, there's flowers . . .'

'So we'll get married on a weeknight at synagogue and Ziva will throw the reception for us here, won't you?'

'I will do no such thing because my daughter will not allow it. You will have a whole hotel *geschichte*. But why not sooner?'

'The weather will be bad before then.'

'But I believe most hotels these days have roofs. A miraculous invention.'

'It's going to be in August, Granny, and God willing you'll be there.'

'Ha. God. For someone who does not exist He has caused me a great deal of trouble.'

Rachel, who chattered to God almost as often as to her mother, was opening her mouth to protest when Ziva continued, 'Anyway, Rachele, tell me about the Goodmans' party.'

'You said,' said Rachel, still faintly petulant, 'that you didn't want to go to it because it would be "a production".'

'Very true, I did, and it was no doubt a production. But it is a production about which, if you will oblige me, I would like very much to hear. He is a nice man, Ethan Goodman, he has in private done very considerate things.

I do not know why it is that he persists in throwing for every Tom, Dick and Harry these parties.'

'They're for charity,' Adam offered.

'They are for social advantage and showing off,' countered Ziva.

The Goodmans were something of an enigma. No one seemed to know how Ethan Goodman had made his money; even those who were also in finance were unable to account for it with any satisfaction. He and his wife Brooke had appeared from California rich and had since got richer after starting several private investment funds in Mayfair. Most of north-west London took no interest in the mechanics of their apparently unstoppable acquisition – of greater relevance was their immediate and unreserved involvement in the synagogue community, that they had been elected to boards and councils, had opened the ballroom of their Bishops Avenue mansion to any organisation or event that needed a large venue, and were almost professionally philanthropic. The Goodman Charitable Foundation was in the small print of every charity letterhead that Adam had ever seen. Brooke Goodman, a gym-honed blonde in her late forties whom Adam's mother admired as much for her triceps as for her generosity, once wrote a personal cheque for a million pounds when the appeal video at a rather low-key fundraising supper for Barnardo's made her cry, and Ethan had been seen paying two hundred thousand pounds in an Alzheimer's charity auction for a painting that he himself had donated. The Goodman ABS Fund was reported to be that rare thing – a safe, low-risk portfolio that had delivered consistently high returns. Ethan

Goodman now managed the assets of a few close friends and they had been, it was reported, greatly rewarded for their trust in him.

The doorbell rang. Adam rose to answer it.

'That is Ashish – will you give him please a pound,' Ziva called after him. Rachel's grandmother could not cook. Instead she took two buses to Golders Green every afternoon to eat lunch at the Jewish Care Survivors' group and, on the rare occasions when Jaffa hadn't cooked and delivered a roast chicken and a side of salmon for the week, subsisted entirely on takeaways.

Fishing out change from his pocket Adam opened the door, expecting to receive a warm plastic bag of foil-wrapped naan bread. Instead Ellie Schneider's hand was in his extended one and she was stepping over the threshold in vertiginous, thigh-high boots that she immediately began to remove, using Adam for balance. A minute black dog scampered in after her and emitted a rasping yap.

'Ellie.'

'Hey, cousin.'

A car beeped twice and she released him, turning to wave. Over her shoulder Adam saw a very old Morris Minor pulling away from the kerb, patches of rust visible on its lurid orange paintwork. The convertible roof was down, exposing the back of a head, bright Scandinavian blond, belonging to the man driving. The hand raised in farewell wore a thick gold wedding ring.

Adam watched the car disappearing around the corner and turned back to Ellie who said only, 'A friend. We've been shopping.'

Nothing followed this. Instead she sat down at the bottom of the stairs and began to massage her toes, exhaling with pleasure. The dog, two bulging eyes deep-set in a mop of long, silky fur, began to yelp and wheel around in circles. Its jerking hysteria reminded Adam of the whining mechanical hare at the dog races.

'Rocky, Rocky! Shh, baby. God, I shouldn't have worn those.'

'For many reasons.' Adam agreed, looking in disapproval at the long columns of black suede on the floor that had clung to her legs until moments ago. Thigh-high, all that set them apart from the classic arsenal of a street-walker were their heels – playful stacks of knotted, polished driftwood. But as soon as the words were out he regretted them. He was six years older than she after all, not sixty, and what she wore wasn't his business. It wasn't as if it was Rachel.

She looked up at him and said nothing, her eyes huge and expressionless, a clear, pale green. She was hunched over, one foot in each hand. Without the boots to distract him, he noticed that the sweater she was wearing was enormous and shapeless, faded black cashmere that hid her body, and her thumbs protruded from symmetrical holes in the woollen cuffs. Her socks were now visible and were blue and ankle-high, and printed with smiling white rabbits. He felt he'd been unkind.

'So, we're going to be cousins,' he said, softening his voice.

'Yup. *Mazel*. Welcome to the family.'

'Thank you.'

'Although you're more a part of it than I am, probably.

I think my aunt has been planning this wedding for about five years.'

Adam smiled. 'More like ten, I reckon.'

Ellie pulled her jumper down over her bare knees and drew her hands back into her sleeves. Rocky leapt up into the hammock of sweater across her lap. 'Weren't you worried about settling down so young?'

'No, I was just pleased to have it sorted.' And then realising this sounded unromantic he added, 'Rach is perfect.'

'Everything here's perfect,' said Ellie, making it sound like an affliction.

'Are you not happy to be back?'

'Just . . . culture shock. I'd forgotten what it was like here. It's a little overwhelming. Everyone's happy and the houses are beautiful and everyone's friends with everyone, and you grow up sweet and pretty and contented and settle down with a sweet pretty boy.' She looked at Adam. 'Perfect.'

'Nothing can really be perfect, there's no such thing.'

'No? Except Rachel, you just said.'

He was annoyed that she'd made him contradict himself. 'Settling and settling down aren't the same thing.'

'I said settling down. You said settling.'

'OK,' he said, stiffly. The intimation of compromise touched a nerve, as it was a fear of precisely this that had made him vacillate for so long over his proposal. Compromise was right, of course. But they had met so young, and in weaker moments he had worried that his lack of experience meant he ought not to trust his own judgement. Not until the end of university had he begun to realise that he'd grown up to be an attractive man; by then it had been too late for him to deploy this advantage to any real purpose. There was no answer; it had taken effort to set aside such nonsense until the certainty of their engagement had rendered speculation pointless.

'OK.' She rested her chin gently on the dog's silky head, but did not look away from Adam. Antagonism hung between them. Eventually she said, 'God, I'm tired.'

He relented. 'Shopping will do that to you. Going with Rachel is like an extreme sport, I'm always tempted to pack a Kendal Mint Cake.'

'Sweet that you go with her.' She closed her eyes.

'Are you all right?' She looked very pale; he crouched down to face her.

She nodded. She opened her eyes and he quickly stood up again hurriedly, feeling awkward.

'Just tired. I'm not a very accomplished sleeper.'

'Always or recently?'

She shrugged. 'Not sure. Just kind of a thing of mine. I can't remember the last time I slept a whole night, or easily. Sometimes it feels like never but I suppose that's not possible.'

'No. But the feeling of never must be horrible. Exhausting. Or isolating.' He stopped. He wasn't quite sure what else to say.

'Both exhausting and isolating, in fact. Exactly.'

'So now do you not sleep at all?' he asked, curious. 'What do you do all night?'

'Interesting question. What would you do?'

'I can't imagine,' he said, and then immediately wondered

why he'd said the very opposite of what he'd been thinking.

'Can't you? How very unimaginative you must be.' Her tone had changed; he sensed that he'd disappointed her.

'Come in and see Rachel. Your grandmother has ordered Indian, it should be here soon.'

'I'll come in a second, I need to get Rocky's eyedrops.'

She stood up with the tiny animal tucked under her arm like a handbag. Looming above him on the stairs she no longer looked vulnerable and had become again the remote model he'd seen across the synagogue – too much exposed skin and clever, knowing eyes. Her sweater had slipped down over her shoulder, and he was acutely aware that her bare legs were at the level of his gaze, peach-soft flesh seamed lightly with long muscle. For one, brief moment he felt an urge, vivid and intense, to reach out and slide a hand between her thighs.

He stepped back and turned away embarrassed, and suddenly infuriated. He had thought himself immune to what was, after all, only a cheap casing concealing an even cheaper mechanism and was troubled to find that he was not. He did not respect her, he told himself, and that ought to render her unattractive.

But however easily he might dismiss Ellie in the abstract, it was different now that she was nearby. His body had responded to the sight of hers, and what he thought of her ceased to matter because he had ceased, in her presence, to think. He had never before experienced anything quite like it. It felt pathetic to watch her walk up the stairs. Compromising.

She turned. 'Wait, Adam, I want us to talk. Will you come back soon?'

'Of course,' he said, wondering if he meant it. He could hear Ziva calling to them and he opened the door to the sitting room, longing for the reassurance of Rachel's hand in his.

THREE

'Is it really true that Rachel's cousin was actually in a porn film? Adam, it's mortifying.'

Adam was driving his mother Michelle home from an early dinner at a sushi restaurant in Chalk Farm. 'It was art house,' he corrected her. 'Don't think about it, everyone will forget it soon, I'm sure.' Michelle had met him with the news that two more boys from the Jewish Free School had been beaten up on their way home – one had a fractured cheekbone, the other was still in hospital but would make a full recovery. Over supper they had discussed other recent hate crimes and the rabbi's wife's prolapsed uterus, and Adam had been drawn into another lengthy analysis of why his sister Olivia might still be unmarried. Why, Michelle had interrogated, as if Adam might be personally responsible for his sister's perpetual spinsterhood, had she not yet settled down? Why did she feel no urgency? Why, his mother had demanded as he had looked down uncomfortably at his salmon roe, why did Olivia not feel the pressing diminution of her reproductive capacity? Adam welcomed this return to lighter topics, but he did not feel like discussing Ellie Schneider with his mother. Or anyone.

'Well, I don't know what the difference is. It must have been obscene to get her in such trouble.'

'She is in trouble,' said Adam, changing the radio station before his mother could object to the loud U2 that had started with the engine. 'She's troubled.'

'Of course I know she's troubled, it's terrible what she went through and such a little girl. I'm not sure there's any recovering from that, you know.' Michelle shook her head. 'Her mother was a lovely woman. Very beautiful and very, very funny. She was famously funny. It was all so awful. But Ellie can't be allowed to throw her life away because of it. I mean, goodness. What's being done for her?'

'I don't know. She's come home, which is a good sign. There's been this older man around for years, Rachel never knew much about him but thinks he's married, but she's pretty sure it's over now. So I guess things are improving.'

'Yes, Jaffa seemed reasonably positive about this visit. I hadn't heard about the married man. Goodness me, that really is appalling.'

'Hang on,' Adam said, feeling a sudden irritation. 'She's not married. If she's sleeping with a married man then surely he's the one at fault. He's the one with a wife.'

'Oh, but Adam, I'm sure she's terribly promiscuous that girl, and she looks predatory, don't you think?'

'Promiscuous doesn't mean the same thing as predatory.'

'Well it doesn't mean anything good.'

'Surely Ellie can sleep with whomever she likes, she doesn't owe anything to anyone. It's not our business.'

He did not normally expend energy contradicting his quietly formidable mother, but this had come out before he could stop himself, and with unexpected vehemence. Michelle was looking at him in surprise. Adam remained dimly aware of the hypocrisy lurking in the corner he defended – Rachel's innocence, and that blank sexual canvas on which he alone had daubed, was a tremendous part of her appeal. Had she half of the sexual history he'd imagined for her cousin, he wouldn't have even glanced in her direction. Still, he found himself going on. 'I mean, aren't women nowadays meant to be emancipated? If she wants to shag around—'

'Adam!'

'Sorry. Never mind. I'm sure she doesn't. And in any case, I'm sure Jaffa agrees with you, if that's any consolation.'

'I'm quite sure Jaffa's beside herself,' said Michelle firmly, flipping down the sun visor to check her neat bob of caramel hair in its mirror. Husbands were a sensitive topic for Michelle, who had been without one for twenty years but could say with pride that she had never once touched anyone else's.

At sixty she still had the light step and ramrod posture of a dancer, a compliment she had received so often that she now took it for granted and had almost come to believe in her own childhood history at the barre, though in reality she had none. Instead she ran many miles in the gym (though never on Hampstead Heath so as not to be seen in undignified Lycra) and ate very little.

This discipline extended to all areas. Raised by Michelle, Adam could fold hospital corners into a bed sheet like an army man, and had been drilled since childhood to be ten minutes early for everything. Almost always in a uniform of freshly dry-cleaned grey cashmere tracksuit and Scotchgarded new black Uggs, Michelle appeared flawlessly, resolutely self-contained. If she were not his mother Adam would have found her terrifying. As she was, he merely found her intimidating. The noisy chaos of Rachel's family had been foreign and wondrous to him, having known only Michelle's emotional and domestic tidiness.

They were approaching Michelle's house on Temple Fortune Lane but she gestured for him to keep driving. 'You can drop me at the corner of Hoop Lane.'

'Are you sure?'

'Yes, absolutely. It's not yet seven. I'm going to pop in and visit your father.'

In the Newman household, the responsibility for upholding Jewish tradition had always been shouldered by Adam's father Jacob, who had wanted nothing more than to transmit to his children a love of Jewish culture. When he'd gone, therefore, Michelle had had no choice but to pick up the slack, furious with him for his abandonment and channelling this fury into perfect Purim costumes and elaborate succah decoration. The cancer may not have been his fault, but for years his dying had been awfully hard to forgive. Olivia had been twelve, Adam eight; there would be bat and bar mitzvahs looming and huge, aching family gaps to fill. But if she was going to do it, as with everything, she would do it properly. The children would not miss a festival.

Jacob had guided her so clearly, shown her by such proud example his stance on culture, on practice, on tradition, and she knew how he would want her to raise his children – as active citizens in a congregation, individuals with a sense of family, of community responsibility and firm, proud Jewish identities. But for all that, Michelle reflected, he had talked to her so little about God. It is not a contradiction to be a Jew and an atheist – on the God question, Judaism might well be the broadest church of them all. There are rabbis (admittedly a rather small minority) who do not believe in Him. You can detest organised religion and still consider yourself Jewish. There is a place for you in a synagogue if you don't believe, if you do believe, if you're not sure, or if you only believe during brief moments of turbulence on aeroplanes or in the final five minutes of a football match in which only divine intervention might save you. But Jacob had never really told her where he stood. What would he think of her talking to him now that he was gone, for example? What had he thought of heaven, or of an afterlife? She didn't know and it was disorienting, for he had been her navigator in everything. At his grave now, it hurt most of all that she did not know whether Jacob, in whatever form his spirit might or might not currently take, would think her silly for perching at the side of Mr and Mrs Lefkowicz to tell him all about recent events on the synagogue charity committee. Or had he believed that it ended in death? That silence and eternal sleep came next, and she was merely confiding in the ether? So many questions she had not had time to ask him and this the most important one of all. And so she was left to keep a Jewish home, to visit the silent Hoop Lane Jewish Cemetery, and to wonder.

FOUR

The prospect of being alone was unappealing on a night when Adam had no desire to be reflective. There were several lines of thought that he was actively choosing to ignore, pushed into the darker cavities of his mind where he felt their menace but could not clearly see their shape. Seeing Rachel would blunt their fangs; would probably banish them completely, just as her deep, untroubled sleep beside him usually made his own release into unconsciousness seem possible. Rachel did not lie awake thinking of sudden death or other calamities. In childhood no one had told her that dying – don't be frightened – is just like falling asleep. Ever since then there had been nights when Adam could not quite let go, even when his eyes stung and his head throbbed with exhaustion. But now he would lie beside Rachel and force himself to breathe to the rhythms of her breath. He would focus on this rise and fall, the warm curve of her back pressed tight against his chest as if he might absorb her calm through his skin.

But as he'd arrived home from dropping off his mother, Rachel had called to say that she was staying at her own flat. Jasper's girlfriend Tanya was upset – Jasper had perpetrated some injustice that would be tedious or incomprehensible when it was later explained – requiring chocolate and ministrations and for Rachel to remain at home to provide them. Adam was disappointed.

He had been imagining her waiting for him as he drove home to Primrose Hill, curled up on the sofa with the television whispering in the corner, mobile wedged under her ear, magazine on her knees on top of a pile of marking, nail file in hand and his laptop open in front of her so that she could communicate in multimedia. Mission control. At the moment she was obsessed with a scandal unfolding in New York – a well-known art dealer named Marshall Bruce was in the throes of a brutal divorce after the *New York Post* had exposed his serial infidelities. Marshall Bruce was tall and silver-haired, and had the oblong jaw and oversized, dazzling grin of an American game show host. He was at least as big a celebrity as the contemporary artists whose work he sold and was known for his signature outfit of a cream suit and a tie in textured Nantucket red, and for having married a distant cousin of the Kennedys. He was a major Democratic Party donor and had, before the scandal, supposedly nursed political ambitions of his own.

One by one, young blondes were coming forward to give interviews and to reveal the 'real truth' about Marshall Bruce. He had sold Hockneys and Hirsts and had made his fortune; meanwhile he had sold himself as a family man who owed it all to his loving wife. His downfall had been this – the endless sound bites given over the years with compulsive frequency, in which he praised his wife and referred, smugly superior, to old-fashioned American family values. Rachel had been transfixed by the crumbling edifice that was Marshall Bruce and had been spending even more time than usual in Adam's living room. He had cable television and therefore the best American gossip channels.

The flat, empty hours of Sunday evening now stretched ahead and Adam had already pulled on a bleached and fraying pair of Arsenal tracksuit bottoms and collapsed with the remote control when it occurred to him that he had almost forgotten to send Rachel a song. Since he had proposed he had emailed her a song every evening, carefully chosen to capture the particular tenor of his feelings that day. A great deal of consideration and energy had gone into these selections. He had begun, elated, with 'You Are the Sunshine of My Life' by Stevie Wonder, and had subsequently included some more soulful, commitment-themed selections such as 'Everything I Do' by Bryan Adams, and 'I Will Always Love You' sung by Dolly Parton (he had rejected the Whitney Houston recording in order, he hoped, to reduce the cheesiness). A few days ago had been an edgier choice, with 'Lovesong' by The Cure. Yesterday he had woken up knowing, immediately, that he would send her 'Every Little Thing She Does Is Magic' by the Police. But the muse was not with him today – for the first time since he'd begun this series of romantic gestures it felt like a chore.

That Ellie could 'sleep with whomever she likes' and it not be anyone's business had been a disingenuous cry. It was merely what one was meant to say; he had come of age in the Nineties when girls around the country were downing celebratory pints and shagging indiscriminately to the encouraging librettos of Britpop – just as they had done for decades perhaps, only now believing that the zeitgeist had finally made it irreproachable. But even if they were right – and the tabloids of intervening years would suggest that they were not – sexual movements left North London's Jews unmoved. The double first of marriage and babies was still the ultimate accomplishment desired of one's twenties. He had been arguing only to grant women vague, hypothetical liberties, for Rachel herself had told him that she could never imagine even *wanting* to sleep with a man she didn't love. But then – growing up where she did, had she ever really had a choice but to feel that way? When Adele Summerstock had done 'everything but' with Dan Kirsch during his seventeenth birthday party (a scandalously precocious age in north-west London, and particularly shocking as they had not been going out for the essential six months that lent respectability to teenage sexual congress), it was not only their classmates and friends from synagogue who knew about it, but also the parents of their classmates and friends from synagogue. No one would ever admit to having confided such things in their mother and father and yet somehow information would leak between the generations, from child to parent to parent to child. Eventually, quietly, everyone in Hampstead Garden Suburb would know.

That night, Adele Summerstock's reputation had not fallen to its knees alongside her – it was not a society anywhere near that condemnatory. But years later when she married Ari Rosenbaum's older brother Anthony, it was probable that 90 per cent of her wedding guests knew the tale, and its unfortunate coda that, in her inebriation, she had subsequently brushed her teeth with Dan Kirsch's mother's toothbrush. It was likely that her new mother-in-law was mentally attempting to suppress these details even as Adele Summerstock was processing down the aisle. In such a climate, of course Rachel would not want anything other than that which she had.

She had been Adam's first too, of course. But later there had been that time at university – those six months in their second year, a glitch of which no one was permitted to speak – when they had broken up, and he had been a single man of twenty. During that dark period Rachel had twice kissed Ari Rosenbaum, with whom she had long ago slow-danced at several bar mitzvahs and had also kissed once before, at an 'evening in' watching *Pulp Fiction* at Gideon Press's house when they were all fifteen. But not even Ari had been granted access to her celebrated assets – only Adam had ever unhooked that hard-working brassiere, let alone removed the matching briefs. When they reunited she was wiser only in the ways of making Adam jealous (at school Ari had been in the first eleven, Adam only in the second). Adam had notched up a one-night stand and a three-month relationship with a girl named Kate Henderson. He was therefore a man of the world.

Rachel as an independent sexual being was a foreign idea to him and not one that she herself had ever encouraged. Instead, she was merely the central benefactress of his own erotic subsistence. But thinking about Ellie's choices not only made him momentarily envious, but also made it seem obvious that Rachel must have wondered. She might even have conjured it, have envisioned the way that her body would respond to another man, a different touch – although he could not believe she would do such a thing while she was actually in bed with him. She wouldn't.

The idea of anyone else with Rachel repelled him – but suddenly, without volition, he could hear her breath as other hands left their imprint on her hips, could see her head thrown back as someone else knelt and thrust. He felt a surge of jealousy so powerful he burned with it. It was sickening – and mesmerising. Who might she imagine? Was this how Rachel felt when she thought about him with Kate? Did she wonder how it had been between them? Kate had been nothing like Rachel – muscled and broad-shouldered from rowing, a little stocky perhaps, she'd had strength that had lent her unions with Adam the controlled violence of a wrestling match. Like Ellie she had been far from virginal – not overtly sexual or flirtatious but instead frank, comfortable in her own skin, easy with her own needs, and far more experienced than he had been. Adam had once arrived at a house party at which Kate had done a single shot of tequila, spun round and whispered to him what she wanted to do to him later, a long low whisper that had ended with him pushing her, he remembered, straight back out of the front door and stumbling with her back to her room and Rachel could never, ever know but later, the third time that night, Kate had let him, told him actually, to—

A song had come into his head, the lyrics aggressive and insistent. Quickly he typed in Akon's 'I Wanna Fuck You', clicked on 'purchase song' and then took the laptop into his bedroom, closing the door firmly behind him.

*   *   *

'Please don't forget that we've got the recital at Rupert and Georgina's this evening.' Michelle was on the phone and Adam had put on his headset. It came out of his desk drawer for conference calls and for his mother – both required lengthy periods on the telephone that otherwise made his neck hurt.

'I know, you emailed me about it yesterday.'

'No, I know you know, but just please don't get stuck at work, they're looking forward to congratulating you so please make sure today that Lawrence knows it's important that you leave on time. You've got to get all the way to Holland Park.'

Michelle believed that, because Adam worked for the firm at which Lawrence Gilbert was a founding partner, the two men spent their days in constant communication about their personal lives. In Michelle's mind, fuzzed with maternal pride, her son spent his days with his future father-in-law in some sort of cosy office-for-two, accessorised with stacks of important-looking ring binders and perhaps behind a smoked-glass door, a team like Holmes and Watson. The reality of thirty employees, of a long corridor carpeted in fading chartreuse and of private, if shabby, corner rooms for the partners, did not gel with her imaginings. Adam stifled the urge to attempt – yet again – to correct this impression, but then stopped. If he did have to work late, it would be helpful to be able to pass the blame on to Lawrence.

'OK. I'll see you there.'

'Lovely, darling. Make sure you wear a suit.'

'I'm wearing a suit! I'm at work.'

'Lovely, well keep it on.'

'I'll do my best. Oh, wait – Mum?'

'Yes?'

'I was thinking, maybe you could get Rupert and Georgina to invite Ellie Schneider this evening? Everyone's been a bit harsh since she arrived. It might be good for her to meet some people.'

There was a rare silence on the line. On the screen in front of him small white boxes overlapped as emails arrived and were ignored.

'Mum?'

'Mmm, yes, I was just thinking. It's a bit of a *chutzpah* to be honest, I mean, and God knows what the Sabahs will make of her, but it's a good thought, I should probably do it for Lawrence and Jaffa. Tell Lawrence I'll take care of it.'

FIVE

They were proceeding very slowly up the Sabahs' gravelled driveway as Rachel was wearing high heels for the occasion, a challenge that she did not attempt often enough to have mastered. Adam couldn't understand why she'd bothered – all evening he would have to be on the lookout for chairs or sideboards on which she could lean if he had to leave her alone. He suspected that it was related to her cousin's arrival. More than once recently he had come home to find Rachel inspecting herself from all angles, arching like a hooked fish and declaring woefully that she was too fat and too short. The fat was her usual complaint; the short was new.

As they approached the front door Rachel squeezed his arm and whispered, 'This house gets bigger every time we come here. I always forget how gorgeous it is.'

'I never forget how gorgeous you are.'

'You're so sweet. I'm not sure, though, are you really sure it's not too low-cut?'

Adam sighed. Preparing an outfit for this evening had preoccupied Rachel since the previous weekend – the dress she was wearing was one of three she'd bought. Anything connected with Rupert and Georgina Sabah made her nervous and finally she had announced that she was going shopping with Ellie who 'knows about clothes', and had indeed returned with the most flattering dress he'd ever seen her in. It was a little more revealing than any garment she'd have chosen alone, but only subtly so, an enhanced version of Rachel's own style rather than a grand deviation. 'I thought you were going to come back dressed like her,' Adam had said when she showed him, and Rachel had screamed with laughter at the very suggestion.

'Sorry, yes, I know it's fine, I'll stop going on about it,' she said now, cutting off his impatient reply, but nonetheless she patted the reassuringly voluminous pashmina that she had herself added to the outfit.

Rachel was not the only guest to consider the evening significant. Unlike the Goodmans, Rupert and Georgina Sabah opened their house only on rare occasions, and invitations to these events were rarer still. As with all of the Sabahs' entertaining the motivation for staging this recital was philanthropic, for Georgina would tolerate the intrusion of other people into her home only when it was for a good cause. But this she did with grace if not with great frequency, for she felt keenly her own privilege and the corresponding responsibility to share it. This time, a Russian string quartet was visiting from Israel under Rupert's patronage and, for a relatively modest charitable contribution, a select guest list was invited to a private concert. The charity was one of the Sabahs' own, a children's music school in Jerusalem dedicated to political as well as melodic harmonies, bringing Muslim and Jewish children together to play their instruments and to learn to play with each other. Next year, Georgina believed, the school orchestra would visit and perform at the Wigmore

Hall, hope-filled and concordant. Already a few of the students had been to rehearse at one another's houses.

That sustaining image of two dark little children bonding over hummus and Handel was all that could have induced the frail and retiring Georgina to stand as she was now, greeting a glossily jewelled and furred procession of guests and saying faintly but earnestly to them, over and over, 'So very good of you to come.' Rupert was nowhere to be seen.

'Look at the fireplace!' said Rachel, and Adam stifled the urge to hush her. She had been here before, had made the same exclamation before and in any case, alone he was far better at affecting nonchalance when he visited the Sabahs. This was ironic, considering that it was Rachel's grandmother Ziva through whom they were all connected. Newly married in 1946, Rupert and Georgina had toured the British Zone and in the Bergen-Belsen Displaced Persons Camp they had made substantial contributions to the makeshift kindergarten and orphanage. It was there that they had met Ziva, a young survivor, fierce and fearsome with pride and rage. She had been their translator, and she and Georgina had been devoted to one another ever since.

Behind Georgina loomed the fireplace in question, dove-grey Italian marble veined with pale chestnut, as tall and broad as the doorway of a ballroom. The grate in the cavern beneath it was stacked with thick logs between which yellow flames licked and wavered, and above its mantel hung a gilt-framed antique mirror of similar proportions, mounted too high to reflect anything but the faded burgundy silk walls of the grand hallway. In the crowd Adam saw Sarah London, mother of Dan and Lisa

London, talking earnestly to a man with a clipped blond beard who Adam believed was the father of someone he'd known from Sunday school. He was related, in some way Adam could not remember, to Rachel's flatmate, Tanya Pearl. Rachel waved to Natalie Cordova, the young rabbi's wife, who still looked alarmingly pregnant for a woman who'd given birth two months ago. She waved back and gestured that she would save them seats. Adam knew her from nursery school and had fond memories of her family poodle Morris; Rachel had been in the same Brownie pack as Natalie and also remembered Morris, though he had by then been an elderly dog. Two years ago Natalie had married Rabbi Cordova whom they both knew from Israel Tour, when he'd just been known as Ginger Josh.

The music room evoked the same awestruck reaction from Rachel as the fireplace. The ceiling was lower here and the lemon walls, glowing in the light of Louis XVI candle sconces, managed to evoke both grandeur and cosiness. The only electric bulbs in the room cast small, neat spotlights on the music stands; the flames of a hundred tapers were left to do the rest. The musicians sat poised, glancing at the Brahms on the pages before them and overseen, in turn, by the oil-painted eyes of Rupert Sabah's ancestors, framed and sightless behind them.

Ellie arrived at the beginning of the fourth movement, and the mounting agitation of the violin stirred the audience into even greater disapproval of her lateness. The doors were not at the back of the room but at the side and her slipping in was visible to absolutely everyone, except perhaps the far back corner. Tonight she had had the decency to cover herself up at least, but her tight jeans and brown leather jacket, aged and cracking at the elbows, made her even more incongruous amid this sea of sequins and velvet than her usual overexposure would have done. She had witnessed Rachel's own anxiety about what to wear this evening, Adam thought in irritation, so the dress code could not have escaped her attention. Sitting between his fiancée and his mother, he heard them inhale in shamed stereo. Ellie looked at no one, merely took the empty seat on the end of the second row and leaned forward slightly to listen. When the music and applause ended she slipped from her chair and crossed the room to the window, and as the audience gathered their coats he watched as she unlatched the French doors and let herself out into the garden. He turned to see Rachel and his mother disappearing into the hallway together deep in conversation and so stayed where he was between the rows of plush chairs, observing Ellie through the departing throng.

Open, the doors framed her, a cigarette between her lips, one hand shaking a gold lighter to encourage its disobedient flame. She stood in a circle of warm yellow light that spilled into the courtyard from the music room, but an icy November wind blew in around her and her hair whipped forwards. A gust of disapproval blew through the chamber with the cold air, and the candle flames guttered. Adam smiled in empathy at those murmuring their objections and crossed to greet her, and to tell her to close the doors.

'Having a fag?' he asked, needlessly.

'To Americans a fag is something else.'

'Aren't you an American?'

'Unclear. Americans would say I'm English.' She hugged her jacket closed and shivered.

Behind her rolled the Sabahs' garden in which lights were hidden beneath rows of heavy yews, the lawn disappearing like vast parklands into blackness. To the right, the courtyard was lined with topiary orange trees in pots, and closed except for a small passage that led round to the front of the house. Between these embodiments of opulent tradition and of nature mastered and manicured stood Ellie, belonging to neither.

'Well, you're definitely not English.'

She raised an eyebrow. 'So we have a dilemma.'

'We do.'

'So.' She accepted the jacket that Adam had removed and handed to her. 'What did I miss?'

'You mean, apart from the first, second and third movements? Not much. Rupert Sabah thanking us all for coming. A couple of rounds of tequila shots. The piñata. Chinese karaoke.'

'Ah, Ziva will be devastated she missed it. She does a great "Bohemian Rhapsody".'

Adam laughed. Moss had darkened the seams between the broad York flagstones; Ellie began to follow one of these cracks with deliberation, walking heel to toe like a tightrope walker. After a few steps she turned and began to retrace the same slow, careful steps.

'You know,' she reflected, 'I really think Ziva's my favourite person on the planet. I hadn't even known how much I'd missed her till I came back. Everything else is worth it just to spend some time with my grandmother again.'

'What sort of everything else?'

'Oh, you know. Family stuff. Reacclimatising.' She stopped pacing and pushed her hair back from her eyes. 'So how go the wedding plans?'

'No date yet. Rachel wants next August, but I'm pushing for sooner. And smaller.'

'Keen to lock things down.'

'Yes, that's a spectacularly unromantic way of putting it, but yes.'

'What's the difference if it's a few months more? Oh –' She laughed suddenly, exhaling smoke. 'God, it's not – I mean, no wonder. You've certainly waited long enough for the wedding night.'

Adam laughed with her but then stopped short when he realised, horrified, that she was serious. 'What?' he asked. '*What?*'

'What what?'

'You can't seriously think that.'

'Don't shout. People are looking at you and I know how much you all hate that here. Think what? That you're getting impatient, or that your love is still pure?'

'The second one. For God's sake.' He was freezing now although he still stood shielded in the doorway, and he wanted his jacket back. He had come outside because he'd pitied her the disapproval of the room, but she had managed within seconds to make him furious. 'Are you insane? It's not the bloody eighteenth century, I'm not some sort of mad retrogressive *frummer. . .*'

'Sorry. What do I know?'

'Something about something, surely. I mean, what tipped you off? My *peyot*? The clank of Rachel's chastity belt?'

'You're mixing metaphors like crazy, or religions at least. I'm sorry, really. It's just that everything here is so . . .' she paused, 'traditional. And so much of it surprises me, and I still don't really know anything about how things work, or at least I don't remember. I was surprised that you and Rach don't live together after dating so long, but when I asked her about it last weekend it was like I'd suggested, I don't know, a threesome or something. And so I had to guess why. And there was that time when you chucked her and went off *"wiz dat shiksa"* – this affected Middle Eastern accent was presumably her impression of Jaffa's outrage and he felt a sharp discomfort at the thought of the Gilbert family discussing his behaviour – 'and back then I thought that it might have been about sex.'

'I didn't chuck her! I just needed some spa— That's actually none of your business. And it's not that, thank you.' Once more he turned to leave her, hot with annoyance and aware that she had pushed him into sounding priggish and defensive, while she remained unmoved by his temper. He was stopped by his mother who had returned to pick up Rachel's pashmina for her, and came over to demand that he do something about the temperature.

'Adam, close those now, please. It's really far too cold, and all the candles are going to blow out.'

Michelle wore a navy silk scarf around her throat, pinned into its perfect whorl with a small gold scarab. She fingered this as she spoke, minutely adjusting its already precise arrangement. 'And you should take Rachel home soon, her shoes are hurting her.' She smiled briefly and unconvincingly into the garden towards Ellie and then returned to her beloved daughter-in-law elect with whom she had been gossiping before the satisfying glow of the immense fireplace. Adam reached up to bolt the left-hand door, leaving the right one open for Ellie.

'Thank you.' She put out her cigarette and came in holding the stub between her fingers, and then stepped back out into the garden. 'I'm going to go, actually. I'll go out this way so I don't disturb everyone.' She pointed at the path that led around from the courtyard to the driveway, and then disappeared down it into the shadows. An usher standing nearby looked quizzically at Adam, who shrugged in answer. Sure, close the doors. Leave her out there, I don't care. And then he remembered—

'You've got my jacket!'

From the darkness she called back, 'I'm in all tomorrow night, you can pick it up then.'

SIX

When her children were teenagers, Ziva Schneider took a position at the Israeli embassy in London and the family moved from Tel Aviv to Temple Fortune. The job was the only possible inducement for her to leave the country that had rescued her. Fresh, vibrant, healthy Israel had healed the body that Bergen-Belsen had almost destroyed; had woven muscle around fragile bone, and had cured her malnutrition with kibbutz ideology and sweet oranges. In the British internment camp in Haifa she had married the second Yosef, Yosef Schneider; the bridegroom a twenty-two-year-old widower, the bride a twenty-four-year-old widow. Both their families had been murdered in Belsen and they had married because they had not died. But that was not enough, in the end, to sustain the union. Like many of the marriages formed in the aftermath of the Holocaust it ended almost immediately, two human beings drawn together by the immensity of their renewed, impassioned life forces and pulled just as quickly apart by the immensity of their trauma. Ziva did not mind very much. The second Yosef had given her the children, Jaffa and Boaz – that was what life force was, after all, and the second Yosef himself was of very little consequence. The love of her life had been the first Yosef, and would now be Israel. Israel meant freedom from persecution. Israel meant Never Again. Israel had nourished her heart, breathed sunshine and hope and comradeship and youthful, optimistic socialism into her soul. She would leave its threatened borders only to represent it, with staunch pride, elsewhere. Rupert Sabah had helped them to find the house.

Ziva's daughter Jaffa had slipped into north-west London and Lawrence's waiting arms with such ease that it was as though she had cabled ahead to arrange it. But Ziva's beloved son Boaz was different. He had caused her trouble in Tel Aviv too; disappearing from school to go surfing at Hilton Beach with the Americans who rode glamorous longboards instead of the wide, cumbersome *hasakes* that the Israeli lifeguards had, or spending her week's shopping money on cigarette filters as an ingenious way to fix some damage to his surfboard. Boaz was bright, his teachers would write to Ziva, irritated, one of the brightest in the class, but he was also wilful and capricious and applied his considerable intelligence only to making excuses, or to surfing. And before they'd even moved there, Boaz had decided that there was nothing for him in London. One day, when he was older, he wanted to learn about balsa wood and fibreglass and polyester and polystyrene, and then he wanted to go back to Israel and make boards. But in the meantime he would not do A levels in England no matter what his mother said – he wanted to travel the world, to explore different countries, and to surf. He came to London, as commanded, but soon afterwards shouldered a rucksack and disappeared.

Ziva found it hard to be angry with him, though he

drove her wild with frustration – he was beautiful for one thing, green-eyed and dimpled and had such confidence, such easy manners, that anyone on whom he turned the warmth of his attention found themselves in total agreement with him, even if later they weren't entirely sure what it was they had agreed to. When he was there before her, charming and feckless, she felt indulgent. He was able and amiable and would, she felt certain, make something of himself one day. But when he was out of sight, no longer reassuring her with his sweet, empty promises, she was left to admit her disappointment, and found his wanderlust inexplicable. What was out there that was so marvellous anyway? Hurt and destruction and echoes of genocides, whether tragically tiny or vast and incomprehensible, were everywhere once you had learned to recognise their reverberations. You're in such a rush, she would ask him, to see the world? What you will see is that people are petty and cruel and can commit epic atrocities in their pettiness. You will see only that it is the same beneath all skin colours, the same in the heat of the tropics as it is below clear, frigid skies. Wherever there is more than one kind of man. Stay in London. Study. Study fibreglass, if you must. But study. Study something.

And then, from New York, Ziva got a postcard, a grainy photograph of a beryl green Statue of Liberty against a clear cornflower sky that had been divided into dotted segments and labelled in black ink with facts: *12 PERSONS CAN STAND IN TORCH* and *LENGTH OF NOSE 4 FT, 6 IN*. On the back, Boaz wrote to his mother that he'd met a girl named Jackie who had given up a place at Brandeis University and agreed to drive across the country with him. The real surprise was that she was so suitable – Jackie was a young and spirited beauty who had grown up playing in the Manhattan back room of her father's kosher bakery. They had married and would come home to live in London, he wrote again from Eureka, California, and the greatest shock of all was that they did. Boaz decided he would study engineering and Jackie, who had promised her father she would go back to college, instead made wedding cakes – elaborate sculptures in ivory butter-cream and painted fondant, and in each of her designs there was always a wreath of sugar ivy at the base. Like art, Jaffa would say, on the rare occasions she discussed her sister-in-law. Curling edible leaves so fine-veined and delicate that they were translucent. In Rachel's early memories Uncle Boaz was a source of sweets and rude jokes and family tension; he was loving and irresponsible, and after family Shabbat dinners – when he remembered to come – would play on the floor with Rachel to avoid sitting at the table with the adults. Jackie had changed him – he still brought forbidden sherbet Dip Dabs and candy watches for his niece but he wore a tie to dinner, and afterwards he sat with the grown-ups. If he was expected somewhere he would arrive there, and he would arrive there on time. He went to college as he was supposed to, and though it was a long way from the dream of designing surfboards still he persevered, encouraged and supported by his wife. When Rachel was six, Boaz and Jackie had baby Ellie – a grandchild so beautiful that Ziva instantly forgave her son his years of idleness. Ellie was achievement enough. Boaz got an apprenticeship with a company in Hertfordshire that made innovative fibreglass sliding doors.

All of them had been on holiday together in Israel when Jackie died, Ziva and Jaffa and Lawrence and Boaz and Jackie, all attending a wedding at which Rachel was a bridesmaid and eight-year-old Ellie was the flower girl. They had been to the party, where the cake had not been as delicate as Jackie's, but everyone had agreed that the girls had been enchanting, and it had happened early the following morning. Rachel had been babysitting, sunbathing by the side of the King David swimming pool while Ellie practised endless handstands and somersaults in the shallow end. And three streets away had been a bomb, on a belt, on a bus, and Jackie on a sun-soaked pedestrian crossing just behind it. Ellie had squealed delightedly at the sudden deep waves that had rippled across the glittering surface of the water; a moment later the sirens had begun.

In the years that followed it became clear that Boaz had not survived the attack. After a death it is understood that one must go on living for the children; after certain deaths, certain horrors, it is simply too much to ask. The family took care of Ellie as much as Boaz would allow them and could do no more, for he did not make it easy. Most of the time he was near catatonic, animated only when he considered that someone else was being too overtly maternal towards his daughter, when he would snarl with territorial rage like an animal. But most of the time he was simply passive. He seemed bewildered by the little girl, as if he couldn't quite remember who she was, or why she was beside him. Father and daughter were isolated, set apart from the world by the fascinating violence of their loss.

Ellie in those years was solemn and pliant. She made it easy for Boaz to neglect her. At Jackie's stone-setting eleven months after her death, Rachel had sobbed against Lawrence's chest until, during a moment between prayers, she looked up to see Ellie holding Jaffa's hand, mute and blank-eyed, and had been shamed into composure. The little knuckles on Ellie's hand were white, clutching Jaffa with all her strength. But her face had shown nothing beneath the glittering tracks of silent tears. Not once did she look towards the new grey marble headstone. When she stayed with the Gilberts they would find her awake at all hours reading comics, watching a low-murmuring television or studying the recipes in one of Jaffa's baking books with intense concentration. After the stone-setting Rachel never saw her cry.

Boaz stayed until an old friend from Israel offered him a job in New York. It was a position with a small software company; nothing he understood or was excited by. But it was Jackie's city, and father and daughter all but disappeared into its maw. Ziva was heartbroken. They all did as much as they could, flying to New York every holiday as Ellie's father would not bring her back to see them, nor allow her to visit without him. But when Ellie turned sixteen Boaz once again shouldered his rucksack. He couldn't care about his child, Ziva saw, because he was no longer capable of caring about anything at all.

Ellie had stayed in New York alone. She had refused to return to London, and there was nothing they could do. During those years Ziva and Jaffa had been beside themselves about the girl and twice Ziva had gone to visit, only for Ellie to disappear. 'We will lose her for ever if we chase her,' Ziva had said eventually, 'and I hope that she will come to us when she is ready.'

Ellie was an odd contradiction. With a modest allowance from her guilty father (who, to his small credit, always worked wherever he was in the world, even if it was hauling crabs in Thailand) combined with her far larger modelling income, she had finished high school and college and finally had begun graduate school at Columbia, all without support or advice, though both would have been forthcoming if only she had allowed the family to see her. In parallel, she had kept up the more conventional curriculum of drugs and drink and self-destruction that one expects of the abandoned, troubled teenager, cries for help that she would then refuse to accept. That she had now agreed to Ziva's offer of if not help then at least somewhere to stay for a while after the Columbia film debacle was seen by the family as proof that she was coming round. Healing, maybe. Jaffa would be the first to say that her brother had been weak and flighty, even before his heart had imploded. He was last heard of selling rose oil to tourists on Varanasi's Assi Ghat and had been silent now for years. But if no good could come for him there might yet be hope for the girl. Whatever life had dealt her, she was still only twenty-two. They wanted to rally round her, if she would let them.

Through Rachel's reports, which were concerned and censorious in extravagantly intensifying alternations, Adam knew a great deal about the surface of Ellie's life. But he wanted the truths beneath it. He thought of the frowning, serious little girl he had met in a synagogue car park only two years after the bombing, and the sardonic and resolutely unserious young woman who had returned from her exile, an unrepentant prodigal daughter. She had known tragedy and was coming through it, in her way, defiant and oddly admirable. It was compelling. He wanted to discover who she was, and retrieving the stolen jacket offered a good opportunity.

Ellie was no longer living with Ziva and had instead set up camp in Bethnal Green, in a flat belonging to a photographer friend who travelled a lot for work. A good friend, evidently, since he'd also left a BMW in her care.

Bethnal Green was not within Adam's usual locus of operations. It seemed like somewhere that should be 'South of the River', that vague designation that conveyed an essence rather than a geographical truth. Several places felt 'South of the River' when they were really north of it – Shoreditch, for example, and her naughty brother Hoxton, places that required satellite navigation and a faint concern over the fate of one's car during the visit. Like all places that were not contained within the bounds of either Central London or the N-prefixed postal districts, it was out of Adam's comfort zone.

By the time he arrived it was after ten. Jasper had kept him in the pub later than he'd planned, and then roadworks had sent him careening around the streets of Whitechapel, while the officious robot-woman who inhabited his GPS sang out instructions that were, because of the diversions, impossible to obey. The address he'd been given led him down a small dead-end street to a broad, iron-studded wooden gate that looked as if it concealed a driveway. But instead he found behind it a cobbled yard in which had been created a makeshift urban garden – a pair of park benches surrounded by carmine, terracotta-footed geraniums. A small red front door stood slightly ajar in the far corner. Beside it was an open window, and when he crossed the yard he could hear, through both door and window, a shower running.

'Hello?' he said, into these apertures.

'Hi, Adam, come in. One sec, I'm just washing this mask thing out of my hair – there's teabags in the fridge, and wine also. The whatever, the opener, is on top.' Her voice was distorted slightly by the falling water, echoing off tiles, but he stepped inside while she was still speaking and looked to his left, where he presumed the bathroom was. Ellie was leaning over the bath with her head under a hand shower. She smiled at him upside down.

'You're very trusting, leaving the front door open in London. Why are the teabags in the fridge?'

'Everything's in the fridge. Roaches.'

'Charming. I didn't know cockroaches took an interest in tea.'

'Well, these are British roaches.' She stood up, tossing her head back violently and there was a squawk from somewhere in the bathroom. Rocky shot out towards Adam, objecting to the spray of water from her hair. 'Hot Rock!' she said, sharply.

'Ah, I've never heard his full name before. Classy.' Adam bent to pick up the animal who had leapt with some effort on to an enormous silver-grey corduroy sofa, but who now leapt, yelping, straight off it again at the sight of his approaching hands. Adam sat down in his place.

The flat was a large single room in a converted stable block, the low ceiling striped with hot water pipes that had each been painted a bright primary colour. One wall, along which stainless-steel industrial units had been haphazardly collected, served as the kitchen – an oven, two glass-fronted bottle refrigerators with blinking red LCD displays and a wide freezer chest that doubled as a desk, with two large-screen computers side by side on top of it. Standard-issue bohemian sleeping arrangements were in evidence: a mattress lay on the floor in the far corner – but made up with incongruously decadent black satin sheets. This was where Rocky now cowered, shivering slightly, bulging onyx eyes fixed mistrustfully on Adam, his fur as sleek and black as the pillows on to which he was no doubt shedding.

Ellie had draped a pink towel around her neck and emerged into the room. She did not kiss Adam's cheeks in greeting as he would expect from the girls he knew. She merely smiled at him as she passed, and crossed to the kitchen where a bottle of red wine stood open on top of the oven. She poured it into two champagne flutes and returned.

'Theo only drinks champagne. It's these or teacups. Anyway, look. I'm sorry I pissed you off last night.'

'It's really OK. You didn't.'

'Well I did, but—'

'My masculine pride will recover. I'll drink some beer, pump some iron, go out bear trapping, the usual. Don't worry.'

'Ah, yes. Nothing like bear trapping to make a man feel like a man again.' She tilted her head and considered him with a serious expression. 'I can actually see you in fatigues.'

'It is quite funny that you thought that, though.'

'Yes, well, no need to rub it in. I get it – you and Rach are swinging from the chandeliers every night. Lucky girl. What do I know?' She sat down beside him on the sofa. 'So apropos of last night, I wanted to ask you for some advice.'

Adam accepted the over-filled glass she offered him and waited; more pressing was the curiosity to discover whether Ellie considered Rachel lucky for living this imaginary endless sexual marathon, or for sharing these exploits with him. He saw no satisfactory way of asking.

'I'm glad I've managed to get you to myself. I want to go native. I want you to tell me what I have to do to fit in whilst I'm here.'

Adam exhaled in surprise, and droplets of Zinfandel fountained from his glass down his front. That she had wanted to talk to him about something he had already guessed; after all, she had taken his jacket on purpose. But whatever it might have been, it was not this that he had expected. Specks of red began to bleed into wider stains on the breast of his shirt, and he swore.

Ellie laughed and handed him the damp towel from her shoulders. 'Surely it's not that amusing?'

'It's quite amusing. You couldn't be more different from everyone here.'

'I know,' she said, taking none of the compliment he had intended nor indeed any of the offence. Instead she leaned over the back of the sofa to retrieve her leather jacket from the floor and fished out her gold lighter and a small cigarette case.

'Is that you?' he asked, looking at the image printed on the case. She extracted a joint that had round chocolate-coloured spots visible on the rolling paper, clicked it shut and then handed it to him, shrugging.

'Yup. Why he thought I would want to look at myself an extra ten times a day . . .'

'Who?'

Whoever it was had obviously put some effort into the gift. The case was heavy gold, and the image of Ellie was perfectly reproduced in enamel. She stood at an open window; behind her an empty sky and a flat grey sea showing the isolation of a girl and her unseen photographer. It was a private snapshot, not something pulled from her portfolio.

'Oh, whatever.' She waved dismissively. The brown spots on her joint revealed themselves to be cartoon coconuts; the air was filling with the heady, cloying scents of coconut and pot.

He waited for further explanation and when none was forthcoming he asked, 'What did you think of Rupert and Georgina's recital?'

'Mmm, they seemed nice,' she said vaguely.

In north-west London the Sabahs were spoken of with the abstract, awestruck reverence reserved for royalty – to have tea with Rupert was as rare and lofty as to be invited to a shooting weekend at Balmoral. Ellie's relentlessly casual posturing was infuriating but surely, he thought, surely she must now be affecting it. It was all very well to remind him at every possible juncture that she knew the world while his was a limited and parochial sphere. But he knew enough to know that the Sabahs were impressive in any circle; ancestors of Georgina's had come over with William the Conqueror and an intimate, candlelit concert at the home of a family so patrician was noteworthy, at the very least. He was opening his mouth to accuse Ellie when she continued.

'So anyway, I've come back, and I think I might stay for a while. And if I'm going to be here then I want to stop putting Ziva in a position where she has to defend me all the time. Ziva's amazing and she deserves more from me now. I don't know how much longer she'll be around.'

'But surely Ziva more than anyone doesn't care how much you conform, or don't?'

'No, I know, she doesn't want to turn me into some perfect little North London clone' – Adam bristled on Rachel's behalf – 'but you know, my aunt's driven by this urge to conform, even if my grandmother's not. Jaffa feels this need to be safe and burrowed into the security of a community and she finds it genuinely traumatic when anything threatens that. That's the legacy, you know?' She brushed a thread of tobacco from her lap. 'The children of survivors are sort of ignored in terms of impact but I think that's part of their legacy. Creating a sense of security and of routine and a very tight circle of friends after a generation when the world turned upside down. So I don't mock it, honestly. It must feel vital to know where you'll be ten years next Tuesday and who you'll be there with and what you'll all be wearing because it's safe, and they all grew up with evidence that the world is anything but. Obviously my grandmother's generation, actually living through what they lived through, don't give a shit about napkin rings.

But for the kids they raised with all their baggage, suburbia feels safe. The trivia matters precisely because it's trivia. Being free to care about napkin rings is a luxury.'

'I hadn't thought about it.'

'Ziva and I talk about it a lot. It's one of the reasons why Jaffa cares so very much what people say about me, I think, and so she goes crazy about anything I do and Ziva takes the flak. And even Ziva must get exhausted defending me all the time. I want her to go to her lunches at Jewish Care and be able to boast to all her friends there about me for once.'

This was the longest and most sincere speech he'd heard Ellie make. Her observations sometimes made her sound as if she had been airlifted into north-west London on an anthropological mission, and each time Adam had taken offence at the implication that his world was so very, very foreign – but now he saw that she was protecting herself. She had set herself apart as a commentator before those whom she observed could exclude her with their condemnation. And she understood them, he thought, far better than they troubled to understand her.

'I don't have to agree with it all,' she continued, and despite his recent insight Adam immediately bridled once again at her implied criticism of anything, 'but if I'm going to be here, then I should try. So come on, tell me. You'll be my mentor. What do I have to do to become a Nice Jewish Girl?'

'Well, you're already Jewish so you're halfway there,' he said, but then realised he had misjudged his tone. She had tucked her knees beneath her and turned towards him unsmiling, awaiting his verdict.

He felt awkward. With Rachel he would have been on more familiar terrain – she was too sensitive for frankness when it was unpleasant, and he knew from years of painful experience and subsequent training that they were both safer when he shielded her with soothing platitudes. Of course the headmaster didn't mind that you missed the staff meeting, darling, he knows that everyone's human; that haircut is beautiful on you, not too puffy at all. It would become the truth. The headmaster would forget; the hair would grow. It did her no good in the meantime to become panic-stricken, which she invariably did. Thus he protected her with forthcoming and predictable reassurances, and he knew that she expected him to. But Ellie, he sensed, was asking for something different.

'OK. Well, I guess if you're specifically worried about what Jaffa's friends think then the most obvious thing is the way you dress,' he said, slowly. It struck him after he'd spoken that he had drawn attention to her bare flesh currently on display as they sat alone together. Her wet hair was dripping on to the enormous grey Rolling Stones T-shirt she wore; the seam around the neck had been torn so that it plunged deeply off one pale shoulder, and although the shirt reached almost to her knees she did not appear to have anything on underneath. The iconic red lips and fat, licking tongue had been rendered in sequins, and the sparkling bow of the top lip aligned almost perfectly with the neat swell of her breasts beneath it. He looked down steadily at his own hands.

She nodded, a serious expression on her face, as if she would like to be taking notes. 'OK. But just help me to understand – why does it matter?'

He hauled himself back to her question, with difficulty. There were always girls who wore short dresses;
whose nails were fake and who posted holiday photos
of themselves on Facebook, cowboy-hatted and barely
contained by tiny string bikinis. But theirs was a superficial daring, for everyone knew that these same girls
still lived with their parents, obeyed their beloved
daddies and, though they had been known to dance on
the odd nightclub table, on Friday nights could always
be found having Shabbat dinner at home. But a girl like
Ellie could not afford the provocative costumes. It was
asking the impossible for everyone to forget what they
knew of her past but if she wanted forgiveness, at least,
then she would be expected to show penitence. If nothing
else, it would be easier for him to concentrate around
her if she covered up.

'It's not really the clothes, I guess, it's more –' He wanted
to say that it was about reputation but that sounded so
antiquated. Still, she seemed, for once, not to be laughing
at him, and so he risked it: 'It's about reputation. Girls
here are very careful about, about knowing their worth,
I guess you could say. And people make mistakes, everyone
knows that, and it's fine that you – you made that film,
for example, or that you've dabbled with . . . substances,'
he said weakly, speaking into his glass to avoid looking at
either the oddly childish flavoured joint in her left hand
or the wine in her right, 'but I guess you want to show
everyone that you've left that stuff behind, and coming to
shul on Kol Nidre dressed demurely would have helped.'

The coconut scent was heady in his nostrils. She set her
glass on the floor and looked down, holding the joint to

the flame of her lighter. Then she said quietly, 'But what if I don't consider those things to be mistakes?'

'You've lived here before, it's not so very different from anywhere else,' he said, changing the subject in order to consider this question before he answered it.

'It's another planet. You're in it, so you can't see it. Those of us who were evicted can compare and contrast.'

'Evicted's a strong word, no?'

'Twice, actually. People couldn't really get past the cinematic horror of the way my mother died, and therefore we were essentially evicted from normal society. I mean, it's not like she died of a heart attack, or something normal. And then literally, when Boaz decided to run away to New York.'

'Couldn't you have moved in with Jaffa and Lawrence if you'd really wanted to be here?' he asked. 'I thought they wanted you to stay with them when your dad went to America.' She was right, of course. For most people who knew of her, the spectacular brutality of her mother's death was her defining characteristic. She could not escape it.

'Oh, and Rachel would really have loved that. I was enough of a pain in the ass being the charity-case first cousin without being foisted on her as a pseudo-sister. That would have gone down very, very badly, I suspect.'

'Is that entirely fair?'

He tried to ask this carefully, as her hostility had surprised him. The way Rachel told the story, she had been in as much torment as her parents – they had all desperately wanted Ellie to move in with them but had not felt able to suggest that she be separated from Boaz.

Whatever he was, after all, he was her father. Had it been up to Rachel, Adam had always believed, the Gilberts would have taken the little girl in a heartbeat.

'Which bit? Oh, I'm sure they'd have said I could move in with them if I'd begged, I do remember a few whispers about it, yes. But it was all crap. Rach didn't exactly push for me to live with them. I'm sure that's why Jaffa and Lawrence didn't ever even bring it up with Boaz, I don't think, in the end. But in any case, my inclination didn't really come into it.'

'Why?'

'Oh, Boaz was pretty formidable then. The more irrational he's being the more determined he is and, anyway, he never asked me.'

'But who was taking care of you?'

'To stop me making all those mistakes, you mean?'

He smiled. 'Or not mistakes then, if you say so. Choices.'

'You're mocking but I do say so. That's exactly what I'd have said. Those "mistakes" you catalogued, the film, whatever else I've done that you secretly disapprove of – I chose to do those things. No regrets.'

'I still think that you deserve someone to take care of you,' he said, after a moment.

'You know the one thing I can't stand?' she said suddenly, and he realised with horror that – out of nowhere – she had tears in her eyes. 'I can't stand the fact that everyone expects me to pretend all the time. Now I'm here Jaffa is really trying and Lawrence is – well, you know, he's such a good man. He's Lawrence. And they're relieved I'm here, I know that, and they want to be allowed to make up for all these things that they feel guilty about but everyone here wants me to leave everything behind and pretend to be something I'm not and abandon my whole life, or at the very least conceal my whole life, which is just so fucking lonely.'

She did not bury her face in her hands as Rachel might have done, nor collapse into emotional submission that might have permitted him to lean over and hold her. She did not even look at him. She sat rigid just as she had before, but for a single, mascara-grey tear that painted a faint track down her cheek. 'You know, they're all so worried about me all the time. I know that when they look at me they feel this . . . *pity*.' She spat the word. Her BlackBerry began to ring, a cheery calypso tinkling, and she silenced it. 'And there's all this guilt for the years that they feel they missed. But they did miss them, for whatever reasons, and they either want me to be perfect like Rachel or expect me to be broken and helpless in a way that would be more . . . palatable, I guess, or sympathetic. I'm not allowed another option. The idea that I don't want to collapse and weep about it, that I might want to live . . . I know that sounds melodramatic but you have to live, because people just disappear. They're there, and then they disappear. Gone. And you can never touch them again. I can never *tell* her anything again. You know?'

Adam nodded.

'You know . . .' She began to comb her fingers slowly through her hair, separating loose tangles that were now almost dry. 'I might not live the way that my family want and God knows I'm not Rachel. But I'm living and that should be enough. Call me a mess if you want but still, you know, I get through the day. Do what you've gotta do. I don't know about someone to look after me, I look after myself OK. But it would be . . .' she paused, 'nice, I suppose, if someone got it. Just a little. Just a part of it.'

The ache that Adam felt at that moment was surprising and acute. He hurt for her. With her self-possession and guarded irony, Ellie did not encourage anyone to remember what she had suffered; until now he had not really let himself imagine. And he felt ashamed – of himself, and of all of them. Minutes before he had been lecturing her pompously about her necklines, and she had shown him that he was ridiculous. She had come home to her family and was lonelier here than anywhere, and that could not be right.

'I'm lonely,' he said, suddenly.

She sighed, and the timbre of her sigh could have resonated with anything from exhaustion to despair. She let her head drop back on the arm of the sofa. Beside him he could see nothing but the curve of a white neck, light gleaming across her jutting collarbone; the shadowed hollow at the base of her throat. There was such exposure in the position that she seemed naked before him and the desire to touch her, which he had battled ever since she'd stood over him in Ziva's hallway, became unbearable. Whatever it was that she had awoken in him, it was both impossible and indefensible. He got up and crossed the small room, heading for anything that might save him.

'Adam—' she started, but her BlackBerry began to ring, a different song this time. Now it was Jay-Z in an Empire State of Mind, and she scrambled to her feet to answer it with more fervour than he had ever seen in her. Jay-Z was barely in his flow when she had snatched up the phone and breathed, 'Hi, baby,' in a voice that made Adam's stomach turn. It was the sight of his jacket hanging by the front door that galvanised him into action, and he was already holding it and striding out into the courtyard before he realised what he'd done. Rocky barked. Through the window Ellie was waving him back but that she did not call aloud to him made him all the more determined to leave. She shrugged and turned away, and as he passed between the moss-green benches he heard her saying, 'But how was the auction, baby?'

That evening Adam had no trouble choosing Rachel's song. 'She's the One' by Robbie Williams was a return to his previous form – a simple melody and an expression of the overwhelming relief that he had felt when, driving home from Bethnal Green, he reached King's Cross and the streets became familiar. He had regained his bearings then and had known for certain that he was heading in the right direction. Rachel was the one. But the knowledge hadn't stopped him from listening to the Jay-Z song that Ellie had saved on her phone in order to glean any clues that it might offer to her relationship with the mystery caller, nor could it erase the memory of her sinking into the sofa, head thrown back, the image of a vast, provoking tongue glittering across her chest. And it did not prevent him, an hour later, from returning to his computer laughing with delighted satisfaction that he had finally been able to capture the strains of a tune that had been tickling at the edges of his consciousness. He found it online, an American blues track called 'I'm Trying to Make London My Home' and sent the song, with its glorious harmonica riffs and simple, apposite lyrics, to Ellie. She might associate Manhattan with the men of her past life, but London was still up for the taking.

SEVEN

The next day the sky was pale November white, and the stiff grass of Hampstead Heath crunched frozen underfoot. The Heath was quiet, sparsely populated with dog walkers and the odd brave, chilly family. A magpie, ink black and striped with azure, scratched and hopped beneath the beeches.

'Thank you for the Robbie song, honey.' Rachel was waiting for him on Hampstead Way as he parked, with her parents' ancient retriever, Schnitzel, collapsed at her feet. 'She's the One' had been a good choice – he had awoken that morning to a long and grateful email. *They're always so different that I know how much thought you must put into choosing them*, she'd written, *and I'm marrying the sweetest man in the world.* He had made up for the ground he'd lost over the Akon 'I Wanna Fuck You' debacle – (the lines about bouncing titties had gone down particularly badly) – which she had found 'just so insulting, to be honest, Ads, did you press the wrong thing?' But today all was harmonious, and her face had lit up when she'd seen him. She and Schnitzel had bounded over to the car with an equal spring in their steps.

'Hey Pumpkin, hello Schnitzel. My two favourite girls.'

He patted Schnitzel's hollow blonde flank. 'Now you see, that's a real dog. Who wants one of those rats when you could have a proper animal?'

Rachel handed him the lead and slipped her arm through his and, pushing past the nettle bushes, they crossed into the Heath Extension. Once they were safely on the grass Adam unclipped the dog, who continued to plod along beside them as if still tethered. The appeal of gambolling had worn off; these days she was happy to meander along at the pace of her human companions.

'Did you see the attachment to my email?' Rachel asked.

'No, I read it on my phone. What was it?'

'Ads! I wanted you to tell me today if you liked it, it was a photo of the function rooms at the Berkeley. They've still got one Sunday slot free next August but they have to know tomorrow.'

'But I don't want to get married in August.'

He realised that this sounded petulant and he was about to neutralise it with a more playful statement, but then stopped himself. Until now, setting the date had been a point on which they teased one another. But he had begun to feel faintly emasculated by his own lack of control, and increasingly irritated that not Rachel, or Jaffa, or even his own mother had taken a second to listen to his thoughts on the subject. Whenever the wedding was discussed the women treated him as if he was a small child clamouring for adult attention, whose conversational contributions were to be indulged and then ignored.

They had reached the bridle path that bisected the Heath Extension, the chips of black bark beneath their feet rimed grey with frost. At the children's play area he stopped and leaned against its wooden fence. Schnitzel flopped to her belly beside him, already grateful for the pause.

'I don't want to wait that long,' he continued, rocking back and forth on his heels, 'I don't understand why planning a party has to take nearly a year,' and then knowing that the trivialising word 'party' might have put him under threat went on quickly, 'I want you to be my wife, Pumpkin, that's why I proposed to you in the first place. I want us to be married, I want us to live together, I want to get on with our life together as a married couple. And if it's the hotel and the guest list and the caterers that are holding it up and take all that time then why do we need that stuff?'

She cocked her head and regarded him for a moment before reaching out to touch his hand. 'We don't need that stuff, Ads, but we'll only do this once and isn't it more romantic to do it properly?'

'No!' He was shouting now, taking full advantage of their isolation. So often when they talked he had to be careful, unconsciously modulating his tones to avoid anyone overhearing. At Rachel's flat Tanya was usually padding around with her ears pricked for gossip, and in the restaurants they frequented Rachel was always convinced – not without reason – that they were likely to be sitting within earshot of someone they knew. To be able to raise his voice was a rare luxury. It felt energising.

'It's romantic to be married! Let's just do it, Rach. Come to Vegas with me and let's get married on New Year's Eve.' The idea had just come to him. It was mid-November already, and they could be married within six weeks. In six weeks there could be an end to the questions. In six weeks he could be safe.

Rachel had been looking on with concern as he'd got louder and louder, her eyes following his hands as he gesticulated as if, when they came to rest, she might be able to divine his mood from them as from a weathervane. But now she was giggling helplessly and collapsed against him, throwing her arms around his middle and squeezing affectionately. They were both insulated in large puffer jackets, his black, hers navy, and her arms barely reached around to hug him.

'What's so funny?' Adam pulled back, trying to see her expression. Her face had been pressed into his coat but she looked up, still laughing.

'Wouldn't that be amazing?' Her eyes gleamed with mischief. 'Can you imagine everyone's faces if we actually did that? Imagine telling my parents!'

Of course she thought he was joking. So convinced was she of the correct path for everything that she was not even aware there was an alternative, he thought bitterly, and felt suddenly despairing. Most of the future guests at his own future nuptials knew, with a fair degree of certainty, what they would be eating at the festivities (roast beef *au jus* with baby vegetables), knew the flowers they would be gazing at while they ate it (cream tea roses in square vases of matte white ceramic), knew the approximate attire of the other attendees, and knew that one of the three bands who performed at London's classier Jewish functions would provide the soundtrack. Why did they have to chug through every benchmark, every occasion, every ceremony as if their lives were one long snaking, predetermined conga line? He could almost see the endless procession of dancers ahead; could feel the sweating hands of those behind him weighing heavily on his shoulders as they bumped and shuffled through the steps. Surely it didn't have to be like this. Why shouldn't they escape from Hampstead Garden Suburb and marry somewhere else, just the two of them?

'I'm not joking!' he said impatiently. 'Let's go. Let's get away from everything here and be just the two of us, and come back married.'

Rachel was still laughing but his tone had confused her and she paused. 'You're not serious?'

'I'm completely serious.'

'Adam, we can't possibly do that.'

They had started walking again, idly, and Adam had picked up a long stick, dead but still pliable, that he was snapping at the naked blackberry bushes as if it were a schoolmaster's cane. It was too long and thin to throw for the dog but still Schnitzel was trotting beside him, fixedly following its movements. Adam began to mime his golf swings.

'Ads.' Rachel had stopped again and was watching him, her hands in her pockets. 'I do know that all this planning is stressful, and that nine more months seems like a long time to plan a, to plan a *party*,' they smiled at one another, 'but you're not being practical. Can you imagine if after everything my parents have done for me, and everything that Michelle has done for you, all that work and love and looking after you and Olivia since your dad died, and then we repaid them all by saying "sorry, you can't see your children get married, they want to do it in America on holiday"? Of course it's our wedding but think how many people would be hurt. And second, to be honest, some tacky, anonymous place in Las Vegas doesn't exactly sound very original anyway. I know it's different from a big Jewish wedding in London but isn't it just conforming to a different sort of tradition? The only difference is that it's not *our* tradition. But it's still the same wedding that lots and lots of other people have. It's not really anything new, is it?'

She had taken the lead from Adam's hand and clipped it to Schnitzel's collar, a sign that she intended to cross back to the road and that their walk – and possibly the conversation – was over. This meant going to Lawrence and Jaffa's house to return the dog and, though he and Rachel had planned to go straight back to his flat to spend a quiet Sunday alone together, someone was likely to be having tea at the Gilberts' who would steal at least two hours from them. He could see the day unfolding; Jaffa's potent coffee would be thrust into one hand, sugar-dusted cinnamon balls would circulate and the visitors, whoever they were, would peer over his shoulder as he was made to look at photographs of the Berkeley Hotel function rooms on Lawrence's laptop. This was all made more galling by the fact that Rachel was right. His suggestions for breaking the mould were as clichéd as the mould itself. That had stung.

But once they were married – which at that moment seemed as far away as the next millennium – he would have to find the means to show Rachel how vital it was that they open their eyes to the rest of the world, for however circumscribed his own horizons might be,

Rachel's were ten times more so. What form this intrepid exploration might take was not yet clear, only that they could, and must, attempt it. He had vague thoughts of travel, of literature and of inhabiting broader social circles, knowing all the while that these had always been available to him had he chosen to reach out for them, and in any case did not contain the essence of what it was he craved. But together, he and Rachel would begin to make real choices for themselves.

He watched her searching for the keys to her parents' house in the capacious depths of her navy blue tote, its leather handles chestnut-dark with age, the fourth or fifth of these identical bags that she had carried since they'd known one another. On Israel Tour, her modest bikini and disposable cameras had been stuffed into a brown one; a version in light caramel had followed, and then they had been either black or deep indigo ever since, more practical, she explained, for day-to-evening. Rachel liked what she knew and was faithful to it. And as Adam watched her walking beside him, swirling her dark hair into a knot and skewering the fat bun with a silver chopstick (bulk-bought at Boots in Brent Cross each time her stock of them ran low), a voice in his head whispered, would she even want her eyes opened?

The following afternoon Adam received an email from his sister. *Deal with mum*, it commanded. *I'm attempting to finish a paper, and she keeps calling me about recreational stimulants.*

Why is mum calling you for drugs? he replied, and almost immediately Olivia's swift fingers had returned,

She's not calling me for drugs, as you well know. She
appears to think that my pastoral role at St Hugh's
might have familiarised me with such matters,
although thankfully these things are left to the Dean.
Rachel's American cousin left a bag of contraband in
Jaffa's downstairs loo, and some person by the name
of Leslie Pearl found it during a dinner party. Gilberts
are understandably mortified. Mum seems to have
connected all of this with a Brahms recital at
Georgina and Rupert's house? Apparently the family
honour is somehow at stake – ours, not the Sabahs',
obviously. Mum is on the warpath. Whatever it is,
please make it stop. She says you're not answering her
messages but for pity's sake, answer them. I've got a
deadline.

Without his sister's plea, Adam would have been inclined
to continue ignoring his mother's repeated and unnecessary
Mayday signals. It was not uncommon for him to impose
a surreptitious communication ban – it had been a
wonderful moment when he discovered that his BlackBerry
possessed a function to send only specific callers to voice-
mail. These days, when he needed to retreat into work his
mother and Rachel were both simply diverted and he need
never know they'd tried. This afternoon he had a case
report to finish and felt enervated even by the thought of
his mother's outrage.

'Leslie and Linda Pearl!' was all that Michelle actually
said, after he had steeled himself to ring. His office-mate,
Matthew Findlay, had popped out to Itsu for a tub of miso

soup and a bag of wasabi peas; Adam had only a brief window in which he could close his door and allow his mother to vent. Matthew was not Jewish and therefore did not have a Jewish mother with whom he was required to communicate on an hourly basis.

'What about them?'

'Of all the people who had to find it, Leslie and Linda Pearl had to be round at the Gilberts' for dinner with that little so-and-so leaving her drugs around.'

'But it's not their daughter, Jaffa needn't be embarrassed. What was it she left?'

'Marijuana, I believe, but that's hardly the point. To have someone actually bringing that stuff into your house – and when they had people round! What does Lawrence say about it?'

Adam sighed. 'Funnily enough, Mum, he didn't mention it in our meeting this morning.'

'Well, ask him if he's all right. Adam, what possessed you to ask me to get her an invitation to the Sabahs' recital? Rupert and Georgina are going to think I've gone completely round the bend, bringing streetwalkers into their home.'

'She's hardly a streetwalker.'

'No, she's worse, she's a junker.'

'Junkie. But I'd hardly say that a bit of weed makes her—'

'Junkie shmunkie. How should I know? Funnily enough, Adam, I've never had to deal with this sort of thing before. I'm very upset,' she added, sounding upset.

'I'm sure the Sabahs are too posh to care about these things. They'll forgive you.'

'I'm quite sure they won't, and I only really know them through the charity committee and it was really a bit much for me to ask them, you know. Everyone saw that girl coming in late, looking like a homeless person, and everyone knows that I brought her. *We* brought her actually, because you're going to have to take some of the responsibility for this. And now thanks to Leslie and Linda Pearl and that awful Tanya who I'm sure has a thing for you, you know, Adam – I have no idea how Rachel has lived with her for so long, and I suppose if Jasper doesn't marry her soon she'll have to find another flatmate to be jealous of – but now that they all know about it the whole of North London is going to be saying that that cousin is still a piece of work and that she was probably smoking God knows what in the Sabahs' bathroom too.'

The diatribe continued until Adam was forced to invent an urgent conference call. He depressed the button leaving the receiver to his ear – he wanted to speak to Rachel and check that she was not also being buffeted through her Monday by high winds of family drama, and to find out whether Ellie was all right. As he was dialling Rachel's number, an email from Rupert Sabah appeared in his inbox. Lawrence was a trustee and legal advisor to one of the Sabahs' charitable foundations that assisted the dwindling, impoverished Jewish communities still remaining in the former Soviet Union. But communication from Rupert was a rare occurrence; cyber communication rarer still. Adam hung up and opened the email with trepidation.

With hope that you have read the minutes and
redrafted the contract in accord with their directions.

Lawrence insists that the work can be in no better hands than yours and I am quite certain of it.

Splendid family into which you are marrying. Ellie joined us for tea this afternoon and she's delightful, she reminds us both so very much of her extraordinary grandmother when we first knew her. Georgina and she have been revisiting some of the documents that we have kept from the days of the Jewish Relief Unit (I'm sure Ziva has told you a little of Georgina's work with that organisation and its actions in the British Zone after the war) and it is gratifying to see a young person take such interest in her history. We are both quite determined to find her a milieu while she's in London so that she might feel a little more settled. One rather suspects that she might be lonely here.

Please do fax the contract as soon as possible. R.S.

Ellie, it seemed, was quite capable of taking care of herself.

EIGHT

The following week Adam was in the office going through the post when Jasper called him. As he picked up the phone, he slipped a slim cardboard box into a drawer.

'It's arrived, mate, but we're going to have to watch it at yours,' said Jasper in greeting.

'What's arrived?'

'The film, you know, Ellie Schneider's film.'

'How do you know?'

'What do you mean, how do I know? I ordered it online, sent some money, someone put it in the post, it arrived, and I've just opened it. Dimwit. Anyway, I had to get it from the States and I haven't got a multi-region DVD player so I'm bringing it over to yours.'

Adam's confusion cleared, but he was still unsettled by the coincidence. His own copy had also just arrived, a guilty and clandestine purchase immediately identified by its American stamps and customs form. Ordering it to the office had been a risk but having it delivered to his flat would have been riskier with Rachel staying over so often, and he had taken the rather brilliant precaution (he thought) of sending it to himself as a gift, with a ribald message from a fictitious male friend. If the film made its way to Lawrence by some horrible error of the GGP post room, he would be able to blame it on his mischievous pal 'Tim'.

He had never wanted to watch it. He hadn't wanted it to exist. But despite the jumble of emotions that the film engendered whenever he thought of it, he now knew that he had to see what it contained. He did not, however, wish to see it in the company of Jasper Cohen.

'I haven't got a multi-region player either.'

'Yes you have, we watched those ripped copies of *Mad Men* on it last week. And Gideon's up for watching it with us, I just emailed him.'

'Oh,' said Adam. 'OK.' He could do no better now than to feign a packed schedule for the next week in the hope that Jasper would get bored waiting and screen it elsewhere. The idea of sitting there while his friends leered at Ellie – particularly performing the acts that were purportedly featured in the closing scenes – it was impossible. He wasn't sure he wanted to see it at all. He had enough images of Ellie alone, with him, with others, images that were bright and strong and cinematic, playing in constant rotation in his head.

There had been no contact from her since he'd walked out of her flat ten days before, clutching his jacket, and clutching vainly at the hope that he could leave his confusion behind in Bethnal Green. He had sent her the Sonny Boy Williamson song about London and had heard nothing back; her silence could be read either as annoyance that he'd left so abruptly, or relief that he'd done so. Or apathy perhaps, the most distasteful and probable of explanations. If she'd thought of him, after all, she could have responded to the song.

There was a knock and Lawrence's secretary Kristine came in, an incongruous splash of colour against the blond laminate door. She wore long skirts of panelled black and plum velvet, usually paired with a loose-necked silk blouse in primary colours, or with a tomato-red woollen cape if it was colder. She had worked for Lawrence for twenty years and in that time, Adam suspected, Lawrence had never summoned the courage to suggest that she represent his law firm in more conventional clothes, or indeed to confront her about anything else. Jaffa, for her part, positively encouraged Kristine's sartorial self-expression. It was thanks to Jaffa that Kristine now completed her outfits with banana-yellow plastic clogs, chosen for her in Israel long before their popularity had spread worldwide.

'Lawrence said if you could pop in and see him when you've got five minutes that would be grand.'

'Now?'

'If that works for you. He's free until the call starts.'

Adam smiled at her, keeping the phone pressed to his chest until she'd departed. Once the door closed he said, 'Mate, I've got to go.'

'I heard. Send my love to Lozza. Tell him to put in a good word for me with his niece.'

'Yup, whatever. Bye.'

Adam set off for Lawrence's office with a sense of apprehension. He was working for Lawrence on two cases and it could be about either of these or, and this was what he feared, it could be that Lawrence wanted to discuss the Gilberts' forthcoming family holiday to Eilat. Every Christmas Lawrence and Jaffa took Rachel to the south of Israel with a shifting group of friends and family, a tradition that had begun when Rachel had still been at nursery school and from which they saw no need to deviate. Lawrence never tired of hiking in the wadis of the Negev, blissful and enchanted by the desert and endearingly unfashionable in his GGP baseball cap, white sports socks and sandals. At other times he would herd his friends into a minivan to see the Roman fortress at Yotvata or tour the dairy farm on the kibbutz nearby, or the ancient mines at Timna where malachite was once mined and smelted into copper for demanding pharaohs, or he would disappear alone to pay a quiet visit to one of the small charitable projects in the region to which he contributed. There was a tiny desert saffron farm working to ease local unemployment whose profits went to fund parallel farming projects in the West Bank; an old people's home at which he and his friends subventioned the running of the organic garden, and a literacy programme set up for the local Bedouin community. At seven each evening Lawrence and Rachel would play tennis, while Jaffa marvelled at their exertions and continued to sit where she had been all day, gossiping on a sun lounger with one of a constant stream of visiting Israeli cousins when the sun had plunged too deep for her to read any longer.

Adam had gone with the Gilberts for the past six winters but this year he was resisting. It was his last Christmas before they married, after which a lifetime of family holidays would lie ahead. The office was remaining open, and he was determined to be in it. But he suspected that this summons would be another gentle attempt to importune him.

Lawrence gestured for him to close the door.

'I've just had a call from Ziva,' he started, and Adam was alerted by his having dispensed with niceties – Rachel's father usually began their exchanges at work with 'All going all right?' and a faint, proud smile at the affirmative response. He waited.

'I'm talking to you about this in confidence now. For the time being Jaffa doesn't know' – he looked sheepish, as such concealment was uncomfortable for a man so determinedly uxorious – 'and I think it best not to upset Rachel with it either at the moment. I don't want to put you in an awkward position but I think the fewer people involved . . .' He trailed off and wheeled backwards in his chair to retrieve from a shelf behind him a stiff, new Manila folder, unlabelled.

'Jaffa's niece is in trouble again,' he said when he faced Adam once more, setting the file down on the desk between them, 'and of course I told Ziva I'd deal with it. I think it requires a litigation specialist but in the meantime I'd appreciate your help with this, a bit of quiet research maybe.'

'Rachel said you were worried that Ellie had been smoking pot?' Adam offered, trying to help Lawrence, who was looking apprehensive, and seemed unable to come to the point. As soon as Lawrence had adopted this uncharacteristic cloak-and-dagger approach Adam had known that it was going to be about Ellie. His pulse had quickened, and he spoke aloud mostly to reassure himself that his voice was steady.

'I can't believe I'm saying this but that's not actually our primary concern right now. I assume you've heard all about this Marshall Bruce business – that schmuck art

dealer in New York with the divorce and the mistresses
. . .' Adam nodded. He had a premonition, screamingly
clear, of where this was going. His stomach contracted.

'Bruce's wife's legal team have obviously been moving
fast, as I suppose one would under the circumstances.
There's been a fourth name linked to his now, a –' Lawrence
glanced down to check some notes on a yellow pad before
him '– Cherry Ripe. That's actually her legal name, she
changed it when she turned eighteen from Maura Miller.
Her claims are much like the others – met in a bar, a few
hotel shenanigans, some smutty messages and emails
etcetera, except that she's also got evidence of substantial
monthly payments from Bruce over the last year or so.
For us, the more important consequence of the Ripe
woman's allegations is that the wife's legal team have since
uncovered more payments, monthly standing orders, to
another girl.' He looked at Adam over his glasses. 'You
see where this is leading.'

Adam nodded, fighting the constriction of his throat.
'How much was Ellie getting from him?'

Immediately Lawrence appeared to ease before him.
His shoulders fell and he exhaled heavily, a man unbur-
dened. He was relieved, it seemed, that the unpleasant
matter was out, that he had not actually had to say it
aloud. Now it was clear to Adam why Jaffa had not been
told – it would have tipped her over the edge. Jaffa in a
true rage was an awesome, terrible prospect and he could
imagine her reaction to this particular family disgrace,
standing in the kitchen in Rotherwick Road hurling curses
like a buxom, miniature Zeus casting murderous javelins
of lightning.

'Five thousand dollars a month for the last five and a half years. She's even paid tax on it – it was all declared.'

'Wait, five and a half years? So she was—'

'Sixteen. Yes. The age of consent in New York State is seventeen.'

'OK.' Adam looked down. 'OK. And how close is this to coming out? I mean, her name?'

'Not clear at this stage, but I would imagine it's only a matter of days. Here, have a look at these. It's all the allegations in the Bruce divorce case so far, some press clippings from the girls, a couple of the telephone transcripts with the first one and some text message exchanges, the financial statements that show the payments to Cherry whatsherface and Ellie and a whole stack of photographs of Ellie with him in various places. The only thing linking her with him for five and a half years is the standing order: the photographs are from various times but all within the last three years. Mrs Bruce got hold of them somehow once Ellie's name came up. So a lot of it will hinge on what Ellie herself says. The wife is *meshugah* with rage, obviously, and wants to absolutely destroy him. I can't say I blame her. If Ellie was—' He stopped. 'That poor, silly little girl. I wish I could say I thought it wasn't true but it was almost exactly the time that Boaz left and she was . . . anyway, look. If Ellie was having sexual relations with that bastard during the entire period of the financial arrangement then Bruce is in trouble of a completely different order – a messy divorce with seedy infidelities is obviously going to pale into insignificance when compared to a statutory rape claim. Third-degree rape in New York State between a minor and a man over twenty-one carries a sentence of up to four years – which is less than he deserves, quite frankly, although the state won't press charges if Ellie wants them dropped. So what she says matters. I don't want her anywhere near all this Bruce divorce business but if she admits she was underage then at least she can remain anonymous in the press reporting. Shall we go for a quick drink after work, once you've read through everything and had a think?'

'Of course. God, OK. I'll start as soon as the call finishes.' They were to be on the same lengthy conference call that afternoon – if Adam was lucky he could remain mostly silent and attempt to read Ellie's files during the more tedious points. But Lawrence looked at his watch and then shook his head. 'Forget the conference call, I'll fill you in. This is time-sensitive and I want you to get a handle on it as soon as possible. Take it back and get on with it now. I'll try to wind up around seven and come by for you. I hope we can help her.'

Back in his office, Adam placed the file on his desk slowly, deliberately, as if careful handing and surgical precision were required to prevent its noxious contents from spilling out. He sat before it with his mind spinning. Half-thoughts formed, rose and sank again, subsumed. There was nothing he could do with this; no justification that could make it other than it was. Until this latest development he had, he realised with discomfort, been weaving his own parallel version of Ellie's life, embroidered to flatter her. The heroine of his story had been naïve and had concealed it beneath postures of brazen knowing. But it turned out that she had actually sold – what had she sold? Something that was worth five thousand dollars a month to Marshall Bruce. That was not romantic. It was revolting.

But her vulnerability remained. She was so very, very vulnerable. And for what she had done – might still be doing, for all he knew – what a price there must be. He was overwhelmed by pity for her, and the pity replaced his revulsion as fast as it had come upon him. She was a broken thing, a marionette collapsed, with strings irreparably tangled so that its limbs jutted and swung. She needed somebody to free her and once the strings were cut, she would need someone to hold her steady. On impulse he reached into his desk drawer and threw the DVD, unopened, into the bin.

'Ready to go?' Lawrence's head appeared around Adam's door. Adam, who had been ready to go for the last half-hour and had been staring blankly at the slow-motion fireworks of his screensaver, stood up. The offending Manila file was already in his bag; its contents were imprinted upon his memory.

They walked together down Marylebone High Street to the Angel in the Fields, keeping pace with easy strides and in a comfortable silence; it was understood that they would begin only when settled into the restful quiet of a corner table and a calming pint. Despite all protestations Lawrence would order and pay, as he had since the days when Adam had been sixteen or seventeen, underage and baby-faced but puffed with pride that he was allowed, in this company, into a pub. He and his friends had been regularly and humiliatingly ejected from the Three Horseshoes on Hampstead High Street, alternating their attempts to penetrate that establishment with failed assaults on the King of Bohemia. But these same places allowed him to remain when he was with Rachel's father and Lawrence, understanding the tremendous significance of the outings, treated him like the man he felt he was (despite the smooth cheeks and flimsy fake ID) and would always buy him a drink. He never even suggested that it ought to be a half.

Adam had loved Rachel from the first, but what had cemented her pedestal in place, what had gilded it and raised her on it high above the reach of other girls, had been Lawrence. Lawrence had sealed the deal. Lawrence had never had a son and wanted one; Adam had had a father once, but it was long ago and it was hard to remember what it had felt like. Jacob was a vivid presence in a dog-eared packet of childhood memories, but they were circumscribed and increasingly abstracted from Adam's reality. Jacob was so very tangible in Adam's memory – snatching him high on to his shoulders and away from an Alsatian that had scared him in Golders Hill Park, or waiting at the school gates for him on Fridays when he finished work early in order to perform precisely this duty – but still, Jacob could not step out of these images. He could not advise his son on whether he ought to shave for the first time the night before his bar mitzvah (he had shaved, prematurely, and the photos showed plump cheeks scraped raw in places by an unlubricated blade, and a cut above his top lip that had scabbed like a cold sore), or help him decide which A levels to choose or teach him how to drive a car. Adam could only play the grainy films in his mind and watch his father perform these vignettes again and again, backwards and forwards, faster or slower, but always the same.

By the time Adam was sixteen, the position of male role model had long been vacant. He had not even known how much he'd longed for Lawrence until he'd found him; he only knew that when, to honour his eighteenth birthday Rachel's father bought him an Arsenal season ticket, the seat next to his own, it had been the happiest day of his life.

Adam had not gone straight from law school to work at GGP – it had not even been discussed. He had instead done what Lawrence advised and fulfilled a traditionally brutal training contract at one of the huge City firms, four six-month rotations in increasingly demanding fields. The unspoken expectation had remained unspoken until the day Rachel phoned her father with great excitement to tell him, 'They want to keep him on after the training contract, Daddy, isn't it brilliant?' and Lawrence, who had been biding his time until precisely this juncture, had invited Adam into his office for a chat. That had been almost four years ago.

'So.' Lawrence placed two pints of Foster's on the table, and a packet of crinkle-cut crisps, the roast beef and horse-radish flavour that he knew Adam liked. '*Nu?*'

'Bloody hell,' said Adam simply.

'I know.'

'Must be a bit weird for you, reading all that stuff about your niece. Weird is a bit of an understatement.'

'Well, we don't know if it's all true.'

Adam conceded this point, faintly self-conscious – he had not even considered this possibility. For a lawyer it was a rather basic oversight. When it came to Ellie his parameters seemed to skew; he knew so little of what to expect that he had become absolutely credulous. For some reason, the realisation that he could suspend his judgement, that conclusions were not yet necessary, was a soothing one.

'Yes, that's true. I'd presumed . . .'

'I know, me too.'

'I guess it's easy to when she's . . .' He trailed off.

'Yes, I know. But then I realised that we mustn't be unfair to the girl. At this stage his wife's got all the reasons in the world to want to make everything sound worse. She's already humiliated, and she'll want him absolutely destroyed. We need to hear Ellie's side and then see what we can do. Half of it might be rubbish. But I think the most crucial thing right now is that she stay close to us in London. I don't want her anywhere near New York for the time being.'

'Do you think it's going to be possible to keep her name out of it?'

'It's not looking good, is it?'

Adam shook his head. 'And whatever the truth is, the money was moving to her account, and the photos are there. She's been on at least three holidays with him. Obviously you can fake those, but who would bother?'

'No, you're absolutely right. The photos are real, I'm pretty sure. But someone needs to sit down and talk to her, and ask her all these questions.'

The word 'someone' was ominous. Adam waited.

Lawrence smiled and clapped him on the back. 'Adam, sonny, I've got a job for you.'

Adam smacked a palm to his forehead. 'Really? Must I?'

'You must,' said Lawrence firmly. He asked little of Adam and gave with quiet and immeasurable generosity; that Adam must do this for him was now unavoidable. 'I think it would just be too uncomfortable if I spoke to her. I've said I'll act for her, if I can, but I'm her uncle and to discuss all this –' he gestured vaguely about him, as if her sins hung in the air like hovering flies '– it's just not right. You're much closer to her age, and Rachel said that she thought you and Ellie were getting along well at the Sabahs' concert. You can talk to her, and then you and I can liaise on everything. But it has to be soon.'

'Sure.'

'Do you think you could get hold of her tonight? It's only eight. If you did then I could have an email drafted by the time New York wakes up tomorrow morning. It might not be such a bad idea.'

'Sure,' Adam said again. He was being assailed by conflicting impulses and it was not yet clear which would triumph – he was desperately certain that he did not want to go round to Ellie's and confront her about Marshall Bruce; the idea of sifting through compromising photographs with her in order to confirm their veracity was distinctly unappealing. But he was also certain that he did not want anyone else to put her through it, or to witness her discomfort. It was this thought that decided him and he reached into his pocket for his BlackBerry.

Lawrence stepped outside to phone Jaffa (he always checked whether she needed anything before he set off

– 98 –

home; on the rare evenings when he and Adam travelled home together he invariably alighted at Golders Green and set off for Sainsbury's instead of his house because 'Jaffa needs muscovado sugar' or some other random item that seemed an improbable requirement at 8p.m.). Adam tapped out an email to Ellie. *When can I see you? Soon – it's important. Are you OK?*

The reply was prompt, and equally brief. *Come tonight,* it said: *After that my week gets crazy.* No indication of whether she was OK or otherwise.

NINE

This time the red door was closed when he got there, and he could hear laughter behind it. It took several knocks before it opened. On top of her usual wisps of black and grey, Ellie was wearing a frilly pink apron that Adam suspected belonged to her absent host Theo; gingham with a candy-striped front pocket and 'Queen of the Kitchen' embroidered on it in glittery lilac stitching. The front sagged forwards and barely covered her chest, which was itself barely covered – beneath a pebble-grey cotton T-shirt the upward thrust of two prominent nipples was hard to ignore. Her hair was held back with a black strip of rolled silk and was standing in stiff and bleach-dried tangles, pillow-mussed or simply neglected. She had dark rings of smudged kohl around her eyes and an air of industry about her.

'Come in, we're making banana pudding.'

The 'we' in question turned out to be Ellie and a small, dimpled man in a pale blue shirt and a pair of mole-grey flannel trousers, who was introduced as Barnaby Wilcox. This was presumably the friend whom Adam had glimpsed driving off outside Ziva's house – the hair was the same sunny blond, the thick gold wedding band still very much in evidence. He looked in his mid-forties but his slight build and round, suntanned face gave him the air of someone much younger, his boyish features currently set and stony, his blue eyes glaring at Adam. He stood in the kitchen holding a large mixing bowl, his shirtsleeves carefully and evenly rolled up, a half-empty bottle of Bombay Sapphire and another of vermouth on the countertop and what Adam took to be teacups of gin martinis beside them. The cups and saucers were delicate bone china sprigged with orange roses and fading violets, twee and incongruous on the stainless-steel counter. A bunch of new, unopened lilies, wrapped in clear plastic and frothing with red ribbon, rested in the sink. Ellie was barefoot.

'Adam, Barnaby's just been made a fellow of All Souls, he's a world expert on pagan ritual. But more importantly he's a very good cook. I've been craving the banana pudding from Magnolia, I know it's such a cheesy place but it's the one thing there I love and it's impossible to get the ingredients in London. Barnaby, Adam is my cousin.'

Ellie seemed animated by the presence of Barnaby Wilcox; positively effusive. There was a bright, hard note in her voice, as if a veneer had locked into place for the evening; a touch of the perky cheerleader or high school prom queen thrown over her usual implacable detachment. Adam began to suspect that she had a different personality for each man she chose to please, slipped on and off as easily as a silk dress. He wondered whether Ellie had made banana pudding with Marshall Bruce. He and Barnaby shook hands, stiffly. It pleased him that, genius or not, the other man was at least six inches shorter than he was. It did not please him to be introduced as a cousin.

'When he's in London Barnaby stays near this place in St John's Wood that sells American stuff and he brought me Nilla wafers for the recipe after I told him I missed them—'

'Panzer's,' Barnaby supplied, visibly eased by Ellie's breezy explanation of his presence in her flat. Neither man looked directly at the other but from the corner of his eye Adam saw Barnaby expanding his chest into an attitude of deliberate, relaxed confidence. He had become the embodiment, suddenly, of a charming, blameless man who was merely delivering groceries. He had squared his shoulders and leaned back against the kitchen counter with his arms crossed, his blond hair tumbling casually into his eyes. He began to regard Adam with an expression that approximated wry indifference and Adam felt a rush of repugnance at this posturing. There was no good reason why a man should be baking, after nightfall, with a woman who was not his own wife. Certainly not baking and drinking.

'Anyway, Barnaby bought me the wafers and Jell-O instant vanilla pudding there. The recipe's got such weird cheapo ingredients in it but it's so, so good when it's made. OK, so now I have to fold that into this.' Ellie took the bowl that Barnaby had abandoned on Adam's arrival and planted it on top of the freezer chest; from one of the fridges she extracted another mixing bowl, which had been wedged perilously between the wine racks. 'Is folding with the mixer, or with a wooden spoon?'

'Wooden spoon,' said Barnaby and Adam together, well taught by their women. Ellie laughed. 'Impressive. You're quite the Betty Crockers.' She slid the contents of one bowl into the alpine peaks of cream in the other. Barnaby Wilcox stood and began to collect various belongings – a large bunch of keys, a wallet of cracked tan leather, a mobile phone and a small paperback, sliding these one by one into the pockets of a brown velvet jacket that he had retrieved from the arm of the sofa.

'I've got to go,' he said, obviously. 'Let me know how the pudding works out. If it's good I'll make it with my daughter this weekend.'

That this statement was probably true did not, in Adam's opinion, make it any less obnoxious under the circumstances.

When the door closed behind him there was a long silence. Ellie was looking at Adam expectantly; Adam was looking at Ellie with the same expression. The stand-off continued until Adam said, 'I don't want to know what he and his bananas were doing here.'

'OK,' she said easily, tipping the contents of Barnaby's abandoned teacup down her throat and putting cup and saucer into the sink. Adam felt an urge to shake her.

'Ziva's spoken to Lawrence, she's worried about you. He told me about the situation with Marshall Bruce.'

In saying this he realised that he was succumbing to his urge to shake her and it proved effective – before him she appeared fleetingly shaken. This result was less satisfying than he'd imagined. She drained her own cup but did not put it with the other one; instead she refilled it and made no move to offer anything to Adam. After a while she said quietly, 'What did he say to you about Marshall?'

'That you were about to be implicated in the whole thing.'

She nodded, but whether it was assent or merely urging him to go on was not clear.

'And that his wife's team has evidence of substantial financial payments going back more than five years.'

'Mmm.' She took a deep breath. 'Will you help me finish making the pudding? We can do it while we talk. I'm not avoiding the subject –' this in response to his look of incredulity, '– but I've started it now and I might as well finish it, I can think at the same time. I've decided I need to *make* things with my hands, it's my new thing. Everything else is just so intangible and bullshit. And I know that really when you get down to it, cooking produces ephemera just like all the other crap we all do, or I do anyway, but at least for a moment there's a *thing*, you know? I sometimes think I'd have been so damn happy working on an assembly line.' She paused. 'Anyway. We just layer the stuff, the Nilla wafers, then the bananas in slices, then the pudding stuff, three times.' She sat down on the grey sofa with the bowl of vanilla-cream emulsion and a large Pyrex dish before her on the coffee table. Adam obediently brought over the open packet of wafers and a plate on which sat a bunch of bananas and a paring knife. He then poured himself a large cup of gin from the open bottle before returning to the sofa. He was going nowhere until he'd got some sense out of her.

'Into rounds?' he asked, peeling a banana and picking up the knife. She nodded, and looked at him, briefly and gratefully.

For a while neither of them spoke. Adam peeled and sliced the browning bananas. Ellie arranged these and the light discs of biscuit on the bottom of the large dish in overlapping fish scales, alternating with satisfying dollops of cream. Her arrangements were neat and careful and she was breathing deeply and deliberately beside him, like a yogi. The end result showed perfect stripes of buff, white, and the pale suede banana slices through the glass sides. They admired it in silence.

'So are you here as a friend, or as my lawyer?' she asked finally.

'Both. Well, it depends on whether you want us to act for you. But of course as your friend, too.'

'A friend would be nice. And I do want you and Lawrence to act for me, if you don't mind doing it. Then I know I can trust my lawyers, which will make for a novel experience. I just want to know I'm doing everything I can to fix this for Ziva.'

'Surely this is about fixing it for you?'

She shrugged. 'The right decision for Ziva is the right decision for me. I don't care what the press write about me, but I can't imagine it's much fun for my grandmother to read it. For me it's not a big deal and anyway, it can't be worse than anything that's been said before.' Her voice was quiet. 'What was it? Bringing my depravity to Columbia University, endorsing the "degradation and humiliation of women" in my "attempts" to be an actress? And that of course means that I'm single-handedly setting back the women's movement by decades.'

'You wield a lot of power, apparently.'

She laughed. 'I know, right?'

'But still, it can't be much fun to read all that about yourself. You can't be unaffected.'

'No. But it's amazing how fast you get used to it.'

'And now?'

'Now it's going to be a bit different. I'm here. I'm supposedly repenting, remember? And I feel bad for Marshall.'

This statement seemed contrary to the point of being disingenuous and after a day immersed in the man's extensive and creatively sordid proclivities, Adam was unimpressed by her apparent generosity. He did not feel bad for Marshall Bruce, or take kindly to anyone else doing so.

'How can you feel bad? He's behaved like a total bastard.' Finding his cup was empty Adam refilled it, and Ellie's, before continuing. 'He's supposed to be a respectable public figure, he's got the whole deal, living the dream – gorgeous wife, kids, an amazing career, three galleries, he's friends with *everyone* – and he's always being interviewed sounding smug saying that his entire success and empire and whatever is down to his wife's support so he looks like the perfect husband, and then he screws it all up like this.' Everyone had become familiar with the story of the Bruces' marriage since the scandal had broken, and Adam's afternoon with Ellie's file had supplemented this information. 'That poor stupid woman. Her family virtually disowned her for marrying him because he wasn't posh enough or whatever, she worked for ten years supporting him while he did nothing except paint crap no one wanted and hobnob at New York charity functions, as far as I can tell, and she was the one who encouraged him to use all her family contacts and start dealing instead, so it *is* all down to her, actually. And then as soon as he's successful and hanging out with politicians and making obscene amounts of money he starts screwing around on her with all these strippers and waitresses and whores.'

Ellie slid a brown polka-dotted joint out of her cigarette case and lit it before replying. She held it neatly between a bitten thumb and forefinger; a plume of blue-grey smoke snaked upwards. 'Well, I'm not a stripper, and I've never worked as a waitress, so I guess by a process of elimination I know what you think of me.'

The passion of his previous speech evaporated in the heat of his embarrassment. 'I didn't mean you,' he said, weakly.

'It's all right. As I've said, I've been called worse. And no doubt will be again once this whole business comes out.'

'It might not all come out, we're going to do our best. Do you mind, though, it would really help to know how much of it is actually, you know, based on fact. I've brought a file.'

'Oh, a *file*. Well, that makes it all official.' The air was heavy with the scent of coconut again. She took a deep drag on her joint and then balanced it on the side of the ashtray, reaching for her drink as she exhaled. Her voice was congested with smoke. 'So, what do you need from me?'

'Well, why don't you read it first and then tell me what happened. And whatever's not true, we can begin by dealing with that. I mean, is it true?'

'I don't know what you've read. It's true that we're good friends. We care about each other, in different ways I guess. I've known Marshall a long time.'

'Was he paying you five thousand dollars a month?'

Adam asked, emboldened by the gin, and Lawrence's two pints.

'He gave me money, yes. He knew I needed it, at that stage. I wasn't modelling during term time. He had it to give.'

'You were underage when all this started.'

'I was nearly seventeen. So?'

'Look, his wife is saying what looks very much like the truth – that you were underage when you started . . . your relationship . . . with him. Were you?'

Ellie made a soft kissing sound with her lips and Rocky scampered over to her from the corner. She scooped the dog into her lap.

'I'm not going to be the means by which Marshall's wife punishes him because she's angry. I don't see why I should say anything one way or the other.'

'It makes a difference. If you really were underage we can keep your name out of the press coverage for one thing – you'd be protected.'

Ellie shook her head, idly stroking one of Rocky's silky ears. 'I'm not going to play that game.'

'Look,' said Adam, exasperated, 'was he or was he not paying you to sleep with him?'

He must now be drunk, he realised, and she was frustrating his attempts to show her that he was different. That men could be different. He wanted her to trust him so that he could take charge and give her the help that she so clearly needed, whether she was aware that she needed it or not. He could never predict any of her interpretations of the world beyond the certain knowledge that they would not be the same as his own.

She sighed. 'It must be nice to see everything so simply.'

'You're so bloody patronising,' he heard himself saying.

'I'm not,' she answered, unblinking. 'I really mean it. You have such certainty. "This is wrong." "This is right." "This should be here." "Thou shalt not covet thy neighbour's whatever." It sounds peaceful. In my life everything is a little less categorical than that.'

'I covet lots of things,' Adam said, slowly, and then looked at her. 'But I know what's important in life, that's all. Values. Family. Love.'

'Family I'm learning to value – it's been a long time since I've felt what it's like to have family batting for you, although I was the one rejecting Ziva's efforts so maybe that's my own fault. Maybe everything would look different if I'd – but you know, I was mad at them all for a long time. Whatever. So yes, I suppose that's new for me. But God, I value love. I value love like nothing else, you've no idea how much. And you know what? I think Marshall values love, too. It just looks a little different to yours. He's not a bad person, you know, although I'm sure you won't believe me. He's been a good friend to me.'

'He's exploited you.'

'How?'

Adam had been furious all day about Marshall Bruce's exploitation of Ellie. Now, with her sitting before him, it seemed as if the idea of exploitation had merely been a construct by which he might absolve her of responsibility. The reality was all far less appealing than the role he had earlier created for her.

'You know,' she continued, 'sometimes people make a

choice because they know it's the wrong one. Self-destruction can be very seductive, sometimes.'

She had taken off the apron when Barnaby left and was wearing only the soft grey T-shirt and tiny, black cotton running shorts. She folded her legs up beneath her and now sat, cross-legged, beside him.

He followed her gaze. On the inside of her thigh extended four faint silvery scars, as fine as blades. He swallowed. As she remained beside him, unmoving, he saw into her. It was as if she had stepped, for a moment, into an X-ray. The fine scars wavered and blurred before his eyes. He saw her head bent with rage, saw her fingers shaking but determined, pressing a razor blade and slicing across her own vulnerable flesh, could see her watching her own bright blood slide and drip. He understood it then – it was a reminder that she was alive, and her penance for living. He wanted, with violence, to protect her. He wanted to crush her to his chest until the images that had tormented her were muffled and invisible beneath his weight.

He took a slow breath and asked, 'Who knows?'

'Only strangers. Lots of them, I guess. Every time I do a shoot they have to airbrush. And no one's ever said anything but I guess anyone who I've . . . But if you mean people who matter? No one.' She shook her head. 'Only you.'

He watched as she ran her thumb lightly, almost fondly, over the fine white scars. Aligned like fingers, they would be perfectly shielded by his hand if he reached out and touched them.

She said, 'I want you to know me. Who I was. Who I am.'

He nodded. He felt the weight of this new secret, combined with a strange, heady gratitude that she had chosen him.

'I want that too.' He paused. 'Did it help?'

'A little. Temporary relief.'

'But you don't . . . any more.'

'No. Not since my eighteenth birthday. Never.'

'That sounds like quite a birthday party.' He risked this joke so that she would know he did not see her differently, would know that he believed it was something she'd left behind and that he wasn't frightened away by what she had confided. He was glad to hear relief in her laugh.

'Yes, I've had better. It was years ago now, though. And I know you don't think so but I'm pretty good at taking care of myself these days. I feel very different from how I did then.' She turned to look at him. 'Which doesn't mean I don't appreciate having a beautiful man appearing to help me out with his legal wizardry.'

Something had shifted between them; a subtle realignment, as though a trauma had not only been confessed but lived through together in fast forward and they had emerged, strengthened and energised by having survived it. She had not taken her eyes from his, and it was only then that Adam realised, from the manic pounding in his chest, how close they were to one another; how right it would feel to lean forward and kiss her; how much she wanted him to. He stood up abruptly from the low sofa to look around the studio.

On the white-painted bricks above the mattress in the corner hung a photograph, the spaghetti-fine curve of a banister soft amid a rigorous grid of straight lines; a doorframe, a table. At the centre of the picture five stems thrust upwards from the bulb of a vase, four leaves and a single flower arranged at perfect angles. A small rectangle of brass tacked to the bottom of the frame said *Chez Mondrian* in small, light italics.

'I like this. The light and dark is beautiful. Who's it by?'

'André Kertész. He's an awesome photographer, Theo's started collecting his work. It's artificial.'

He paused. He could feel her behind him, though he knew she had not moved. 'What's artificial? The photograph?'

'No, the flower in the middle. Mondrian coloured it to match his studio. I don't know what it means but it feels significant. Or maybe significant precisely because it doesn't matter. Does that make any sense?'

'No.' He remained with his back to her and breathed deeply.

'I suppose I just thought – it made me think that it's one way of saying that substance isn't important. Only the appearance.'

'That's so superficial.'

'It doesn't need to be, it can be precisely the opposite. It can also mean that what matters is the face you show to the world and the way you treat the people in it, and that your private inner life isn't judged. It resonates with Jewish thinking, actually – that actions are what truly matter, and thoughts aren't sins unless you act on them.'

'Well, I certainly hope that's true,' he answered. The pounding of his heart had slowed; he was suddenly exhausted and turned back to her to take his leave. For the last few moments he had been tormented by the thought of her lips on his skin; it was time for him to be safely away, at home. He would walk until he found a cab. 'I'm going to leave the file with you. Call me when you've read it.'

'OK.' She stayed where she was, looking up at him. 'I trust you. Whatever you tell me to do, I'll do.'

TEN

Adam met Jasper at Belsize Park Tube station on the way to Dan and Willa London's Christmakah party, an event that had begun partially as a joke and had since burgeoned into an institution. Willa had converted to Judaism when she had married Dan, and they had since decided to combine the best of both families' traditions into a single hybrid.

'Hi, mate. Right, let's go.'

They set off up Haverstock Hill, Jasper rubbing his hands together in the cold. His round face was chilled pink; Adam had a startling preview of what his friend might look like at sixty, puce and multi-chinned.

'God. It's freezing. Remind me why you didn't go to Eilat again?'

'Too much work this year.'

'You've been shagging the boss's daughter for a decade, surely he would have given you the time off.'

'He would have,' Adam conceded, 'but I don't like asking. And we're going to end up taking loads of time off for the wedding in the summer and so I thought . . . Anyway, Rachel didn't give me any schtick for having to go without me, she actually didn't seem to mind when I said I was staying here. Once we're married we might not end up going away with them every Christmas –' at this Jasper snorted in disbelief, which Adam ignored '– so it's her last year to go away alone with her family, blah, blah.'

'Whatever. If Tanya's parents wanted to pay for me to be lying by the pool at the Hilton right now you wouldn't catch me saying no.'

'Leslie and Linda would probably pay you to stay away from their family holidays.'

'Mate – I don't know what you've been hearing. The Pearls love me. They can't get enough.'

They had turned off the main road and were now descending Pond Street where the looming bulk of the Royal Free Hospital, newly enlarged by a refurbishment almost as hideous as the original concrete architecture, dominated the sky. Its front was uplit in garish violet; the huge Christmas tree blinked with red and yellow lights that flashed only a little more slowly than the rotating blue strobes of the incoming ambulances.

This was the first time Adam had gone to the Londons' party, as he had always been in Eilat with Rachel. Indeed, it was the first winter holiday they were spending apart in many years, and so far it was as exhilarating as he had thought it might be. They were engaged – there was no need to waste energy missing her now that he knew they were to spend eternity together. Two weeks, in the meantime, stretched ahead of him as a rather welcome break. He planned to work less and drink more, had tickets to weekday football matches and two away games, and had accepted invitations to parties that Rachel would usually have vetoed ('It's miles away, Adam! It's in town, how will we park on a Saturday night?' or 'Yes I know, but your university friends are a bit . . . and anyway, it's Tanya's birthday and I said we'd be there so we can't'). That afternoon he had driven the Gilbert clan to the airport – piloting Jaffa's beloved thirty-year-old Volvo station wagon to accommodate their refugee-style packing – and had been guiltily unaffected by Rachel's tears at Departures. She was going on a beach holiday after all, not being cast into perpetual exile. With a recently rediscovered Sonny Boy Williamson album blasting out of the fizzing, ancient speakers he had driven back, abandoned the ailing car in the Gilberts' driveway and had gone straight home to change for the Christmakah party.

They were mounting the stairs outside Dan and Willa's building when a distinctly un-celestial voice spoke to them from above. 'A-dam! Ja-sper!'

'Li-sa!' Jasper mimicked and a laugh returned from the balcony.

'When did Lisa get back?' Adam asked as the buzzer sounded. Lisa London was Dan's twin sister, a famed beauty in the last years of summer camp who embodied that rare alchemy of a tomboyish ease among her brother's friends with more distinctly feminine advantages. At twelve (when she was not yet beautiful, though the accolade benefited him retroactively), she and Adam had declared themselves boyfriend and girlfriend for two halcyon weeks until – it was too galling to remember, even these many years later – she had dumped him for a pre-pubescent (although admittedly not yet fat) Jasper Cohen. It was Jasper who had claimed the triumph of being Lisa London's first kiss – on a rain-slick pavement, behind the graffitied photo booth in Golders Green Tube station – even though she'd then gone out with Adam again shortly afterwards and had subsequently bestowed upon him the same favour. Which one of them had technically 'got there' first was therefore under contention. For the last year she had been on a general surgery rotation in a Manchester hospital and it had piqued both Jasper's and Adam's interest to learn that she'd finally broken up with a little-seen non-Jewish boyfriend who had been around, in rumoured form at least, for some time. She was a tremendously accomplished and gratifying flirt, a valued commodity for men as long attached as Adam and Jasper.

'Didn't she call you, mate? She's been back two weeks. Ha. She clearly can't keep away from me, whereas you . . .' Jasper made a wavering hand signal.

The door of the flat was open. Dan had made whiskey-laced hot apple cider, which he was distributing in red plastic pint glasses. Willa circulated behind him, her blonde hair hidden beneath a red felt Santa hat, offering Chanukah doughnuts. From the speakers Harry Connick Jr was crooning, sultry and smooth, that it was the most wonderful time of the year. The living room was hot and crowded, noisy with voices and laughter. Adam recognised almost everyone – either the long-known dramatis personae of north-west London's social scene or familiar faces from Willa's birthday parties; her school friends and colleagues. The evening had a nostalgic feel to it – the Londons were not unduly concerned with keeping their soft furnishings pristine, and had for many years been the only couple willing to throw a party of this scale. Most of Adam's other friends from the Suburb had years ago begun hosting determinedly sophisticated dinners and admiring one another's kitchen Corians and spotless carpets (this placed rather clear limits on entertainment, as their guests were required to use coasters, and often to remove outdoor footwear). Adam and Rachel had oohed and aahed obligingly along with the rest of them and, unable as yet to display their own home improvements, had rallied by conjecturing about them instead. But the Londons, it seemed, were still actually having some fun.

'Hey, stranger.'

Adam turned unsteadily, and the third pint of gin and tonic that Jasper had pressed on him moments before splashed over his wrist. Ellie stood on the balcony from which Lisa London had called down to them. A small heater glowed on the wall beside her, casting a strange orange light on her skin. He squinted at her blur in the darkness. He had earlier considered the possibility that she might be at the party and had dismissed it as there was no reason that she should be; it now felt as if he had conjured her appearance simply by willing it.

'I didn't know you knew Dan and Willa.'

'Rachel introduced me to Willa on Yom Kippur, at the break fast. I thought you'd be in Israel with the in-laws.'

'Too much work,' he said, joining her on the balcony. His head was spinning from loud music and gin, and the cold air whipping through his shirt felt fortifying. He stepped away from the heater.

'Ah. Your girlfriend has too many troublemaking cousins making paperwork for you. Sorry about that.'

'Fiancée,' he corrected, sitting down heavily in a folding garden chair.

'Quite right. Fiancée,' she said, softly. She seemed impossibly tall that night – Amazonian, he thought, and it was as if the word had never been so perfectly embodied. She looked like a warrior princess, lifted high again on those impossible driftwood heels and looking down at him. Several moments passed before he broke the silence.

'You smoke too many of those.' He nodded towards the joint in her hand, still unlit.

The cigarette case was on the small aluminium table beside her; she returned the joint to its place and clicked the case shut again, dropping it into the pocket of her leather jacket. 'There. I told you I would take your advice.'

'Actually, you said' – what had she said? – 'you said you would do whatever I told you to.'

'So I did. I wonder if that was wise.'

'Bollocks to what's wise,' said Adam with sudden heat.

'Are you drunk?' she asked, incredulous. 'Don't tell me Adam Newman is anything other than sober and controlled.'

'Hell no. Sober as a judge.' He took a swig from his gin and tonic and squinted up at her. 'I'm not allowed to drink. Rachel hates it. So of course I don't.' This was unnecessarily disloyal, but Ellie rewarded his minor betrayal with a sly half-smile. He could say what he wanted to her; anything at all, he realised. It was intoxicating.

What he actually said was, 'I can't sleep.' He surprised himself with the confession. She had once told him that she couldn't sleep and he had not admitted it then; now it seemed important that she knew she was not alone. 'It's like torture, sometimes. So I know you think – I know you think you're the only one. But you're not. It's an illusion.' He could hear himself elongating these last words, particularly *iloooosion*, as if he were doing a voiceover for a haunted house at the fair, and surmised that he must indeed be very drunk.

'Yes. I know about that. Rachel told me.'

'Told you what?'

'A while back. She said you never sleep, she worries about your insomnia. She said you have nightmares.'

'That's not for her to talk about.' He felt a sobering flash of anger that Rachel had betrayed his confidence and also, irrationally, that she had appeared between the two of them in the conversation, laying claim to private knowledge of him from which Ellie had been excluded.

'She worries. I guess she doesn't understand it or you or something.' Ellie picked up Adam's glass from the table and took a sip.

These words hung between them, immediately turned over and analysed by Adam with forensic care. He rotated them, peered into them, under them, searching for their subtext. This line of thought danced away ahead of him, leading him into danger like a tantalising and treacherous Tinker Bell, and he was freed from its siren call by Jasper crashing on to the balcony with Tanya.

'Hey, kids.' Jasper put an arm around Ellie; Tanya threw herself into a chair. 'Ellie. Long time no see. How the devil are you?'

She was nearly a head taller than Jasper; his casual attempt at flirtation left her hunched over into an acute scoliosis, his shoulder straining almost directly upwards.

She extricated herself firmly and stood upright once more.

'Oh, you know. Trying to make London my home.'

At these words Adam glanced up as she continued earnestly, 'I find the people here, they really do treat you warm; so kind and cool.'

Jasper looked bewildered but Adam was transfixed – she was almost quoting the lyrics from the song he'd sent her. They locked eyes, and Adam was once more alone with her in the exclusive and delicious privacy of this reference.

Tanya then shattered the moment by asking, 'Are you really going to live in London for ever? But you're so American.'

And Ellie smiled, kissed only Tanya goodnight, and excused herself.

ELEVEN

Once Ellie had left the party Adam no longer felt like staying. Lisa London joined them on the balcony, perching on the wall next to him and whispering, 'Hello, you big gorgeous thing' in a voice at once seductive and unthreateningly free from intention.

The customary conversations were resumed. Tanya asked Lisa about Manchester; Jasper asked Lisa about her hospital's supply of 'hot nurses'. Tanya asked Jasper why he was such a pig; Jasper replied that it was what she loved him for. 'That, and for my enormous . . . personality,' he finished, swinging back on his chair, legs splayed so that anyone who had missed the subtlety of his joke might be helped along by the illustration. His jeans strained over large, womanly thighs. It was business as usual. Adam felt tired, and strangely lonely amongst these people whom he had known for so long. Ellie had taken with her the fresh air that he had been sucking deep into his lungs. What remained was a fug of claustrophobia; of the perennially predictable. He was waiting for a break during which to make his exit when a man emerged through the doors, looked around in search of someone and then retreated. Adam was cheered.

'Nick!' he shouted, and the man returned.

'Adam! I didn't see you lurking in the shadows out there. How are you?'

Nick Hall stepped out to join them. He was a tall, lean man with strong features and subtly lopsided eyebrows that gave him a permanent expression of ironic disbelief. At university, where he and Adam had met, he had generally been considered attractive. But more and more these days he had a look of narrowed and appraising cynicism in his blue eyes, and didn't seem to have adapted his wardrobe since his student days. He had come to this particular party in a T-shirt once white and now stained a dingy beige, and a pair of ripped corduroys of an indistinct mushroom grey. These hung from a carelessly malnourished frame, a body whose chief physical exertion was lifting a wine glass or a fag. Nick considered exercise to be for morons or Americans, preferring to fester thoughtfully and smokily in his office, his living room or his local. All this was manifest at a glance. Adam saw that Lisa, who assessed all new men she met with unabashed interest, had judged and found him wanting.

'Nick, this is Lisa, who is Dan's sister, Tanya who is Rachel's flatmate and Jasper who just is. This is Nick. We were at university together.'

'Nice to meet you,' Jasper said and, rising from his chair, he stepped back over the threshold that Nick had just crossed. Jasper's awkwardness with strangers surprised Adam afresh every time he witnessed it. That a vast ocean stretched beyond Jasper's little tide pool was especially evident when someone tall and affable washed in from elsewhere. Nick was effortlessly and somehow charmingly rude, and slightly shambling where Jasper, hunting for his own self-defining hallmark, was forced to settle for being an ostentatiously ethnic self-parody. Jasper was neurotic, hyperactive, driven to unconvincing self-aggrandisement where Nick would have more effectively wielded witty self-deprecation. This schtick worked only with old friends. 'I'm going in to get another drink,' Jasper said, to explain his departure. 'Anyone want anything?'

'I'll come, I'm cold.' Tanya followed him. Lisa, who had assumed Ellie's position beneath the small beam of the heater, jumped to her feet.

'I'm so sorry, babe, you should have said! Come stand here.' She stepped aside to cede her place under the orange glow but Tanya shook her head.

'It's fine, honestly, I want to get a glass of water in any case. Do you want to come? I wouldn't mind finding something to eat, too. Willa made strudel, there's loads in the kitchen.'

Before answering, Lisa looked at Nick in a swift, final evaluation. He had some attractions, but was altogether too gaunt and grubby for her taste. She followed Tanya.

And so they had all disappeared almost as soon as Nick arrived and for Jasper, parties would continue to be what they had always been – opportunities to spend time with exactly the same people he spent time with everywhere else. Jasper was safe in the knowledge that the companions with whom he had sat tonight on a cold balcony in South End Green were precisely the same as those with whom he had sat in someone's family's kitchen fifteen years before. An iPod provided the soundtrack instead of a CD player; the place belonged to his friends and not the parents of his friends. Instead of a six-pack of Strongbow between twenty they had Dan's spiced cider, made with cinnamon sticks and slices of fresh red apple. He was allowed to stay past midnight (though Tanya did not often let him take advantage of this freedom). But these discrepancies were merely superficial. Disaster averted – at core, all had successfully remained the same as ever.

Adam was genuinely delighted to see Nick, and had forgotten that they might meet at Willa's party. As teenagers Nick and Willa had been at Bryanston together and it was Adam who had reintroduced them years after they had lost touch. In the meantime Willa had fallen in love with Dan London and had converted to Judaism, a decision confusing to her girlfriends as Dan himself was so clearly unobservant. But the traditions, if not the beliefs, were important to the Londons, and they had decided to raise a Jewish family; if nothing else the conversion classes, taken at a cosy Reform synagogue (and therefore gentler and far more inclusive than anywhere Orthodox) were an excellent primer for life with a Jewish man, with all the attendant relatives, quirks and customs. The Londons now threw Shabbat dinners for friends and spent their Sabbath afternoons like most Jews, in fervent and near-religious contemplation at White Hart Lane. Willa was as happy and exemplary a convert as Adam had ever seen, and their marriage equally inspiring. She had fallen in love with Dan and everything about him – the Londons were a warm and chaotic family, and she had become one of them wholeheartedly. With Sarah London as her mother-in-law, she would return from every holiday for the rest of her life to find her flat clean, her ironing done, and a pint of milk, a moussaka and a crème brûlée in her fridge. There were certainly worse fates.

Nick, by contrast, believed in only two things: atheism and the Labour Party. He had grown up in the country. His mother was lapsed Church of England, his father was Jewish and had been, for many years, the only Jew Nick had ever met. He had never ceased to find Adam's north-west London Judaism amusing, with its bar mitzvahs and weddings and festivals and endless series of family meals and obligations. Nick had never experienced anything like it. In his own Fens village he'd been known, only half in jest, as 'Jew-Boy'.

'So how goes life in the ghetto?' he asked Adam now.

'All good. The usual. How's everything with you?'

Nick stretched out and crossed his ankles revealing odd socks beneath the frayed corduroy. 'All right. I'm working like a bitch at the moment, which hasn't done much for my Sisyphean extracurricular writing attempts. Still trying to push this bastard novel up the mountain.'

'But it's brilliant that you're doing it,' said Adam with enthusiasm. 'You're going for it, it's shaming for the rest of us who just sit around in offices like monkeys.'

'Yeah, well it won't be brilliant if the damn thing rolls back and flattens me. And Emily's great but writing with a kid –' here he shook his head, 'we don't get five seconds' peace.'

'How old is she now?'

'Nineteen months.'

'Bloody hell. I can't believe it's been that long since she was born.'

'Ah, well. Time flies. No doubt in the meantime you've

been busy being a moral pillar of the *shtetl* whilst I've been battling the conflicting tugs of literary glory, dissipation and parenthood.'

This *shtetl* jibe had its origins in an old argument between them. Nick's position was that religion was the root of all evil; Adam's that fundamentalism of any sort was not to be confused with the faiths it subverted and that organised religion provided morality and community, and encouraged precisely the tolerance that Nick believed it lacked. It was hard to object to the Judaeo-Christian attachment to the Decalogue when its suggestion not to murder, steal or tell porkies seemed to be incontrovertibly sensible. Adam thought Nick was a hypocrite to criticise moral guides when his uber-left-wing politics equally abhorred the more libertarian suggestion that people would do good if left to themselves. But this evening he was not in the mood for a debate, and Nick was welcome company. He lived with his girlfriend Marianne and their little daughter Emily in a flat in Stepney Green, hours away from his parents in Cambridgeshire, and nearly four hundred miles away from Marianne's mother in County Cork. Nick wrote for the *Independent*; Marianne had worked on *The Sunday Times* until Emily arrived and it transpired that she earned less than the childminder they required for her to go back to work. She now freelanced from home and wrote fiction, perennially unpublished. They had chosen their own paths. Their mothers did not have one another on speed dial. They were free.

'How's Marianne doing?'

'Very well. Going a bit stir crazy at home with the baby but very well. Emily's sleeping better now so she's getting a bit more writing done. But not much. We're both too knackered.'

'I'm impressed you're doing it at all.'

'Brutal. It's brutal. Hold off a while, that's my advice. Worth it, but brutal. Still, weekends are all right. Marianne gets Friday nights out and I get Saturdays.'

'So you don't go out together?'

Nick looked at him, head cocked. 'What do you want us to do with Emily? Order her a pizza and leave her to it?'

'Babysitter?'

'On whose trust fund?' Nick demanded, somewhat bitterly. 'Even kids now expect ten quid an hour, we can't afford it. I just saw Josh Cordova inside, do you know where his kid is this evening? At his parents' house – where she is every Saturday night. Every single one, and she *stays*. They drop her off at six and pick her up at lunchtime every Sunday. Every bloody week! I couldn't believe it – and he said it was his mother's idea! My parents were happy to get me off their hands years ago, they're not about to start slaving over my own kids now. Every time she's in her cups my mother threatens to make me pay back my school fees with interest. She worked it out once and claims they could have had a yacht instead. Can you believe Cordova's parents take the kid every week?'

'Yes,' said Adam, simply. There was nothing remarkable in Josh Cordova's arrangement. In north-west London, grandchildren were considered the source of life's highest pleasure; more, Adam sometimes suspected, even than the children who begat them. He knew without ever having considered it that if his own mother lived where Nick's parents did, two hours away from Adam's children, she would still offer to drive down to look after them so that Rachel could go back to work; she would offer to take them home with her for a night; if none of those things were possible she would offer to pay – nay, insist upon paying – for the babysitter. Aunt Judith and Uncle Raymond would not be far behind. Michelle's older sister Judith was a rounder, softer version of Michelle, wild haired and mostly unkempt. She worked as a GP in Stanmore and was married to full-bellied, cinnamon-bearded Uncle Raymond, who was a GP at the same practice. For reasons the family never discussed they had not been able to have children; their devotion to Adam and Olivia was therefore redoubled. I have, you need. So take. It was the way with all the families amongst whom Adam had grown up. When he and Rachel had a baby they would have to fight off Jaffa's offers of assistance, he imagined, so effusive would be her outpourings of love; she would be desperate to squeeze soft cheeks and parade, alight with worshipful triumph, through the streets of Temple Fortune. There was no life event – marriage, birth, parenthood or loss – through which one need ever walk alone. Twenty-five people were always poised to help. The other side of interference was support.

The following Monday at work was particularly grim, and the ritual of beginning a new week seemed merely to emphasise how very similar this week was to the ones that preceded it. On Monday nights Adam usually played five-a-side football with the boys, but tonight most people were away.

Lawrence was in Israel, the office was quiet and Adam had little pressing work with which to divert himself. He was meant to be finishing a pro bono review of a charter for a new homeless shelter. Instead he sat morosely at his desk, staring at the BBC Sport web page and brooding. It would end in a late night, to compensate.

Since the party he could not stop thinking. It had served his purpose until now to reject all evidence of alternatives, and to uphold the simpler belief that it was required to marry a Jewish girl whose mother had for years bumped into one's own mother in Waitrose and who was therefore known and parentally endorsed. Michelle had been alone for a long time and there was nothing about that state that he envied, for in the Noah's Ark of Temple Fortune it was best to go two by two. Since Jacob's death he had grown up believing in dark, looming uncertainties, and fearing them. It wasn't obligatory conformity; simply a question of joining the majority, a subscription to desirable traditions that allowed one to remain supported and cushioned in the bosom of north-west London. And he had subscribed wholesale, firm in the belief that his childhood friends had done the same. All were happily settled in conventional relationships, married, engaged, or well on the way. Jasper was with Tanya. Josh Cordova was married to Natalie. Noah Cordova (Rabbi Josh's first cousin and son of Simon Cordova, Rachel's dentist) was engaged to Lucy Wilson, whom he'd met on Israel Tour like Rachel and Adam, although Noah and Lucy had started going out only two years afterwards. Even Gideon Press, who was gay and therefore awarded nominal points for unconventionality at the outset, had been in the same relationship since he was twenty, cohabiting contentedly with a man called Simon Levy who was from Glasgow and who played golf every Saturday with Gideon's mother.

Adam had always assumed that to pursue independence was to sacrifice security. But thinking, really thinking, about Dan and others he could see that it simply wasn't true. Dan London had gone up to Cambridge with his virginity and a Tottenham duvet cover and come down with a blonde-haired, green-eyed girlfriend called Willa Hope-Christopher and the world had gone on turning. Gideon had brought home a nice Jewish boy. The community was liberal and elastic, far more than he'd allowed himself to admit. It was he who had been rigid. It was his own insecurity that had constrained him. If only he'd known, Adam reflected with a throb of indistinct regret, he would have stridden forth without fear – but then he had already walked so very far following the old rules.

He composed an email to Ellie.

If you're really trying to make London your home then we should go out and drink to it. Are you around this week? We could even have something that doesn't come in a teacup. Adam x

Send.

The sense of having taken action restored his humour and imbued him with enough energy to answer, belatedly, a long email from Rachel that detailed every particular of the Gilbert family's holiday thus far. She was a bit rusty playing tennis but it was coming back and she'd won the night before; their rooms had been noisy but they'd moved two floors up and now they were perfect, the sun was shining and she missed him. It was so nice to have a break from the stress of school and marking homework. The food was amazing as usual. Did he remember those ice cream sandwiches they'd had by the pool? They had them again this year except with caramel swirled in the vanilla.

His resurgence of energy and the unfounded sense of optimism turned out to be just a flash, however. When days later he had received no answer to his offer of a drink, he slumped back into melancholy. All the communications, the loving messages and voluble effusions that poured from Rachel by phone, text and email were drowned out by the single deafening silence of her cousin.

TWELVE

Adam oscillated between despair and relief before finally settling into the less exhausting equilibrium of a moderate, resigned depression. For almost a week each vibration of his BlackBerry had caused an equally strong vibration in his heart, and nervous anticipation would shiver through him until he saw that the email was merely a smutty joke forwarded by Jasper (*WHAT'S THE DIFFERENCE BETWEEN MARSHALL BRUCE AND SANTA CLAUS? SANTA ONLY HAS THREE 'HO'S' – HO, HO, HO*); an article urging the awakening of his political consciousness from his office-mate Matthew Findlay, sitting only four feet away from him (*Iran's Ticking Bomb: President Ahmadinejad boasted of the installation of 60,000 'third generation' centrifuges for the enrichment of uranium. Time is running out – world leaders must act now to prevent nuclear terrorism*), or a daily update from Rachel (*Weather here still gorgeous and Yael coming down from Tel Aviv to visit tonite. She's bringing her baby, yay! I switched bikinis from the white one to the pink one because yesterday I fell asleep and now I've got tan lines – nooooo! I need u here to rub in my sun cream ☺. Down to factor 4 now, kisses from your pumpkin*). This roller-coaster of anticipation and disappointment had continued for days. It was after he had given up hoping for a reply that the reply eventually came.

He was in the Roebuck on Pond Street watching Chelsea play Fulham. It had been a gloriously bad December for Chelsea and today Fulham had scored in the first five minutes. When his phone began buzzing he did not even think to reach for it. Much heated discussion with Jasper and Gideon followed (Arsenal's title challenge was no longer a joke, Adam had claimed – the quest for the Premier League became ever closer each time Chelsea faltered. Gideon maintained it was still a joke). It was an hour later that he thought to check his messages. An email had arrived from Ellie Schneider. Its subject was 'Escape'.

Sorry for radio silence. I just needed a break and some breathing space from everything. Georgina and Rupert went to their place in Oxfordshire at the beginning of December and they invited me to stay a couple of times as they're not back in London till January. They are so awesome – and appear to be the only people who don't pay any attention to the crap said about me or if they do, it only seems to make them want to be kinder to me. I suspect Georgina thinks it's painfully middle class to care about someone else's private life (and Ziva thinks they both secretly love a little bad behaviour to liven things up – it's true, Rupert seems positively gleeful about 'taking in a black sheep', as he's started calling me). I feel very lucky to know them. They're so generous.

I wasn't going to leave the city but the day after I saw you at that party I just had to go. So I've been out here since then just thinking and getting some air. It's so, so peaceful and beautiful – nothing like a bit of bucolic winter splendour to put our choking urban lives into perspective. In a quiet way, the English countryside is at its most awesome when it's stripped and naked like this, I think anyway. White sky, bare, black trees – it's all so clear out here. Wouldn't it be nice if everything else was black and white?

Anyway, I'm becoming quite the country girl, going for long bracing walks and Rocky is loving the space out here. He's fallen for Rupert's pointer but she's not showing much interest. I wish I could tell him that love just screws things up. He should go back to being the Casanova he used to be in the Washington Square dog park, he got a lot of pedigree ass back then. I guess he's lonely these days. Well, he can join the line.

I take it you know that Marshall and his wife are officially reconciling? If it works out good for them – and I'm sure Lawrence is right that the best place for me while they're figuring it out is anywhere but Manhattan but God, it's nice to be away from London for a bit, too. So I'm going to stay here for a while. Begin the New Year with a bit of tranquillity for once. Fresh starts, or whatever. Maybe I'll even sleep. So when you're out partying, think of me in Oxfordshire, re-potting orchids and listening to The Archers with Georgina . . . Ellie

There was a great deal in this email. More, much more, than the words themselves. Adam was perched on a rickety upholstered stool and surrounded on all sides by looming beer-warmed men in sweaty polyester club T-shirts – under these conditions, discerning the significance of the communication was too great a challenge for his concentration. He excused himself from the table and pushed his way towards the front door so that he could focus.

Outside the pub the winter sky declared that night had fallen, though his watch told him there were several more daytime hours to go. London's hours of light are weak and few in December; his BlackBerry glowed brightly in the darkness like a beacon. He looked at her message again.

It was not clear what had happened on Dan and Willa's balcony, that strange and trivial drunken conversation, thickened with subtext, interrupted by Jasper and Tanya and then left, like all the somethings and nothings that had ever passed between them, unresolved. This message was nuanced too, in a way that he did not fully understand. And that final sentence – her joke about him at a party imagining the incongruity of her days in Oxfordshire; he felt stung by it. How could she not know by now that all he ever did with an acute and all-consuming energy was think of her wherever he was, wherever she was, all the time? Had she ever, as he had now more than once, lain alone in midnight silence and imagined her hands were his hands, eyes closed to the solitude of reality in favour of another secret, deeper place where they were touching? Whispering? Fucking? He had been so close to her in these moments, it was appalling to believe she didn't know it. 'When you're out partying, think of me' was so trivialising, it was an insult. In these last weeks, to think was to think of her.

Behind him there was a rap on the window and he turned to see Jasper inside the pub, lifting his eyebrows and tipping an imaginary pint to his lips. Adam nodded his assent to another but then instantly shook his head. 'Two minutes' he mimed with a raised victory sign, and Jasper gave him a thumbs-up and retreated. Adam placed the flat of his palm against the pub door but took a breath before he pushed inside and returned to his friends. An idea had come to him; less an idea, in fact, than an urge. He would go home tonight – and, if it still seemed possible the next day, then he would act.

As it turned out, the drive to Oxfordshire gave him less time for preparation than he'd hoped. He had envisaged hours alone with a clear road and a clear mind, composing his impassioned (yet logical, comprehensive and persuasive) address to Ellie as the gentle curves of a winter-coated Buckinghamshire slid past soothingly. And the M40 was indeed icy and deserted so early on a Sunday morning, but it did not produce a corresponding calming of his thoughts. Instead it served to deliver him to his destination, still unprepared and increasingly apprehensive, long before he'd expected. It was not yet eleven when he turned into the broad drive of yellow gravel that curved in a wide arch up to the Sabahs' house.

Built in the late 1600s, the Sabahs' country residence was a red-brick manor house; grand, bay-windowed, and constructed with loving homage to Christopher Wren. When they inherited it in 1951 it had been in use for many years as a school and then empty just as long; Georgina had quietly restored its interior to its former, understated glories and the result had greatly pleased the village.

Georgina's family had been English since 1656 when Oliver Cromwell had reversed a banishment of 366 years and officially allowed the Jews to resettle in England. Rupert's ancestry was similar; not for the Sabahs this Yiddish, these *shtetl knishes* and *lokshen* and bagels. Not for a good few British Jews, in fact – though it might surprise their fellow countrymen. Apart from the period between their unfortunate banishment by Edward I and Cromwell's enabling their return, there have been English Jews since Roman and Anglo-Saxon times. In 1066 William the Conqueror was busily encouraging the Jewish artisans and merchants of northern France to cross the Channel; among them an ancestor of Rupert Sabah's. That Jews should 'go back where they came from', a suggestion so frequently proposed by those who brandish St George's flag and fear the dissolution of 'true' English culture, is bewildering. Lawrence's parents, for example, came from Winchester.

Adam's plan took him only thus far. The Sabahs were not a family on whom one popped in; invitations were issued in writing, and in advance. But the dilemma was resolved for him when he heard footsteps on gravel and saw Ellie, growing nearer and nearer in his rear-view mirror. He performed an undignified scramble out of the car and was standing beside it when she reached him.

'Stalker,' she said, but her eyes were alight with pleasure.

'You know, mountains, Muhammad . . .' He shrugged, trailing off.

'I'm glad you're here.' She stood still before him, arms crossed over her chest, and her head cocked. They faced one another like sentries, smiling.

'Let's walk. Have you seen the gardens?'

Adam nodded. 'Years and years ago they had a charity thing here.'

'Let's go down and walk along the river then, there's a path at the side through the woods.'

She made no mention of Rupert and Georgina; Adam did not prompt her for fear she would invite him into the house for coffee and questions and an exchange of pleasantries with the Sabahs. She led him across the lawn that sloped down on three sides of the house towards an iron gate and he followed behind her, trying to emulate her calm.

It was only now that he dared to look at her properly. Old jeans tucked into high green wellingtons; several bulky layers of faded black beneath her familiar leather jacket; a long college scarf of blue and yellow wound high around her neck. For once there was colour in her cheeks, her face animated by the cold. She looked tired as she often did but her face, make-up free, seemed younger. Tucked up in stripy scarf and wellies she could have been a schoolgirl, sixteen and tramping out to feed her ponies.

They did not have to go far. Twenty feet beyond the gate was the river, olive green and barely moving, the bank sloping down steeply from a path of terracotta-coloured mud. Bare ash trees spread vast dendrites above them in the sky, each trunk marking ten yards along the towpath. Adam's thin-soled tennis shoes began to squelch quietly beneath him as they crossed towards it; the hems of his jeans grazed puddles as he walked and the bottom inches were slowly saturating with cold brown water. Ellie strode on ahead of him towards a narrow wooden footbridge. The boards were mottled green and slick with damp moss and in the middle of this she sat, folding one long denim leg beneath her and dangling the other over the edge.

Adam looked down at her. 'How inviting.'

'Your jeans are filthy anyway.' She nodded at his ankles, which were level with her gaze. Adam sat beside her and they both looked down into the murky waters beneath, riffling in the wind. Until this point they had been in motion, and moving with purpose. Now they had arrived somewhere, wherever it was, and an awkward, expectant silence fell between them again.

'So how have you been keeping yourself busy out here?' he asked.

'Writing a bit, actually. There's not much to distract me, which is good.'

'Have you always wanted to write?' He felt tense, the reason for this visit not yet acknowledged between them, and could hear himself sounding like an interviewer on Radio 4. But he couldn't help it.

'When I was really small I wanted to be a baker. And then – and I know how ridiculous this sounds, believe me – then for a couple of years I wanted to be a rabbi. God, I'd forgotten that.'

Adam suppressed a smile. It was such an innocent fantasy; a little girl's fantasy. 'I wanted to be a Premiership footballer. Still do, actually. Why a rabbi?'

She shrugged, biting at the cuticle of her thumb. 'No one believes anything any more. When my mom was killed everyone kept going on and on about heaven, that her soul was eternal, all the stuff that people say to kids. And

I wanted it to be true, more than anything, I was desperate to be convinced. But I knew even then that no one really believed it, they were saying it because I was little. And Boaz never even said that stuff. He was honest with me, at least, I'll give him that much. Nothing else, nothing after. All over. But I remember Rabbi Isobel coming to see us – did you know her?'

Adam shook his head.

'She moved back to California a few years later. Anyway, she took me to the park for cherry brandy lollies a couple of times that summer, and she once took me ice skating, I have no idea why. She talked a lot about the indestructibility of energy, like, in physics rather than religion, and also about souls, but not the way other people did. I knew she really believed it, she wasn't just making up stories for my benefit. I guess I felt like if I became a rabbi I might start believing something. Nothing very noble. No great urge to serve the people, or anything.'

'She sounds lovely.'

'She was. Is. She still emails me, sometimes. She has a congregation near San Diego somewhere, and she and her husband also keep donkeys. She's awesome.'

'I have no idea what I believe in except randomness,' Adam said, after a while. Beside him lay a slick of wet black leaves and he began to shred one carefully, dropping it piece by piece into the water. 'It seems hard to reconcile randomness with any idea of a deity.'

'Randomness is comforting, isn't it. I've long thought that a firm belief in randomness is the only way not to feel persecuted. But do you need a deity to believe in heaven?'

'I suppose not. I suppose heaven could just be another – phenomenon.'

'Do you talk to your dad?' she asked.

He paused. 'Yes. In the last few years, only ever when I'm in the cemetery though, for some reason.'

'Maybe you needed to make some space for yourself, so that there are times when you're just you, alone. That's OK. It's a lot, thinking that someone is everywhere. And nowhere is unbearable.'

Adam glanced up at her profile, watching her watch the river. Then he said, 'I can't stop thinking about you.' That awful cliché was the truth – he had tried to stop, and failed.

Ellie did not move. Beneath them their reflections blurred and rippled side by side.

'I can't stop thinking about you,' he said again. 'All the time. I've been going crazy.'

'Me too,' she answered softly. 'I miss you. I know that sounds stupid.'

Adam felt his heart contract. He was aching to touch her. Behind him he heard the crunch of tyres on gravel; Ellie's head snapped up.

'Shit,' she said softly. Her expression had altered and he turned to follow her gaze.

Through the trees he could see the Sabahs' driveway; beside his own car there was now an elderly Morris Minor, pumpkin orange.

'Adam . . .' she started, but he did not look at her. She had scrambled to her feet and looked impatient that he should do the same, but he stayed seated where he was. 'Adam, please, I've got to go back so that Rupert and Georgina don't . . .'

'Go.'

'No but I want to talk to you, just wait.'

She was already walking backwards away from him, torn between staying to explain and an urgent need to intercept Barnaby Wilcox, who was even now adjusting his collar in the reflection of his car window and turning to approach the front door. At the gate Ellie called out and Adam, abandoned and obscured on his bridge by distance and iron railings, saw Barnaby turn and grin broadly at the sound of her voice. Adam saw her say something in greeting, and then they both disappeared around the far side of the house heading, he presumed, into the gardens.

Whatever she might be she was not mendacious; her look of horrified surprise when she'd seen his car made it clear that she had not expected Barnaby to come, or wanted to see him. But the interruption made Adam see his own visit in bleak terms. It was reckless, pointless – and reprehensible. His feelings for her were foolish, and he was not alone in having foolishly cherished them. Look at yourself, he thought, with sudden bitterness. Look at yourself, crouched here in the damp like an animal. So he'd not slept with twenty women before he settled down – so what? He was lucky to have Rachel, he was lucky to have Lawrence and all their family, and if he'd lived those years he so envied – the invigorating uncertainty and freedom; the sex, the possibility of sex, the thrill of possibility – if he'd had those things he would not have these. Had Barnaby Wilcox married his first girlfriend, too? Was that the excuse he gave himself for being here, slavering for what he thought he'd missed, chasing around after a *nafka* half his wife's age? It didn't matter – Adam loathed him, and all that he represented. That was not the marriage he'd dreamed of, growing up. That was not the union he had longed for. It was not who he wanted to be.

When he was certain they had gone he squelched back to his own car and left, driving as slowly and silently as he could until he reached the road and then accelerating angrily. He retraced the route by which he and Barnaby Wilcox, two equally stupid men, had both arrived.

THIRTEEN

In the early evening of the last day of the year, Adam landed at Ovda Airport. The flight had been crowded and the taxi queue was formidable, a line of passengers anxious to reach the city to begin their New Year's celebrations and now shuffling their trolleys forwards inch by inch, glancing repeatedly at wristwatches. But the Gilberts had a driver named Shachar whom they used every Christmas, and Adam had called him. Shachar, in stonewashed Levi's cut-offs, a string vest and a pair of purple plastic sandals, leading him towards an ancient white van, was currently the only person who knew that Adam had flown to Eilat.

On the plane, the rest of his row had been a family whose three blonde teenage daughters had boarded already dressed for New Year's Eve, and who had managed to spend almost the entire five-hour flight on their make-up. Ceremonial unction, goo and glitter were passed from one to the other, the elder two obviously an inviolable pair while the third, maybe just fourteen, leaned eagerly across the aisle to participate. Adam had been unable to exclude their chatter even with his earphones turned up high, and so gathered that she had been permitted to join her sisters at the hotel club that night, provided she walk in ahead of them – if she was asked for ID then the elder two – less obviously but still underage themselves – didn't want to be dragged down with her. These were the conditions, and the only other choice was to spend midnight with mum and dad and their friends. Teenage girls ruled a principality with nakedly Darwinian governance. He watched the youngest accept without complaint, applying yet another layer of warpaint for the battle ahead. Not for the first time he felt grateful to be a man. Rachel and her girlfriends had made one another cry improbably often when they were teenagers, and for reasons he had found incomprehensible. Not that women had become easier to understand in subsequent years.

Adam was also already dressed for the night ahead. Rachel had told him that they were having dinner at the hotel and he hoped to arrive while they were still ordering, and to surprise her with her family. He slunk through the lobby with the air of a celebrity or politician travelling incognito, hiding his face beneath a baseball cap. The flame-haired, polyester-suited girl at the reception desk caught his eye and he fought the urge to wink and raise a silencing finger to his lips in complicity, as if everyone around him was in on the surprise.

In the end it came off beautifully. The Gilberts were at a long table down the centre of the restaurant and he had posed at the bar, sending over a bottle of champagne from a secret admirer. Rachel, in a white linen dress, had been sitting with her back to him, her dark hair loose and glossy over suntanned shoulders. He saw her look up at the waiter, turn in confusion and then leap to her feet with a scream that drew the attention of the room. The choreography of the entire evening from then on could not have been better. After some unfortunate – but luckily not fatal – mistakes, it was the right way to end the year.

The setting for all this romantic excitement was a hotel on the North Beach, command centre for Eilat's British tourists. Amongst the London Jews who wintered in Eilat, everyone and their mothers were in attendance (literally, in many cases), and even those who stayed in the other, quieter establishments had come for the New Year's Eve party. With each passing hour more people accumulated in the floodlit beach bar, piling out of cabs on the forecourt or appearing in clusters from out of the darkness having walked along the sand. In one group Adam recognised Gideon Press's sister, Louisa, twenty-one and on holiday with three girlfriends, lodged no doubt in a dingy but far cheaper youth hostel away from the water. Across the bar Adam had seen Adele Summerstock's mother talking to Jaffa's cousin who had come down from Tel Aviv. Adele herself – née Summerstock now Rosenbaum – he had greeted earlier, sitting on a beach chair with legs spread to accommodate an unwieldy, pregnant belly. The sisters from the plane were all there, united in a happy threesome by the giddy triumph of their admission to the bar and dancing together barefoot in the centre of the dance floor. The youngest one, he noticed, was looking sleepy. Perhaps she wished she'd spent midnight with her mother and father after all. Behind them was a man to whom Adam nodded a greeting at least one morning a week in the England's Lane Starbucks who might have been a distant cousin of Tanya Pearl's, and to whom he had never actually spoken.

Louisa Press waved cheerily and was lost again in the crowd, amid others known or unknown but recognised – familiar faces plucked from around the upper branches of the Northern Line and deposited on the banks of the Red Sea. Shortly after midnight Adam had found Anthony Blume, a barrister who now occasionally joined them for Monday-night football. Rachel was talking intently to one of her cousins, retelling the story of Adam's surprise arrival.

'Well, it was just damage limitation in the second half, wasn't it?' Anthony was saying, when Rachel appeared. She was flushed from daytime sun and night-time cocktails, and her eyes were still bright with the pleasure of their unexpected reunion. She tripped over to them with an impish smile, half a piña colada in a tall, neon pink plastic cocktail glass clutched in one hand. This was her third of the evening but she usually drank so little and so infrequently that she was now unquestionably drunk. Her shoes had been abandoned in the sand beneath one of the tables. Anthony kissed her cheek in greeting and Adam opened his arms to her. She fell into them, giggling. She still could not believe he'd come – every few minutes she would reach out for him, or lay her head on his shoulder. At dinner she had found it impossible to go more than a few moments without turning to him and exclaiming, 'I just can't believe you're here!' Jaffa had spent much of the meal beaming at Adam with her hands pressed to her bosom, presumably to still a heart beating wildly at the romance of the gesture. For every time Rachel had expressed her disbelief, Jaffa had exclaimed to her daughter, '*Ach motek*. It's a good man, that one.'

'What are you boys talking about?' Rachel asked, burrowing her head into Adam's chest and turning to look sideways back at Anthony.

'Man U, Wigan,' he explained.

'Oh.'

She paused, and then turned back to Adam. 'Let's go,' she said in a loud stage whisper and began noisily and enthusiastically kissing his neck, unselfconscious before a bemused Anthony Blume. Over her head Adam could see Lawrence and Jaffa sitting on the plastic beach chairs with a dwindling group – the younger guests had colonised the upper levels of the bar, taking over as the voluble and big-haired Israeli DJ upped his volume and dimmed the lights and began playing electronica instead of mild summer reggae, driving the middle-aged guests to retreat to the quieter seats near the water. Later they would retire completely and the beach too would be taken over by their children; to wax philosophical on their plans and resolutions as the new year entered its fourth and fifth hours, to watch the water, and eventually to watch the sun rise.

'Let's *go*,' Rachel said again, insistently, and then turned back to Anthony who was exchanging indulgent smiles with Adam. 'We're going to go and have sex now,' she told Anthony, seriously. 'We're getting married.' Adam covered her mouth with his hand and laughed. Behind it she stuck her tongue out, so that it protruded between his fingers.

'Charming, Rach.'

She blew a raspberry on his hand and giggled. 'Come *on*. Let's go and do it.'

'Keep your voice down, your parents are just behind you.'

She shrugged and stumbled slightly, steadying herself on his arm. 'So? We're getting married. We're allowed to do it. We have to practise making babies! They *want* us to be doing it now, we have to practise making their grandchildren. Let's *go*.'

Adam turned to Anthony, who was laughing. 'I'm going to take her back, I think.'

'Good luck with all the baby-making.' Anthony clapped him on the back and raised his bottle of Goldstar.

'Thank yooou!' Rachel interjected, and began to drag Adam up the beach towards the hotel.

The whole Gilbert family had been touched by his coming. Lawrence's delight had been greatest of all when a confused (and, back then, sober) Rachel had seen Adam sitting on a bar stool, his holdall still at his feet. Lawrence's expression alone had been enough to make the trip worthwhile – he had looked quite misty-eyed. To Lawrence, there was only ever one thing that was important, and that thing was family. For his own family Lawrence would cross not only oceans but continents, stratospheres – galaxies, if necessary. What he would not do for Jaffa and Rachel could not be done. He had known that Adam had turned the holiday down in order to man his, Lawrence's, own office. He had understood that this drive to work hard was a drive to provide for a future with a new wife. Still, he had been disappointed that the young couple were to start the year apart. Success was important for the security it provided, Lawrence knew that, and if it protected his girls then Lawrence would work until he fell. But nothing was more important than being together. Adam had realised it, acted, and Lawrence was tremendously proud.

Adam's appearance reaffirmed a secret plan that Lawrence had long been hatching. Once they were officially related, he would find a way to fly Michelle out to Eilat with them each Christmas without embarrassing her, and Olivia too, though it was an imaginative stretch to picture Adam's sister on a beach. But she would appreciate the Neolithic excavations at Nahal Ashrun, he thought, and if she came he would take her to them.

Until now he had been holding back, not wanting the Newmans to feel so keenly the imbalance between the sides – Michelle and Olivia teetering high on a seesaw that was weighted heavily on the other arm by all the Gilberts and Schneiders, heaped and jostling on top of one another. It was an improbably large family in which relatives kept appearing like clowns tumbling out of a Mini, and Adam had been lovingly enveloped by the flock. But there was room for Michelle and Olivia too, and now that Adam had demonstrated his commitment to Rachel's every happiness, Lawrence was determined to bring them into the fold. The evening had been a magical one. For his part, Adam was equally pleased with his decision. It had worked out better than he'd even imagined, although the family's elation had done little to assuage his guilt. If recently their praise seemed sometimes to evoke a mild claustrophobia, now he pushed this aside with deliberation.

'Do you want to say goodnight to your parents before we go up?'

'Oh.' Rachel stopped and pushed her lip out in an exaggerated sulk. 'Do we have to?'

'No, we can just go to bed. I thought you might want to.'

They had reached the decking that led through the restaurant back into the hotel and Rachel spun round, a mischievous smile on her face. 'I want to see you! You're here now, I still can't believe you're actually here. Oh – let's go back down to the beach, let's go and have sex on the beach!' This was so loud that he feared she'd been overheard by the patrons around them – among them no doubt several members of their synagogue, a neighbour, or a young cousin of her father's squash partner – but no one appeared to react. He had never seen Rachel so uninhibited, and her behaviour had been out of character from the start of the evening. He was uneasy about this unfamiliar, daring Rachel, sensing a nervous hysteria simmering beneath her new, bold exterior. He felt a dull throb of shame and anxiety, and for a moment he wondered if she had suspected something and was competing to out-sex her cousin. Still, it was not an offer he was willing to turn down. He followed her back through the bar, circumnavigating a constellation of yellow plastic beach chairs that contained Lawrence, Jaffa and assorted Schneider cousins. They walked together into the darkness that fell on either side of the hotel, padding across the hard, wet sand near the water's edge. At one point Rachel stopped and, leaning on Adam's forearm, pulled off her knickers, tripping as she stepped free of them, and flung them into the air towards the sea with an accompanying shriek. They fell anticlimactically, six inches in front of her, where they lay sopped and wavering gently in the shallow water like pink cotton seaweed. Adam and Rachel carried on walking.

They had been stumbling together for a while, Rachel's hand groping unsteadily at the waistband of his trousers, before they reached anywhere with privacy. The sand had widened and low dunes had appeared, standing between the empty beach and what looked like the dark staff quarters of a big hotel. She seemed to have sobered a little and her gleeful laughter had subsided to awkward, intermittent giggles. Before the sand dunes he picked her up and she squealed as he carried her into the black shadows of the palm trees. There was hope then, he reflected, for adventure with this girl whom he loved so tenderly. Maybe she'd guessed nothing. Maybe it was the long, long awaited engagement ring – glittering even in the deep blue desert night – that held magic for her that might yet free her like a djinn. Perhaps it really was enough to make her feel safe, liberated under its protection to be someone bigger, someone braver. And why shouldn't she change? Here was the evidence. This was a new Rachel for him – more adventurous, less careful, and now on her back on the cool sand, pulling him on top of her with urgency and parting her legs beneath his weight, driven by needs that he hadn't seen in her since they were teenagers. He pushed aside her fumbling hands to undo his buttons himself.

But when she kissed him the taste made him shiver. The piña coladas on her breath and the traces of suncream still on her skin filled his nostrils with the sweet scent of coconut, and took him suddenly and painfully elsewhere. And as he knelt over her in the darkness, it wasn't Rachel's gasps he heard.

Israeli hotel breakfasts have their origins on the kibbutz, where breakfast comes at the middle of the working day – if you've risen with the sun to pick fruit or tend chickens, by eight o'clock in the morning it's time for a substantial meal. At centre stage are the least exciting elements – rectangular catering trays steam-heated and steaming with scrambled eggs, oily roasted tomatoes, pancakes (both potato and blueberry); the customary glass bowls of slippery pink grapefruit segments, and the slickly purple-brown prunes sodden with syrup and ubiquitous in hotel dining rooms. Beside the yoghurts, cheeses and smoked fish are cut vegetables; tart young purple olives; small, dry Middle Eastern cucumbers; fresh, chopped tomatoes, sugar-sweet and drowned in salted lemon juice. And beyond these the firm cheesecakes, iced lemon cakes, poppy seed coffee cakes, brownies, Hungarian sponge cakes with walnut icing and bowls of whipped sour cream. In no other country had Adam ever seen chocolate mousse served for breakfast (piped into champagne glasses, a black chocolate musical note perched proudly on each swirled peak). Glistening neon-red carrot jam; bowls of shredded halva, chocolate-covered almonds, candied orange peel, glossy, flaking baklava. It is all there in an emulation of the exhausted farm workers' reward, laid on for holiday-makers who will exert themselves only in the harvesting of souvenirs, and the picking of lunch from the pool menu.

The Gilberts breakfasted at one end of a table for twenty. As Jaffa's cousins had set off late the night before, in typically intrepid fashion, to drive the six hours back to Tel Aviv, their numbers were depleted to a more modest sixteen. Brunch on New Year's Day was extended until eleven and so they had all assembled at ten o'clock, a jaunty and cheerful crew. Not for this family the traditional morning cocktail of Alka-Seltzer and regret; Rachel's was the only hangover at the table – quite possibly the only hangover in the dining room. She sat white-faced behind her sunglasses and nursed the orange juice that Adam brought her.

'I feel wobbly,' she whispered sadly.

'That's OK, Pumpkin, you'll feel better soon.' Next to the orange juice he set down a *café barad*, a slush of coffee, sugar, cream and crushed ice that swirled beneath the revolving blades of a self-service granita machine. She sipped some feebly from a teaspoon.

At the head of the table, Lawrence began tapping his coffee cup with a fork to command attention, but to no avail. It would take a far greater sound than that to be heard over the symphony of shouting and laughter, the clink of spoon in bowl and fork on platter. The soundtrack of three hundred breakfasting Jews, hungry and unleashed in a room of unlimited carbohydrate. 'Hey!' said Lawrence eventually, tapping louder. His family looked up.

'I would like to propose a toast,' he continued, lifting up his coffee. 'I for one was tremendously touched that

Adam took the trouble to come all the way to Israel and surprise Rach when we all know what a tyrant his boss can be –' here everyone laughed except Jaffa, who after thirty years of marriage no longer pretended to be amused by her husband's most over-used jokes '– and as it's the first day of the new year, the year in which you're getting married . . . the year in which my little girl is getting married . . . sorry.' He paused, and swallowed several times. 'Sorry. Yes, as I was saying, this is the year that the rest of your lives are beginning and I just wanted to say, well. It seems crazy to welcome you to the family, Adam, when you've been part of our family for such a very long time, and such a very welcome part of it. So instead I will say we love you, and *thank you*, for joining our family, and for making our Rachel so very happy. I wish the two of you many happy years together and Adam, I wish the two of us many happy years together at the Arsenal. *L'chaim.*'

Cappuccinos were raised; Adam clinked his orange juice with Jaffa's iced tea; Rachel clinked coffee slush with her younger cousins who were drinking the same concoction through slim red straws. Jaffa, despite her eye-rolling during the opening words of Lawrence's address, was now sniffing loudly and reached with one plump hand for her husband and with the other for Rachel.

'*Ach*, my family,' she said, and then released them and strained over Rachel for Adam, cupped his face between jewelled fingers and squeezed. Rachel, trapped in the middle, objected.

'I can't breathe, *Ima*, get off, leave Adam alone.'

Jaffa sat back with the benign expression of a woman who was, despite her family's recurrent exasperation with her, completely secure in their love. 'OK, OK. I leave him. But my new son will go and get me another *boureka*, yes? Potato, not cheese.'

FOURTEEN

How does anyone know when it's right to marry? Around the pool were sun loungers in pairs; on them couples sleeping, chatting, passing drinks and suncream and books and babies to one another in a constant exchange of thoughts and things. In the pool a broad, tattooed father with a stubbled face and wet-shaved head was throwing a gleeful toddler high in the air while his young wife swam lengths, her lean body dark and muscled and barely concealed in a white bikini. Two long black braids trailed behind her in the water. In the shallow end was a modern Orthodox couple (identifiable as such because, although they were Orthodox, they were liberal enough to swim together), he in a Hawaiian print shirt and baseball cap in addition to his baggy swimming trunks; she in a long-sleeved T-shirt that ballooned around her in the water, her hair modestly stowed beneath a rubber swimming cap. They also had a baby with them but this one was smaller, smacking the water with tiny fists as mother and father held her together and smiled encouragement. And sitting on the side of the pool was another young couple, he with carrot-shaped blond dreadlocks and she with the lower half of her hair shaved and the rest cut short as if they might have only a certain amount of hair between them, though both had an equal number of piercings. They sat on the damp concrete with their legs in the water and their arms around each other. And looking among these couples, on every left hand there glinted a gold wedding ring. Adam fought the urge to go to each man he saw branded thus and shake him and demand to be told: how did you know? Are you happy? What might you have had instead?

'I'm feeling sooo much better.' Rachel flopped down next to him, restored to life by a long nap and a swim. She pulled at the silver chopstick in her hair and arched backwards to let it fall over the back of the chair – it was crucial to keep dry hair away from wet shoulders. She remained in this position for several moments until satisfied that the midday sun had evaporated all potentially frizz-inducing droplets from her skin. Lawrence appeared before them, careful to adjust his positioning so as not to interrupt his daughter's access to the sunshine.

'Pedaloes?' he asked. 'I think the Wilsons are going down, they've reserved four of them so you two could take one.'

Rodney and Charlotte Wilson were old friends of the Gilberts. Rodney had been at school with Lawrence and was now his squash partner; their elder daughter Lucy Wilson was Rachel's age and had also been in her class at school. Leonora Wilson was much younger and had been at school with none of the Gilberts but had been in the same Sunday school class as Tanya Pearl's sister Hayley. Charlotte Wilson's cousin, who had become religious and upset the family, had studied in Jerusalem ten years ago with Jaffa's cousin who had also become religious and upset her own family. Rodney Wilson was an orthopaedic surgeon and had once helped Adam's mother with her back. Numerous other tangential connections united them.

'Great.' Adam answered before Rachel could opt to remain supine. 'It'll be perfect for your tan, Pumpkin, we'll stay in one spot and just go round in circles so you can get all angles covered.'

Rachel pulled a face at him without opening her eyes. Lawrence laughed and continued along the row to issue invitations to other friends.

The last time that Adam had captained a plastic boat he had been in Hyde Park, desultory swans drifting past as he and Rachel explored the motionless expanse of the boating lake beneath a lead-grey sky. The long ago date had been a success, however. Boats were romantic even if the weather did not hold and the swans, close up, were raggedly dirty and bad tempered and just slightly menacing. It was all rather different on the Red Sea. They pedalled away from the pontoon, powering slowly through clear turquoise water towards the red hills of Jordan. On the shore behind them tall palm trees threw perfect fluted shadows on the sand.

'I've found a dress, I think.'

'Cool. What's it like?'

'Well, obviously you're the last person I can say what it's like to when you're not meant to know anything. But it's gorgeous. Yael and I were looking at Vera Wang online yesterday, and there's one that I really think is it. And Tanya knows someone who used this brilliant seamstress in Belsize Park who can copy anything so I'm going to try it on in Selfridges and if it works then she can make something similar. And it's perfect because that way I can change it a bit too.'

'How long does it take to make a dress?'

'She thinks about six weeks, depending on how busy she is. But six weeks probably, until the first fitting.'

'So, in theory it could be ready by the middle of February.'

'Yes, if I find the right fabric for her too. She's given me the names of a few places to go.'

'Hmm. How are you ever going to choose a colour?'

'Yes, ha ha, Ads, I know, all wedding dresses look the same to you but I actually do have to choose a shade.'

'What about red for Arsenal?'

Rachel ignored this, as she did so many of his jokes. Her selective hearing became particularly selective when she deemed his frivolity to be in poor taste as it saved her the bother of getting annoyed. 'At first I thought maybe oyster.'

'Not kosher.'

'Or ivory, maybe, or something in the middle, like cream. But I think I'm going to go for white-white. I do tan quite dark.' This with some pride. 'And once I've chosen that she can start.'

'So then please, Pumpkin, will you consider changing the date of the wedding? I really don't want it to be in August, that's still almost a year away—'

'Eight months.'

'Eight months but still, it's ridiculous. I know how important it is to you to get married in the perfect wedding dress and you deserve it, absolutely. But you've found the dress, which you've always said is the hardest part, so now

I really don't see why it can't be late February.' As he spoke he felt lighter; after all, there was no need to have worried when put like this it was all so simple.

'Just think about it, all our family and the friends who really matter to us will make sure they're free whenever, and I want it to be *meaningful*' – he spoke this with emphasis, a shield held up pre-emptively against accusations of callousness – 'and I don't want to wait. And now we really don't have to. And all the rest of it, I'm happy for you to have anything you want, really, any way you want, but can we just at least talk about making it at the end of next month? Last weekend in February, say. Eight weeks is more than enough time to plan . . .' He trailed off, realising that Rachel had been sitting still and his own pedalling, rhythmic and synchronised with his emphatic speech, was powering them in circles. They slowed and began to drift.

Rachel gazed ahead of her for a moment, and then pushed her sunglasses up into her hair. 'Ads, what's going on?'

'What do you mean? Nothing's going on, I just want us to take back a little control of this wedding, that's all. It's about what we want, not anyone else. I think people forget that sometimes and—'

She interrupted him. 'And I really, really don't understand this big rush all of a sudden. I mean, it was sweet before when you were all impatient and saying that you wanted me to be your wife and everything but I've been thinking about it and Ads, we've been together *thirteen years* now. Why is it such an emergency all of a sudden? Are you actually sure you want to marry me?'

Adam stiffened. 'Don't be silly, Pumpkin, of course I want to marry you.'

'Don't tell me I'm being silly, I'm not. I'm not an idiot. You've been acting differently ever since we got engaged, and it feels like maybe you're having doubts.'

'I'm not having doubts!' he said, quickly.

'Well, something's going on. And if your heart is somewhere else –' at this point Adam's heart felt as if it was somewhere else entirely: contracted with fear and lodged in the region of his throat – 'then it's not right not to tell me. If you're still thinking about Kate then . . .'

'Kate?' He could not keep the surprise from his voice. Kate Henderson! He had barely thought of her at all in the last years, and when he did it was mostly because Rachel herself had a habit of bringing her up in the middle of arguments. In Adam's mind, Kate was filed away somewhere in the catalogue of sexual memories through which he occasionally rifled, cross-referenced with mild domination and dirty talk and appearing only at moments when his imagination required such supplements. But she did not feature elsewhere. He'd been fond of her; he had even loved her once, maybe. But he had never pined for her, even back then. Kate!

'Yes. I'm not stupid, I saw how you were with her. I met her, remember? And you said it was nothing but I've always known it wasn't. You loved her. And you broke up with her because she wasn't Jewish and I know that your dad had always wanted you to marry a Jewish girl and you felt guilty, and that must have been very hard because you can't feel OK about rebelling against someone who isn't there. And I know you think "Oh, Rachel's so conventional and she doesn't understand anything" or whatever, but I understand *love* because I know the way I love you, and if you want to be with someone then I know that religion shouldn't get in the way. And nor should what your family would say, or anything you feel towards me that is a –' she was almost in tears now but he watched her steel herself to continue and her bravery moved him more than anything in her words '– a responsibility. I don't want you to marry me because you feel like you have to. We have a choice here, you're not stuck. And I don't know if you've been in touch with her or . . .'

Adam finally found his voice. This conversation was preposterous and it was preposterous to have it in a pedalo, separated in their moulded plastic bucket chairs and unable even to face one another properly. He could not let it continue.

'Stop, Rachel! I mean – stop. I don't even think about Kate from one year to the next! This is crazy. And you're . . .' He paused and then continued. 'It's so wide of the mark, it's madness. I want to marry you. No one else. Why would I be begging you to move the wedding forward if I was thinking of anyone but you? Let's take this stupid boat thing back now. Don't you see that doesn't make any sense?'

She shook her head. 'No, I don't think it makes no sense, it makes sense to me. Yes, let's go back.' They began to pedal slowly in unison. 'Sometimes if someone's worried about something, they want to just do it and get it over with so they don't have to keep questioning their decision. If you're really sure that you want to be with me for ever then why does it matter when we get married?'

This was a more apposite observation than even she realised, he thought. He was grasping for certainty. The sooner they married the sooner his vacillating and torment would end, and on that point his reason and his instinct had been in harmony. She had cornered him. Although he often felt that he was the one to back down in arguments, during which Rachel would contradict herself frequently and wallow in the irrational, he was not used to conceding logical points to her. To concede was usually to indulge. But there was nothing he could say in answer to her question except, 'You're right, of course it doesn't matter. I don't care if it's ten years, Pumpkin. I don't care if it's another thirteen. I could not be more certain – I want to be with you for ever.'

'Are you sure?'

'Of course.'

'Are you sure you're sure?'

'Yes, I'm sure.' To his own surprise he heard his voice breaking and felt the odd sensation that, for reasons that he could not articulate, he might cry.

'Ads!' Rachel reached across the moulded fibreglass gulf between them and stroked his cheek. They were approaching the little bobbing pontoon from which they had set out; the pedalo man was semaphoring that they should come in on the left side and behind him stood Lawrence and Jaffa, waving at them and squinting into the sunshine. As they drew nearer Adam could see Lawrence reach for the camera around his neck and aim it at their little craft.

'Ads, don't be upset, I love you, I'm sorry. I know you don't want to be with Kate.'

'I want to marry *you*,' he said, with feeling.

'I know.'

Together they turned to look up at a beaming Lawrence who extended his camera towards them, capturing for posterity the moment at which they arrived together, back on to dry land.

FIFTEEN

'Friday night dinner' is one of the most evocative phrases in the vocabulary of any Jew – up there in significance with 'my son the doctor' and 'my daughter's wedding'. In the Newman household Friday night dinners had been, like everything else, divided into the epochs of Before Jacob and After Jacob, both defined by distinct but equally fixed practices. In the early years of Adam's life, his father would collect him and Olivia from school on a Friday and they would go home via Carmelli's to buy the *challah* for the blessing of the bread, unless they had made dough the night before and were baking it themselves. To buy *challah* so late on a Friday is controversial. Most of North London's housewives have already queued for theirs well before midday – by three thirty there is always a moderate risk that they'll have sold out (one is meant to have two *challot* on the table beneath a decorated cover to represent the double portion of manna that God bestowed on the Sabbath, a clever suggestion on the Lord's part that ensures there will always be enough left over for French toast the following morning). By the afternoon the bakeries are either feverishly crowded or stripped bare.

But Adam and Olivia both loved to go to Carmelli's Bakery with their father, to breathe in the warm steam of fresh bagels and admire the glass displays of cakes and biscuits, the loaves of *challah* and black rye heaped on blond wooden shelves behind the West Indian shop assistants, all of whom now spoke Yiddish by osmosis. If Adam was lucky, these outings also offered the opportunity to ruin his dinner with something that he and Olivia had nagged Jacob to buy them. Olivia favoured the apricot-glazed Danish pastries, shiny as glass; Adam's most coveted treats had been the broad, dry gingerbread men with piped white faces, their clothing implied by a series of miniature Smarties. Adam had passed many walks home to Temple Fortune trailing behind father and sister, absorbed in rendering his gingerbread man's howls of protest during a slow and violent consumption. Sometimes the captive biscuit was a Nazi, at other times merely a non-specific villain whom Adam's cunning had defeated. At the door crumbs were brushed off chins. Ruining one's dinner was a sin punishable by swift but potent guilt-inducement. Michelle did not work a long day at the office and then slave to cook their meals for her own health, you know.

After Jacob, the visits to the bakery had ended and instead the remaining Newmans had begun to go to synagogue every Friday – religiously, as it were. Through the modern wizardry of delayed-timer ovens and Slovakian au pairs, Michelle had managed to parboil potatoes, roast a chicken, pâté its liver and the livers of many of its cousins, steam vegetables and bake amaretto-soaked peaches, all while she accompanied her offspring to *shul* and remained with them therein, praying for them to stay anchored and supported at the bosom of a community. Adam fought temptation each week. His friends from Sunday school were inevitably sitting together in the back row or were outside gloriously unsupervised in the dark playground, but as the eight-year-old man of the family he knew what his father would expect of him. And so he remained standing beside his mother throughout the service, braced for the two inevitable danger moments – the *misheberach*, the prayer to heal the sick, and the Kaddish, the mourners' prayer. During these – the first a sweet, lilting melody, the second chanted in mysterious and haunting Aramaic – it was always his worst fear that his mother might cry. She had never done so but each week he felt her stiffen beside him, and watched as her left thumb crept to stroke her wedding band under the partial cover of a closed fist. He would not leave her side, though he longed to escape. Olivia was spared such temptation by having no friends she wished to join.

The dinner that followed would inevitably be strained, and strange. It was for Jacob that all was arranged as it had always been – the starched white linen tablecloth, the elaborate courses, the blessings over candles and wine and bread – but Jacob wasn't there. And so Michelle, ramrod straight, did not look very thankful as she lit the candles and intoned her blessings to God for the light of Shabbat, and eight-year-old Adam raised a wine glass and squeaked a version, woefully inadequate, he felt, of the prayers that his father had sung each week. A man ought to do it, and he was the closest thing to hand. When they invited other families to join them, as Michelle did more and more in the years that followed, someone else's father would sing the blessing over the wine and that was worse, usually. They always did it wrong, not knowing that in this house you were meant to pour little glasses of sugary boiled Kiddush wine for the children to raise along with you, or that the 'amen' at the end was meant to be said with a deep Southern Baptist twang – 'ay-men' – to make Adam giggle and Olivia roll her eyes.

In Rachel's family there were no notable absences at Friday night dinner, only many, many presences. As a Mediterranean people Jews tend to be expansive by nature – as for Greeks, Italians or Turks, a meal is not a meal unless you sit down to it with twenty people you love (or if that's too optimistic, twenty people you are at least related to). But even amongst Jews, Jaffa hovered near the upper end of the scale. She owned several sixty-litre stockpots of the sort found in school kitchens; Rachel had grown up thinking it normal to buy chickens six at a time.

By Jaffa's standards this particular Friday night dinner had almost negligible attendance. In addition to the Gilberts there was Rachel's grandmother Ziva who came every week and therefore did not count as "having people"; Adam's mother Michelle who came almost as often; Adam's sister Olivia, down from Oxford in another of her strange embroidered get-ups and an especially peculiar bottle-green and burgundy striped woollen hat; Leslie and Linda Pearl, Tanya and Jasper, and all four Wilsons, who had brought with them Leonora Wilson's pouting French exchange.

Unable to break a habit so long established, Jaffa had catered for approximately forty guests, and the menu was traditional Ashkenazi by way of Marks & Spencer – much like Michelle's Shabbat dinner, and the Shabbat dinners of innumerable north-west London families. Jaffa's version was compiled with loving intuition, with minimal aesthetic concern and a great deal of care for flavour and balance, infusing, tweaking, marinating, improvising; Michelle prioritised expedience and presentation and cooked, always, to a precise recipe. But the building blocks were the same. Chopped liver topped with a spaghetti heap of translucent golden caramelised onions; egg mayonnaise streaked with shreds of bright green spring onion to be eaten with the *challah*, followed by chicken soup. This was succeeded by a main course of chicken stuffed with whole lemons and onions and cooked, at Jaffa's house, in *zatar*; roast potatoes and *tsimmes* – soft carrots long baked in honey and cinnamon. The menu was predictable but there was safety in the weekly appearance of these foods – security, continuity and love. For a people whose history is one of exodus and eviction, the luxury of repetition is precious.

'You must read *Trials of the Diaspora*,' Olivia was saying to Ziva, who had been asking her something about Chaucer. 'It's a conflation of ideas, of course, by necessity, but excellent and essential. If you're at all interested in the Prioress's Tale you must look at it.' Olivia was animated for the first time in the evening as the seating had shifted slightly since dinner and her earlier position, between Lucy Wilson and Rachel, had exposed her to conversations in which she could not hope to participate – Lisa London's rumoured new boyfriend, for example, and what had possessed Adele Summerstock and Anthony Rosenbaum to call their new son Zebedee. Women like Rachel (like her own mother, in fact) bewildered Olivia, and she did not know how to talk to them. Her knowledge of north-west London's complex social networks had been limited when she had lived there, and now she was unable to recall the relationships even between people she'd known since infancy. It was a defence, Michelle theorised, against recalling a childhood of rejection by the cooler, less cere-bral girls. Olivia had simply forgotten them all. During the reshuffling at the table Olivia had gravitated towards Ziva and Lawrence.

'Is that the one by Anthony Julius?' Lawrence asked. 'I've heard good things about it.'

'Yes, I can send it to you. There's another article in the *Journal of English and Germanic Philology* that's relevant too called "Wordsworth and the Jews".'

'I would like very much to see that,' said Ziva. 'I have recently re-read his translation of The Prioress and her Tale which is interesting, of course, when considered beside "A Jewish Family". Please, if you might email me the reference.'

Lawrence, his arm around Jaffa who was dipping a shard of black chocolate into his coffee cup, wore his habitual Shabbat expression of beatific contentment. He had been to synagogue to mark the transition from week to weekend, from work to rest, and there had greeted the approaching Sabbath with joy, as was customary – as one celebrates the arrival of a bride. Lawrence had a quiet faith and he liked to reconnect with it like this, once a week. He would come home from *shul* and stop Rachel wherever she was, placing his hands on her head and blessing her softly, father to daughter. Before they ate he read aloud the words of the *ayshet chayil* to Jaffa: 'A woman of valour – who can find her? Her value is far beyond pearls. Her husband's heart relies on her.' He would recite this in poor Hebrew and then in English every week with, it had always seemed to Adam, no diminution of sincerity or passion as he looked across the table at his glowing wife. Lawrence was a happy man. A grateful man. By the time he reached grace after the meal the French exchange had decamped to the kitchen where she was on the floor feeding scraps of chicken to the dog.

Jasper had the week's *Jewish Chronicle* before him, open to the Social and Personal pages.

'Sadie Levine,' he read.

Olivia looked unimpressed. 'Dispatched, clearly.'

'Correct. That was a warm-up. Lisle Kupermann.'

'Dispatched,' said Olivia and Adam together. Jaffa tutted in ostentatious disapproval and began to clear the plates, noisily.

'Wrong. Hatched.'

'Hatched, really? Lisle? Oh, that's terribly old-fashioned these days, poor thing,' said Michelle, standing to help Jaffa.

'Jonathan Cohen.'

'You're giving us nothing to work with,' Leslie Pearl complained. 'Matched.'

'Well done. OK. Coco Winter Freedman. Too easy,' he added, over the collective shout of, 'Hatched.'

'Maurice Leonard Pinsky.'

'Dispatched,' said Ziva, who until that moment had shown no sign that she was listening.

'Matched,' Jasper corrected. 'Although possibly a second marriage.'

'This game is not very respectful,' Jaffa called from the kitchen.

'Feyga Baumel?' Jasper shouted in reply.

There was a silence, during which everyone looked expectantly towards the open door of the kitchen.

'Dispatched,' Jaffa called eventually.

'Indeed. May she rest in peace, poor woman. What a life she must have had, with a name like that.'

'She was no doubt a *frummer*,' said Ziva sagely, 'and so probably did not realise that she had been so inconsiderately encumbered. Very good. I will now go home.' No one was surprised by her abrupt announcement; Ziva did not believe that social niceties were required with family – or indeed, with most others.

'OK, *Ima*, Adam will take you back,' said Jaffa, who had returned from the kitchen with a bowl of tangerines, just in case anyone was in need of a little something.

'Adam, thank you. I am ready to go now.' Ziva pushed her chair back and stood stiffly, her handbag already on her arm. Into the front pocket of this she placed a single Bittermint, slipped in to join the other discs wrapped in frog-green foil that accumulated there from week to week. Beneath the foil the chocolates would whiten and seam with hairline cracks like glazed pottery, eventually making their way to one of the bowls scattered around Ziva's sitting room, decanted there each time the pouch on the front of her handbag was full. Adam had been caught out by these antiques before.

'Of course we'll take you, Granny,' said Rachel.

Jaffa objected. 'No, *motek*, you stay. I need you to help me with the guest list this evening and you're away all weekend you said, so it must be now. Adam will get you on the way home, OK?'

'Of course.' Adam reached for his jacket. Michelle, who had driven herself to the dinner just as she had driven herself everywhere else for the last twenty years, was unimpressed. She did not see why her son should be presumed chauffeur to these assorted women. Paragraphs of censorious commentary were written on her face, discernible only to her son – if Jaffa wanted Adam to drive Ziva to Islington it was one thing, she was an old lady, but it was utterly unreasonable to ask that he then come back again to collect Rachel. Michelle was fond of Jaffa, but this perceived exploitation tapped into a long-held objection: as a woman who already had one man at her beck and call (and Lawrence was a man who did a great deal for his wife, whether it was demanded of him or not), Jaffa had even less need to commandeer the services of a second. But it did not seem to work that way. Accustomed as she was to men in the role of drivers, lifters, bankers, shleppers and errand boys, she employed them all the same way and with ease. Her role was merely as controller of the fleet; God forbid, thought Michelle with heavy sarcasm, she should actually have to do any of these tasks herself. Why did Adam never say anything? Why did Rachel never disagree with her mother about these commands? And while we're on the subject, it wouldn't actually kill Rachel to get behind the wheel herself once in a while. Adam shrugged at his mother in response to this silent communication. Michelle shrugged back with an expression of elaborately feigned innocence. What? I didn't say anything.

In the car, Ziva enquired, 'You did not want to stay and

help with the guest list to your wedding? They will no doubt invite many people you do not like if you are not there.'

'That'll happen whether I'm there or not. The way things are going I'm not even sure I'm on the guest list.'

Ziva cocked her head. 'You are not happy with Jaffa's plans for the *chaseneh* of the year?'

'I wanted it smaller. And sooner.'

'Ah, yes, I remember. But let us be serious for a moment, you knew always that would be impossible. Jaffa perhaps has been planning this ever since Rachel was *in utero*. They said it was a girl, and my daughter began to call caterers.'

'I know. But I hoped.'

'Ah, well. In all pleasures hope is a considerable part,' Ziva quoted, 'but in this instance hope is perhaps best abandoned, yes? When you reach my age, a few months here and there will not seem so very long to have waited. And a few people you don't know, a few sandwiches you don't like at the reception – it is not what you will remember. You will remember a life together. One day is one day, wedding day or no. These days young people marry less, I think, and I cannot disapprove of it. These contracts seem antiquated even to me, and I myself am antiquated.'

They had drawn up outside her house.

'You will come in please for one moment, I have a photograph that Rachel wanted, if I do not give it to you now I will forget. At my age one must strike while the iron is hot or risk senility in the interim.'

The lights were on in Ziva's hallway. Loud music throbbed from the sitting room – Adam had heard faint strains of it as they'd approached the front door.

'Tosca,' said Ziva. 'For the burglars I usually put Radio 4. And so I believe that my granddaughter is here.'

In the sitting room they found Ellie, stretched out on the sofa, her long legs hooked over the back of it, ankles crossed and flexing gently in time to the music. She did not seem to hear them as they entered. No doubt she had been invited to her Aunt Jaffa's for Shabbat, but the prior engagement that had kept her from coming appeared only to be a date with Ziva's CD collection. Her eyes were closed; Rocky was curled in the crook of her arm. She looked like a little girl cuddling her doll. Together, Adam and Ziva regarded girl and dog.

'She is beautiful, my granddaughter, no?' said Ziva, beside him in the doorway.

Adam merely nodded. The energy with which he had avoided seeing Ellie had been all-consuming these past weeks – that he had second-guessed her whereabouts and planned his own movements only to come upon her like this shocked him, though with hindsight it should not have done. His heart was in his throat. He gestured to Ziva that he would sneak out and leave them. But at that moment Rocky scrambled across his owner's stomach and leapt to the floor to greet them, and Ellie opened her eyes.

'Sleeping Beauty,' said Ziva, fondly.

'Not sleeping, listening. Isn't Gheorghiu awesome?'

'I favour Callas myself, this one I do not like so very much, she is too . . .' Ziva filled in the missing adjective with a gesture, a rotating of her wrist that resembled a royal wave. She approached Ellie, who jumped up to hug her in greeting.

After embracing her grandmother, Ellie then turned to Adam. 'Hey, stranger.'

'Shabbat shalom,' he replied, and then instantly regretting his pomposity added, 'Hi.'

'I will go and get the photograph for Rachel, it is somewhere on my desk.'

'I'll get it, Granny.'

'No, you will not know where to look. One moment. You may instead make Adam a cup of coffee now that he is obliged to wait for my scrabbling.'

'No coffee, thanks,' said Adam when Ziva had begun, painfully, to climb the stairs in the hall behind him. He relinquished his place in the doorway, stepping farther into the room so that he could not see her struggling. In place of help Ziva always preferred privacy.

'No. No coffee. Apparently there's nothing I have that you want.'

This was a response both unreasonable and untrue, and they both knew it. Adam did not reply.

'You didn't answer my emails,' she said eventually.

'What do you want me to say? I shouldn't have come to Oxfordshire.'

'I wanted us to talk. There was stuff I wanted to explain.'

'I don't want excuses.'

'I didn't say excuses. I don't have anything to excuse. But I at least wanted you to know what was true and what wasn't.'

Adam looked away from her. It was one of those moments, he knew, in which he teetered on the edge of something vast and incalculable. On one side rationality, security and honour. On the other terror, oblivion and possibility. He felt her nearness as if she were touching him.

'Can I see you tomorrow night?' he asked. Rachel was going to Lucy Wilson's hen party in Paris and he, Jasper, Gideon and Simon had tickets to see Jeff Beck and Eric Clapton at the O2. They could go without him.

Ellie nodded and then smiled, widely and brightly, a smile that was directed over his shoulder. 'Did you find it?' she asked her grandmother. Softly, to Adam, she added, 'Come to Casa Blue on Brick Lane at ten.'

Ziva shuffled forwards. 'I have found it. I do not know why it is of such interest to her but there you are. Ancient history. My family all now seem to be nostalgic for things they never themselves knew and I want to tell them, *ach*, it is all so much better now. Or rather, not so very bad as it was. Still, she can do with it as she wishes.'

'Let's see?' Ellie held out her hand for the photograph. It was small and square, printed in sepia on thin paper that curled at each corner. Adam looked at the image over her shoulder.

At the centre of thick white borders was a picture of a young girl standing beside a piano. She was delicate-featured, skin bleached white by the faded photograph, a thick plait of dark hair coiled and pinned around her head. She stood facing the photographer proud and erect, her hands by her sides and her feet crossed a little awkwardly, one over the other. Her dress was straight and plain, its light colour now lost to the monochrome of the image. She was not smiling, but she looked very happy.

'Is that you?' asked Adam.

'Yes,' said Ziva. 'I was very beautiful, no? But anyway,

that is me on the morning of my wedding to my Yosef, the first Yosef. Take it to Rachele, she remembered it from when she was a little girl and wanted to see it again. Tell her she will be just such a beautiful bride.' She paused. 'When I remember that day, you know, I remember most that after the *chuppah* a man spat at my father. One of the Austrians. But not a peasant, not one of the big, angry men who worked in the fields near to our farm and who would shout at us always, always throw things. This was an educated man, a landowner. And I think – so. Things change and change again. I did not think I would or could ever again live in Europe and nothing ever can be certain. It is right that we should celebrate, that your wedding day should be a happy one.'

SIXTEEN

The route to East London was now becoming a familiar one but each time he passed the pink brick expanse of the British Library and the grey-tipped neo-Gothic spires of St Pancras, Adam would begin to get nervous. From that point east it was Ellie's territory.

The first half of this drive he had already done once that day, delivering an excitable Rachel to the station where she was met by an equally excitable group of her girl-friends, all in the customary hen party attire of matching pink T-shirts (in this instance emblazoned with a photo-graph of Lucy Wilson, the bride-to-be, taken when she was a toddler with plump, creased arms raised towards the camera and a towel on her head like a veil). In addition they each wore bouncing glittery deeley-boppers extending from pink headbands. Rachel's were fished out of a plastic bag by an officious Tanya Pearl (who was this weekend operating under the designation of Head Bridesmaid) and issued to her as soon as she stepped out of Adam's car.

Clustered on the pavement beneath the sleek glass flank of the Eurostar terminal, they were a swarm of fuchsia bumblebees fizzing and buzzing around their collective heap of luggage. These were the Nice Jewish Girls who populated Adam's world; young, modern women, many fiercely bright, several equally ambitious; strong and forthright and intellectually emancipated. Among them, Rachel was the least conflicted. The rest were contradictions, these creatures, and that they did not see it was the wonder. Lucy Wilson herself was an excellent example – with an intercalated MD–D.Phil. from Oxford, she now worked at University College Hospital as a clinician and researcher but her highest ambition, Adam knew, was to be Mrs Noah Cordova. She was a strange faun like so many of the others, with the head of a consultant oncologist and the heart of a *shtetl* daughter. And here they all were, preparing to send off one of their number into the halcyon paradise of matrimony. It was the thirteenth of February – nine girls were on their way to the city of love, crossing the Channel to celebrate Lucy's love-themed Parisian hen party, marking her passage into wifehood. Emotions of all hues would be running high: tenderness, nostalgia, sisterhood and womb-twisting envy. In London, nine corresponding men had heaved a sigh of relief that, for this year at least, they were released from the pressure of arranging a Valentine's celebration.

'Passport?' Adam had checked, leaning across the passenger seat and shouting through the open window. In return Rachel had waved it at him and blown him a kiss, nodding her deeley-boppers so that they danced cheerily. The others had waved and blown him fond kisses alongside her, for they were old friends of his, too, and now doubly woven into his life as the girlfriends and wives of other childhood friends.

And then later for the second time, he navigated through the dark back streets of King's Cross to the Euston Road where he would turn east, towards who knew what. He did not know what he was doing as he drove to Brick Lane – only that he felt impelled to be doing it.

Nothing had happened that he could not yet reverse. As the City Road nosed east in to the bleak expanse of rotating traffic at Old Street it was easier to pretend that he had crossed the Rubicon, but it was far from true. Since he'd left the Sabahs' in December, shamed and confused and angry, he had stayed safe by avoiding Ellie and he could stay safe still, by continuing to do so. He did not need to keep driving. He could keep away from her until he was married. But now he was round the corner and had found a parking space behind a Tesco's van where two men in reflective jackets were unloading pallets of Evian and 7up on to the pavement. He was early and she, he imagined, would be late. He would order a drink and collect his thoughts. He would try to understand why he was there, a question he had not yet asked himself.

What had not appeared, when he had scanned through a kaleidoscope of imagined beginnings to the evening, was the possibility that she might already be there with someone else. The time and location she had whispered to him turned out to be not an intimate assignation quickly invented; rather it had been a suggestion for him to join her on an evening already planned. He walked into the bar and saw Ellie immediately, perched on a low, crushed-velvet sofa and addressing a woman and two men with animation. That she had been on a shoot that day was evident even from across the room – her hair was back-combed and stiff with streaks of black that looked like tar; she wore false eyelashes so thick and heavy that their spidery tips reached her eyebrows. She looked as if she was in the middle of an anecdote, gesticulating with the nozzle of a shisha pipe held delicately between her fingers. Adam approached the group, irritated with himself for the shyness and embarrassment that had surged suddenly on seeing them all. Ellie's face lit up when she saw him and she handed the mouthpiece of the pipe to the girl beside her in order to commence introductions.

To her left, she said, was the famous Theo in whose studio she had been living ('my lovely squatter', he called her, and blew her a kiss) who had coincidentally been shooting her that day, and was nothing like Adam had imagined – in reality, he was a tiny man and extremely thin, with a severely trimmed black goatee, kohl-rimmed eyes and a sequinned porkpie hat. On Ellie's other side was a stout girl she identified as Theo's assistant Anoushka, now sucking greedily on the hose of the tall shisha, her wild red curls cut short into a cloud, and a great deal of green glitter around her eyes. She wore a dress as short as Ellie's usual attire, but with a far less appealing result. Flesh strained at the holes in her artfully ripped fishnets; from his position standing over their low sofa Adam could see directly up her skirt to the expanse of black lace beneath. He averted his eyes.

On a stool opposite them was Chris ('He's a talented social commentator,' Ellie said by way of introduction. 'I write the odd London piece for *New York* magazine,' he amended), a square-jawed man with greying hair and the triangular build of a swimmer, his muscles visible beneath a faded white T-shirt that depicted – with deliberate irony, Adam assumed – Ellie in a controversial advertising campaign from several years ago. How she might feel about her friend wearing her own unclothed image on his broad chest Adam could not imagine. He felt instantly protective of her, but then so very little offended Ellie.

'You've escaped NW11,' Ellie observed, pulling up a stool for Adam. On a low, scarred wooden table a candle burned in a wine bottle fattened and distorted with tumours of wax; beneath this was a cocktail-sticky menu that she extracted and handed him. 'How does it feel to break free?'

He sat down. 'It feels pretty good.'

'Then we must toast your night of freedom.'

'What are you all having?' Adam looked at the table where four identical cocktails stood at various stages of consumption, raspberries floating on their surfaces.

'Chambord and bubbles,' said Anoushka, offering him the shisha, which he refused. 'They're nice, a bit sickly. But Theo will only have champagne or champagne-based liquids.'

'Theo and Anoushka I've known for ever through work, and I know Chris from Norwood in New York,' Ellie explained. 'And I don't know how you all met each other. Not through me?' she asked.

Chris shook his head. 'No, Noush and I met at a book launch at Lutyens & Rubinstein, and then we bumped into one another again the same week at the Lit Salon at Shoreditch House.'

'Yonks ago,' confirmed Theo.

Adam nodded, uncomprehending. Just as when he spoke to Nick Hall, he had the sense of other Londons swirling past and beneath and above him of which he was only liminally aware. In these places his contemporaries were photographers and poets and musicians, publishers and editors and foreign correspondents, and people who worked for think tanks. And they were there to be found – North London was awash with Jewish writers and artists and intellectuals, more than seemed probable from a population that constituted less than half a per cent of the country. He wondered, for the first time, how many lives in Hampstead Garden Suburb were actually as homogeneous as his own. Fewer than he'd always believed, no doubt.

Ellie put down her glass. 'I'm having candy cravings. What's the closest thing to Swedish Fish in England?'

'Ooh, I love Swedish Fish!' Theo exclaimed, uncrossing and recrossing his legs for emphasis. 'There is nothing here I can think of that's nearly as delicious. Maybe wine gums?'

'What are Swedish Fish?' asked Adam.

Theo looked appalled. 'They are *ambrosial*,' he whispered, and left it there.

Ellie pulled her leather jacket from the pile slung over the back of the sofa and stood up. 'Wine gums will do. OK, I'm going round the corner. Amuse yourselves, kids.'

As she clambered over Anoushka to get out, Adam said, 'I'll come with you.'

'No problem, I'll be back in a second, stay here.'

'It's late, I'll come.'

'No, thank you, really. And in any case, I need to make a phone call. I'll be back.'

Adam felt distinctly uncomfortable. Rachel and all the other women he knew would go nowhere at night unchaperoned – even if they'd driven themselves out for the evening they were likely to ask a man to walk them back the short distance to their cars. When he dropped Rachel – or Tanya or Jaffa or Michelle, or any woman – home, he would always remain outside until the front door was safely closed and she had waved goodbye to him from an upstairs window. He would do so even when the front door and window in question were on a Neighbourhood Watch cul-de-sac in Hampstead Garden Suburb whose residents had also clubbed together to employ a private security firm. Twenty-first century or not, Adam upheld these precautions and approved of them. Mothers, sisters, girlfriends – they should be protected, and he liked to protect them. Ellie was the one he felt the strongest urge to protect and she was the most resistant to his efforts.

'I literally mean around the corner. You can count to a hundred and I'll be back.'

Her legs were bare; she hung her jacket over her shoulders and then disappeared half naked to the corner shop, her phone already raised to her ear as she left.

Anoushka turned blinking, green-glittered eyes to Adam, regarding him like a curiosity with which she could entertain herself in Ellie's brief absence. Jade spangles had fallen on her cheeks, which looked acceptable, and also on her nose, which did not. She addressed him. 'Ellie says you're her lawyer. Are you going to be able to get her back into Columbia? What are you doing about Marshall Bruce? Is it true that the wife has threatened her if she goes back to New York? Surely she can't do that?'

'I can't really talk about it,' said Adam, surprised that that wasn't self-evident.

She shrugged. 'OK. She'd tell me all of it anyway. She'd tell anyone anything. She's a crazy one, that girl.'

Theo shook his head in what looked like a combination of awe and disapproval. 'She is definitely crazy. What was she doing with that terrible Marshall Bruce?'

Chris laughed. 'Do you mean actually, technically – *what* was she doing? You'd have to ask her yourself, Theodore. Get some pointers.'

Anoushka sighed, heavily. 'She doesn't value herself. It's a question of self-respect I think, or self-esteem, and she's just not able to separate her value as a woman – as a person, actually – from her value as a sexual commodity.'

There followed much earnest analysis. Chris believed that the tragedy of her mother's death had not only deprived her of a female role model but had taught her a destructive fatalism. Theo sniffed, 'That father, Boaz. I called him Bobo the Clown. I saw him in New York, he was just never there for this splendiferously wonderful daughter even when she needed him, and she was always coming alone on jobs even when all the other girls still had their mothers tagging along and quite rightly too. Now she doesn't even know where he is, I don't think.' Anoushka believed that all this was true and was compounded by a lack of self-worth derived both from a double parental loss and from teetering on the brink of flawlessness – there was a theory, she explained, that very beautiful, very intelligent women suffered because absolute perfection felt tantalisingly attainable for them, just beyond reach of their beautiful, capable fingers, whereas for normal mortals it was abstract, impossible, and therefore not worth worrying about.

It was several minutes before Adam identified what was bothering him about this conversation. The surprising element was the utter lack of surprise: he had heard these discussions about Ellie, held in these terms and this tone, many times before. What he had not expected was to hear them from these people.

Chris had just finished saying that Ellie had cheapened herself irreparably with some of her editorial campaigns even before he'd known about Marshall Bruce, and was pointing to the image on his own T-shirt by way of illustration, when Adam finally entered the conversation.

'Isn't it a bit off to wear it then, if you think it cheapens her?' he asked, surprised by what he took to be such clear hypocrisy on the part of someone who moments ago had claimed liberality above all other virtues. Chris's disapproval bothered him much more than Jaffa's, or his mother's, or Rachel's. More than that of anyone in North London whose clucks and tutting he could dismiss. In her own circles at least, Adam had imagined that Ellie would not be judged for her actions. 'After what you said before about the diminishing importance of marriage I thought you'd be the first person to speak out against adherence to empty convention.'

Chris looked at him with a strange expression. 'I hardly consider a sense of self-worth to be empty convention.'

'She has self-worth, but she's choosing to discard conventional expectations. She's brave. Just before, you sounded like you were advocating for us all to break free of cultural and social expectations.'

'Again – bravery –' here Chris raised his left hand, cupped as if holding in it the virtue he discussed '– and stupidity.' He raised his right hand in the same way, and then separated the two hands to illustrate the difference between them, the distance between them. 'I like Ellie, she's a great girl, but I can't agree with you that she has an adequate sense of her own value and as a result of that lack she's made some absolutely moronic decisions. Destructive, stupid, generally unwise. Just because I don't believe two people need a legal contract or a discriminatory tax advantage to join their lives together doesn't mean I applaud the girl for rogering a married man for money. That's not at odds with, as you say, objecting to an adherence to empty convention. *Empty* convention, yes. Of course I object. But there's a place for meaningful, constructive social convention and principles. I'm not actually an anarchist, whatever misleading impression I might have given you.'

He was laughing a little as he said this but it was clear that he was affronted. Adam in turn felt foolish. That something was condemned by north-west London's gossiping mothers did not, he realised, automatically make it brave. They weren't wrong about everything – their censure was not, in fact, an endorsement. But why had that never occurred to him before?

SEVENTEEN

It was not turning into the evening that Adam had expected. Shortly after Ellie had disappeared she sent Theo a text message to say that she would be gone for longer than she'd thought – she had remembered that she had to speak to someone in New York before they went into the theatre and it was getting late. Adam found himself sharing a platter of garlicky, paprika-dappled hummus and oily stuffed vine leaves with Anoushka and Chris, while Theo pursed his lips and nibbled unenthusiastically on a stiff triangle of pitta bread. Around them the bar had slowly filled with big-haired boys in women's jeans and short-haired girls in Ray-Bans and even here, in the heart of the laid-back hipster East End, there was a charge of Valentine's Day madness in the air. Everyone in Casa Blue was too hip, too cool, too ironical and counter-cultural to care about greeting-card holidays and yet – gazes were roaming; eyes were meeting. If you were out tonight, you were probably looking for some action.

Adam stayed on, sampling meze and listening to Theo tell an unflattering story about Marshall Bruce's soon-to-be ex-wife (Anoushka, who had met her once on a photo shoot in Cape Cod, said that tale was untrue and that Mrs

Bruce was charming). He wondered whether Ellie was outside on the phone to Marshall. At half past eleven Theo produced a comically oversized pocket watch and rapped it impatiently, like the White Rabbit.

'Tell Madam we had to go, the guest list shuts at midnight. She'll be back soon, I'm sure, but we can't wait any longer.'

'Where are you off to?' Adam asked, confused.

'We've got tickets to a gig at the Ivy Club, we've got to get over to Covent Garden,' Anoushka explained. From beneath the table she produced a slim patent leather handbag. 'Will you hang on to Ellie's stuff?'

'Is she definitely coming back?'

'Oh yes,' said Theo, adjusting his hat in the tarnished mirror across the bar. He snatched the small bag from Anoushka and flipped it open, reached in and produced Ellie's enamel cigarette case. 'Her beloved coconut sweeties are in there, see? She'll be back. So sorry to leave you here, we're such ungracious little things. But what a pleasure to meet any friend of Miss Ellie's. Tell her we said happy Vee Day.'

They were all standing now – Chris was even taller than Adam had imagined from his seated frame, looming over Theo who looked positively Lilliputian beside him, at eye level with the graphic photograph of Ellie that was stretched over Chris's pectorals. Anoushka tugged at her skirt, which had bunched and ridden up over pudgy stock-inged thighs. 'Send her our love,' she said, and the three of them began to make their way out through the crowded bar, having left on the table a patently inadequate contri-bution to the bill. Adam sat down again, this time on the velvet sofa that the others had vacated. It had suddenly become the moment he'd expected: waiting for her alone, drink in hand and heart in mouth. The evening could begin again.

'What the hell did you say to them?' asked Ellie when she returned. In the short interim other larger parties had expanded from the tables on either side of Adam and had appropriated the stools, one by one; she sat down next to him on the sofa.

'I told them they were in the way.'

'That's right. They were.'

'They were going to a gig. Weren't you meant to be going with them?'

Ellie wrinkled her nose as if the very suggestion were distasteful. 'Nope. I loathe that atonal experimental horse-shit that Theo's obsessed with, I have more than enough dissonance in my life without listening to it. It's like the Emperor's New Clothes but without the diversion of male nudity to keep me awake. Never.'

'I don't know anything about it, to be honest.'

'Nothing to know. Pretentious Royal College graduates up on a stage gratifying themselves, and only themselves, by making a freaking racket. They always look overcome with a sort of masturbatory self-satisfaction at their own supposed creativity. Half the time they have their backs to the audience and just gaze in adoration at each other.'

A vague recollection stirred. 'Didn't your father play professional jazz saxophone?' Adam asked her.

'Whether Boaz has ever done anything professionally is up for debate. But he certainly plays a lot. At sea, on land, it's always playtime for Boaz. Did you meet my father ever?'

'Once, a long time ago.'

What he did not say was that he had met her mother that day too – Boaz and Jackie had come to the synagogue and given a *challah*-baking lesson to Adam's Sunday school class, a young, happy couple who had seemed so old to seven-year-old Adam, though they could not yet have been thirty. As the baker's daughter Jackie had led the class and while she kneaded had taught them phrases in Yiddish that she said were too rude to repeat to their parents; Boaz had been her assistant, had made jokes and pulled faces and had shaped his dough into a heart that he had presented to his giggling wife, who kissed him in front of the whole class while the boys had made vomiting noises. Adam's *challah* had been more like a pancake, he remembered; he had been too ashamed to take it to show Jacob when they'd gone to visit him at the hospice later that day. Adam had been baking *challah* with his father for years – he should have been able to do better for him, he'd felt.

'A long time ago sounds about right. Anyway.' She sat back and closed her eyes, pulling at one of her heavy false eyelashes. Adam winced. Her eyelid flickered as she stretched it; the thick spidery fronds began to peel away slowly. 'So now you're speaking to me again, it seems.'

'I was never not speaking to you.'

'I'm not sure that's strictly true, but we'll let it pass for now.' She opened her eyes and regarded him. One set of the lashes was now in her hand like a small black comb.

Without it her face looked strangely distorted, her eyes vastly different sizes, as if she was a Picasso portrait of herself. She set to work on the other side. 'So how was Israel with the perfect family?'

'Fine. A little strained, to be honest.'

'Why strained?'

'Rachel asked me if I was in love with someone else,' he said, bluntly. This statement coincided with her detaching the second set of eyelashes and so he could not identify the source of the brief discomfort that flashed across her face. He took a deep breath. 'Only she was asking about someone, this girl Kate—'

'Ah yes, her great rival from college,' Ellie said, but now that he had started to speak he would not let her divert him with mockery and he continued, tense but determined, 'Look, obviously I've not even thought about that girl for years. It's bullshit.'

She nodded, almost imperceptibly, but did not look back at him. On a chain round her neck she wore a slim gold ring and was sliding it on and off each finger in turn.

'I can't stop thinking about you,' he said, and somehow despite everything it was just so easy to say it, so simple. The rest came out in a rush. 'I've been trying to stay away from you since Christmas and just stop – but then I saw you yesterday and it was like – I realised how impossible it is for me to stay away from you.' His own ineloquence was maddening and with it the certain knowledge that when he relived this speech later, too late, the right words would flow, simple and powerful. But he had finally reached his point and he concluded with a sudden rush of triumph, 'I want to be with you. I know it's a mess and I know – I don't know how it could even ever happen or how you feel, although I think, I hope – I, I know that you feel *something*. And I can't marry Rachel and feel the way I feel about you. I want to be with you. If there's even a chance it's what you want.'

'But Adam,' she said, and the sweetness when she spoke his name was unbearable, 'that's impossible.'

He had expected protest at this point but had thought no further. Now he prepared to convince her. Logic and romance were both on his side; you must not dream of one woman and marry another. It is noble to follow your heart. She needed him. We must be together because we must.

'Why?'

'Do you really need me to tell you that?'

'Yes,' he said stubbornly. 'Nothing is impossible. Things are difficult – so, so difficult, I can't even imagine but – but not impossible. Just, we have to try. If it's what you want.'

With one finger she began to stroke the deep, ruby velvet of the sofa back and forth; dark to light; rough to smooth. 'You'll probably think I'm a psycho but I swear I knew you, I saw who you were, that very first time I met you. I'll never forget it. You were standing there with Rach with her enormous duffel bag on your shoulder like it was nothing and you kept making her laugh, and you both just looked so – you know, I don't think she even knows how *safe* you make her feel when you're beside her. How could she, I guess? She's got nothing to compare it to. But I saw the way you looked at her.' She began to draw slow circles in the nap of the fabric. 'And then I think maybe I – we could be happy together. And I haven't ever really been happy, I don't think. I don't really do happy. Not like she is all the time. But ultimately I'm telling you – that's the point. You're going to protect Rachel, just like everyone always does, and you'll do what's right for everyone. You know you have to. God knows she wouldn't know what had hit her if you didn't. So I'll follow your example and learn to be a good girl, and you're going to forget me and marry my darling cousin.' She raised her head and looked at him, steadily. 'But if things were different I would try – I would be with you, if I could. It probably doesn't help to say, but it's true.'

Adam thrilled – if this was true, and he no longer doubted that it was, then she could be convinced.

'I can't marry Rachel,' he said again. Over and over in his head he was hearing Ellie say 'I would be with you if I could'. I would be with you if I could. I would be with you if I could. He had heard nothing else.

'You're only saying that now. We both know that's not true.' Ellie sounded gentle but there was a warning in her voice that told him not to make false promises. Even as he had spoken he had begun to see that she was right. He still believed he couldn't marry Rachel. But he felt equally certain that he couldn't not marry Rachel, either.

'This is a nightmare.'

She smiled. 'You've had an easy life if this is the worst thing that's happened in it.'

He looked away, hurt. 'This is not,' he said deliberately, 'nor could it ever be, the worst thing that's happened in my life. My father died when I was eight –' the same age as you were when your mother died, he added silently, have you never realised? Have you never thought about it? '– and there you have it, the worst thing that could happen happened and nothing will ever be that painful again. But that's the whole point – life is so short. If you really mean that you'd be with me, then be with me. I'm not going to marry Rachel.'

'I know that life is short.' She dropped the ring she'd been playing with and with one finger began to trace the wishbone of blue veins on the back of her left hand. 'Just as I know that you think it's too short to hurt the people you care about. Be practical. You don't mean that you can't marry her. You're going to. You're going to marry Rachel and give her the perfect life that she expects.'

'I do mean it.'

'You don't.'

He breathed deeply for a moment. 'I don't.'

'I know.'

And then she reached up and laid a cool palm against his cheek, touching him for the first time, tracing the line of his jaw with her fingertips. His skin burned as if she had touched him everywhere; he felt certain there must be a blazing handprint on his cheek just as surely as if she'd slapped him. He took hold of the hand near his face and, turning, pressed her wrist to his lips. He heard her sharp intake of breath and in a moment she had drawn away. The urge to have her was almost unbearable.

'This is bullshit, we should go. Or – I should go.' She

sounded calm, as she always did, but he saw now that her eyes were alight.

He glanced at his watch. 'Stay here till midnight. Start Valentine's Day with me.'

'Valentine's Day? God, you really are conventional,' she said, but with tenderness. 'OK. I'll stay the . . . twelve minutes.'

'OK.'

'OK.'

A silence fell between them, lost beneath the din of the crowd and the throb of a pounding beat. Ellie watched the clock above the bar. Adam watched Ellie, a dull ache building beneath his ribs. He glanced away only when his phone beeped.

HAPPY VALENTINE'S DAY FROM PARIS!!! MISSING U LIKE CRAZY. THE GIRLS SEND LOVE. BEING AT HEN MADE ME THINK, IF U WANT 2 MAKE WEDDING SMALLER LET'S DO IT. I JUST WANT U THERE, I DON'T CARE ABOUT ANYONE ELSE. BEING MARRIED MORE IMPORTANT THAN WEDDING. SMALLER AND SOONER, IF U WANT. KISSES XXX R

Adam stared at this message for a long time before he set down his phone. Now it was Ellie who reached for his hand, gently, and he did not pull away. With her fingers she traced circles, feather-light, in his palm. A charge of electricity surged up his spine. 'Rachel is a very lucky woman,' she said, softly.

– 199 –

PART TWO

PART TWO

EIGHTEEN

The marriage of a Jewish son is a bittersweet prospect. There is relief, always, that he has navigated the tantalising and plentiful assemblies of non-Jewish women to whom the children of the Diaspora are inevitably exposed: from the moment he enters secondary school there is the constant anxiety that a blue-eyed Christina or Mary will lure him away from the tribe. Jewish men are widely known to be uxorious in all the most advantageous ways. And so each mother fears that, whether he be short and myopic, boorish or stupid or prone to discuss his lactose intolerance with strangers, whether he be blessed with a beard rising almost to meet his hairline, he is still within the danger zone. Somewhere out there is a *shiksa* with designs on her son. Jewish men make good husbands. It is the Jewish woman's blessing as a wife, and her curse as a mother.

But that is the outward fear, and the one to which they will admit. After all, who doesn't believe in continuity? Who doesn't fear cultural dispersion, collective forgetting, assimilation? Such concerns are forgivable and expected. But beneath them are murmurs of a more complex ambivalence. For when a son does it right and chooses, early, a good girl like Rachel Gilbert with a good family, and good, symmetrical features, a different fear whispers into the sleepless nights of the woman who raised him. A *shiksa* might keep him apart from his community and feed him shellfish and make their children, God forbid, celebrate Easter – that day when a historical scapegoathood was cemented for ever by the singing of Roman hammers on iron nails – but a nice Jewish girl, if she's nice enough, holds deeper terrors. If she's all that they dreamed of for their beloved boy, *she might make the mother redundant.* If she cooks and she reads to the children she bore him and she picks up his underpants and remembers the cousins' birthdays and on top of that she's there in the bedroom where you have never been and can never go, then what's left? She's won. You may have created him but it is she who gets to reap the benefits.

Adam's mother Michelle had thought about it a great deal, and with much shame, for she loved Rachel. She knew she had it lucky – Rachel Gilbert was the envy of all her friends: the dream daughter-in-law who loved her boyfriend's mother and never so much as peeped in complaint when Michelle rang Adam at midnight to say that she couldn't stop her computer from typing in italics, or that the Sky+ had stopped recording halfway through the second episode of *Vanity Fair* reruns. But she had lost her beloved Jacob almost twenty years ago this summer, and Olivia was wonderful of course but her darling eccentric Olivia was a girl, and that she'd still never had a boyfriend was a constant source of worry rather than solace. You never lost a daughter when she married. But Adam was the only man in her life.

In some ways it was hard not to envy Elaine Press. Back when the children had been teenagers they had all felt a little sorry for her; they had seen it coming, of course, and the sweet, open boys they'd raised had been concerned only that their school friend Gideon should feel comfortable enough to confide in them what they had always known anyway. (If you're going to come out as a sixteen-year-old then Jewish North London, with its endearingly quaint guitar-strumming, 'Kumbaya'-singing liberal youth move-ments, is the place to do it.) But if the sons had taken it in their stride, in those days the mothers had felt sad for Elaine and Roger. Life as part of any minority becomes more difficult (God knows, the Jews can relate to that) and grandchildren had seemed impossible once he had confessed that girls weren't for him. But these days, Elaine Press was flourishing. Instead of having Gideon on a timeshare with another woman she had actually gained the devoted Simon Levy, and if there were to be no grandchildren (of which Michelle was by no means certain, given how long the boys had been together and the increasingly favourable adoption laws) then Elaine at least had the solace of a guaranteed life partner for golf and – thanks to Simon Levy's mother living in Glasgow – an unrivalled role as matriarch in a family of men. Jacob had wanted another baby – would it have been so terrible to have had a third child, to have had a boy who liked boys? To have had one man in her life she would never have to part with?

Despite Michelle's conflicting emotions, however, in the end Adam's wedding was widely acknowledged as a tremendous success. Whatever ambivalence she had felt in the hours preceding it, when the two families had stood together beneath the *chuppah* she had known that her baby was in the right place. Rachel Gilbert adored him; Lawrence and Jaffa could not have loved their new son-in-law more if he had been their own flesh and blood. She saw what they had given him and it softened the vicarious envy she'd always felt at Jacob's absence; in Lawrence, Adam had support and a mentor for life. It could never take away what he had lost but it had filled a different space and buoyed him through the times when Jacob should have been there for shouts of praise, gentle censure, shoves of encouragement. The Gilberts were a family who rallied round – with this allegiance she knew that nothing would ever happen to her, or to Adam or Olivia, that Lawrence Gilbert would not put heart and soul into fixing. Adam had done a wonderful thing for all of the Newmans, not only for himself.

Throughout the many years of their children's courtship Michelle Newman and Jaffa Gilbert had not always seen eye to eye, but on this occasion Michelle had had to concede that Rachel's mother (under the conscientious and painstaking management of Rachel herself) had arranged a beautiful wedding. They could all be proud. Jaffa's more flamboyant Middle Eastern tastes had been successfully reined in – on the bride's suggestion, for example, they had offered the dill-poached salmon and the roast beef as alternatives rather than nestling together on every plate and had forgone the reusable silk flowers that she had thought so classy and practical. ('*Motek*, they look just like real only not with the smell and this is nothing, this you can fix with a little *schpritz* of something, and you can keep them for ever. Beautiful! People can take, they can keep and remember the wedding! You and Adam can put them in the house.') Instead, the ballroom had been fragrant with Madagascar Jasmine and huge puffs of hydrangeas had softened and scented every surface like creamy snowballs. The grand master of kosher catering, a man whose name was virtually synonymous with having a 'do', had arranged equally delicate petals of sushi on clear platters for the canapés: there were heart-shaped salmon rolls on beds of pansies with pink tongues of tuna sashimi laid plumply between them. For the generation who had not kept pace with the Japanese food revolution they had served fishballs and chopped liver on crackers, and the waitresses had been instructed to keep the unfashionable food circulating only among the elderly. Glass plates and edible flowers for the young people; silver platters and doilies for the old. Everyone was happy.

And everyone was happy. Ziva was happy, watching a union two generations on from her own, a future that had once been unimaginable. Lawrence and Jaffa were happy, seeing the happiness of their beloved little girl – now undeniably a woman. Tanya Pearl (soon to be Cohen) was happy because Jasper had surprised nobody by proposing in July, and going to weddings is a favourite pastime among the newly engaged. Olivia was happy because the quotations she had selected for her brother's Order of Service – a Stoppard line from *The Real Thing* on love, another on a wedding from the Song of Songs – had been much admired.

And Adam, watching Rachel process up the aisle between her parents (Jewish mothers would never be left out of such a moment – why should the father get all the *naches*?), living the moment that he had imagined so many times before, Adam was happy. Why would he be anything else? Walking towards him was the most perfect girl in north-west London. She had always been lovely but in the last few months Rachel had become absolutely radiant. Much to the consternation of her seamstress she had lost weight and her features had sharper lines, her full Cupid's bow more prominent now in a slightly streamlined face. She looked more refined; less child-like. Her skin was luminous and clear, and her eyes shone. Today, in her wedding dress, she was incandescent.

At a Jewish wedding, a groom's first sight of his bride is not this public entrance as she walks towards him. It is a private moment earlier during the *Bedeken* ceremony in which all the men – the fathers, the rabbi and the groom's closest friends – dance him towards his waiting bride for him to lower the veil over her face. It was the first of innumerable moments when Adam had ached for Jacob to be there – but Lawrence and Uncle Raymond had led the dancing and singing and clapping and foot-stamping and thus they had swept him towards the room in which Rachel waited with Michelle, Jaffa, Ziva, Aunt Judith, Olivia and the bridesmaids.

Everything else had fallen away. Here was Rachel, his childhood sweetheart; his childhood; his future. All he'd wanted growing up was there in her eyes. Tears had brimmed and settled as she saw him approaching, perfect diamonds on her lower lashes as he stood before her to recite a blessing from Genesis, given to Rebecca by her family before her marriage to Isaac: *'Achotenu: at hayi le alfei revavah.'* Our sister, be thou the mother of thousands of ten thousands. All his life he had felt self-conscious reading Hebrew prayers aloud: on that day he had meant every word he spoke, and had spoken them with pride. My darling girl, be thou the mother of my children.

No one else had been there. They were in a room filled with family chanting wedding songs and snapping photographs but he had seen only Rachel, their eyes locked together as he blessed her. He had not known if he was laughing or crying – she was surely doing both – but as he'd bent over her to lower her veil, Rachel so tiny and fragile now in the meringue peaks of duchesse satin that stood in thick folds around her, he had whispered the only thought that filled his head: 'God, my dad would have loved you,' and the diamonds on her lashes had slipped, first one and then the other, down her cheeks. She had nodded fiercely at him, smiling through her tears. 'I know. We'll make him proud,' and he could say nothing before Lawrence and Uncle Raymond and Jasper and the other men began a new song behind him, their rhythmic stamping grew louder and louder and he was surrounded once more by the scrum who escorted him to the *chuppah* for the wedding to begin.

There had been a brief time some months ago when he had not been sure that he would get here. The great machine set in motion by their engagement had frightened him; he had feared that he might be crushed beneath it, his voice drowned out by its volume. Around that time an email had circulated – one of those entitled, *SO YOU THINK YOU'RE HAVING A BAD DAY???* and describing a man who had been scuba diving off the coast of southern California, minding his own business, and in a freak accident had been swept up by a water-spraying helicopter used for fighting forest fires as it dipped its scoop into the ocean. Tiny and helpless, Adam imagined the man clinging to the lip of the bucket, peering over the edge as the ocean got farther and farther away beneath him. And the flying machine that had snatched him up in its beak like a giant hunting pelican would never hear his screaming in the din of its propellers. Adam pictured him as minuscule, no bigger than a lead soldier, and for that little scuba diver there was no escape – just the bobbing and sloshing until the inevitability of his expulsion over an inferno. The machine, lumbering blind and deaf, had him in its jaws.

The email had popped up on Adam's phone when he'd been in the middle of a meeting, a stupid and unconvincing urban legend, but the image had haunted Adam for days. How fast had it happened? Would there have been time, had he known, to jump out of the scoop? Or would his first realisation have come when he was already thousands of feet in the air? What had he felt? Disbelief. Panic. Claustrophobia. Terror. And perhaps, if he was very lucky, a final few seconds of pure calm as the unalterable truth of his fate had dawned. There had been a time when these questions had consumed Adam in his idle moments, sneaking into whatever space he left unoccupied. He had taken up jogging again and would play over the possibilities as he ran, circling each time round the same factors:

sizes of water-collecting buckets, speeds of helicopters, speeds of swimming in flippers, heights from which a man could fall and live – into water and on land. He'd worried at these things and worried that he worried. And then gradually, he had forgotten the email.

There had been a brief time when he had not known but six months on, he barely thought of it. He found it easy to dismiss at a distance. Ellie Schneider had merely been a repository for emotions running high – he could see that now. He had not spoken to her since that February night in Casa Blue and now in the bright sunshine of high summer there were no dark corners for shadows, merely a faint embarrassment that he'd said what he'd said. But it was surprisingly easy not to think about her. She had gone to Paris on a job and had not come back, even for the wedding; instead she had sent them a KitchenAid mixer complete with the ravioli-making attachment that Rachel coveted – one of the more expensive items on their wedding list. Ellie was to be the new face of Balmain leather and was shooting an entire season's campaign for them, living in Le Marais in an apartment owned by a friend of Theo's. Another man jumping to the rescue. Lawrence had surprised them all by his great enthusiasm for the move – Adam had expected disapproval that she was once again to be on her own in the world. But Paris was a good place for her to be, Lawrence maintained.

For a while after the scandal broke, the New York papers had been filled with images of Ellie and Marshall Bruce just as they'd feared; ones Adam recognised from Lawrence's file in the office and others that had come out once the story emerged. It had seemed only a matter of time before the financial arrangement between them became public and Ellie's tattered reputation was completely destroyed, and yet somehow it hadn't happened and all had gone oddly quiet. Almost immediately afterwards, Marshall Bruce and his wife had made their reconciliation official and were once again appearing at New York functions together, hands clasped and smiles wide and rigid. Lawrence had confirmed with the solicitors in writing that there was to be no divorce case and that Ellie's testimony was no longer required; a more complex telephone conversation had left him with the distinct impression that it would be better for Ellie if she steered clear of Manhattan and the newly reinstated Mrs Bruce.

'The wife had them dig up all sorts of stuff when they were building a case, and her lawyer more or less implied that Ellie would be better off keeping her distance for a while. It's virtually blackmail but she's on such thin ice with all this and it would do us no good to be litigious. At least no one knows he was paying her, thank God. The Balmain contract has another two years on it, and by then she'll be safe again,' Lawrence had said, and Adam had thought to himself, By then, so will I.

Remembering his own private histrionics made him cringe a little. But he had needed it, whatever it was. It had jolted him into seeing that he wanted more from life. There was a world outside NW11 and with every month that passed he had become more and more convinced that – once the all-consuming wedding mania was no longer occupying Rachel's every waking moment – they could discover that world together. Once they were married and life was their own again they could travel, they could go to new places and meet new people, and live. Why shouldn't she become worldlier? Why shouldn't they both? They could grow together, and he could teach her as he learned. Once the wedding was over.

NINETEEN

'I bought *US Weekly*. And I was going to buy the *National Enquirer* but then I figured Tanya can get it in London now so there's no point.'

Rachel was kneeling up, talking to him over the back of her seat. As a surprise Lawrence had upgraded them to First Class and so they were separated into individual pods replete with everything except easy communication with one another. Rachel had twice come over to sit on his footrest but now, six hours into the flight, she had resorted to peering over the top of her seat.

'Haven't you read them all already?'

'New ones came out today, the old ones are in my suitcase too just in case she wants them. And I got *People*, *Star* and *In Touch*. She was so excited that we're bringing them all back.'

'Poor Jasper, you've probably ruined his sex life – Tanya's going to be in bed with a heap of crap Brad Pitt magazines for weeks.'

'Ads,' said Rachel, as if she was explaining what he ought already to know, 'Brad Pitt has gone off, he looks vile these days and anyway Jasper probably reads all the tabloids too, you know, you always steal mine, I've seen you. I was just about to offer you *Grazia* but I won't now.' She stuck her tongue out at him and flumped back down in her seat, disappearing.

Adam laughed. It was true that Rachel's magazines had been intermittently instructive over the years; apart from observing Rachel herself, he had derived the best part of his understanding of women from their pages. He went round to where Rachel was curled in her pod, smiling behind her magazine, and kissed her.

'Pumpkin, I love your magazines, they've taught me all sorts of important things. I know that Marshall Bruce's wife has had breast implants, for example.'

'And that she might have been sleeping with her assistant.'

'And that she might have been sleeping with her assistant. They're very informative. But personally,' he leaned forward and nuzzled his face against her cheek and she giggled loudly and then clapped a hand over her mouth, 'I think we've made far better use of our honeymoon so far.'

They had spent ten days in Maui. Ten days of traditional honeymoon pursuits – of sunset beaches and cocktails of chilled Hawaiian rum and fresh fruit; of surfing lessons and whale watching and infinity pools and private dinners on the balcony of their suite. Rachel had sunbathed and had, two days before the end, arrived at a shade that she considered to be suitably enviable. Adam had discovered audio books (the Wilsons had given them an online subscription as part of their wedding gift) and had gone for evening runs along the beach listening, contented, to Ian McEwan.

It had been the most relaxed that either of them had been

for as long as he could remember – certainly since their engagement. Rachel had spun and twittered for the first few days, disoriented without a wedding as the epicentre of her near future. But the pleasure of the post mortem and of being, finally, just the two of them, had aided her recovery. By the end of the first week she was almost convincing when she said brightly, 'I'm so glad it's all over and we get to get on with normal life!' She had repeated this assertion a lot since they'd arrived, but that had been the first time she hadn't sounded crestfallen. Calling her Mrs Newman helped cheer her, Adam discovered. It had evolved, yesterday, into the more aspirational 'Mrs Pumpkin-Newman', which had made her giggle and this morning he had tried out 'Mrs P', which she had liked less, as she said it made her sound old. But all in all, she was perkier. She asked questions when he talked to her about what he was listening to. Mealtimes were glorious because she would finally share desserts with him again and had stopped shooing away every breadbasket as if it was a malarial mosquito. And she had gone down on him three times in the last five days, which was something of a record. Married life in Hawaii was no bad thing, Adam had discovered.

'Where *is* Newark?' Rachel asked, moving her handbag so that he could sit down on the footrest in front of her.

'New Jersey. *Noo Joisey.*'

'Why are we flying to *Noo Joisey*? We always flew to JFK.'

'It's just as close, half an hour in a cab and then we'll be in your shopping mecca. I'm glad I'm well rested.'

'I'm so excited!' Rachel clapped her hands. 'It's so nice to finally be going with you, I can show you all my favourite places and stuff. Every single time we would always go to the Second Avenue Deli at least once, and have the most enormous sandwiches I've ever seen, and pickled green tomatoes. But I haven't been back since it moved.'

'I have a date with one of those sandwiches. Turkey and pastrami on rye with Russian dressing. Your dad gave me instructions. Shall we go later today?'

'Ads, you don't know what you're saying, you'll be sick if you eat a whole one.'

He stood up and stretched before walking back to his own seat. 'You don't have to start worrying about what I eat just yet,' he said, moving aside the seat belt to sit down. 'We've only been married ten days.'

The honeymoon was over. They had another full day together in New York but the tranquil Maui spell had evaporated the moment they joined a queue of a hundred angry, time-pressed New Yorkers waiting for cabs in jungle-thick humidity. The city was smoggy and boiling and a warm rain fell intermittently but did not break the heaviness of the air. Rachel's energies were devoted to doing battle with her hair in the humidity and to buying a series of items, both for herself and on commission for other people, from a list so long and so randomly assorted that it felt as if they were on a particularly tedious scavenger hunt. Adam did not see that they needed to chase around a sweltering SoHo looking for organic suncream for his mother, nor could he imagine that Michelle had really insisted they find it. But Rachel was tremendously excited to be in New York and a great part of that excitement, he could see, came from the opportunity it offered for beneficence. She could bring back coveted moisturisers and eye creams and lip balms and vest tops and CDs and cupcakes and iPad accessories for the poor people back home, the underprivileged who did not have the chance to shop the Big Apple as she did. Bringing gifts for others made Rachel feel cosmopolitan and she approached the task with gravity and a minute attention to detail, as if she was scouring the rainforest for rare, healing berries. Along the way she would say things like, 'I'm sure they stock Kate Somerville products at Henri Bendel,' and all Adam could extract from these explanations was that strange people, Kate Someone and Henry Something, were making him spend the last days of his holiday loitering in department store cosmetics halls. He had suggested that they briefly separate so that he could at least retreat into the air-conditioned paradise of MOMA for an hour or two – when they'd booked the tickets he'd had a vision of himself in New York, standing in contemplation before Jasper Johns's American flag; coming face to face with Warhol's Marilyn screen prints and understanding for the first time the subversive brilliance that a postcard, a T-shirt, a mouse mat reproduction could never convey. He'd even have been happy to sit round the corner and have a cold beer while she shopped – but Rachel had looked wounded. 'We're on our honeymoon, Ads!' she'd exclaimed. To leave her side for a moment would not, it was clear, be correct honeymoon protocol.

But finally, on the penultimate day, they were following Adam's wishes and meeting an old friend for brunch. Zach

Sabah was the son of one of Rupert Sabah's first cousins and had been at the same prep school as Adam, Dan London and Gideon Press, after which Zach was promptly whisked off to Eton. Then, because his mother was American, he had disappeared to Princeton and had never returned. He turned up in London every now and again but hadn't visited for over four years – precisely the length of his employment at a New York hedge fund. His parents had retired to Israel where his mother had instantly been moved to come out of retirement and had opened a nursery school. Lisa London would be jealous they were seeing him, Rachel confided happily, because she'd always fancied Zach, and these days he was almost never in NW11.

'Ten days' holiday a year,' he explained, sitting on the pavement outside Cafe Cluny in the West Village. The benches were all full; even with a reservation they'd been told that it would be another half an hour for a brunch table. Impatient New Yorkers would be patient only if there were eggs Benedict on the horizon.

Rachel was sitting on her bag to avoid getting marks on a new cream dress and was biting the straw of the iced coffee that she would press, intermittently, against her cheek to cool herself down.

'That's awful!' she exclaimed. 'Daddy and Tony give everyone at GGP twenty days, don't they?'

'Christ, I should move back to London. Sorry, Ezra should be here any second and then they'll seat us. We need "all of our party"' before they'll give us the table. I wanted you to meet him, though, I think you'd get on, he used to be a lawyer too but he jacked it in a couple of years ago and you've never seen a happier man.'

Adam thought Zach himself looked pretty contented. He had made no attempt to assimilate and seemed actually to have become more English during his tenure in New York – he was wearing a pink and white striped shirt, the neck open, the collar turned up, and had grown a foppish shag of hair that fell into his eyes. The boys on their football team would never have permitted this in London and would have ridiculed him until he had a haircut and turned his collar back where it belonged, but Adam imagined that the English dandy look probably went down quite well with New Yorkers. In any case, as a Sabah, he was more qualified than the others. Adam noticed that his signet ring, never aired in north-west London unless he was going to see his grandfather, was back on the little finger of his left hand.

'Anyway, it's good here, I swear, I wouldn't keep you waiting otherwise. Great eggs.'

'Brioche French toast with berries for me!' said Rachel happily. She had studied the framed menu in the window when they first arrived and, Adam noticed, was embracing carbohydrates as long-lost friends.

'Ezra. Ezra!' Zach stood from the pavement and gestured to a very tall man who was ambling towards them across the cobblestones, a white keffiyeh round his neck and shoulder-length dark hair held back in a plastic Alice band. He was holding a scroll of newspaper and had a very large Polaroid camera hung round his neck. Adam stood to shake his hand; Rachel stayed perched on her bag and waved shyly.

Ezra lifted the camera from round his neck and handed it to Zach. 'I just found this in a consignment store on the way. Isn't it amazing? The mirror's jammed but I think I can fix it.' He turned to Adam and Rachel. 'So *mazel tov*, you guys. Zach says you're on your honeymoon.'

Adam nodded. Rachel glowed.

A girl in an extremely low cut black top leaned out of the door of the restaurant and called into the small crowd, 'Zachpartyoffour?' She led them in, gesturing with a clipboard, and they were settled at a table in the window under the envious eyes of the crowd still waiting and sweltering outside.

'So how's the play?' Zach asked Ezra, and then explained, 'He's written a really cool play in collaboration with a scientist at Harvard about the synthetic genome, and it's been on in Brooklyn for the last month or so.'

'They've just extended the run actually.'

'A play about science?' Rachel asked, dubiously.

'It's genius,' Zach reassured her, taking a monogrammed handkerchief out of his pocket and polishing his sunglasses. The handkerchief, Adam thought, was going a bit far.

'What's it about?' asked Adam.

'It's about that guy, Craig Venter, he's a sort of entrepreneurial geneticist, and his lab created a synthetic genome, the first synthetic life—'

'I remember that, it was terrible!' Rachel interposed.

Adam noticed Ezra's eyebrow twitch.

'What inspired you?' Adam asked him, quickly.

'It just consumed me, when I read about it.' Ezra turned away from Rachel to Adam. 'I got obsessed and I started emailing this biologist guy I knew at Harvard to learn a bit more about it. It was the most beautiful feat of bioengineering and it's created a taxonomic shift in everything – the way we see life. It changes the very definition of it. On a practical level, what Venter achieved has brought us closer to a time when we'll be able to create bacteria that make biofuels, or clear carbon dioxide from the atmosphere, or are, like, miniature factories for specific vaccines. On a far more crucial level though, and what I was interested in, he's pushed the boundaries. He's changed the definition of what it is to be alive. What life means. He's shown what can be achieved if scientists – if people – are open-minded and think outside the prescribed boundaries of what conventional morality or religious doctrine might say is acceptable. He's actually playing God.'

'That's awful!' Rachel said again. 'He should stop!'

Adam resisted the urge to clamp his hand over her mouth but Ezra merely shrugged. He slid off the Alice band, shook his hair out and then replaced the band higher up. It was an oddly masculine version of a familiar female gesture.

'Why? I believe in intellectual freedom. He has a right to ideas independent of the dictates of a particular community. I think I'd take the right to think freely and pursue new ideas over almost all else. Venter agrees and the outraged collective will come to see in the future that he was right.'

Adam looked expectantly at Rachel. This hypothetical place that Ezra was describing to her – a place free from communal values and where there was no collective judgement to fear – was as foreign to her as the moon. North-west London was a place of open minds when it came to science – and politics and literature and sexuality and art – but Rachel did not usually trouble herself with such thoughts one way or the other. When it came to making life choices, other people's expectations were of paramount importance to her. They made her feel safe, because she always knew what to think. Her world was one in which her own highest aspirations had always been those wanted for her by a community, and the concept of innovation at a cost of isolation (or even mild disapproval) wasn't worth it. There was security in their social dictates. She was also unused to having men disagree with her. He watched her reaction with interest but she merely pouted slightly and poured syrup on her French toast.

After a moment Ezra said to Adam, 'You should come; I'd like to know what you think.'

'We'd love to,' he said. Rachel was still busily cutting a slice of French toast and he could not catch her eye.

'Great, hit me up tomorrow and I'll leave tickets on the door for you.'

Adam exchanged looks with Zach, who was smiling at him with an expression that said, 'I told you you'd like him'. There was no corresponding look of appreciation for Rachel.

On the way back to the hotel they stopped to pick up frozen yoghurt at a do-it-yourself ice-cream shop that Rachel had read about in their guidebook. A row of nozzles offered fat-free confections in flavours from lychee to cupcake batter; Rachel got particular pleasure from anything fatless, though to Adam these tasted like air and artificial sweeteners. As they were walking back along

Bleecker Street, Adam humming the Paul Simon song and peering into the windows of the cheese shops and fish-mongers and Italian delis, Rachel said, 'I couldn't think of a single excuse to give that man about his awful play.'

'Why? I thought we were going. It sounded interesting. It's actually a kind of brilliant idea for a play if it works.'

Rachel laughed, stroking her spoon over the crest of her yoghurt to collect the chocolate chips sprinkled on top. 'Seriously, Ads, it sounded like the most boring thing *ever*! We can't go all the way to Brooklyn tomorrow to see a play about a crazy man who grows bacteria. If we were planning on going to a show here it should have been something real, like a Broadway musical or something.'

'Brooklyn's not that far, they both came up from Brooklyn to meet us for brunch today,' Adam pointed out. He was irritated with her. He had been determined to go to the play and yet he'd known, even as he'd been setting his heart on it, that Rachel would refuse. He had enjoyed talking to Ezra. Adam wanted to see him again and imagined the play would be intelligent. And even if it wasn't, he thought with annoyance, it was something different to do. It was something they would never do in London. Rachel smiled at him with her spoon in her mouth, raising her eyebrows and holding out her tub of yoghurt to him.

'It was self serve,' he said crossly. 'If I'd wanted vanilla I'd have got it myself.'

'Ads.' Rachel pouted at him. 'Don't get your knickers in a twist, we met your friends today and that's already quite a lot of other people to spend time with on our honeymoon.'

She stood on tiptoe and kissed his cheek, ruffling his hair as if he could be jollied out of a sulk. He smiled back, feeling weary. This was how it would be, he realised, and giving in was easier than trying to explain. When Rachel didn't want something there was no sensible discussion to be had, because she couldn't even see that other people might feel differently. He threw the rest of his frozen yoghurt into a bin.

'Ads, I wanted to try the peanut butter flavour!' Rachel protested.

'Then you should have got it yourself, shouldn't you.' he said, as jovially as he could, but he meant it.

TWENTY

The first time Dan London had brought Willa to the Gilberts' for Shabbat, Willa had expressed her interest in converting to Judaism and Lawrence had advised her, 'There's really not much to it. Any Jewish holiday can be described the same way. They tried to kill us. They failed. Let's eat.' On Purim it was Haman, an evil Iago in a three-cornered hat, who had attempted the killing, and whose failure is marked by the eating of three-cornered pastries. Along with these *hamantaschen*, sweet dough glossed with egg and filled with poppy seeds, the day is marked with a great deal of drinking, attending synagogue in fancy dress, and a theatrical reading of the Book of Esther in which, whenever the name Haman is mentioned, the congregation boos and heckles like a football crowd to drown it out. It is the one day of the Jewish calendar in which cross-dressing is not only permissible but actually encouraged. The closest equivalent is a Christmas pantomime.

The Purim story's heroine was Esther, new bride of the Persian King Ahasuerus. Shortly after their marriage, the King's advisor Haman decided to murder all the Jews of the region and Ahasuerus agreed to the genocide. It was only when Esther threw herself on her husband's mercy and confessed that she herself was Jewish that he revoked his consent, and sentenced Haman to death.

As a bride herself only six months earlier, Rachel had been cast to play Queen Esther in the English performance of the Purim *shpiel* at synagogue. Adam had not seen her on stage since she played Lady Bracknell in the upper-sixth production of *The Importance of Being Earnest*. (She'd been the best actress in the production by far, but had been refused the coveted role of Gwendolen because the director had complained that her inescapably large chest would make her look more matronly than the scrawny teenage girl playing her mother. She had cried about it and had begun the first of her many preliminary investigations into breast reduction surgery – not for the last time Adam and Jaffa had talked her out of it.) He was intrigued by the idea of his new wife taking centre stage. She had been an excellent Lady Bracknell but he'd always thought that her own natural sweetness would have made her an ideal Cecily.

Greeting the arriving guests at the Young Adults Purim party was the freckled junior rabbi Josh Cordova, dressed as a milkmaid with a bosom large enough to rival Rachel's, blonde woollen Heidi plaits concealing his curly ginger hair, and a black and white stuffed cow under his arm that he introduced as Moo-ses. Tanya Pearl's younger sister, Hayley, stood beside him, dressed as Mata Hari as far as Adam could tell, decked in bells and anklets and displaying a rather startling amount of fake-tanned midriff. Unlike Tanya, she was rail-thin and had been wearing a full face of make-up, complete with false eyelashes and equally voluminous hair, every day since she was twelve. She worked at a respite centre for disabled children and taught in the synagogue Sunday school, and if discipline was required for these roles, then Hayley Pearl was the ideal candidate. She had put her face on every morning even when they camped in the desert on Israel Tour.

'Rachie!' Hayley embraced her, wrists and feet jangling as she moved. 'Come with me, we've got a five-minute rehearsal in the kitchens and then you're on. Did you really bring it? Is that it? Ah, we had a spare one from the fancy dress box just in case you didn't want to wear it again!' She reached for the garment bag that Adam carried but Rachel shook her head.

'It's been dry-cleaned and packed so I couldn't but I've got a white dress and a crown for the costume instead.'

Adam squeezed Rachel's hand before passing her the hanger. There was no need for Hayley Pearl to know that the wedding dress had remained at home because now, only six months after the wedding, it no longer fitted. Rachel's wholehearted return to carbohydrates had had its inevitable consequences. The discovery had been made that morning; the tears had ended only recently.

Hayley pouted. 'But you looked so gorge in it, what a shame! Ah well. You'll look gorge in anything. Come in with me. I've got my whole class here to see you, they're going to be so excited. And it's Natalie Joseph's seventh birthday today so don't forget to give her a cuddle.' She drew Rachel away from Adam and they disappeared together through the back doors of the synagogue. Adam remained outside with the milkmaid. His own costume – a hat and magnifying glass to be Sherlock Holmes – was already feeling rather half-hearted.

The little plastic gemstone tiara that she wore to be Queen was comical but Rachel on stage was not – she was captivating. Rachel's Queen Esther was sweet and solemn. Her innocence and gentleness lent a grace to her quiet courage as she risked her life before her all-powerful husband, a grave expression in her wide, dark eyes as she pleaded. It was all there in Rachel's lovely face – a young girl unused to confrontation who, in defence of her family and her people, had found steel within. As she prepared to come before the King unbidden – a crime punishable by death if it displeased him – it was all Adam could do not to walk on stage and enfold Rachel in his arms. She looked so frightened, and yet so determined. She had mesmerised the room.

The performance ended and Adam joined the rest of the audience in a standing ovation for the players. Rachel was glowing with pleasure, taking her bow between Haman (Jasper Cohen) and King Ahasuerus (Anthony Rosenbaum). Adam had not been able to take his eyes off his wife throughout the performance and he now saw that the rest of the congregation felt the same: the whoops and whistles of approval were all for Rachel.

'Isn't she gorge?' Hayley Pearl whispered to him during the standing ovation. Her bells and bracelets jangled as she clapped. 'Every man in the room right now is mad about your wife.'

Adam swelled with pride. 'I know,' he said, immodestly.

Rachel was as proud of herself as Adam was of her, and in the car her excitement was infectious. She sat, clutching the *hamantaschen* that Rabbi Cordova had insisted that they take home, a bag of fifty from the caterer. The rest of the leftover food was going to a homeless shelter in Camden – Rabbi Cordova would deliver it to the same place he took the spare *challot* every Friday on his way home. But he had been desperate to show his appreciation for the star actress of the night and had only pastries with which to reward her. Refusing had not been an option.

Rachel shifted the bag on her knees. 'Shall we take these to Ziva? It's only nine and we could just drop them off if she's going to bed.'

'That's a lovely idea, Pumpkin.' They were about to turn into England's Lane; Adam continued down Haverstock Hill instead.

'And we'll still be home for you to watch *Match of the Day*.'

They stopped at a junction and he turned to look at her, her eyes bright in the tawny streetlight, pleased by her own suggestion. In Rachel's early childhood Ziva had been a source of painful embarrassment, Rachel had once confessed to Adam. At her first primary school play, Amy Thomas had seen Rachel's grandmother swaddling fairy cakes in napkins and putting the bundles into her handbag. It was not theft of which she stood accused – Laura Young's mother had been manning the refreshments table and at the end of the night had been giving them away. But everyone else's parents had taken one and peeled off the paper case and handed it on to a child, or had simply refused the offer of pink-iced cupcakes unevenly studded with silver balls. Even class six, whose chubby fingers had decorated them earlier that day in Home Ec, knew that they were not good enough to justify wrapping them in shredding tissues to take home. The next day Amy Thomas had suggested that Rachel's grandmother probably didn't want to pay for her own cupcakes because Jews didn't like to spend money, and this had been Rachel's first gentle brush with bigotry. She knew this only in hindsight – at the time it seemed to say less about the world view to which a precocious Amy Thomas had been exposed at her parents' dinner table and more about Ziva herself, who was now a source of humiliation and was perhaps also mad. Rachel had nursed these fears alone until the school carol concert when, forced to explain why she did not want her snack-filching grandmother to come and hear her solo in 'Silent Night', Jaffa and Lawrence had told her about the Holocaust.

'*Kinderlach*?' Ziva squinted at them from the doorway. '*Vos is dis?*'

Adam held the plastic bag aloft in his fist like a giant funfair goldfish. '*Hamantaschen*, Ziva.'

'Wonderful. Come in! *Ach*, this is a lovely surprise. Come in. We have just been having crumpets.'

'Oh, do you have people here, Granny?' Rachel had stepped across the threshold and begun to follow her grandmother across the hall but stopped. 'We don't want to disturb you.'

Ziva continued towards the sitting room. She had momentum; pausing to reply would make the walk more difficult. She addressed Rachel over her shoulder. 'First of all, Rachele, with nobody in the world could I be disturbed if my visitor was you. And secondly, I am now alone in any case. Come. Sit. Bring plates.'

'*Hamantaschen* with your crumpets?' Adam asked, moving an ebony-handled toasting fork from where it lay on the coffee table and returning it to a brass stand by the mantelpiece. Although it was already March, a fire burned high in the grate and the butter dish, also on the coffee table between three grease-slicked plates, was now a pond of buttercup-bright oil.

'Thank you, Adam, but I have crumpeted already quite enough. But please make tea. *Ach*, ten minutes earlier and you would also have seen Ellie.'

Adam had been trying to make the toasting fork stand upright in its place beside the poker and a pair of brass fire tongs; he tightened his grip on it to prevent it clattering to the ground.

'Ellie's here?' he and Rachel said together.

'Why didn't she tell me she was in London?' Rachel continued, sounding hurt.

'She is here only for tonight and then she has I think a

lunch with the Balmain directors and *Tatler*, and is going straight back to Paris in the afternoon.'

'But she's here this evening.'

'Yes, and I know that she would be very sad to miss you. She wished to have more time to see the family, this I know. But it got late and now she has gone to the pub with her friend Melissa who is also staying with me here. She is a model also, one of those peculiar looking ones. Very heavy features, and the big thick brows. Androgynous a little, but also attractive. I have been feeling very diminutive, especially now with you also, Adam, looming over me.'

Rachel, who had shot up to five foot two in primary school but had since got no further, did not smile. 'Ellie shouldn't bring her friends to stay with you, Granny, you'll get tired.'

'And what is it precisely for which you think I should be conserving my energy? Nonsense. I like to have life in the house. Melissa is very charming, and she speaks excellent French.'

During this exchange Adam had remained facing the fireplace. He was not sure what he felt now, only that the idea of her proximity was disturbing and when Ziva had said that they had missed her by moments, his disappointment vied with an equally powerful relief. His cheeks felt hot. He stepped back from the fire.

'Adam, you know Prebend Street from here, yes?'

He turned around, forcing a smile. 'Yes.'

'Ellie and Melissa are in a pub, I believe, it is called I think the Duchess of Kent. It is cream and red brick, there is nothing else near it. It is not a very exciting one, Ellie said, but glamour I suppose they have in Paris, and this one she is able to take the dog inside. Her phone is I believe charging upstairs. Would you mind very much to go and fetch them, just for a little? Rachele is upset but Ellie I promise you will also be upset not to see her cousin now that you are both here. She has been asking me all about you this evening, and how you were. I showed her photographs from the wedding.' She patted Rachel's hand and Rachel smiled, tentatively reassured. Ziva would not flatter her unless this was true. 'It was just so short this time and she was a little *meshugah* to get everything done. It is only very close. Would you mind?'

Adam shook his head.

The Duchess of Kent was full, the windows blurred with condensation. It was impossible to see anything through them but smudges of moving colour and so Adam steeled himself and pushed open the door. He was hit by a fug of heat and humidity. Above the threshold a heater whirred and blew and he stood in its hot gusts feeling faintly dizzy and scanning the room. Whether he hoped to see her or hoped she was elsewhere he had no idea – only that he was hoping something, fervently.

Ellie was standing at the bar. Despite the dense crowd, it seemed as if every group he looked at was oriented towards her. Melissa was beside her, precisely as Ziva had described – angular and heavy-jawed, wearing a slash of red lipstick and hair gelled into a black Teddy boy quiff. Ellie was conspicuous everywhere but together with

Melissa the effect was exponentially exaggerated. Every man in the room had found an excuse to face in their direction.

Ellie had changed since last he'd seen her. She was leaning on the bar, Rocky at her feet. He could see her profile and the long curve of her body, one foot resting on the brass rail, as if she were a cowgirl leaning casually on a fence. Even from across the room it was obvious that she had lost some of her haunted look: her skin was clearer and her face and arms were tanned caramel-dark, as if she'd just returned from the tropics. She wore a black vest and loose grey jeans that hung so low they showed a band of tanned skin and the violin curve of her hipbone. He imagined reaching for her, his hand on the small of her back where he could see the neat beads of her spine as she leaned forwards. His palms were sweating and he remained where he was, wiped them on his jeans and told himself, without sympathy, to get a bloody grip.

She was laughing – the bartender was firing something from a soda nozzle into two glasses in front of them and was chuckling with her. As Adam watched, Melissa leaned a hand on Ellie's shoulder and whispered something in her ear at which Ellie threw her head back and laughed harder, her eyes briefly closed. Her leather jacket was slung over a bar stool between them and when her hand went to its pocket he thought, 'She's reaching for her lighter and her cigarette case. She'll go outside to smoke,' and the intimacy of predicting her most trivial movements sent a thrill through him. He stayed rooted where he was. It seemed impossible that one glimpse of her could petrify him into a dumb silence in a doorway, and that it could still happen after so long – yet her proximity had electrified him. Remembering the light touch of her fingers in his palm he stared at her, willing her to turn. If she looks at me, he told himself, it means something. It was a stupid, infantile conviction – the same kind of bargain he'd made with himself as a child. If the first train is for Charing Cross and not the Bank branch, then it means that Arsenal will win today. If I can fit four Hobnobs in my mouth then it means I'll make the First Eleven. If the rain stops before we get to the hospice then it means they're wrong about Dad. He knew that such bargains did not pay. Still, when Ellie didn't lift her face towards him he made no move towards her. She had taken out her lighter and cigarette case, just as he'd known she would, but instead of moving to the door where he waited she had simply placed them on the polished bar and continued talking to Melissa. A group of people were leaving; Adam stepped aside to let them pass and when the last girl left, wrapping her scarf high around her ears and squealing at the cold night, he followed her outside and kept walking. Ellie hadn't seen him. He had had a fortunate escape, he thought, breathing in cold air that burned and cleared his lungs. Seeing her could only harm him now – he had stupid, unilateral fantasies that could never bear any relation to reality and apparently those feelings were still lurking just beneath the surface, however much he'd silenced them until now. But it would be fine. He was married. If anything, it had been a test and he had passed it because he'd extricated himself before anything had unsettled him beyond an initial jolt of memory. She looked well; she didn't need him. Once and for all he would get over it. In the meantime he would tell Ziva and Rachel that Ellie was nowhere to be seen.

TWENTY-ONE

The months that followed were distinguished only for being unremarkable. Summer edged reluctantly into London; broad saucers of Queen Anne's lace balanced on tall stems across the Heath Extension and buttercups splashed the parks with sunny, yolk yellow. Optimistic barbecues were planned, rained off, and planned again. Adam was given directorship over two new trainees, which tripled his workload because giving them assignments and explaining them took far longer than doing it himself. Michelle bought a neat Burberry mackintosh for the upcoming autumn. Tanya and Jasper got married. The football season began.

Adam had been in a meeting with Lawrence and Jonathan Pearl, one of the other GGP founding partners, when he had noticed three missed calls from Rachel. The fourth time she rang he had excused himself and stepped outside to answer. 'Hi, Pumpkin, what's up? Are you OK?'

'I'm good. How are you? How's work?' He could hear noises behind her, voices and beeping, and the line was crackling.

'Work's good but really busy, Pumpkin; do you need anything?'

'Oh – yes. I'm just in M&S and I just wanted to catch

you before I left. Do you feel like salmon tonight? Or I could do a leg of lamb if you wanted? It's still early enough if I got a small one, or did it in bits maybe. But I'm in the queue now, though, and I went for the salmon because you loved that one we had the other night at Café Japan so I thought I'd try to copy it for you. I looked for ages on the Internet and I found a recipe that seems like it's right.' She sounded jubilant. 'Yes please, double bags. Sorry, Ads. But I can easily do lamb and freeze the fish. What do you think?'

Rachel did not, Adam imagined, want to know what he thought. What he thought was that they had had too many of these conversations during the thirteen months of their marriage and that what slender novelty they'd had was fast waning. Rachel had never been a striving career woman and for many years had been candid with him about her aspiration, one day, to give up teaching and be a housewife. But he could not have envisaged that she would become one quite so soon after their wedding, nor that she would apply herself to the role with such all-consuming energy. Rachel had always been generous and considerate but as the only daughter of devoted parents, she had never been a low-maintenance girlfriend. Adam had done it all willingly. But now, confusingly, she required constant tending to in her incessant tending to others. Shortly after Purim when she had told him that she couldn't endure another minute teaching in the Portakabins at the back of the playground under a headmaster who she was convinced was having a nervous breakdown ('Honestly, Ads, the whole maths department is like a loo on a building site, it's horrible and the kids get so depressed out there they can't even listen'), he had not objected to her giving up work. It was a few years and a baby earlier than he'd expected but if they were prudent, he'd estimated, he could keep them both on what he earned already. If she could have stuck it out until he'd made partner at GGP it would have been better but it wasn't the end of the world. If it made her happy, he would go along with it.

He had imagined having to be a little more careful with his spending, and for a while having to be a lot more careful with their holidays. What he had not imagined was this – that in giving up work Rachel had given up a great deal of what made her days differ from his; had given up a great deal of what broadened her life beyond the bands of it, morning and evening and weekends, in which he and she cohabited and related. What he had not understood was the tremendous vault of free time that Rachel had unlocked, and how much of it would be dedicated to activities concerning him. And this commitment to him had realigned her priorities still further away from his own. He was touched that she wanted to do it for him, touched every time he came home and saw that she had laid the table in advance and had folded white calla lilies horizontally into glass bowls of water like a lobby centre-piece and that she had made a pudding every day – real puddings like tarte tatin and trifle and crème caramel so that he was already beginning to worry about his waistline – but within weeks it had begun to feel faintly oppressive. Despite discouragements, Rachel had always called and texted him during the day but now the communication was almost hourly – did he think she should take back the cafetière that the Wilsons had given them to John Lewis and exchange it for a smaller one? It was still in the box from the wedding but of course she didn't have the receipt. Did he think Michelle would like a copy of the lovely new Philippa Gregory? She had popped into Waterstone's for it and there was a 3-for-2 on but there were only two books she wanted. What were those papers he'd left on the kitchen table? Did he need them? Could he sort them out when he got home?

'Salmon's brilliant, Pumpkin. I've really got to go, though, I'm in a meeting.'

'Okay.' Rachel was unperturbed. 'Say hi to Dad and tell him if the salmon works I'll make it for them next week. Love you.'

'Love you too.' Adam slipped his phone back into his jacket and returned, sheepishly, to his meeting. This time, fortunately, no one questioned his absence. Lawrence was on the phone asking Kristine to reserve a conference room and Jonathan was standing over Lawrence's desk reading something on his screen. He was Tanya's uncle; still, he was the most remote and formal of the senior partners and the one Adam worked hardest to impress. Adam resumed his seat and kept his head down, reading an article on his BlackBerry until they addressed him again.

The following Saturday, Adam packed his sister into the car to keep him company as he ran errands. She was in London for the weekend, preparing for imminent noughth week and the annual descent of stumbling, giggling drunken freshers. Michelle had greeted her daughter's return to London as she often did, presenting her with a pair of optimistically purchased jeans or a small, encouraging pile of make-up – a mascara usually, and a lipstick. One day, she hoped, her daughter would give up the strange clothes and would accept these gifts. After all, why not demonstrate that women could be both intelligent and feminine, both intellectually voracious and visually pleasing? Why not dress normally? Why not have a good haircut? Why not get a nice boyfriend?

Olivia was unmoved by these exhortations. The jeans were bemusedly accepted and then forgotten in an upstairs bathroom whenever she went back to Oxford; on this occasion she'd been unable to hide her distaste for a particularly slinky, particularly expensive pair and Michelle was currently at Selfridges returning them. Olivia had agreed to run errands with Adam because it seemed preferable to running such errands with Michelle.

'Why precisely are you doing this?' Olivia asked her brother as they circled Hampstead for the third time in search of a parking space.

'Because Rachel's grandmother asked Rach to pick it up for her, and it's heavy so I said I'd do it.'

'Yes but, forgive me, I barely see you, and Rachel could do it during the week.'

'You sound just like Mum. Why are you both obsessed with her not working?'

'I'm not obsessed, I'm bewildered. I cannot fathom it.' She shook her head and the strange necklace of green and yellow woollen pompoms that she wore over a purple Fair Isle sweater bounced with the movement. 'Don't misunderstand me, if she had a brood at home and was busily channelling her energies into moulding the next generation of Newmans I would absolutely see her purpose. I don't think the raising of children should only be performed in allocated slots between board meetings. But really, Adam, what on earth does she *do* all day?'

He shrugged. He had already had this exchange with his mother when Rachel first decided; since then he had come to understand the choice less and less.

'Dunno. Cooks, reads, she's planning to redecorate the flat so that takes up a lot of time, I think. She's helping Jaffa with some of her charity stuff.'

A parking space directly outside the frame shop rescued him. He left Olivia in the car with a copy of last week's *Jewish Chronicle* to examine – she enjoyed expressing outrage at its contents when in London – and went in to collect Ziva's picture.

There was no one inside and he stood for several minutes admiring the assortment of images on display in the tiny shop, a glimpse through keyholes at living-room walls across Hampstead, private family exhibits brought here for mounting, or framing, or retouching. To his left an enormous canvas of a purplish-black tulip stood awaiting attention, and against the other wall were four small Indian tapestries mounted and framed in delicate gilt. A series of black and white photographs of the same laughing baby, her dress and the bow in her hair digitally coloured in pale pink, had been arranged behind glass with whimsical asymmetry. There was nothing else in the room. Radio 4 played quietly and Adam listened, waiting for someone to appear. Then a voice called from downstairs, 'What name?'

'What? Oh, Ziva Schneider. She said Ian called to tell her it was ready.'

A man raised his head from a low spiral staircase that disappeared into a basement. 'Ah yes, the photograph. I'm Ian – hello. I'll get it for you, it's all paid for. One sec.' He disappeared again. Moments later he was back, carrying a large oblong swaddled in bubble-wrap.

'Would you like to check it? Best if you do. She wanted a mount around the picture but I haven't added it because the proportions really looked better without, but if you think she'll mind . . .' He began to slash at the plastic wrap with a small blade, peeling it away in layers.

'I don't really know what she asked for, to be honest,' Adam said. He was anxious to get back to Olivia, to deliver Ziva's print to her and then to get on with his day. He had offered to take his sister to a screening at the ICA that was to be followed by a discussion of psychoanalysis and cinema, an afternoon hosted by the Institute of Psychoanalysis. It was the sort of excursion he had spent years avoiding but for once he had not dismissed his sister's suggestions as affectedly cerebral and had instead booked the tickets himself. Rachel would not have come with him and that seemed, somehow, an important reason to go.

'She wanted the frame in brushed stainless steel and a cream mount which I agreed with when she first brought it, but once I'd lived with it for a day or two I saw that it didn't need a mount at all and that a gunmetal grey was far more suited. But if she disagrees just bring it back.' As he spoke Ian had been unwinding the padding from around the photograph and now he leaned it in front of the tulip canvas for Adam to inspect. Adam glanced at it without much interest, expecting to see a reproduction of a Chagall like the four others that hung in Ziva's hallway. Instead it was a photograph of Ellie, almost life-size, bathed in grey-green shadow and chlorophyll-green light and looking more extravagantly sensual than he had ever seen her. It was a simple picture. She stood leaning against a tree trunk, her hair long and wet, her body wet and oiled. He felt a shock of pain beneath his ribs; his stomach contracted. For one strange, lurching moment he felt an urge to be sick.

'It's got lovely balance,' Ian observed.

Adam continued to stare without speaking. He knew at once that it was the picture taken for the Pirelli calendar and he would have given all he had in that instant to track down and destroy every copy. It was far worse than imagining a Times Square billboard on display before millions. That a few thousand men should feel ownership of her or any sort of private, exclusive access to her, even to this single photograph, was nauseating.

He had known that she was in it – Jaffa had made a disapproving reference over dinner months ago. Ziva had been the only one at the table to defend the decision and had been staunch in her defence: 'I have been researching it on the Internet. The photographs I have seen from the Pirelli are on occasion extremely elegant, and she will insist, she has promised me, on keeping some control of the styling. The most beautiful women have posed for it in the world. Why should my Ellie not claim her place among them if she was invited?' Beside him, Rachel had wilted.

Ellie had implied that Rachel might have resented more

than just her beauty. Yet it had always been so clear to him that Rachel was the enviable one, and that she might have begrudged the attention that her parents had paid to a bereaved little girl was not a sympathetic portrait. But almost as soon as he'd considered the idea he'd dismissed it. Despite a natural insecurity during moments when she measured herself against her cousin, Rachel adored Ellie and had always worried about her; he could call up a decade's memories of her affection and concern. Ellie was resentful, and he understood why. But Rachel was blameless.

And so during the Pirelli debate he had wanted to make her feel better and had disagreed with Ziva for the first time in his life, saying, 'Yes but Ziva, if she wants to be taken seriously then she has to stop doing this stuff,' and beside him Rachel had sat up a little straighter and he had been glad he'd spoken. But it seemed that Ziva had taken a stand against the general disapproval – there was a space cleared above her sitting-room mantelpiece for this picture that she'd asked Rachel to collect, a flag waved in public support of her favourite granddaughter.

Now, standing before the photograph itself, he was awake and feeling for the first time in his life. Ellie was there in front of him and the sight of her had stopped his heart. Her eyes, huge and green and filled with shameless challenge, seemed to be staring only at him. They followed him. It had to be for him, for he could not bear the idea of her looking at anyone else with her heavy-lashed lids lowered, her face alight with the mockery he recognised and the yearning he'd only dreamed of seeing.

'Is she your grandmother, Mrs Schneider?'

Adam blinked. 'No, my wife's grandmother.'

'So Ellie Schneider is your wife's sister?'

'Cousin.'

Ian whistled. 'Wow. Have you met her?'

'No.' Adam shook his head. 'I'm all right, thanks,' he added as Ian tried to help him carry the photograph to the car.

Olivia glanced up as he struggled to fit it in the boot but made no move to help him. She had given up on the *Jewish Chronicle* and had a stack of undergraduate essays on her lap and a green pen between her teeth, one hand entwined absent-mindedly in the woollen pompoms round her neck.

'We can go now. Let's just run this over to Ziva and we'll head into town.'

Olivia nodded. She had a fine streak of green pen on her chin and written on her hand in the same colour were the words, 'Danube crossing? NB.'

'So will you come up to the gaudy next weekend with Mum?' she asked, as they drove down Haverstock Hill. Her annual college garden party was approaching, an afternoon of strange speeches and dry, triangular sandwiches filled with neon Coronation chicken, an event always scheduled just a few weeks too late in the year to be pleasant. But it was one of the few chances to see his sister in her element, a glimpse into her world of scarlet robes and Latin epigrams. He was faintly jealous of her in these moments; faintly jealous and fiercely proud. Olivia had forged her own path, had ignored their mother's silent (and not-so-silent) disapproval and had sought a place in which she thrived. Olivia in Oxford was a fuller, richer version of herself, even when she was only walking down Cornmarket Street or having tea with Adam in the café she liked in the Covered Market, rickety tables across a narrow aisle from the butcher where haunches of venison and skinned, pale rabbits hung on steel hooks in the window, uplit like art. She made sense in Oxford and it suited her. In London Adam worried for her, unwittingly imbibing his mother's fears for her increasing eccentricities and seemingly endless romantic vacuum. When he saw her in her own world he regretted his patronising assumptions. Olivia was more fulfilled than most people he knew.

Adam took a deep breath and then practised his nonchalance on his sister.

'I'll try. But there's a chance I have to go to Paris next weekend.'

TWENTY-TWO

'Who did you say was running in this race?'

Rachel was awake when Adam tiptoed out of the bathroom, lighting the way to the door with the screen of his phone. In the small, white light he saw that though she had barely moved she was stretching, her arm locked and straightened for a moment, her fingers flexed and curled around the edge of the bunched sheets. Her mouth was pressed into the pillow but the faint flaring of her nostrils betrayed a yawn. Surprised by her voice, he went back over to the bed and kissed her.

'Why are you awake at five in the morning? Was I too loud getting up?'

'No, just am.' She pushed her hair back from her face. She looked like a little girl roused too early from a nap, drowsy and pliant, and the pillow had imprinted a network of pink creases across a cheek flushed with sleep. 'When do you get in?'

'Ten thirty tonight. I'll be back here by eleven, just a whirlwind trip. You won't notice I've gone.'

He had found himself doing this in the last few days – adding attenuating statements every time he talked about his journey. To his own ears it made him sound guilty; no one else seemed to have noticed. When explaining this impromptu visit to Paris he found it very hard not to babble.

'No, I mean when do you get there?'

'I think around ten a.m. French time.'

'Oh good, so you get a little time to play in Paris.' Her eyes were closed again but she smiled at him as he bent again to kiss her forehead. 'My phone's charging on the floor in the other room if you want Ellie's French number.'

This was the third time Rachel had suggested that he call her cousin. The previous times he had said that it was a good idea and that he would do his best, hoping she would forget. Now he felt his back pocket for his passport and said, 'I don't think I'll have time, to be honest. I'll try to make it to Galeries Lafayette and pick up some macaroons or something, like the ones you brought back from Lucy's hen, and maybe a nice bottle of wine for us. But other than that to be honest, the day will go pretty quickly I think.'

He had half closed the door when he saw Rachel turning over, the sheets tangled around her legs and her hair fanned out on the pillow behind her. Watching her he felt a sudden surge of vertigo and rushed back, kneeling down to hold her. She kissed the shoulder closest to her and then pushed him gently away, murmuring, 'Too hot.'

'Have a lovely day, Pumpkin,' he said. He felt homesick looking at her, and a maudlin nostalgia for her untouched perfection.

'Mmm, OK,' she murmured. He closed the door as silently as he could, though he knew that she could not yet be sleeping.

*   *   *

It had been easy to make it happen, once he'd set his mind to it. Starting with that moment in the car a week ago when he had answered his sister's enquiries with the lie about the race across the Paris bridges as easily as if he'd been rehearsing it for months. Seconds before, he had wanted to shatter the glass to climb into the image of Ellie and seize her. He had not been thinking coherently when he told Olivia about Paris – providence had provided the answer.

It was only by chance that he knew about the race; a colleague's sister-in-law was running it for Cancer Research and had forwarded him the sponsorship email. He had matched the bids on her web page and then days later, thinking of his father, had gone back and donated again. It should have been sacrosanct, and yet it was an email raising money to find a cure for cancer that had seeded his first lie, had given him a reason to dash to Paris and the means of seeing Ellie. And although fingers of guilt had crept into the corners of his mind he had not allowed them to take hold. The guilt had been easy to push aside, a discovery that was itself both frightening and energising. All week, his overwhelming sensation had been of impatient excitement. He could not believe it was all so simple. He was actually on his way.

The train drew up in the Gare du Nord and he looked again at Ellie's message:

Curiouser and curiouser. I hope your friend runs fast enough to justify his fan club travelling so far. I'm working all afternoon but I'll meet you for a coffee at

the Gare du Nord at eleven. Sorry not to show you
the best of Paris but needs must . . . A bientôt.

For all he knew she was in love and playing house with a Parisian, or was having an affair with the rage-inducingly pretty male model who was fondling her in the first Balmain editorial campaign, her stillettoed heel resting on his thigh as they lounged together on the bonnet of a vintage Porsche. Months before there had even been a photo in the tabloids of Marshall Bruce skulking beneath a New York Yankees baseball cap and leaving a hotel in St-Tropez. Far too close for comfort. Even so, something in Adam's guts told him not to let it stop him. Whatever might be happening in Paris – and he could not, however much it repelled him, delude himself that there were no men – he would not believe that her heart was taken. Yet he had lied to her, too, about his reason for coming. If he'd told her the truth she might not see him and it was possible, then, that he might go mad. So he had been casual and had suggested a coffee, but only if she had time. That had been on Monday. And now it was 10 a.m. on Saturday and he was walking through the Gare du Nord and somewhere in it, Ellie Schneider would be waiting for him, if only for a few hours. Outside the station café he took a single breath and went in.

Ellie was sitting on a red banquette behind a row of small square tables, bent over a novel. A large mirror above her head reflected back his own anxious face and he had a brief moment to adjust his expression before she looked up and saw him. The deep tan he'd seen in the Duchess of Kent had gone and she looked as ashen as he first remembered her, with dark circles of exhaustion under her eyes. She had no make-up on and her full lips had the same pallor as her cheeks. She was twenty-four now, almost two years older than when he'd seen her on Kol Nidre, but she could have been sixteen, or thirty. Already, fine lines were forming around her eyes and yet she still looked vulnerable, fragile, brittle. She took the fingernail that she'd been biting out of her mouth and smiled.

'Hey, stranger.' His voice sounded high and unsteady to his own ears; his pulse was racing. 'Hi, Rocky,' he added, noticing the dog curled in her lap.

'Hey.'

Ellie was all in black, her only jewellery that single gold ring on a fine chain round her neck. He sat down on the rickety mahogany chair across from her and smiled back. His pulse slowed.

'How are you?'

'Happy you're here,' she said, simply.

'Me too.' He paused. With Ellie, always, he had a simple compulsion to speak his thoughts aloud, uncensored. It drew him to her. 'Everything just – realigns – when I see you. Straight away.'

She nodded, almost imperceptibly. 'So.'

'So.'

She picked up the laminated menu that lay between them but then asked, without looking at it, 'Will you have a hot chocolate with me?'

Adam nodded. He wasn't going to tell her that since Rachel's pudding campaign he was trying to diet when he was out of the house. The waiter approached.

'*Deux chocolats Viennois, s'il vous plaît. Merci.*'

'How's your French?'

Ellie laughed. 'Spectacular, as you can see. If I only order items that appeared on my high school vocabulary lists then I speak flawless French. But actually it's getting better. It comes back fast.'

'Assuming you ever had it. We had this French teacher, she must have been in her first or second year out of university. Poor woman. Jasper and I did nothing but play Fantasy Football in the back. I made it through five years of French lessons entirely unscathed. I learned nothing.'

'That's an achievement in itself.'

'Yes, I'm very proud. No, that's not true, actually, I did accidentally learn how to say *le chien a mangé mon devoir.*'

'Impressive. And how did you do in the football?'

'Oh – brilliant. Top of the league two years running.'

'Did you at least buy French players?'

'Erm, only Cantona. But he was one of my stars, until he retired.'

'I had no idea you were such a rebel.' Ellie shook her head. She had been fiddling with the menu, opening and closing the concertina of its folds, but then set it down with a decisive action as if telling herself, firmly, to stop. 'Well, I don't know about their soccer players but I do love it here. Which is lucky, as I can't go back to New York.' A strand of hair slipped out of her ponytail and she pushed it back idly. She was white-blonde at the moment and her hair looked dry and unkempt, longer than he'd ever seen it but just as neglected. He wanted to scoop her up and take her somewhere with sunshine and feed her fresh fruit and vegetables. Instead he asked, 'Why not?'

'It's complicated. I've been in touch with Marshall a little – not like that,' she said, interrupting herself as Adam looked horrified, 'and it's become this very – awkward situation. Lawrence must have told you that he and his wife are back together now and trying to make it work, and I guess I hope for him that it does, but it's obviously a little delicate. Anyway, in the course of the investigations when they were apart her lawyers have done some pretty extensive research into my life. It's not really in her interests to draw too much attention to me any more, I suppose, so they've not done anything with it, but Marshall said that if I came back to New York then he couldn't say what she'd do. She doesn't want me around because I'll remind people that her marriage is – not exactly perfect. She works in television now, she's pretty well connected and she's put together this list . . .' She trailed off. The rest of the sentence was unnecessary. 'Other people would be hurt,' she said finally.

Adam extrapolated, unhappily. An image of Barnaby Wilcox flashed into his mind, seducing Ellie with his dimples and erudition, and his wondrous tales of pagan ritual and folklore. Adam did not care if Barnaby Wilcox, or any others like him, got hurt. But then there was Mrs Wilcox. And Wilcox Junior. And of course there would be other men, probably someone else in the public eye, probably someone else with a family. And Ellie herself, at the centre of all this.

'So you can't be in New York,' he said, pushing a series of images aside with effort. 'Will you come back to London?'

'I can't be there either.'

He briefly considered a joke here, something about other angry wives, and then reconsidered. Instead he raised an eyebrow, inviting her to go on.

'It's just easier for me to be here.' She looked at him and paused. 'For many reasons. Don't you think?'

The waiter had returned and Adam sat back, moving his arms from the table.

'No. I don't. I think you should be in London. There are people in London thinking about you. Missing you.'

'In which case – *merci*,' she added, accepting a glass of creamy hot chocolate. On top quivered a drift of whipped cream the size of a tennis ball beneath a mound of shaved chocolate curls. 'In which case, why didn't you come over and talk to me when I was, in fact, in London? In the pub?'

'Oh, Ziva told you I looked for you? I couldn't find you anywhere . . .'

She paused with a spoonful of whipped cream halfway to her mouth. 'That's horseshit. I was standing at the bar, I saw you. I knew you were there.'

Adam felt himself redden. 'Well, if you saw me there . . .' He trailed off.

'Because you had come looking for me, remember? And if you wanted to stand there in the doorway, if you wanted to stay away from me you must have had your reasons. And I was going to come after you when you left but I figured it would be selfish. You decided something else was more important, I guess. You were fighting with something, I could see it. I didn't want to stand in the way of that.'

'I was fighting with something.'

'Me too. And we both won.' She smiled again, but without warmth. 'Right? We both won. Everything's as it should be.'

'But it's not. Nothing's as it should be.' Adam pushed aside his glass and reached for her across the table but she reared back, spoon in hand and held aloft as if to defend herself.

'What the hell are you doing?'

'Sorry, sorry,' he mumbled. He pulled his saucer back towards him and, for lack of anything better to do with his hands, clasped them around the hot glass.

Ellie sat forward again and said, softly, 'I'm sorry. I am – I didn't mean to talk to you like that. But, Adam, everything's different. You're married now. To my cousin. You married Rachel. You chose.'

He ignored what he felt to be the unfairness of that comment. 'I know. But just tell me—'

'Let's not talk about it now. Is that OK? I've only got another hour. Can I have you till then? Can we just have a little time not talking about how fucked up everything is? I promise – I'm not avoiding anything. I'm not pretending anything. I am well aware that you're Rachel's. But I just want to,' she dropped her spoon on the saucer with a clatter and circled her hands, searching for words, 'I just want to enjoy having you here for a while. Before either of us says anything out loud that means it's not okay for us to sit here together. OK?'

He nodded. The rush of humiliation that he'd felt when she'd pulled away from him was subsiding.

'OK.'

'Good. So let's talk about other things.'

'OK,' he said. 'You go first.'

TWENTY-THREE

They had left the station café and now stood outside so that Ellie could smoke. After the first cigarette she had moved on to a joint, covered as always in coconuts. Adam was holding Rocky's lead and trying not to worry about being arrested, but he could not help wondering what the precise implications would be for a lawyer caught with someone smoking pot in the middle of a Paris street. It had taken all his self-control not to tell her to put it away but he was loath to waste a second of the time they had together, and he wanted her to learn to trust him so that she would allow him to guide her when it was important. He wanted to be a protective influence in her life. He would not give her an excuse to push him away by fussing like a Jewish mother. Let her be as she was. Instead he breathed in the sweet smell so evocative of Ellie, and tried to focus on what she was saying.

'It's inane if you make it inane. Or it can be creative and inspiring and collaborative.'

'Don't you get bored?' he asked.

'I'm not going to say that only boring people get bored because I hate when people say that, it's such a boring thing to say. But I guess it's what you make of it.' Adam was leaning on an empty bike rack watching

Ellie as she paced before him on the pavement. Rocky sat between his feet. 'You can sit like a vegetable sending text messages while you're in hair and make-up for three hours, or you can see it as time you're being paid to sit in a chair and educate yourself. I'd read all of Dickens – including the non-fiction that most people never bother with – by the time I was twenty-two, and I was paid to do it. There's no way I'd ever have ploughed through *Our Mutual Friend* if it hadn't have been for Chanel, but then I was in Rome for them a few years before that and they also gave me *Martin Chuzzlewit* and, I mean, what a fucking page-turner! And now it's all there marinating and I hope – God, I hope – it will make me a better writer one day. At the moment, Balmain are paying me to read Tolstoy. I'm up to 1889 and *The Kreutzer Sonata*.'

'So you still want to write,' he said, carefully. Jaffa had talked a lot about Ellie 'throwing away her opportunities to make a smutty film' – he had heard it so many times that he had, he realised, assumed it was true.

She laughed. A wind picked up, blowing her hair across her face. She turned up the collar of her leather jacket. 'What, you mean do I still want to be a novelist even though Columbia University decided I was just a little bit too creative to get a Master's in Creative Writing? Yes. I know it's crazy but I guess I just figured that some people have struggled by and managed to write fiction without a degree in it.'

'Point taken. But why did you want to do the course in the first place then, if it's pointless?'

'It's not pointless. It's just not necessary. It was a

time-killer. I love learning, I love writing and I didn't want to do a Master's in Literature that would have sucked all the joy for me out of any writer I chose for my thesis. And so it was a little counterweight to the modelling which always makes people assume you're stupid. It was enriching my fabric, or whatever. Life experience.'

It was Adam's turn to laugh. 'I'd say your fabric was pretty enriched already.'

She smiled back. 'Maybe. But who wants to hear the ramblings of a twenty-four-year-old? Give me a decade more and I'll give it a shot. Maybe two. In the meantime I'm preparing.'

'So what do you mean "up to" 1899 and *The Kreutzer Sonata*? Do you always read chronologically?'

She nodded. '1889. Always. I've always done it. I like to evolve with the author, I don't want to know their future before they do and if I'm really reading a writer, like, committed to reading their whole *oeuvre*, then I want to move through their life with them and their work. If I love someone I want to walk beside them from the first to the last.'

A silence fell between them. Adam began to stroke Rocky's fragile belly, gently, with his toe. The dog rolled on to his back, tiny legs splayed in undignified bliss.

'My little comrade,' Ellie said, fondly. 'You've won him over.'

'How old is he?'

'Five. I got him when I was on a job in LA. They have this pet shop in the Beverly Center where they'll let you play with the dogs. There was no way I was going to get a puppy and if I did then I wanted an Airedale, and a rescue, but then I met Rocky and it was done.' She looked down appraisingly at the small animal as if reminding herself of his attributes; cataloguing the charms with which he had conquered her. 'He's been all over. He was in a shoot with me once. For some cheap sunglasses commercial thing.'

'We had an Airedale when I was younger,' Adam told her. 'Called Norman Levene.'

Ellie threw her head back with sudden laughter.

'I never actually knew why his surname was different from ours. I suspect my sister had something to do with it.'

'Your sister's so cool. She told me to read *The Line of Beauty* when I met her and it was honestly life-changing. I'd never even heard of him and there he was – my favourite writer just waiting to be found. It was like the perfect *shidduch*.'

Adam was surprised that Ellie had ever spoken to his sister; even more so that she had endorsed her, improbably, as cool.

'I wouldn't talk to Olivia about *shidduchs*.'

'Yes, I had the impression there was some anxiety bubbling about her love life. I didn't really get why it was anyone's business.'

'Everything is everyone's business,' said Adam, and then in case he'd sounded bitter added, 'but if you know an eccentric medieval historian then give him my sister's number.'

'Not gay?'

'No. Not to the best of my knowledge. My mother asks her once a week.'

'Hmm. Well, I should find her a sexy French model

then,' Ellie mused. 'No need to condemn her to a man in tweed just yet.'

Adam could pursue this line of thought no further, in jest or otherwise. The idea of Olivia with a male model was beyond the flexibility of his imagination.

'Will you stay here in Paris, do you think?'

She affected a nonchalant French shrug. '*Qui sait?*'

'Don't. Move back to London. Come back.'

'Stop saying that when you know I can't be in London,' she said, suddenly. 'It hurts.'

He looked up. Her voice had changed; she was no longer smiling. Her hands were in her pockets, and she looked cold. It had begun to rain but she made no move to go back inside.

'Don't you think I would? But this isn't about me, or about what I want. Who knows, maybe those people who seem like they get everything get it because they do the right thing and deserve it.'

'You don't mean that, surely,' he asked, incredulous. 'You don't believe in karma and all that crap. What was it you said? "A firm belief in randomness".'

'God, I don't know.'

'It's crap. Fine, you're right in the sense that we should all work harder to be better but you can't follow that argument through. It's too cruel to say that bad things happen as punishment for things we've done, you can't possibly believe that. It's rubbish. Life is random.'

'OK, maybe. But there's nothing wrong with saying that the looking after other people, the morality, that those things will make your life better, indirectly, because then you deserve better. There is so much bourgeois bullshit in Hampstead Garden Suburb and gossip and whispering but you know what? People there have values that make you sit up straighter.'

'As long as it doesn't leave you believing that you deserve the bad things,' Adam repeated, stubbornly.

'No one deserves bad things.'

'No.'

'But some people seem like they are worthier of the good things than others,' Ellie observed.

'Do you think?'

'I don't know. When I was younger I used to be so jealous of Rachel that I thought it would kill me.'

Adam crouched down to stroke Rocky again, hiding his surprise.

'Her life seemed so easy and perfect, and she gets everything she wants and it felt like my life was just the opposite. Like, I was watching her get everything that I wanted. She had Lawrence, who worships her. And then she got you. I just – I wanted to be her; I wanted everything she had. And now I think, well, maybe to be her I would have had to be her – remembering everyone's birthdays and who doesn't like mushrooms and volunteering in old people's homes and teaching Sunday school and whatever else she did. Not karmically or mystically or whatever. Just – be good, think of other people, and maybe other people think of you. So this is me, thinking of other people.'

By some unspoken agreement they had begun walking slowly back inside and through the station, and when they reached an empty bench in the concourse Ellie sat down and scooped the tiny dog on to her lap. Adam wanted to say – Rachel's life isn't perfect. She doesn't have everything.

After all, I'm here with you. Instead he said softly, 'I'm sorry.'

'Me too.' She began to pick at the graffiti paint that flaked from the bench beneath them. Then she asked, 'Is she happy, at least?'

'Yes. I think she's happy.'

'I'm glad.'

Adam snorted. He had felt so close to her seconds ago; now he felt light years away. 'How can you be so bloody stoic all the time? How can you be glad she's happy? Are you happy? I'm not happy. I'm fucking miserable.' He looked at Ellie who had her little finger between her teeth, tearing at the skin around her nail. A bubble of blood formed and he winced; it was all he could do not to slap her hand away from her mouth to stop her hurting herself. She said nothing and he continued, 'You – you showed me just this tantalising glimpse of how it could be and at the same time you expect me to keep everything from before exactly the same, everything I thought I wanted before I even knew that life could be any other way. I didn't know, don't you see that? I thought I wanted it but that was because I didn't know there was anything else. You said I chose, but it wasn't a real choice. She was all I knew.'

It was a shock, when he finished, to realise that Ellie was crying. Rachel cried all the time; he was virtually immune to it. But Ellie crying – he could hardly bear it.

'This is so fucked up,' she whispered, clenching her fists. A tear slid down her cheek and she wiped it angrily with the sleeve of her jacket. 'This is so fucked up. I can't be near you. But I don't want to go far away either.' She stood up to leave.

He sprang up and caught her wrist, and her half-hearted struggle gave him courage. He had to make her promise; had to know that she'd see him again.

'You punish yourself with comparisons but no one has everything. Rachel's life is hardly perfect, is it? I'm here. I'm with you.'

A strange expression came over her face; one that he didn't recognise and couldn't quite identify, but at his words he felt her slacken in his grip. She took a step closer to him. She had relented; he had won.

'I'm coming back next weekend. I don't care – cancel everything. I'm coming back next Saturday and I'm staying here, with you, and we're going to be together. Enough talking.'

He pulled her towards him until he could feel her breath, could smell perfume and smoke and the rain-wet leather of her jacket. He leaned forward and kissed her neck. And then with all the strength he had, he turned and walked away from her, back towards the platforms.

Behind him he heard her say, quietly, 'OK.'

'Adam!'

Adam jumped. He had made it on to an earlier train – in the end, he'd spent less time in Paris than it had taken to get there, and all in the Gare du Nord. Still, it was worth it. He had leaned against the window as the French countryside slipped past him in a blur and for the whole journey he had played their conversation over and over in his head, and the tears that had made him ache to comfort her now seemed like a victory. Ellie had been hurting too.

He had stepped straight off the train and crossed St Pancras, heading for the ticket office to book his seats for the following weekend. At the sound of his name he spun round, sure that his elation was written all over his face. He could feel it on his lips; it was in his stride across the station, pulsing in every cell. In front of him was Zach Sabah's friend Ezra.

'Adam Newman.' Ezra held out a hand to shake.

'Ezra. What are you doing here?'

'I'm everywhere, dude.' Ezra slapped him amiably on the shoulder. 'I've been filming in Paris. Gay Paree – or at least it was for the two days I was in it. I love that city. I want to eat Paris.'

'It's beautiful.'

'As are some of its inhabitants. I didn't know you knew Ellie Schneider.'

'How did you know I—'

'I saw you two gossiping in the station café. I was going to come over but I was carrying all this gear –' he lifted both arms, from which hung a tripod in a case, several camera bags and his luggage. On his back was a huge rucksack with a water bottle tucked into a mesh pouch on its side, so that he looked as if he was about to go hiking – 'and I didn't want to interrupt.' This was said without apparent subtext; still, Adam wondered how much he had seen. He tried to think back to any moments in the café that might appear suspect – only that single second when she had pulled away as he'd reached out for her.

'How do you know Ellie? Or did you just recognise her?' Adam asked.

Ezra began to lift off his various bags and pile them on

the floor with relief. Adam saw that he was in for a longer conversation than he had the strength for. After having spent days irritated for not insisting that they go to Brooklyn to see Ezra's play, he now wished that the man was anywhere but in front of him. His mind was still full of Ellie and he had not yet come up with a convincing explanation for why they had been together. And, in truth, he didn't want to. He couldn't bear the idea of sullying their perfect morning by lying about her.

'No, I know her, I've known her a long time. Trust me, there was a time when everyone in New York knew Ellie. Now you can't sneeze without tripping over a poster of her but Ellie herself is nowhere to be seen. I was the photographer's assistant on one of her first shoots.'

'Oh, cool.'

'It all looked very serious back there in the café – are you guys close? She's behaving herself now, isn't she?'

'No. I mean, yes she's behaving I think but no, not close.'

'I sure hope she is. Sweet kid. Where are you going now? Do you have time for a drink? At six thirty I've got to meet with an accountant about some charity stuff I'm doing, but I'm totally free till then.' As he spoke he inclined his head first one way and then the other, stretching his neck and wincing.

Adam mumbled an apology and left Ezra collecting all his bags again. He had hours before he was expected at home and he wanted to think his way back to where he'd been, in his head, before Ezra had called to him. He bought a ticket for the following weekend and then, instead of descending into the Tube station, he left St Pancras, turned up his collar against the rain that had started and began to walk home. It was only when he reached Camden Town that he remembered he had forgotten to bring back the macaroons for Rachel.

TWENTY-FOUR

Ziva's birthday was a major event in the Gilbert calendar and Adam had always been moved by the enjoyment that it gave her. Ziva – ferociously rational and contemptuous of most other frivolities – glowed with pleasure at the sight of her own candlelit cake. This year she was turning ninety and despite many offers from Lawrence and Jaffa, was throwing her own party at home. No one else, she believed, would do it just so. Jaffa had worried about several aspects of this plan – about the elderly guests travelling so far when most of them lived in Golders Green; about her mother's terrible cooking and also about the alternative, that in all probability Ziva would commission the local takeaway to cater the party and that her ninetieth year would be honoured with lukewarm curries in polystyrene. In the end, compromises were reached. Jaffa was granted permission to cook; Lawrence arranged for each of the younger guests to chauffeur the less mobile ones. Rachel ordered a new book of pastry recipes and had been fussing in the kitchen for days. Ellie had not been able to get out of a shoot for Balmain and so was still in Paris but had sent a towering, violet-iced cake from Ladurée, covered in scallops of cream and pearly sugared almonds and placed at the centre of the dining table where Ziva would glance at it, intermittently, with pride.

The older contingent were the fellow members of the Jewish Care Holocaust Survivors' Group. Often at the lunches they did not talk about their experiences, Ziva told her family, often nothing was said at all. They spoke of politics, of literature, of their grandchildren. But to be there together was restful, in a place where volunteers ensured there would always be bread on the table. There was balm in their silences together, just as their listening offered balm to those among them who did decide to talk. Others thought they could imagine, but no one else could know. And here they all were – Ziva's daily lunch companions; men and women shrinking with age but strengthened with pride at their own continued existence. To celebrate ninety when they'd faced death at nineteen, it was not nothing. They ate and they joked and they argued. And always in English, even among friends who shared a mother tongue.

With unspoken consensus, everyone had converged on an Austrian theme to their catering. Lawrence had collected three old ladies from an assisted living centre in Hendon, one of whom had thrust into his hands, without explanation or ceremony, two heavy oblongs of silver foil. These warm, sagging parcels turned out to be wide coils of apple strudel, rich with nutmeg and moist raisins. Michelle had bought Linzer tortes from Carmelli's, filled with plum butter and sour cherries. From the new book, Rachel had made Sacher torte with bitter black chocolate and home-made apricot jam; another of the formidable Austrian ladies from the Jewish Care group had brought a box of rum-soaked petits fours iced in strawberry-pink fondant and painted with arabesques of dark chocolate, Viennese delicacies that were apparently called *punschkrapfen*. Lawrence and Adam had both suppressed a smile at this name; Ziva had tutted and called them infantile and though the word *punschkrapfen* had been only mildly amusing, her chastisement ensured that when they next caught one another's eye they both emitted infantile, strangulated giggles. Ziva, entirely aware of the effect this would have said again, 'Really, I do not see what is so amusing about *punschkrapfen*,' and left Adam and Lawrence collapsing with laughter in the kitchen.

Later, when Lawrence's BlackBerry began to trill on the sideboard Adam, who was closest to it, peered at the number.

'It's the switchboard.' He handed it to Lawrence who was amongst a group listening to a very tiny old man tell a story, confused and hilarious, about buying a beagle in Frankfurt in 1929.

Lawrence took it, mouthing 'sorry, sorry' at Jaffa and heading for the hall. Michelle looked disapproving. It was a work call – of course he should take it, she thought, without the need for an apology. Michelle had turned back to hear the beagle punchline when Lawrence's voice was suddenly audible in the hallway.

'Shit.'

His family exchanged worried glances. Lawrence did not believe in profanities. Adam had last heard him swear when Arsenal had lost to Barcelona in Paris in the final of the 2006 Champions League. Adam and Lawrence had gone over with Rodney Wilson; Barcelona had scored twice in the last fourteen minutes. Then, Lawrence had said 'bollocks'. It was possible he'd even said it twice. Now Jaffa half rose to go to him but Ziva checked her with a glance.

'Leave him to talk, Jaffale.'

Lawrence returned to the dining room looking pale.

'Nothing to worry about,' he said before Jaffa could ask him. 'But one of our clients has had . . . a bit of a situation. Adam, I'm sorry, but I'm going to have to ask you to come back to the office with me.'

Adam had been on his feet as soon as his father-in-law returned, scanning his face for clues. Lawrence bent over his wife and kissed the top of her head. 'Nothing to worry about,' he said again, 'but I think it's going to be a late one. I'll call later if I can with an update but don't forget to set the alarm when you go to bed. Happy birthday, Ziva, so sorry to run.'

Kisses were exchanged; Rachel and Jaffa in almost perfect synchrony tipped some desserts into plastic bags (Rachel the brownies, Jaffa the meringues) and pressed them fervently on the men. Adam demurred, with no idea of the emergency he was about to attend to; Lawrence accepted them in order to speed up their departure. Once in the car he threw them on the back seat and said to Adam, 'I don't actually believe what's happened. Shit. I can't actually believe it.' Lawrence swearing again was more unsettling than almost any other development.

'What happened?' Adam's first thought had been of Ellie; his panic had been steadily rising.

'Ethan Goodman.'

Adam breathed freely again until Lawrence said, 'He's lost everything, Adam. Everything. Not just his own investments – everything.'

'God. What do you mean? How?'

'I just – I don't know anything. But it's all gone. His fund's collapsed, or it was with an Austrian bank that's collapsed – I don't know. Tony was saying something about the forint but we'd never have done anything as risky as investing in Hungary so I don't understand how it's happened. Ethan doesn't take risks. My staff. The pensions! This has to be a mistake.'

Adam was unable to keep the horror from his face and then felt immediate regret that his first reaction had not been more supportive, or at least more calming.

'It has to be a mistake,' he echoed. 'Substantial losses maybe, but he can't have lost everything. Tony's panicking.'

But if it wasn't a mistake it was horrendous. His father-in-law would be ruined. The money they held for clients would be safe, but GGP's debts would be crippling. Fatal. They would have to sell the company for pennies.

Ethan had taken on the GGP Pension Fund as a favour when Lawrence had been looking for safe, reliable fund managers. Adam remembered the conversation – it had been more than five years ago and all three of the GGP founding partners had been elated by the move. Surely it wasn't possible for a pension fund to just disappear? An inventory of GGP employees began to form in Adam's mind; those with families, those who'd recently bought houses, were pregnant or were approaching retirement. He began to imagine them in a line, men and women in single file stretching away into the distance. The future of each one and all their dependants had been entrusted to Ethan Goodman. Along with his own fund, Ethan had managed the GGP Pensions and the savings of one or two private individuals – not people with a lot of money, but those whom Ethan had gone out of his way to help. And what help it turned out to be! Adam was fairly certain that Ari Rosenbaum's father had given his money to Goodman and—

'Poor, poor Ziva,' Lawrence said, just as Adam's realisation dawned. She would lose everything.

Not since his first year at Linklaters had Adam worked through two consecutive nights at the office. They were seeking to obtain a freezing injunction against the Goodman Funds and he was almost cross-eyed with exhaustion, fuelled only by caffeine, adrenalin, a fierce urge to protect Lawrence who was looking a decade older with each day that passed, and an even fiercer urge to punch Ethan Goodman and keep punching him until he was on the floor and screaming for mercy. Then, he imagined, he might move on to kicking him in the face. That his train for Paris had departed that morning without him on it was a frustration he did not yet have the emotional resources to address.

Goodman had begun proceedings to liquidate his two ailing investment funds, The Goodman ABS Fund and the associated Fairman Fund, and as a result had lost, personally, many millions. The Goodman ABS Fund had been in trouble for a while and as the Fairman Fund had a 40 per cent stake in it, it could not continue to trade once the Goodman ABS closed. Understanding the interdependent entities was more challenging than it should have been, made even more so by the fact that Lawrence had so far been unable to get hold of Ethan Goodman himself.

'It looks like the banks that lent him money will get it back but there's almost nothing for the investors. You know, it wasn't just me and Tony who wanted this, the trustees jumped at the opportunity back then. They were all in favour and now they've had collective amnesia. If one more person asks me why I wanted to invest with that schmuck,' said Lawrence, taking off his glasses and pinching the bridge of his nose as if to stave off a headache, 'I think I'm going to throw myself out of this window.' He was standing at the back of his office staring out blankly at Marylebone beneath them, rocking back and forth on his heels as if he was on the ledge itself and about to do just that. Michelle's vision had become a reality – very late the previous night Adam had moved himself into Lawrence's office so that they did not need to bother picking up the phone to speak. The other GGP partners, Tony Gould and Jonathan Pearl, were each in their own adjacent rooms and Kristine had come in to answer their now incessant phones. Adam was the only other employee yet to be included in the council of war. It was Saturday night.

Lawrence turned back into the room. Neither man had

shaved since Thursday morning, and his father-in-law's beard, Adam noticed, was coming through grey. Had it always been? He couldn't remember him anything other than clean shaven. For a moment he tried to imagine Lawrence when they had first met, almost a decade and a half ago, but that long-ago Lawrence appeared as a child's memory, unchanged and unchanging, always substituted with a current image so that Adam's devious unconscious could deny the alteration. The thought of Lawrence getting older was an intensely painful one.

Two phones began to ring outside. Kristine was trying, valiantly, to answer every call. It had been impossible to work since the news had become public – either it was a GGP employee hysterical that Ethan Goodman's fail-safe investments had failed, or it was a friend, full of pity and offering to help. Questions from the frantic staff were heart-rending, and they had no answers to them. Was it really possible that everything was gone? What would happen to the company? To their mortgage? Would they have to sell their house? Would their husband have to come out of retirement? Lawrence had begun by taking all of these calls himself, speaking for hours to his senior associates, his mailroom men, the secretaries, until Tony and Jonathan had intervened. Every hour on the phone was an hour in which he was unable to look for a solution. Equally disruptive were the well-meaning friends – was there anything they could do? Did Lawrence need a loan? Advice? A barrister? An accountant? A break in the countryside to clear his head (this from a concerned and paternal Rupert Sabah)? Their support was touching but their pity was, Adam could sense, intolerable. It was these charitable offers that finally led Lawrence to cede his mobile to Kristine.

Only Adam had kept his own phone. He had not wanted to overload Kristine, he'd said, but in truth he hadn't wanted her to answer if Ellie called him, though he was almost certain that she wouldn't and hoped, in fact, that she wouldn't. He had only the strength remaining to help Lawrence. Rachel too had added a bewildering dimension to the last few days by sending him provocative text messages in which she promised to reward all his hard work just as soon as he got home. He did not have the energy for her, either. Whether it was the thought of her man soldiering at the front like a hero that was doing it for her he didn't know; only that his wife seemed to have rediscovered her sex drive at the last moment in the world when he could think about sex.

'We've got to find a way. This is people's lives. It's an insult to tell them I don't know anything – but I don't, I don't know any more than they do. And they're all calling. Everyone's calling us. I have to be able to tell them something. We'll have to have a meeting on Monday morning with everyone and tell them – what? What can I tell them? Why the hell won't he speak to me? Why . . . ?' Lawrence shook his head. 'Why the hell hasn't he called me back? Surely he couldn't have seen this coming or he'd have told us. I mean, it wasn't some hare-brained high-risk investment, it was a pensions fund, for God's sake. I understand that people make mistakes, but a real man, a *mensch*, shoulders his responsibilities and faces people and at least *explains*.'

Adam hurt for Lawrence, still resolute in his

determination to see the best in everyone. It had been glaringly obvious since the beginning of this fiasco that Ethan Goodman, whilst he was many things – stupid, cowardly, irresponsible, possibly even criminally negligent – was not a *mensch*. A *mensch* would not have gambled with the money of people who didn't have it to lose.

'And what about this Brooke business?' Lawrence continued. 'Do you believe that Brooke didn't know any of this was happening? What husband doesn't at least warn his wife that their lives are about to fall apart?' Jaffa knew Lawrence's movements as clearly as if he wore a tracking bracelet – he himself made sure of it. That Ethan's wife had been, the rumours alleged, as ignorant as the rest of them seemed unfathomable to him. But that was apparently the case. Brooke Goodman was in shock, people said, rigid and silent upstairs in the house on the Bishops Avenue that they would soon be forced to sell. Neither Ethan nor Brooke had been seen to leave the house since the news broke.

Adam considered the question. 'I think she really didn't know. I think he's that big of a *putz*,' he said. It was what his instinct told him and he felt strangely protective of poor Brooke Goodman, trapped in her collapsing golden cage with a man who had just told her, out of the blue, that he had ruined her life.

'Yes. A *putz* he certainly is.' Lawrence sat down at his desk, resuming the position that he'd been in for most of the past two days, hunched over, his head in his hands. Beside him was the email that the Goodman Fund had circulated to its investors, the only communication that Ethan Goodman had offered anyone:

I have been working ceaselessly in recent days, inves-
tigating all feasible methods by which to alleviate this
current crisis. The situation has been further strained
by the recent and well-publicised alterations to the
circumstances of the credit providers who have
resorted to draconian terms, without considering the
creditworthiness of firms in each individual case. I am
devastated for my investors by this unavoidable
liquidation.

Goodman was no doubt devastated – and certainly in
financial terms. It looked as if he had put several million
pounds of his own money into the funds in recent days
in a desperate attempt to prevent a fire sale and to keep
them trading, but it had, in the end, made no difference.
This had not made anyone feel any happier.

Lawrence was reading the email for the hundredth time
when Kristine appeared in the doorway dressed in a sort
of black woollen muumuu, covered in Hawaiian orchid
prints in pale peach and dove grey. She had insisted on
coming in and her presence lent a reassuring normality to
one of the strangest working days they'd ever had.

'You should eat,' she directed. Adam and Lawrence
laughed; she sounded as if she was speaking from Jaffa's
lips. 'I'm going to order something in for you lot. Tony
and Jonathan haven't eaten either. What about Lebanese
from Fairuz?'

'Perfect, thanks.'

'Half an hour in the conference room. You'll all be
there.' She had raised her voice for this last statement so

that the other two partners could also hear – they would not get away with starving themselves on her watch, financial crisis or not.

'You should go, Kristine, honestly, it was so kind of you to come in on a Saturday and it's getting late.'

She drew herself up, offended. 'Kind of me to come in on a Saturday? Lawrence, the world has gone mad and you're talking as if you're at tea with the Queen. Of course I'd be here. And I'm going nowhere for the time being, thank you. I'll stay till ten when you've eaten and hopefully the phones have quietened down a bit. I'll do my part. It's all our pensions that man has lost, in any case. We should all muck in.'

It was then that Lawrence, to Adam's horror, began to cry. He couldn't be certain, for Lawrence had returned to the window and had his back turned to them. But he had lowered his head and his shoulders were shaking and it felt to Adam, watching helplessly, as if he was witnessing the destruction of the Temple.

He exchanged glances with Kristine and she left, closing the door behind her. When he heard it shut Lawrence turned to face him, exhaling heavily. He looked exhausted and rumpled somehow; not simply his clothes but all of him.

'What am I going to do?' he asked Adam. 'We have thirty-seven employees and the pension fund . . . we made that decision, Tony and I. We thought we were doing something safe. He's such a community-minded man, or we *thought* he was such a community-minded man,' he corrected himself, 'a responsible man, a *father*, a great philanthropist, and honestly it seemed as if we were doing the right thing. And you know the most ridiculous part? We had to beg him to take the fund. Do you remember? Beg him. He didn't want to do it, he was so modest and kept saying he wasn't a fund manager, he'd just done some favours for some friends, we really had to schmooze him to do it. The trustees all approved it. Thirty-seven pensions, for which I am personally responsible. And now there'll be a takeover. What am I going to do?'

'Surely they'll recover it somehow. Surely he still has something of his own, in America or something.'

'Maybe. I only *hope*,' Lawrence rubbed his eyes again, 'I only hope that we get this done in time before he actually starts getting rid of assets. He wouldn't – I'm sure he wouldn't. He wouldn't. But without picking up the bloody phone to me, he's left us absolutely no choice. God, this is a mess. Poor man. What a mess he's made.'

Adam had abandoned his shirt the day before and was now in the Thierry Henry Arsenal T-shirt from his gym bag, but the office still felt stifling. Rachel had offered to bring him things from home but he'd lied and said he had everything he needed, to avoid the interruption. He considered, briefly, whether it would be more restful to stay at work again rather than to go home and fend off his inexplicably randy wife. She would also, God help him, want to talk about all of this. It was exhausting just thinking about it. But it was not something he had to decide yet – many hours lay ahead before any of them could consider going home.

Tony Gould came in, wearing jeans and an ancient University of Bristol sweatshirt. Until yesterday Adam had rarely seen Tony without a tie.

'Affidavit's looking good, I think. It's going to be monstrously big. Kristine's got dinner set up. Fancy stopping for a bite?' Tony asked.

'Yes.' Lawrence pushed back his chair and threw down the sheaf of Goodman ABS Fund statements that he'd been poring over, the same documents he'd been reading with forensic care all day in order to draft the application for the freezing injunction. The others had all been doing similar, painstaking examinations in a frantic bid to complete the supporting affidavit setting out the assets and the imminent threat of their dissipation.

'Good man. Might be the last time the company credit card works, might as well go wild on the expense account. I'll tell her to order extra baba ghanoush. Let's go crazy.' Tony put a weary arm around Lawrence. Adam was glad Tony had come back in as he seemed to be the only one who could raise even a fleeting smile from Lawrence.

Lawrence laughed and shook his head, patting Tony on the shoulder. 'Why not? Nothing like baba ghanoush to take the sting out of financial ruin.'

Adam followed them to the conference room watching the two men as they walked, talking softly, still with their arms round one another, old friends who had supported each other through school and university and marriage and children and were now, together, facing the challenge of their lives.

Adam was gratefully inhaling a lamb kebab when Kristine burst in, thrusting a phone at Lawrence. Lawrence set down the piece of grilled chicken that had been halfway to his mouth.

'Mrs Gilbert's mother's not well,' she said, 'they're at the Royal Free. Ziva's had a stroke.'

TWENTY-FIVE

'How is she, Pumpkin?'

Rachel had met their cab on the forecourt of the Royal Free Hospital, waiting between a man in a wheelchair and blue hospital gown smoking and shouting in loud Arabic into a mobile phone, and two women, one also in a hospital gown and the other in pyjamas, also smoking. Rachel's nose was red but she was composed, offering a wobbly smile as they drew up. But when Lawrence had paid the driver and stepped out she took one look at her father and all attempts at bravery disappeared.

'Daddy, she's not conscious,' she sobbed, throwing her arms around him. He stroked her hair.

'Take us in, poppet, let's see what the doctors have to say. No use thinking the worst at this stage. How's your mum?'

'*Ima*'s OK.' Rachel drew back and sniffed, and then turned back to Adam. She tucked herself under his arm as they waited for the lift and he squeezed her. 'She's been talking to the consultant. She knows more than I do, I've been outside calling people.' She wrinkled her nose and gestured back to the unwelcoming entrance to the hospital. They walked together down a long corridor of shiny buff linoleum, an exhibition of floral oil paintings displayed on the white walls. Rachel sniffed again and looked upwards, wiping under each eye with a forefinger in the vain hope of clearing her smudged mascara.

'She found out about Ethan,' she continued when they were in the lift, pressed between two pushchairs and a man on crutches. 'We tried our best but we couldn't be with her all the time and so she found out about everything last night. *Ima* didn't tell you because she said you had enough to deal with and so we'd look after Granny – and she seemed to be fine about it this morning when we left her. She was even joking that it didn't matter because she never had much money to start with. But if it's really all gone then she's got nothing at all, he had everything, Daddy, and she'll have to sell her house – and so she must have been so upset, and then Ashish called us—'

'Who's Ashish?' Lawrence interrupted.

'You know, the Indian takeaway guy. That's who found her. She called and ordered something and he went round to deliver it and she wasn't answering the door, so he called the police because he'd just spoken to her so he was worried, and then when they let him in and they found her he called us. He came with her in the ambulance.'

'Thank God. And what did he say? How long did they think she'd been unconscious?'

'Not long, because he said he was very quick going round. Not more than ten minutes, he was positive.

Thank goodness Granny can't cook.' Rachel smiled weakly.

'Ziva will be fine,' Adam said suddenly, with vehemence. He had no basis for saying so – but it seemed impossible that it could be otherwise. Ziva was unconquerable.

The lift doors opened, a nurse on reception smiled and pressed a button to unlock the security doors for them and Rachel led them down a waxed corridor to Ziva's cubicle.

'*Ani ayefa*, Jaffale,' said Ziva, squeezing her daughter's hand.

'I know, *Ima*. I know you're tired. *Shluf, Ima*. We're here if you want us.'

Ziva had been awake and able to talk, albeit slowly, for the last few hours, and although the consultant had kept her on oxygen the mask was frequently round her neck so that she might communicate something, carefully, to Jaffa.

Adam and Rachel had gone home, on Jaffa's insistence, while Jaffa and Lawrence had stayed overnight at the Royal Free. Lawrence was looking white with exhaustion when they came back on Sunday morning but he met them in the corridor, smiling with relief.

'She's going to be fine. She's not very mobile at the moment but she's absolutely clear, not remotely confused, thank God.'

'Will you get some sleep now, Daddy?' Rachel had asked.

'Later. Later. I'm going to run to the office in a bit.'

'You'll be more use to everyone if you get some rest,' Rachel had scolded and Lawrence had laughed and kissed the top of her head.

'That's exactly what your mother just said to me. I'll be fine. Let's not waste energy worrying about me just now.'

For most of the morning they had all been assembled around Ziva's bed, sitting quietly as instructed. Every now and then a nurse would pop her head around the curtain and suggest, gently, that one or two of them might like to step outside and give the patient some air, but this was met with such ferocity from Jaffa that their efforts had become more and more half-hearted.

'She needs the family,' Jaffa would say stoutly, waving away the nurse like a fly. 'I want to make sure you don't kill her with that terrible *drek* you feed to these old people.'

'*Wo ist sie?*' Ziva mumbled. '*Wo ist meine eynikl?*'

'She's here, *Ima*, Rachel's here.' Jaffa pointed across the bed to where Rachel sat beside Adam, holding his hand, her gaze fixed anxiously on her grandmother.

'*Nein*, Jaffale, I'm not demented,' Ziva said irritably. Adam considered the irritability a good sign. It was a return to form and she was also speaking English, which was a relief. So far it had been German, Yiddish and Hebrew, and sometimes a mixture of all three. Only Jaffa could understand all of them, although Rachel caught about half. 'I can see that Rachel's here. *Wo ist Ellie?*'

'We've been trying to get her, Granny, she's not picking

up her phone but I'm sure she'll call back soon,' said Rachel. She looked crestfallen that she had not been the granddaughter that Ziva wanted. She turned to Adam. 'Will you go down and try her again? And has my uncle answered?'

'Pumpkin, I tried her twenty minutes ago, I think her phone's off or something. Your dad emailed Boaz and it bounced back. Unless someone has a newer email address for him I don't know how else we can reach him.'

'Please try her? Or I'll ring her – will you come down with me?'

'Of course but really, I'm sure if she'd got the message she'd have called by now.'

Rachel had stood up to leave, clutching her phone, but she spun round suddenly. 'Ellie's such a selfish bitch.'

Adam started, and he saw Ziva close her eyes with pained exhaustion.

'Rachel!' said Jaffa sharply.

'It's true. Where the hell is she? We've been trying her since yesterday. She doesn't care about her family at all, she's probably holed up in some filthy hotel with some man who's paying her to do God knows what. She's such a slut, she's disgusting.'

Adam stiffened with anger and then checked himself and glanced away. Jaffa looked apoplectic. Rachel's venom did not frighten her. 'Rachel, *tafsiki*!' she hissed. 'I will not have you raising your voice in this place. People are trying to heal. Go out and compose yourself. *Eze meshugas*?'

Rachel burst into tears and fumbled her way out through

the plastic curtain that encircled them. Adam squeezed Jaffa's shoulder and followed his wife.

'Rach, what is going on?' Adam asked when they were outside. They had left the hospital and were sitting on a bench by the memorial in the centre of South End Green, next to a row of idling, belching London buses. It was a favourite place for a well-established coterie of Hampstead drinkers to enjoy early-morning lagers, and a neat row of empty Foster's cans was arranged at the foot of the monument.

Rachel shrugged, rolling a Coke can back and forth with the toe of her trainer.

'I just hate her.'

'You don't hate her.'

She looked up. 'I do sometimes, actually. Sometimes I really hate her. She's so – it's like she's untouchable. Nothing affects her, anything could happen and she's just – fine, she's just perfect. Except she's not. She does every- thing wrong and she's selfish and still everyone thinks she's perfect.'

Adam tried to ignore the sirens of warning that were wailing in his head. They hadn't talked about her cousin in any detail for months; he didn't want to say anything that might betray that he'd seen her. And yet there were odd echoes of a conversation he'd had with Ellie. He said carefully, 'I don't think her life is particularly perfect.'

Rachel shrugged again. She looked like a sulking

teenager, her shoulders rounded in self-defence, her hair falling forwards over her face. He felt sorry for her.

'I know, I know. I'm a terrible person because she's had a hard life and I'm jealous of her and so what does that say about me, blah, blah, blah.'

'It says you're human, Pumpkin, and that families are difficult sometimes and you're all under stress right now. We're all worried about Ziva.'

He rubbed her back but she twisted away from him in annoyance.

'You sound like you're reading from a textbook. I know families are difficult, I'm not an idiot.'

'Sorry.'

'It's not just about right now. It's always. Like, where is she this weekend? She hasn't even bothered to call.'

She was meant to be in Paris with me, he thought, and shivered.

'I'm sure she—' he started but she cut him off.

'She hasn't even bothered to call us and I'm here all the time, helping and worrying and it's so unfair. I could stay with Ziva and sit with her all day every day – all year – and she would still ask for Ellie at the end of it. Everyone would, probably even my own parents. She's beautiful and clever and troubled and needy and soooo charming and I'm . . . whatever. She gets everything I want.'

A seagull landed in front of them and Adam watched as it rummaged greedily in an abandoned bag of cheese and onion crisps. The pigeon that had been hopping nervously closer to the foil packet, eyeing the crisps with curiosity, flapped suddenly and flew to the top of the monument. It sat at the pinnacle, looking down with its head cocked at the lost prize. Adam felt the breath catch in his throat.

'That's not true,' he said.

Rachel turned to him, her eyes glistening and ringed with smudged mascara. 'Yes, Adam,' she said, 'it is.'

TWENTY-SIX

'I know I sound like Rachel but Lawrence, you've got to get some sleep.'

Lawrence looked up blearily; he had been nodding off, a coffee cup in one hand and the mouse in the other. 'I know. I know, I know.'

'Will you go home now, for a bit?'

'I just want to check this through again before I go anywhere.' Lawrence raised a copy of the draft claim form, waving it in slow motion like a white flag of surrender. Adam wasn't fooled; his father-in-law was angrier than he'd ever seen him. There would be no surrender until Ethan Goodman, who had still not answered any of Lawrence's communications, had been hauled out of hiding and made to account for himself. All traces of pity had disappeared. Lawrence was going to succeed with the injunction if it killed him.

'The barrister is going before the judge tomorrow and he had some guidance, some comments on the . . .' Lawrence trailed off.

'You're actually slurring. Go home! We spent two nights here and then you spent last night at the Royal Free. It's in good shape, it's basically finished and I'm staying here in any case to work on the final amendments for Jonathan. So now I'm staging an intervention.'

'Hear, hear.' Tony had appeared in the doorway looking dishevelled. His hair on one side stuck up as if he'd been clutching at it in frustration. Adam looked down. He would never have spoken to Lawrence with such familiarity if he'd known that one of the other partners was in earshot.

'I propose,' Tony said to Lawrence, 'that we meet at seven tomorrow. It's – almost midnight. Not too late. We might know more by then in any case, at least about what he's been up to since Friday. We've got a call with the accountants at nine thirty and we'll speak to the barrister again before he goes in. Adam, do you know what you're doing? Clear on everything?'

'Yes.'

'Good. Crack on then, phone me any time and after the call tomorrow you can nip home for a couple of hours. Jonathan will be here all night, I imagine, so ask him if you've any questions.'

'OK.'

On his way out Lawrence patted Adam's shoulder. 'Doing all right?'

Adam nodded.

'Good. I'm very proud, you know. You've been a real asset these last few days. Kept your head. Well done. However this turns out . . .' He trailed off and patted Adam once more before he went, leaving Adam to complete the thought. How might this turn out? It was absolutely impossible, at this stage, to be certain. The worst case scenario meant financial decimation for Lawrence and his partners who would, Adam knew, use every penny of their own to repay what they could to their employees' fund. Unless the money could be recovered, there were some people for whom this would turn out very, very badly indeed.

The fourth time Jasper had emailed Adam could not ignore him any longer. He had no time to stop, barely any time to think, but Jasper was frantically, touchingly worried about the Gilberts and Adam's silence seemed to be confirming his worst fears. Adam reached for the phone.

'Adam! Where the hell have you been, mate? I've been bloody stalking you. I'm going out of my mind. Are you OK? You're alive? You haven't jumped off anything?'

'I'm sorry. Yes, I'm alive. You can't imagine how things have been here.'

'If they're anything like they are everywhere else then I can. Is it all true? He's trying to flog it all off?'

'Yes.'

'So that bastard screwed GGP, right?'

'Not intentionally. But yes, effectively. And effectively,' Adam joked, joylessly.

'But surely it's negligence, surely you can sue or something. What has Ethan said to Lozza? How can he even face him?'

'He can't, Lawrence hasn't been able to get hold of him, Ethan's too spineless to speak to him. He's holed up at home, I think, with Brooke. He's lost pretty much everything, I reckon.'

'He deserves to,' said Jasper bitterly, 'for what he's done to Lawrence. Bloody hell, what I'd give to be a fly on the wall in that house right now, Brooke must be going absolutely mental. But I mean, whatever, forget that for a minute. What about you lot?'

'We are all,' said Adam, quoting Lawrence's rousing battle cry in a meeting earlier, 'going to have to help each other. It's a crisis. We're going to have to support each other in a crisis. We'll all do what we can, not that I can do much. But I think Lawrence and the other two partners are going to remortgage to try to get something back into the pension fund. It's a nightmare, I don't know where it leaves them all.'

'God.' Jasper whistled. 'Well, I'm here if I can do anything. If you need another accountant . . . or anything. Oh, which reminds me, I saw Ginger Josh and he said he was going to call you and Lawrence. He wants to help you, be there for people to talk to or whatever. I know he saw Jaffa when he popped into the hospital to visit her mother.'

Adam twined the cord of the phone round his finger absently. 'Not exactly sure how a rabbi is going to help anything but tell him thank you.' He had been sitting still too long – the office lights, controlled on motion sensors, turned off and left him in blackness. He waved an arm above his head and they blinked back into life.

'Well, he can pray or something. Have a quick chat with the big man and sort out this mess. Dunno, I guess he wants to counsel the people who are desperate.'

'Everyone at GGP is desperate, he's got his work cut out. Jas, I've got to go, it's bloody late and I've got a long night here. We're making an urgent claim, it's going before the judge tomorrow morning.'

'OK, mate. Good luck with it all, I'm thinking of you.

It's good to hear your voice. Tanya's mother is dropping something into the Royal Free for Ziva tomorrow, by the way. Some audio books, I think.'

'Thank you.'

Adam put down the phone and picked up the end of a Mars Bar he'd abandoned many hours earlier. It had melted on to his desk; a string of caramel slid sensuously from it and stretched across his mouse, as fine as spider's silk. He swore, loudly, his voice a satisfying volume in the empty office. He balled the front of his T-shirt in his hand and rubbed the mouse irritably, threw the chocolate in the bin and glanced at his screen.

Two new emails had arrived while he'd been speaking to Jasper. Matthew Findlay had sent him an article about Ethan Goodman from the archives of the *LA Times*, describing a charitable donation that had halted the eleventh-hour closure of an old people's home and had guaranteed that its residents would never have to move. A local councillor was quoted describing Goodman as a hero. *Odd*, Matthew had written, *how people are not of a piece.*

The next was from Ellie.

When you wrote you weren't coming I went down to the Camargue to stay with a friend for a few days. I can't pretend that I was surprised you bailed – let's just say I had a backup plan in place. We were in the middle of a lavender field, I've had no reception till an hour ago. I'm devastated about Ziva – will be on the first train tomorrow but Adam, how is she? Rachel barely explained anything. All I know is that she's conscious. In the morning please tell her I'm coming as fast as I can. E xxx

He saw only one thing clearly: she would be here tomorrow. In the morning, Ellie would be in London and he could snatch a moment with her – legitimately – in the Royal Free basement cafeteria, where white-hatted staff ladled endless stir-fries and cubes of gelatinous lasagne on to white plates. They would be allowed, he felt, to sit there with propriety.

Ziva's OK, I promise, he wrote back. *She's going to be fine except maybe have a little more trouble walking. She misses you but she knew you'd come as soon as you could. You can't imagine how it's been here. Get some sleep, see you tomorrow.*

He considered this and then deleted the last line and wrote, *I can't wait to see you tomorrow.* But she was coming because her grandmother had had a stroke. He wavered for a moment and then wrote instead, *Call if you want a lift from the station. A xxx.* When she could see his face he could make her understand that he'd had no choice but to stay in London. In those three kisses he chose to see hope.

TWENTY-SEVEN

Adam had worked straight through until 10 a.m. on Monday morning when Kristine had loaded him into a cab and sent him home. He had gone past fatigue into hyperactivity and the final few hours, making the last amendments to the affidavit advised by the barrister, had been some of the most productive of the weekend. Jonathan, overseeing him, had been pleased with the work. But when he got back to the flat the exhaustion had resurfaced and redoubled, weighing on his limbs until he felt as if he was wading through thick mud. He was asleep before he had time to eat or to call Rachel at the Royal Free or even remember to plug his phone into its charger. When his alarm went off early that afternoon he felt more exhausted than before he'd slept, but the sensation of heaviness had gone at least, and his only assignment from Lawrence had been to pop in and check on Ziva. The partners were now locked in a council of war in Tony's office. Later that day they had a call scheduled with the trustees of the pension fund and until after the call, Adam was on standby.

He arrived at the hospital just after Rachel had left it. She and Jaffa had spent the weekend at Ziva's bedside overseeing a constant stream of well-wishers – the community had mobilised, and a rota was required to manage the deliveries. If left alone, it was possible Ziva might actually be walled in behind boxes of Marks & Spencer biscuit assortments. When Adam had said he could visit her, Jaffa and Rachel had both jumped at the opportunity to go home, briefly, and cook. '*Ima* wants to make some chicken soup to bring in because the food's so disgusting, and Granny likes my brownies so I wanted to make some. I know millions of people keep dropping stuff off for her, but there's so little we can do for her that makes a difference, and nice things to eat must help,' Rachel had told him on the phone. Adam was inclined to agree. Even if the hospital meals hadn't been quite so execrable, Jaffa's chicken soup and Rachel's brownies were good enough to heal for.

Ziva had been moved up a floor, the ward sister told him when he arrived, because she was doing so well.

'I am now officially classified as geriatric,' she told him when he found her new room. 'Not that I had before delusions of youthfulness, but now it is on the door of the ward it is official. We get our own zone. It is quite an achievement, no?'

She was sounding better, but nonetheless Adam felt awkward. She wore a floral nightgown and a fleecy, royal-blue bed jacket. The nurses had washed her hair and it was combed back on her head in thin white strands, pink scalp visible in small, vulnerable patches. He had never seen her without it set into a high, proud puff around her head. She looked shrunken and her hands, resting on ruthlessly bleached hospital covers, were mottled with liver spots that he'd never noticed before. But just twenty-four hours earlier she had been speaking a strange salad of languages and slurring a little when she did remember to address them in English, whereas today her speech was laboured but clear. The difference was remarkable. He forced himself to focus on her eyes.

'How do you feel, Ziva? You look great,' he said, carefully avoiding the trailing plastic tubes as he leaned over to kiss her.

Ziva laughed weakly. 'I will not call you disingenuous because I presume that you are using the term relatively. I did not, I understand, look particularly "great" when Ashish found me. I am feeling not so bad, Adam. But still I cannot walk. They tell me maybe never. I will have to be carried in a litter like an empress.'

'Well, being treated like an empress is no more than you deserve,' he told her. In the previous cubicle the Gilberts had appropriated chairs of blue plastic from all over the ward and had lined them up at Ziva's bedside; in this room there was only one, light wood with a fraying wicker back, and it had a bag of fruit from Marks & Spencer on it. He moved the bag to the bedside table and sat down.

'Have you been sleeping?' he asked.

'*Ach*, I can sleep in the grave. For me it has been far more healing to have Ellie here.'

'Is she here?'

Involuntarily he cast an anxious glance around the small room, as if she might have escaped his notice.

'She is having a cigarette and making some phone calls. She had of course work today that she is missing. She will be back in a minute.'

'She smokes too much,' he said, with feeling.

Ziva considered this for a long time and then said very slowly, 'That is probably true, but my darling battles bigger demons than nicotine, and so if these *papirosn* keep her steady then it could be worse. She's back with us, you know. And she was gone for a long time. So everything is – whatever she needs, it is OK.'

Ziva seemed exhausted by this speech. She closed her eyes and they had been silent together for some time when Ellie came back, wearing reflective, gold-framed aviator sunglasses and holding two takeaway cups. Ziva held out a shaking hand to her and Ellie put down the drinks and went to her side, sitting down on the bed and steadying Ziva's outstretched arm in a firm clasp. Adam jumped to his feet. She hadn't called him from the station. She hadn't called him at all, though she must have been in London for hours.

Ziva grasped her granddaughter with a desperation that Adam had never seen in her. She seemed frightened, and he was ashamed of where his mind had been only seconds before.

'*Bubele*, I missed you so terribly just now. Time is doing strange things to me. Ninety years feels like its gone *chik-chak* but you go out for five minutes and already I'm missing you. Perhaps it is that one experiences time as a fraction of what one has left rather than what has gone before.'

Rachel would have squawked a protest to this, insisting that Ziva had many long years ahead of her. She never permitted Ziva to discuss mortality – her own or anyone else's. But Ellie merely said, 'Is that your own?' She had not yet looked at Adam.

'I believe it is mine. Formulated just now. Certainly it

is a new theory to me even if others have thought of it first.' Ziva looked down, watching her own hands stroking Ellie's on the thin hospital sheets.

'I think if you've started philosophising it means it's soon time to get you out of here. Too much thinking time. I brought you a hot chocolate from Starbucks.'

She turned, finally, to Adam. 'I didn't get you anything,' she said levelly, 'because I didn't know you were here.'

'No problem, I don't want anything.'

An eyebrow arched above her sunglasses. 'You don't want anything? What a painless life you must lead if there's nothing at all that you want.'

'There are very few things I want,' he said, staring at his own reflection in her glasses. He could not look away from her, nor could he stop himself from adding, 'But the things I do want, I want more than anything.'

'And what if you have to choose between those things? What if you can't have both?'

Ziva had been sipping slowly on the hot chocolate that Ellie held to her lips but her eyes moved between her two visitors, quick saccades from one to the other. When Ellie put down the cup for a moment Ziva struggled to sit up.

'What can I get for you?' Ellie asked her. She took off her sunglasses and began to look at the sides of the bed. 'There must be a button here if you want to sit up a bit more comfortably.'

'Adam must do a favour for me, a little thing, if he does not mind so much. I have on the table there a list of things that I will be needing from the house. Would you mind so much to get them for me? You have just arrived, I know, but my granddaughter will stay with me.'

Adam nodded, feeling a dull rush of disappointment that he had been dismissed without a chance to be alone with Ellie. 'Do you need them now?' he asked.

'If you please.'

There was a rap on the door and a nurse came in wearing a faintly nervous expression. Adam wondered if she was looking around for Jaffa.

'It's time Mrs Schneider had a bit of a rest, if you don't mind. She's had a real party going in here all day, haven't you, Mrs Schneider?' She spoke very loudly and cheerfully, in what Adam imagined to be the prescribed geriatric ward bedside manner. It was probably driving Ziva wild with irritation.

Ziva didn't answer but closed her eyes again. She looked very tired, and as if she was in pain.

Ellie had unpacked the fruit and arranged it on the bedside table that loomed high on its practical wheels above the bed, and was now collecting rubbish – the Starbucks cups, yesterday's newspaper, some free scratch cards and fliers that had tumbled out of a magazine – into the plastic bag. 'In that case,' she said, 'I'm going to let you rest just for an hour and pop back to the house with Adam. I've got to make sure that Rocky isn't wreaking havoc. You know what he's like when he's left alone. I'll just feed him, close him in the kitchen and come back. I'll be back really soon.'

She stroked her grandmother's cheek. Ziva exhaled heavily and nodded, but did not open her eyes. She wore an expression of defeat.

*　　*　　*

They did not speak in the car. For twenty minutes they drove in silence. They did not speak as Adam parked near Ziva's, nor as they walked down the shade-dappled path to the house. They did not speak as Ellie fumbled for the keys in the pocket of her leather jacket, opened the door and stepped inside to calm the high, threatening shriek of the alarm. And they said nothing as they came together in the dark hallway, finally, drawn into each other's arms with angry desperation, grappling and clawing like adversaries, stumbling together through the drift of denim and cotton and leather discarded at their feet and finally, finally, enfolding each other like mingled flames. There were bright spots on his vision though his eyes were closed and Adam felt himself for the first time wholly consumed, soul and blood and flesh, swallowed in the heat of her until he was only this, only now, lost for ever to everything that had been before her skin. They did not speak until they lay together, wet with sweat and Ellie's silent tears, and even then, the only word he ever spoke aloud was her name, over and over with the rhythm of her breath as again and again he bent to kiss the tiny tattooed Hebrew letter *samech* hidden beneath her left hip bone, a secret mark that he had never known was there.

TWENTY-EIGHT

'Rachel? Rachel?'

It was still early when Adam got home and he was certain that Rachel would be back at the hospital delivering the brownies. He hoped so, desperately. In that moment he could not imagine ever being alone at home with her again. There was no answer and he breathed with relief. He wanted to lie down somewhere – he had an urge to be connected to the ground; to lie on grass or in a field, but if it could not be then he wanted instead to collapse on his back on the floor of the sitting room and stretch and unfurl like a starfish. Alone, he did not feel in turmoil.

The Tupperware container of brownies was still on the table in the kitchen, however, and when he went into the sitting room he saw that Rachel was asleep on the sofa. When he came near her she blinked and smiled. She yawned loudly.

'Hi, Ads. Why are you being all formal all of a sudden?'

She sat up sleepily and began to rearrange herself, pulling down the T-shirt that had ridden up over her stomach and swirling her tousled hair into a bun.

'What do you mean?'

'Calling me Rachel.'

Adam felt suddenly, urgently ashamed. 'I – I don't know. I hadn't even thought about it.'

She lay back down again, her knees pulled up to her chest, and her hair fell across her cheek. She pushed it away. 'Mmm. I'm so tired. How's work?'

'I've not done much today since I spoke to you earlier, I'm waiting to hear from your dad. And Ziva's doing well.'

She smiled. 'She's soooo much better. She's going to be able to go home really soon, they think. She had a good sleep after you left this afternoon apparently, and then the physio tried her walking with a Zimmer frame and she could do it. Only for a minute before she got tired, but still.'

'That's such great news, Pumpkin.'

'I know, she sounded like herself again, all strong and determined all of a sudden.'

'Who was at the hospital just now?'

'Just *Ima* and me, and Ellie called and said she was on her way back and nearly there so I – just when I was leaving.' She rubbed her eyes. 'And I forgot to take the brownies back! I made them and then walked out without them – I'm so knackered. We should probably take them later.'

'Pumpkin, you've had so much on, if you're this tired let's have supper at home and you can take them in first thing instead. Jaffa's there, and your cousin.' Even her name was sacred now; he would not hex himself by speaking it aloud to Rachel. He could not go back to the hospital, obviously, nor could he allow Rachel to go. But he was surprised when she nodded.

'That's a good idea, and I think it gets a bit much for

Granny anyway, when we're all in there at once. I can't be bothered to cook, do you mind? Shall we curl up here and get a pizza?'

Rachel tipped her face up and held her arms out to him, like a toddler asking to be carried. In recent months he had begun to notice how many of these tics and mannerisms she had; had seen how a lifetime of her parents' infantilising worship had meant that her default posture was to be cute. Once he had noticed, it had been difficult to stop. His irritation had only increased, compounded by embarrassment, when he realised that her dependence and innocence had been traits that he'd once found appealing. They were deeply, intractably ingrained, but how could he have known it? When they'd met they had both been childish because they were children. More than once since they'd married he'd had to stop himself from snapping at her to talk in a normal voice, to act her age. But today he felt pity, and the same lurching vertigo he had felt when he'd left her to go to Paris. Poor, sweet Rachel. She loved him with such loyalty and such simplicity. She was so unprepared for the havoc that his betrayal could wreak in her perfect, simple life. He went to her and held her as she asked him, burying his face in her shoulder. She stroked his back.

'Poor little Ads,' she whispered. He lowered himself to sit beside her, his arms still locked around her, his face still hidden. 'Poor Ads. You've been working so hard. What a mess this all is.'

*   *   *

The claim was not going well. Lawrence had been philosophical since the hearing and did not hold out hope that they would receive very much, if anything, he told Adam as they ate bagels together in the small office kitchen. Although he remained committed to pursuing the case, Adam could see that most of his energies were diverted, in private, to finding another solution. Justice done to Ethan Goodman concerned him less than seeking justice – and reimbursement – for his own staff.

Tony had brought the bagels, having decided on the way to work that his team needed cheering sustenance. But they were from the supermarket rather than Carmelli's and there was something not quite right about them: too similar in texture to bread rolls – too light and airy, with an outside that needed very little jaw strength to penetrate. A real bagel should have a touch of India rubber about it, Lawrence had said sagely, holding up one of the impostors, and should be heavy enough to induce a soothing catatonia. Despite the chaos, Lawrence and Tony found time to argue this point for some five minutes before going back to their own offices. Adam was relieved to be at work. He was grateful to give himself over to it.

A nuzzling, cooing Rachel had climbed on top of him early that morning and, already half roused by vivid waking dreams of Ellie, he had been too weak-willed to push her off. He had spent a long time in the shower after that and had sat morose on the Tube, feeling more disgusted with himself for sleeping with his wife than he had felt the day before after sleeping with her cousin. Aware that this was staggering hypocrisy, he nonetheless resented Rachel for having sullied something. She had interposed herself, and now when he called up those private, precious moments with Ellie it was as if there were fingerprints smearing what had been inviolable.

Yesterday's dizzy elation had given way to a queasy hangover, although beneath it he felt an instinctive certainty that all between him and Ellie was as it should be. Everything else, however, was a mess.

The return date was looming. Matthew Findlay had also been put on the case and now worked quietly and steadily across from Adam, clicking the top of his pen. Until deep into the afternoon the two men read together in near silence.

A text message arrived. Adam had been completely absorbed; Ellie's name took him by surprise. All it said was, *What now?*

Kristine popped her head round the door. 'Call's been moved forward, Lawrence wants you all before the barrister rings.'

'Coming.'

He tapped quickly, *I don't know but we'll work it out. I know you have to stay near me,* and then went to join the others in the conference room.

When the meeting ended Adam went back to his desk and was checking for the tenth time whether Ellie had answered him when Lawrence came in.

'Ziva's being discharged today, she's able to go home in about an hour.'

'That's brilliant news. Do you want me to go and pick her up or anything?'

'No, that's fine, stay here, Jaffa and Rachel will take her back.'

'Is she going to be OK at home?'

Lawrence did not look convinced. 'Well, Ellie is staying with her for a bit.'

'That's a great idea!'

Adam's voice sounded high and false to his own ears. 'I mean, how brilliant for both of them that they can sort of, take care of each other. Ziva's going to need lots of hands-on help by the sounds of things and she can make sure that Ellie doesn't go off the rails again, I suppose, it might be good for her to be living with Ziva and good for Ziva to be living with Ellie. Nowhere near Marshall Bruce or his wife. So good for everyone,' he finished. He wanted to fall through the floor. For the first time in twenty-four hours he could no longer feel Ellie's skin, could not summon the shivers of pleasure that had buoyed him all day at the slightest thought of her yielding body. All he could feel was his father-in-law's comforting, familiar presence before him and the vacuum that would open between them if Lawrence ever found out the truth. Until now, his intermittent shame had taken Rachel's form. Suddenly Adam felt with equal force how profoundly he had betrayed a man who loved him.

'Is it?' Lawrence asked. When he looked at Adam, Adam felt the urge to look away. Lawrence held his eye. 'I'm not so certain that it's good for everyone.'

TWENTY-NINE

She was staying for him. He knew that she was staying for him. He knew it even before her text message arrived that morning – the one that stopped his heart with the single sentence: *Now I'll be near you*. What now? He didn't care. Whatever it was would be difficult and yet he felt sure that there was a way. A way now to see her whenever he could; maybe one day a way that he could be with her and her alone, somewhere else and always. He was walking home from the Tube station. The Jewish New Year, Rosh Hashanah, began once again that evening and she would surely be in synagogue with her family and he could sit in the men's gallery and look across at her and start the new year knowing that, however fucked up it all might be, the woman he loved loved him too. In the meantime, walking home to Primrose Hill past the bright graffiti and high, copper-green girders of the Chalk Farm footbridge he felt sick with lust and manic with possibilities. Maybe Rachel would fall in love with someone else and leave him. He almost laughed aloud at the possibility. But – wouldn't it be incredible! It would all be so easy. She could marry Dan Kirsch – no, not that *schlemiel*, someone he didn't know and couldn't picture but who nonetheless made her happy – and he could be blissfully and openly with Ellie, life would begin afresh, and when he and Ellie came to visit London from their loft in Tribeca then the four of them would have dinner in Notting Hill in an easy bohemian way while Hampstead Garden Suburb marvelled at their amicable divorce. Stranger things have happened.

And then he thought, No, actually, they haven't. That was the most improbable scenario, maybe ever, maybe in the world. It would happen when pigs, or any other earth-bound, un-kosher creature, could fly. So what? He didn't need dinner in Notting Hill. There would be a way and they would find it and right now he felt recklessly, bound-lessly joyful.

Rachel was out when he got home, which surprised him. It was already six and they had to be at synagogue at seven thirty for the *erev* Rosh Hashanah service; usually she would have been at home for hours checking her outfit, blow-drying her hair, trying different angles for her married-lady hat – this year a neat charcoal cashmere beret from Jigsaw in Brent Cross – and generally preparing herself to appear before the community.

Half an hour later he heard the key turn in the lock.

'Ads?'

'Hi, Pumpkin.' He had already changed into a suit for *shul* and was waiting in the sitting room. He got up to meet her in the hall. She looked tired. Her dark skin usually had a glow to it, as if her cheeks were lit from beneath the surface. Today she looked pale. She put down her bags and hugged him.

'Where've you been? We've got to go quite soon.'

'I know. I went to Islington to wish Ziva a *shana tova* and see how she's doing at home.'

'How is she doing? I'll go and see her tomorrow afternoon, after *shul*.'

'I sent her your love, don't worry. But she'd like to see you so that would be nice, we can both go. She's really well, she's so happy to be back at home instead of in that horrible hospital. And I had such a nice chat with Ellie.'

Adam's blood ran cold. He could almost feel it as it slowed, freezing into ribbons of ice beneath his skin. He'd never seen Ellie rattled by anything but still – the idea of the two of them alone together made him panic. 'Really?' he said.

'Yes, the lovely agency nurse was helping Ziva have a bath and so we had a really good catch-up. I've been a bit – off her, I suppose, recently, and you know I get a bit jealous, over Ziva and I suppose even my parents, too, which I know is so silly. But she is my first cousin, and I do love her. We're just different. But we really talked. It was nice to feel close to her again. I've missed her.'

'Let's go, Pumpkin. We've got to get to your parents' to light candles.'

The next day was Rosh Hashanah, the start of a new year in the lunar calendar, a time for renewals and fresh, clean beginnings. The *challah* is round instead of braided to represent a perfect cycle, and Jewish families eat sweet things – *teigelach*, tiny dough balls boiled in honeyed syrup, honey cake and apples dipped in honey, wishing for a sweet year ahead. The Day of Atonement, Yom Kippur, is ten days later and this time marks a period of re-evaluation, of repenting broken promises and of atoning for sins.

Ellie had not been in synagogue either last night or that morning. She had stayed in Islington with Ziva and no one, Adam noticed, had mentioned her. He thought it odd that neither Rachel nor Jaffa had offered to visit Ziva during either of the services so that Ellie could go to at least one but perhaps, he reasoned, they did not think she would care about honouring the festival as much as they did.

After the morning visit to *shul* all the Gilberts and Newmans had gathered for a buffet lunch at Leslie and Linda Pearl's house on South Hill Park ('just be wherever you like, stand, sit, all very casual,' Linda had greeted them at the door, though it was clear when they went into the dining room that she had been cooking for several weeks). Dominating the conversation was the question of whether Ethan Goodman was repenting for his sins (Jasper argued vociferously that it *should* be a sin to be so stupid). Taking such risks with people's futures – all agreed that it was unforgivable. Rachel worried aloud about Brooke Goodman, and the children. No one, it seemed, had been able to get hold of her and there was great concern among the community about their welfare. Adam was surprised to discover that his wife had been among those who had tried. 'Those poor things will suffer because their father was so irresponsible,' Rachel said, quietly. 'Brooke needs to be helped so that she can help them through all this.'

Michelle and Jaffa were in a particularly amicable phase and were in the kitchen together making and distributing cups of tea. Olivia was in the hall, talking to Leslie Pearl and Lawrence about the ramifications of Ethan Goodman's idiocy.

'The repercussions reach beyond those financially affected, he's done damage to the entire Jewish community,' she was saying, animated. 'It won't matter that he didn't steal, history shows us that it's enough that a Jew was involved and money was lost.' Her voice grew louder and she began to enunciate more distinctly, as if addressing an auditorium. It drove Adam wild with irritation when she slipped into lecturing mode like this, which interfered with his ability to appreciate her – usually very astute – theses. He noticed Leslie Pearl stifling a yawn as Olivia continued, 'It's a truism, of course, but that's one of the fundamental rights afforded by true freedom, the freedom to be just like everyone else. For each man to be judged as a man and not as a Jew. But we're not there yet, we still have to be *better* than everyone else just to be tolerated. That's the reality of anti-Semitism – we have to be unimpeachable. We can't be normal, be average. What a gift Ethan's misjudgement has given to all those who hate us.'

Lawrence was nodding sadly. Leslie Pearl was scanning the room behind her for the brownies.

Adam looked at his sister earnestly lecturing the two men and gesticulating. Olivia had come down from Oxford but had not brought any clothes that Michelle considered acceptable for the High Holidays and had been forced, during an argument of such screeching vigour that it reminded them both of long-ago teenage years, into a suit of Michelle's. The sharp navy tailoring was too short for her and very much too tight, but otherwise was unremarkable apart from the hiking boots she wore beneath it, scuffed brown leather decorated with Olivia's own oil-paint butterflies. She had been girdled and squeezed into her mother's clothes but nothing could be done about fitting her size-six feet into Michelle's size-three pumps. They had been late for the service and Michelle had given up. At least in synagogue the boots had been hidden behind a pew.

Adam and Rachel were sitting in one corner with Jasper and Tanya.

'In any case, you're meant to say you're sorry to the people you've wronged before God can forgive you,' Tanya was saying.

'Goodman's going to have a very expensive phone bill if he calls everyone whose pension he lost. In any case, I bet you anything they go back to America within the month. They'll have to sell the house and they won't stay here,' Jasper said with confidence, helping himself to another stuffed date. These were among Linda Pearl's specialities and had been much applauded – plump Israeli dates filled with soft, mint-green pistachio nougat. Every few moments Jaffa would come over for another one or sometimes two, with rueful jolly laughter that did not quite disguise her embarrassment. A complex dance had sprung up around these dates – Michelle, who would never have allowed anything so calorific to pass her own lips, had twice picked up the tray to offer them round; Jaffa would raise a hand in polite refusal when Michelle brought her the sweets but once the plate had been returned to the coffee table she would swoop back as subtly as she could, unable to resist.

'They shouldn't have to be banished,' Rachel disagreed. 'He made a mistake, he's not a criminal. People make mistakes. Human beings make mistakes.'

'He should be ashamed to show his face here,' said Jasper, who had no time for Rachel's show of generosity to the man who might have ruined her father. 'He should piss off back to the States as soon as he can scrounge up the money for the plane ticket. They could go to New York. I know – Rachel's cousin could introduce them to Marshall Bruce if he's looking for a new business partner. They could launch a chain of brothels. It's perfect.'

Beside him, Adam felt Rachel stiffen at the same moment that his own fists clenched with anger. Before he could answer he heard Rachel say, 'You will *not* talk about my family like that.' There was a break in her voice. Her ferocity made him turn to look at her in wonder and he saw tears brimming in her eyes. 'How dare you say that to me? You will *not* be so disrespectful about my cousin.'

'Jasper,' Tanya scolded.

'Sorry, Rach. Sorry. I didn't know that you – I mean, I was only joking. I'm sure she's got nothing to do with Marshall Bruce any more, I wasn't saying that.'

Rachel sat, white and rigid, and fumbled for Adam's hand. Jasper's apology was interrupted by Leslie and Lawrence who came over to the 'young people', as Linda Pearl insisted on calling them, to say that they were all about to set off for *tashlich* on the Heath, to atone for their sins at a corner of the Hampstead Bathing Ponds.

Lawrence looked at Rachel anxiously. 'Are you OK, poppet? You look upset.'

'I'm fine.'

She stood up and Adam, still holding her hand, stood with her.

'Let's all go and say *tashlich* now, and then I'll drop

Jaffa and Rachel at Ziva's so they can take her a honey cake and have some girls' time,' Lawrence said. There was no suggestion of the men going with them, Adam noticed, with a mixture of disappointment and relief. He desperately wanted to see Ellie and to meet her eye for just a moment of complicity or reassurance, but he also felt that it would be impossible under those circumstances not to betray their feelings.

'Jasper's going to be there till next year if he casts all his sins into the water,' said Tanya as they were putting their coats on.

From the Pearls' house they walked down towards South End Green, stopping briefly outside the Magdala pub for Rachel to check her reflection and to adjust her hat, with which she was not entirely comfortable. They carried on until they could leave the road and turn, opposite the station, into the quiet of the Heath.

When they reached the banks of the closest pond they waited, as Rachel's parents were dawdling behind, talking in low murmurs. There was already a suitor for GGP, a midsize American practice keen to expand their London offices and with the resources to take on the pension liability. What few decisions remained had to be made in the next weeks; Adam imagined that Lawrence was explaining the structure of the potential new company and the GGP partners' diminished roles within it. Lawrence and Jaffa were holding hands in a way that Adam had always thought touching and Rachel found embarrassing; Jasper and Tanya were even farther back, their heads together in an intense but less harmonious exchange. Adam suspected that Jasper was being told off for what he'd said about Ellie.

Tashlich had always been evocative for Adam – not necessarily of religious thought or of spirituality, but of his father. Until he was eighteen and had begun spending part of the High Holidays with Rachel's family he had not performed the ritual for ten years, not since Jacob had brought him here, to the Ponds, to recite it. After Jacob's death, Michelle had felt conflicted about whether she was able, with any sincerity, to talk aloud to God. Such a vulnerable, exposing action – to stand by flowing water and to ask Him to cast her sins into the depths – had felt impossible without Jacob. Michelle didn't do anything with the children that she couldn't do with honesty and she could not read the *tashlich* prayers, she once told Adam, because the only thing she ever asked God for was an explanation. Between Michelle and God, *she* was not the one who had something to apologise for. Until she'd cleared up that business between them there was nothing else to say. So they hadn't done it. They'd stayed at home and stained their good clothes counting pomegranate seeds at the kitchen table because their Sunday school teacher had told Adam that there were 613 in each pomegranate, one for each of the 613 Jewish *mitzvot*, and Olivia had said it was rubbish.

This year they stood, a little group huddled self-consciously on the balding grassy bank while joggers passed them and on either side mothers led their toddlers to throw small fistfuls of bread for the glass-eyed, red-beaked moorhens that bobbed and slid across the black pond. Jaffa linked her arm into Lawrence's and he kissed the top of her head; Leslie and Linda Pearl stood proudly behind Tanya and Jasper who had resolved their dispute and had their arms around one another, her hand resting comfortably on the plump swell of his hip. Michelle and Olivia stood behind the Pearls, shoulder to shoulder and also friends again since Michelle, picking her way across the wet grass, had conceded that Olivia's hiking boots at least had practicality to recommend them. Rachel slipped her hand into Adam's coat pocket with his and he squeezed the tips of her fingers. Lawrence began to read.

'"Who is like You, God, who removes iniquity and over-looks transgression of the remainder of His inheritance. He does not remain angry forever because He desires kindness. God will take us back in love, and He will conquer our iniquities, and He will cast off our sins into the depths of the seas. Give truth to Jacob, kindness to Abraham, like that you swore to our ancestors from long ago."'

As Lawrence spoke the words 'He does not remain angry forever because He desires kindness', Adam had watched him. He was not stooping in apology – today, Lawrence looked like a patriarch. Tall and erect in the old black overcoat that Jaffa had brushed with extra care for the occasion, Lawrence had his arm around a *zaftig* and voluble wife he worshipped, a beautiful daughter beside him listening with respect and adoration, his prayer book in his hands as he read – and Adam breathed and hoped and prayed, fervently, that Lawrence meant those words for him. You are my family now; I will not remain angry for ever. He would deserve Lawrence's anger when it came, though he did not know if he could bear it. At the wedding

Lawrence had taken him aside and had helped Adam to adjust Jacob's prayer shawl around his shoulders. He would never replace Jacob, he knew that, nor did he want to, he'd said softly, fastening the fine wool folds together with a small silver *tallit* clip – two delicate Stars of David set in deep indigo enamel shields. But Adam was his son too. We love you, he'd said. We love you like our son.

It was around the words 'God will take us back in love' that Adam understood that he would have to leave Rachel; would have to leave Lawrence and that he was losing this beautiful, precious family that he and his first love had brought into being and that would be broken by his betrayal. He could see his own father standing on the same bank, hear him reading those same words, and his sense of shame was overwhelming. This was not the man his father had wanted him to become. Now he could make it right only with honesty. He turned and began to walk away so that they would not see his face.

'Ads.'

Rachel came running after him.

'Ads. What happened? Are you OK? I know you miss him, it must be so hard. I was thinking of your dad too.' She caught up with him and grabbed his arm to slow him down. One hand was pinched at her waist as if she had a stitch. He was already at the road when she reached him; as soon as the path had turned out of sight he had begun, mindlessly, to jog. He would tell her tonight, he decided. He would tell her now.

'Let's walk back to our flat instead, we don't have to go back to my parents',' she added. They were walking together through South End Green, passing the station fruit vendor, piles of autumn apples and green punnets of blackberries arranged on flowing sheets of bright plastic grass. Adam nodded his assent.

'Rachel . . .' he started, and then fell silent again. They had reached the tiny triangular memorial park outside the hospital. Two defunct red phone boxes stood on one flank, leaning towards one another companionably. The benches were all empty. It was sitting here that Rachel had told him she hated Ellie, only days ago, it felt like another lifetime. His life had fractured as Ellie touched him – now there was only before that moment, and after it.

Rachel stopped and looked at him intently. For a moment her brow was creased and her eyes were dark and grave, and he felt certain that she could read his thoughts. But then she smiled brightly and said, 'Thank goodness Granny is out of this horrible place. And I really think that she'll be happy with the lovely agency nurse after Ellie goes.'

'But she's not going, she's staying in London.'

'No, of course she's not. Her whole life is in New York, she can't *do* anything here, and it was silly to stay away just because Marshall Bruce's wife was threatening her with something she might never even do.' Rachel shook her head with an expression that looked, to Adam, like fond exasperation that he would believe something so outlandish. 'Daddy said he will make sure that it's not too terrible for her if that woman does try to do anything with her horrible list. She's moving back next week. There was never really anything here for her to stay for.'

'I don't understand.' Adam took a step backwards away from her, away from the source of this revelation. He had a strange feeling in the pit of his stomach. 'Lawrence – your dad told me the day before yesterday that she was staying in London.'

'Mmm. I suppose then she thought she was. But when I saw her last night at Granny's house she told me she's definitely going. It's all sorted, she's booked her ticket and told Balmain and everything – she told me that the tenant in her flat there only needs a week's notice so she's leaving the day after Yom Kippur. Once she goes back there,' Rachel paused to catch the silver chopsticks that had loosened and were falling out, swept her hair up again and then continued, 'once she's in New York again I can't imagine she'll come back.'

THIRTY

She wouldn't take his calls. She wouldn't answer his messages. And she wouldn't leave Ziva's side, so there was absolutely nothing he could do about it. He sat at the kitchen table staring miserably out of the window, the pile of blue and white paper napkins that Rachel had given him still untouched. He was meant to be rolling each one round a knife and fork and heaping forty of these cutlery sausages on to an ornate Moroccan tray, but so far he had done only three. Behind him Rachel was drizzling the icing over her lemon drizzle cake and humming snatches of *avinu malkeinu*, which she'd said earlier was always stuck in her head from Yom Kippur almost until Succot. The Yom Kippur fast had just ended and any minute the doorbell would ring.

In the days between Rosh Hashanah and Yom Kippur Adam had had brief intervals of Buddha calm, when he had envisaged an almost telepathic connection with Ellie. By this means he determined that she had retreated into silence until he was free, and free to communicate honourably. So it was all better, really, better that she was safely away from London and waiting for him while he found a way to leave. And leave he would.

But he veered from these moments to far, far longer

periods of wild distraction. Because most of the time he did not feel calm, nor did he believe that nothing had changed. Most of the time he agonised over what might have caused her sudden and inexplicable silence, and why on earth she was going back to New York when her return was almost certain to bring about another cataclysmic series of revelations about her past.

Meanwhile he felt gripped by a coiled and threatening energy, battling the urge to stand outside Ziva's house and bellow and demand that Ellie come down to him. All traces of sleep disappeared, and he could not even lie still long enough to pretend. He became obsessed with the idea of standing beneath her window and each night he would prowl the flat, wild-eyed, having the same conversation with himself – Ziva had the hearing of a cat, he would set off the security lights on the path and terrify her and then get caught; in any case, Ellie's bedroom was at the back. And in truth, the problem was not to attract her attention, for he could do that in multimedia. The problem was to make her answer him.

This evening's Yom Kippur break fast at their flat, an idea that he had tried to veto without success, had now become the only bright spot on his horizon. Rachel had leapt at the chance to host her first real 'do' as Mrs Newman, though Adam had privately been troubled by the idea. What would people say when they looked back, after he'd gone? What would they think when they knew the truth? But he had been unable to offer Rachel a convincing reason not to do it, could not tell her that she would feel retroactive humiliation in this public role of happy hostess, and so it was all going ahead. Adam had the familiar sense that events were moving beyond his control.

The cake iced, Rachel had become a dervish of activity, wiping tables, arranging wine glasses, distributing bowls of mixed nuts and whipping off sheets of protective cling-film with the confidence of a performing magician.

'The bagels and the *challah* are in the oven for the moment but I don't want them to crisp so can you just keep an eye on them for a bit? And the smoked salmon is all plated up but I've left it in the fridge because I figured it should come out last. But do you think I'm right about the cheese?'

'What about it?'

Adam took his assigned place beside the oven. Now that it was happening he wanted, mawkishly but with fervour, for Rachel's break fast to be a success. He tried to remember what she'd said about the cheese.

'What I asked you before. I think it should all be room temperature, no? So I took out the Brie and the other one and put them on the breadboard on the dining table and put the grapes out already in that nice mango wood bowl that the Londons gave us. But do you think the cheese is OK?'

Adam looked at his watch. 'Yes,' he said decisively.

'Oh, good. In that case there's room for the egg and onion to stay in, and the chopped liver. Or do you think they should be out now, too?'

'In,' he said firmly. He had no opinions. But what simple relief there was in solving problems, in offering solutions. Rachel looked up from washing her hands and smiled at him, and then set off to deliver another platter to the sitting room. As she bustled past him, absorbed and purposeful, he had a sudden urge to kiss her. He bent to touch his lips quickly to her cheek but she clucked and kept moving, raising the tray of cold salmon fillets that she held and saying, 'Ads, it's heavy!' She had been zesting lemons for the cake and the scent mixed with the light citrus of her perfume.

A moment later he heard her call, 'The bagels!' and so he took them out of the oven and began to arrange them in concentric circles as he knew she liked them, in a big wicker basket. He felt utterly transfigured, and yet the surface of everything was the same. Plain, sesame, poppy seed. Plain, sesame, poppy seed. Plain, sesame, poppy seed. Ellie was flying the following morning and after more than a week of silence his desperation had begun to feel like a mania.

The doorbell rang.

The first guests were Michelle and Olivia who arrived in the midst of a heated debate about whether it had been inappropriate for Michelle to try to make a *shidduch* with her daughter and the new rabbi during the very short pause between afternoon services.

'Darling, he's perfect for you,' Michelle was saying, pausing briefly to kiss Adam hello. 'He gave a very thoughtful sermon, he's clearly an intellectual.'

'She corralled him on his way to the loo,' Olivia hissed to Adam, unwinding a violet mohair scarf from around her neck, 'it was mortifying.'

Before the front door had closed behind them Tanya and Jasper Cohen arrived with Dan and Willa London who had come straight from the Liberal Synagogue and had bumped into them in the hall. With this batch of new arrivals there were already enough people to feel celebratory and Adam saw Rachel's smile of relief as the machinery of the evening began to turn; Michelle gravitated to the kitchen to help with the final preparations and Dan, Willa, Jasper and Tanya launched unabashed into the cakes on the coffee table, with Rachel's chocolate brownies nominated as the best morsel with which to break a fast. 'Give Tanya the recipe,' Jasper bellowed, in Rachel's direction.

'We met a friend of yours,' Tanya told Adam, ignoring Jasper, 'Ezra, from New York. Zach Sabah put him in touch with Jas about helping with the accounts for a film scholarship thing he's doing. He was in London. He said he knew you.'

'Oh?' said Adam. He swallowed.

'I'm not sure Jasper liked him, to be honest, but I did. He seemed interesting. Small world, anyway,' she finished, considering him over the rim of her teacup. Adam had nothing to say to this, and nodded distractedly. He rose and returned to his post in the hall.

Linda and Leslie Pearl came next with the extended Pearls – Lawrence's GGP partner Jonathan wearing an expression that Adam recognised from Lawrence and Tony in recent days; the careworn, beleaguered look of a man whose robust natural optimism is straining beneath a load almost, almost too great to bear. This evening Jonathan was valiantly smiling, arm in arm with his South African wife Lydia, and soon afterwards Dan London's sister and parents were on the doorstep apologising for their lateness and bearing extra honey cakes that they'd popped home to collect. There was a short lull in arrivals before Aunt

Judith and Uncle Raymond appeared, each holding a caterer's disposable foil tray heaped with mini Danish pastries and *rugelach*, Aunt Judith almost hidden beneath an enormous beribboned hat. Uncle Raymond, ginger beard trimmed and marshalled for the occasion, wore the pained expression of a man who has driven half an hour from Stanmore with a car full of food that his wife hadn't allowed him to touch so they might 'break the fast with family'. It was a brave woman who would come between a fasting Uncle Raymond and a tray of *rugelach*, but Aunt Judith was equal to the task. They reported seeing Elaine and Roger Press and their daughter Louisa parking outside, although Gideon and his boyfriend Simon were not there as apparently they'd gone to Simon's family in Scotland and *apparently* Elaine was furious. Did they know – Aunt Judith leaned closer, whispering loudly beneath her hat – did they know that Louisa Press was going out with Dan Kirsch? Dan was a cardiologist now and Louisa was finishing medical school and it was a very nice match, although Uncle Raymond had had an eye on Louisa for his nephew Johnny. Hadn't Dan Kirsch been the little boy who had followed Rachel around everywhere on tennis camp? Adam accepted the foil tray from his uncle. '*Nu?* Open them, open them, this one is starving me to death,' Uncle Raymond told him, fondly patting his wife's large bottom with one hand and his own large stomach with the other, an impressive feat of coordination. 'I must eat something or I will disappear.'

The flat felt full, and cosily chaotic. The Wilsons were all on their way. Lawrence and Jaffa would be last as they had driven to Islington to collect Ziva and Ellie.

It might take a while to get Ziva in the car, Lawrence had said, and Rachel and Adam were to start without them. Adam felt as if he was watching the scene from behind glass, and his own participation seemed most alien of all. There he was, greeting Elaine Press and asking after Gideon; carrying a plate to Leslie Pearl and recommending the meringues; embracing and being embraced; shaking his head sorrowfully at yet another whisper of commiseration about the sad fate of the GGP Pension Fund. And all the while he was thinking that Ellie was on her way to him, that a second would be all it took to whisper a time and place that they could be alone together. It was extraordinary that such dissonance could exist between inside and outside; he felt almost crazed by it.

'We made it, poppet,' he heard Lawrence say behind him and he turned, his heart thudding. Ziva was between Lawrence and Jaffa, leaning on both with an expression of fierce determination. And beside them, Ellie and Rachel were hugging. Adam, moving towards them, stopped.

To reach her cousin, Ellie was bending over as if to a child, her narrow back a long arc, her eyes cast down. Though Adam stared at her she did not lift her gaze. 'You look absolutely beautiful,' he heard her say to Rachel, but could not hear the soft reply. Rachel did look lovely that night – he'd noticed it himself earlier, her cheeks flushed from the warm kitchen and her eyes bright with the anticipated pleasure of generosity, of bringing everyone she loved into her own home. She looked, he thought, like a woman who had everything. She would have enough, even without him. Ellie – with Ellie there was no promise that she would ever be fine, he knew, and it would be foolish to pretend otherwise. But he would give everything he had to make it so. She needed him – anyone could see it. And Rachel didn't. Not really.

Next to Rachel, curved and tiny and shining with health, Ellie seemed gaunt, like a spindly creature of an entirely different race. She had come in glasses that he had not known she needed, square tortoiseshell frames that emphasised the sharp angles of her face, and she wore an old sweater that he'd seen before, a huge woollen sack in funereal charcoal and black that hung off her frame in folds. If he picked her up in his arms she might fold perfectly in three, like a collapsible walking stick. And yet despite the glasses, the utter lack of adornment, she was spectacular. Her very carelessness was compelling.

Behind him he heard Jasper whispering over his shoulder, 'It shouldn't be allowed to be that hot. She's a hot mess,' and Adam gave no answer, flinching as if a fly had buzzed past his ear. He stood rooted to the ground, staring recklessly and fixedly at her face so that she would have no choice but to acknowledge him.

Jaffa surged towards him and took his face between her hands, squeezing hard. 'Ah, everything is beautiful. We will not stay long because my mother, you know, she will be very tired. But she is in good shape, no? And Ellie, she must travel very early, so just a *shana tova* to you both and we will have to go.'

'*Shana tova*, Jaffa,' he murmured. But it would not be a good year for her, he thought, and it would be his fault.

'*Shana tova, bubele*. She did a beautiful job with the

party, my girl, no? What a hostess.' Jaffa gestured around the room with a balletic sweep of her arm, a thick tube of plastic bangles clicking as she did. Her hair was a particularly bright shade of aubergine, freshly hennaed in honour of the High Holidays. 'What a hostess,' she said again. Adam nodded. He wanted her away from him, this plump, smiling aggravation of his guilt.

'She gets it from you, Jaffa,' he told her, hating himself. He cast about over her head for something to draw him away.

'Yes, this I know. The cooking I gave her, and the short-ness also, and the bust. But the beauty,' Jaffa looked across at Rachel who was offering a tray of mini bagels to the Wilsons, 'the beauty she did not get from me. That is all her own. And the goodness, that is my husband.' She turned back to Adam and looked up at him intently. 'It will be a good year for you both, I know,' she told him. It sounded like a command.

Across the room Ellie was sitting on the side of her grandmother's deep armchair, leaning towards her so that they were touching, shoulder to shoulder. Ziva reached up and gripped her granddaughter's hand, her head sinking heavily towards her chest as if its weight was too much for her. Intermittently she would speak and Ellie would lower her own head, her ear close to her grandmother's lips, never letting go of her hand. A group stood around them chatting idly, clinking teacups on saucers or forks on Rachel's treasured lace-patterned side plates, but Ellie's attention was only on Ziva. Occasionally she glanced up at someone to answer a question and then looked down again.

The throng that had formed was entirely composed of women who had never, to the best of Adam's knowledge, spoken more than two nervous words to Ellie before now. Emboldened on her last night among them and no longer able to hide their fascination, they had all flocked to her side; Elaine Press and Leonora Wilson, Linda Pearl and Tanya Cohen, all asking enviously about life in Manhattan, about her apartment and her friends and the castings she went to – questions that they would never have dared to ask her until this, their final opportunity. Later, among themselves, they would discuss Ellie Schneider's hair, her clothes, her manner; later they would remember and misre-member things she'd said. They had enjoyed watching her and her return to America was depriving them of glamour, and of someone about whom they could be comfortably scandalised. Little did they know that her return was likely to prompt yet more scandal, though they would not be able to observe it at close range.

Adam leaned in the doorway and watched. He no longer imagined that he could be alone with her before she left – it was clear that she would not leave Ziva and even if she did, the others were unlikely to leave her. But still, she could not avoid his eye for ever. All he needed was a single second to tell her that soon he would be following her. She might not even know that she needed rescuing but still, he would rescue her. They would rescue each other. 'If I was lucky enough to move to New York,' Adam heard Tanya say to Ellie with possibly the first words they'd ever exchanged, 'I'd never, ever come back here.'

Ellie did not respond but instead whispered to Ziva

who laughed, softly. Tanya, who had evidently been about to say something further, fell silent. Elaine Press took the opportunity to tell Ellie about her own recent visit to New York with Gideon and Simon, where she and the boys had gone to a service at the gay and lesbian synagogue in the West Village and someone had thought she was only fifty. Can you imagine! Lawrence, standing beside his niece, was nodding politely at Elaine's gesture-heavy anecdote and holding a plate of his daughter's spiced honey cake, untouched. What happened next was unimaginable.

Adam knew Lawrence. For fifteen years he had watched him intently at dinners, at football matches, in meetings and on holidays, in celebration and in crisis. He had studied him to learn and he had studied him to emulate. He understood him. And at that moment Lawrence looked at Adam and the world realigned. In his eyes, Adam saw that Lawrence knew.

He could not say how he'd arrived in the bedroom. Yet somehow he was there, battling to open the window and choking down sharp, cold breaths of air. Coats were piled high on Rachel's crisp, ironed sheets and on the bedside tables were two vases of blushing stargazer lilies with which Rachel had replaced their usual clutter of books and mugs, jars of moisturiser and hair clips. Her fluffy purple dressing gown, usually on a hook in the corner, had been hidden away in the closet; her fluffy purple slippers had been paired up, invisible under the bed. The room was faultlessly tidy and he felt certain that if anyone were to mistake a cupboard door for the bathroom they would find order within as well as without. His wife would have thought of everything.

Adam closed his eyes and steadied himself, leaning his cheek against the window frame. There was no longer a question of extricating himself carefully, of choosing the right time in the coming days to tell Rachel that his heart had left their marriage. Everything was different now. He might not know the whole of it – he could not know the whole of it – but somehow, Lawrence had sensed the danger. Adam knew Lawrence but Lawrence, in his turn, knew Adam. What could Lawrence think of him now? He had loved Adam devotedly, enfolding him in the warmth of his family, and Adam had repaid him by forfeiting everything. For the first time Adam understood, with a sudden bright pain, that he was not entitled to a son's unconditional love from Lawrence. His love was conditional, and it was conditional upon Adam's loving his daughter. Adam felt an irrational flush of rage, as if it had been Lawrence who had somehow deceived him. But it was momentary, and he was then gripped by a deep, sickening shame. He felt dizzy with it. He could not bear to face Lawrence again. He would have to tell Rachel tonight. He would have to go immediately. He had only to make it through the next few hours.

THIRTY-ONE

'Bye! *Shana tova!*' Rachel called from the window, waving with both hands at the last guests to leave. Uncle Raymond and Aunt Judith waved back up, and Aunt Judith raised the blue plastic freezer bag of bagels that Rachel had pressed on them at the door. Uncle Raymond was making room on the back seat for a Tupperware of chopped liver and for his wife's boat-sized hat.

Lawrence and Jaffa had driven Ziva home earlier, taking Ellie with them. Adam had not been able to bring himself to look at Lawrence again, though Lawrence had kissed him on both cheeks and had wished him, with gentle gravity, a *shana tova*. Adam had simply bent his head and nodded. He had not cried, as he'd feared he might.

And a moment after that, he had had his chance. He had watched Ellie take her jacket from Lawrence who had collected the family's coats from the bedroom, had watched her slip it over her shoulders like a cape, and hold it tightly around her by crossing her arms. After an evening of willing her to turn to him, she had turned to him, at last, in the doorway. But when she'd looked back at him he'd felt frightened. In her eyes he'd seen such sadness – and something else; something fleeting, that might have been longing, or pity.

He could hear Aunt Judith calling from the street. 'Bye, Rachel! Bye, Adam! *Shana tova*! Thank you!'

Rachel left her post at the window and sank gratefully on to the sofa, wrapping her arms around a cushion and closing her eyes.

Adam swallowed. 'Rach, are you falling asleep? Can I talk to you?'

'Oh Ads, I'm so tired, do we have to talk right now?'

He looked at her. She did seem tired; her earlier glow had gone and since her parents had left she'd seemed uncharacteristically weary. She had emerged from the bathroom in tracksuit bottoms half an hour ago, even before Uncle Raymond and Aunt Judith had begun to take their leave.

'Yes,' he said. He had stood up and paced the room but now he sat back down on the coffee table in front of her. An image of Lawrence's face swam before him and he fought to replace it with Ellie. It was easy to fill his mind with her.

Rachel struggled to sit up from between the soft cushions and wriggled a little, rearranging herself on the sofa. She had been curled in the centre but now she sat opposite him, her knees between his, a serious expression on her face. He could smell the clean citrus of her hair.

'OK. In which case I need to talk to you about something first.'

'Rachel, I—'

'Ads, I didn't fast today. I ate. At lunchtime.'

He started. Her confession was so ludicrously minor, such a grotesque contrast to the one on his own lips. He felt the bubbling of a violent, hysterical laughter. Maybe there was more, he thought wildly. Maybe she didn't fast because she's feeling too guilty about leaving me tonight for her tennis instructor, or she's going to tell me that she's a lesbian, or that she's always thought we met too young and she still loves me but thinks that we should both be free to see the world. Maybe she'll hurt me so that I don't have to hurt her. Maybe she's letting me off the hook.

Rachel leaned towards him and took his hands between both of her own and gently, with a mother's tenderness, she placed them on her stomach.

Rachel looked at him, her dark eyes joy-filled, the same trembling diamonds on her lashes that had moved him at their wedding. She flung her arms around him and he held her, numbly, shielded from her gaze in the embrace.

Something was dawning on him, swirling and tickling at the edge of his vision, something too big, as yet, for him to see in its entirety. He strained to understand. It felt like trying to see a whale from the tiny porthole of a submarine; six inches at a time. But it might not be a whale. It might be a shark. Or a cruise liner. Or a mine. Or anything at all. He caught glimpses through the miasma, but the whole evaded him. He stayed like this for several moments, his chin still on her shoulder, her arms still tight around his chest. He did not yet trust himself to speak.

Rachel pulled away, wiping the tears from her eyes.

'Big news,' she said, smiling. Then she settled back on the sofa, tucking her legs beneath herself neatly and watching his face.

'Big news,' he affirmed. Somehow he was smiling back, though his face felt frozen. Rachel picked up the cushion again and began to toy with the fringing and her movement shocked him out of his paralysis. He heard himself ask her, 'Who knows?'

Rachel flushed, twirling the little plaits of blue silk round and round her fingers. 'Oh Ads, I know I should have told you first. But I wanted to give it another week to make sure sure sure – you know these things can be – it's just so *early*. And,' she looked down at her nails, 'I guess there's just something so natural about talking to women, this instinctive thing.'

'So who,' he tried to repeat the question but it suddenly felt as if everything was moving very, very slowly, the vast bulk of something drifting in slow motion past the tiny window of his cell, 'who did you tell?'

'Well, *Ima* guessed straight away – she noticed when we were checking Granny out of the hospital two weeks ago, she could just tell, it was so strange. And so I had to tell her and I know she told Daddy although she promised she wouldn't, and Tanya and I have told each other everything since we were at school, you know we always have, and so I couldn't not. And I was so worried about Granny, I really thought she'd die, Ads, and it would have been so awful if she'd never known, God forbid, so when I went round on *erev* Rosh Hashanah I told Granny and I know it was the right thing because it made her so happy, it made her want to get well again. And then that night she was in the bath and Ellie and I were – we had such a lovely talk. And I told her then.'

And there it was. His submarine had blown into a

thousand pieces and he could see the whale – no more tiny glimpses through a window, because instead he was drowning. Ellie was leaving because Rachel had told her. And Rachel, staring at him unwaveringly though her fingers still combed idly through the fringing of the cushion, Rachel's proud, straight posture and the light of triumph in her eyes told him all the rest. It was not only Lawrence who had guessed. Tonight, in that crowded room of friendship and family and history, there had been no secrets – Tanya and Jasper and the Wilsons and Linda and Leslie and Elaine and Roger Press, and Ziva and Jaffa – they all knew, because that was how it worked. And they had all moved together like fronds of coral, to expel the predator. They were shielding Rachel. And no doubt, they thought, they were shielding Adam from himself.

PART THREE

THIRTY-TWO

They had all worked tirelessly to make it happen. It seemed extraordinary that so many people felt themselves to be a part of it; touching to see the true quotidian magnificence of the community. But there it was, and they had all moved together with the effortless choreography of lives long interwoven. It takes a village to raise a child, and the village of Temple Fortune had begun its work immediately and with diligence. Although the new owners had so far kept on all of the employees, Lawrence and the others had been forced to sell GGP for a song; given the family's altered circumstances it was agreed that, if it could be managed with sensitivity, the Gilberts ought to pay for nothing.

Linda Pearl had made a few discreet phone calls. Those who sent flowers all sent white arrangements so that they would coordinate – tall orchids or velvety roses in sprays of white baby's breath. Where possible Linda had gone further, steering those who asked towards gladiolus and lisianthus and hinting that, if they waited and sent them a few days late, the arrangements would be perfectly timed for the party. Roger Press had a cousin who owned a catering supplies website and Elaine rang Jaffa with the news that this cousin had an overstock that he was desperate to shift. All he needed was someone to collect it all, and they would actually be doing a *mitzvah*. Roger would do it, as he was popping round in any case; she believed that there were some blue and white helium balloons and canisters, a box of napkins printed with blue nappy pins, and six white ceramic cake stands, each of which had already been painted with a little blue '*mazel tov*!' No one wanted them, he'd assured her. These days everyone seemed to be having girls.

Sarah London knew someone who made rich sugar cookies, hand-iced, individually wrapped in iridescent cellophane and tied with satin ribbons. These came in assorted shapes – creamy rocking horses with curling, pale blue manes; chocolate teddy bears with coal black eyes and marshmallow-pink paws; pale lemon yellow bootees laced with lilac, and smiling storks in royal blue peaked caps, their happy bundles snuggled in white buttercream. Each of these biscuits had a designated space on which could be iced the baby's name, and the date. After some consideration Linda Pearl, who had been in the kitchen with Jaffa when Sarah London had delivered her gift, went through the box and tactfully removed the storks. It was not known whether a reference to this myth of baby-delivery would be considered profane by the *mohel*. Best to err on the side of caution. The rest were arranged in white wicker baskets, and it was hoped that the guests would take them home.

Jaffa had catered herself, of course, and would brook no contradiction. Tanya Cohen had tentatively suggested that she and the Wilson girls might like to be allowed to take care of the breakfast, to which Jaffa had drawn herself up to her full five foot two and declared that such assistance would happen over her dead body. She had been folding *bourekas*, whipping rings of chive into cream cheese, and slicing smoked salmon into ribbons since sunrise.

Outside, it showed the promise of a perfect August day. The sky was clear. In the front garden, Elaine's balloons had been tied to spokes of the trellis to form a festive arch around the front door, white and robin's egg bobbing in alternation against the starry pinwheels of pale lilac clematis that covered the house, and over everything lay a fine, gold mesh of hazy sunlight. The climbers had bloomed late; the baby had come early, and both marked a new and precious season. Tanya Cohen, idly stroking her stomach as she and Jasper circled the Gilberts' house in search of a parking space, had remarked that it had been, hadn't it, a perfect summer. Their own baby was due in December, by which time the Suburb might be muted and pillowed with snow.

Early that morning Adam had walked to Carmelli's to buy the *challah* for the *seudat mitzvah*. After the circumcision everyone would stay for breakfast, though Adam, his stomach knotted with anxiety, could not imagine his appetite ever returning. But it was a tradition to connect the joy of a new life in this world with the joy of breaking bread with family and friends. Jaffa had catered for fifty and on this occasion it was not unreasonable to assume that fifty might actually come. Michelle had offered to stop at the bakery on her way, but Adam had been insistent as it had felt, urgently, like something he had to do. He had not even really known why until he'd got there.

The gingerbread men had been on the top shelf of the display, stacked between a baking sheet of white chocolate Florentines bright with green and amber candied cherries, and on the other side a row of white paper cases filled with sweating marzipan fruit – bananas dusted with cocoa, clove-stemmed apples and rosy strawberries textured with granulated sugar. On the back wall, slotted shelves were piled with black rye, bagels freckled with sesame and poppy seeds, and yolk-washed, mahogany-dark *challot*. When he'd ordered the loaves he had found himself pointing into the glass case. 'That one, on the far left.' It was the only one with red buttons set in little pools of white icing; the others, each with three buttons, were multicoloured. This one wore only red, as he had always chosen, for Arsenal. And without knowing precisely why, he had snatched the paper bag with sudden jealousy, had dropped a twenty-pound note on the counter and had left, abruptly, without waiting for his change. Walking back to the Gilberts' house with the warm *challot* under his arm he had pressed the small bag to his face, inhaling the scent, suddenly familiar, of spicy ginger and cinnamon.

And it was then that he had started to cry. He had cried for his father, on whose lap the baby should rightfully be cradled throughout this upcoming ceremony – a grandfather's ultimate role of honour. That Lawrence would take on this and all other duties could never, Adam had finally admitted in these last months, make right that loss. He had cried for his new son, who at eight days old would endure his first trial on the path towards manhood, who was fragile and perfect, and whom he could not protect from all future suffering and from mourning his, Adam's, own death, one day. Walking through Golders Green, past the kosher cafés serving *café barad* and microwaved *bourekas*, past the Iranian grocer and Polish deli and discount factory outlets of the high street he had cried for Rachel, who he had never believed could understand his loss and so he had never honoured with his confidences. And for the first time, as though uncovering a chasm long obstructed, he had cried for himself. He had been trying since his own childhood to be a man, had tried to teach himself and had failed, sometimes spectacularly, to live up to an example he could only ever strain to imagine. For months now he had been trying to understand the seismic shifts of impending fatherhood within himself – that he would be to a tiny creature that which his father had been to him. As the weeks had passed and he had dreamed, night after night of Jacob, it had come to be the only single thing that mattered in the world. They were having a child, and the depth of that miracle obliterated everything that had ever come before.

He missed his father; missed him in ways that he'd never even had time enough with him to know. And since then he had lost his way and no one – not Michelle, not Lawrence, not Rachel, not even Ellie who he'd once believed could alleviate his loss by sharing it – no one could make it better. The only things that he could fix now were those that he himself had damaged along the way. His father should be here today and was not; Adam had been angry for almost his whole life, he realised, always doing the right thing and meanwhile raging and resentful that no one saw the magnitude of that sadness. And he had punished Rachel, because she didn't and couldn't understand. But then, he had never even let her try.

His pace quickened as he turned on to the Finchley Road. As he crossed the street beneath the railway bridge he tucked the gingerbread man into his inside pocket, its head and arms protruding as if to see out from its vantage point. He pulled his jacket closed, smoothing it down over the slight obstruction. In half an hour the house would start to fill; the community would come to celebrate with them and to learn the name that they had chosen for their little boy, as he entered into this covenant of Abraham.

It had been there, knotted and silent, for more than twenty years. But something within Adam had shifted in that moment eight days ago when he had first held his son. No one could make it better. It could not be made better. But it could be made – bearable. If not acceptable then accepted. In moving on, he had then understood, in letting go, he was taking nothing away from Jacob. Until he no longer believed it, he hadn't known he'd feared that healing meant forgetting. Instead, with the certainty of fatherhood, he now knew that by finally healing, he was honouring the man who would have raised him with generosity, if only he had lived long enough to do so.

When Adam got back to the Gilberts', Michelle and Jaffa were side by side in the kitchen in companionable silence, Jaffa creating mess, his mother, in purple rubber gloves, neatly eradicating it. Jasper and Tanya had arrived and were sitting at the kitchen table, both folding paper napkins around plastic cutlery. Adam raised a hand to them in greeting, but continued past the door into the garden. 'Did you know,' Jasper was demanding of Michelle, 'that there are opiates in breast milk?' Jasper these days was full of baby knowledge – mostly unhelpful but all enthusiastic. It seemed probable – certain, almost – that the impending Cohen daughter had been conceived of and then conceived as a result of the impending Newman son. Emulation, competition, or perhaps simply coincidence. Lucy Wilson was no doubt also trying.

Rachel had retreated to the bottom of the garden. The sun was behind the house and cast a long shadow over the lawn. At the end, two chairs were still in bright sunshine; she had turned one of these and sat with her back to the round iron table; with her back to the house. At her feet the baby slept in a carrycot, tightly swaddled in brushed blue cotton. A muslin cloth draped over the handles shaded him. Rachel's eyes were also closed, her face tipped up to the sun.

'Pumpkin,' he said. 'Rachel.'

She opened her eyes. 'Hi, Ads. Are people arriving?'

'Rachel,' he said again. She looked up at him.

Rachel had not wanted this party. She had not wanted anyone to gather at her parents' house to honour the circumcision of their son; she had wanted it done privately, in hospital and by a doctor. She had sat for days on the Internet, laptop balanced precariously on ever-dropping bump, reading about statistics, about pain relief, about techniques. Adam and Lawrence had been subcontracted to conduct similar searches and they had all eventually reached the same conclusion – that the *mohels'* experience surpassed the doctors' many hundreds of times, and it would be less traumatic, less clinical, to conduct the circumcision at home. Prince Charles, Google informed them, had been circumcised by a *mohel*. The baby could be on a lap instead of an operating table and would be soothed by tender, loving hands. Still, Rachel hadn't wanted to make it a party. It had been Jaffa's suggestion, Jaffa's wish; Jaffa's impetus.

'Is everyone here?' Rachel asked again, sitting up. She swirled her hair into a tight bun and let it fall slowly, unfurling across shoulders she was now squaring in readiness. She looked around for her shoes. One was under the seat of her chair, the other by Adam's own feet. He handed it to her.

'Thanks.'

'Not yet. Jasper and Tanya are in the kitchen, I didn't see anyone else.'

'I wish it was all over. I want everyone to go away.'

He moved the second chair so that it was next to hers and sat, heavily. 'Me too. You can take him upstairs the second it's done. Will you? We don't have to pass him around like a parcel, they can all take care of themselves.'

'He's so . . .' She was leaning down, buckling the thin strap of a bronze leather sandal. Her hair fell forward, hiding her face. 'It just seems so weird that everyone feels like this is something for all of them to celebrate. I mean, I know it's not a big deal and everyone does it in America and people keep saying it's tiny surgery and everything but to turn it into a *party*.' She shook her head, still buckling. They had had this exchange, in various forms, ever since the scan at twenty weeks had introduced them to their son. '*I* wouldn't want to go to a circumcision and then stand around eating bridge rolls.'

'People want to celebrate the baby though, I suppose.'

'I know. I'm being mean. I'm just scared for him, I'll be so happy when it's over.'

'I know,' said Adam, with feeling. 'Me too.'

Her sandals were on and she straightened, her mouth set, a slight frown creasing her brow. She was wearing one of her maternity dresses, a navy cotton wrap that tied with wide black ribbon at the waist, modest and adjustable. It had fitted her at nine months and now it fitted still, pulled only slightly tighter around a healing body still softly slackened, though contracting daily; a body remembering its tighter contours, and already no longer sore. She had rejected out of hand Jaffa's offer to pop up to Hampstead for her and pick up a new dress for today.

'Well,' she said. She reached down to brush the cream-pale cheek of the sleeping infant with her fingertips. 'Little one, there are people in there waiting to meet you.'

'The whole family's coming,' Adam added.

Rachel did not look up but still looking at the baby said, steadily, 'Not the whole family.'

Adam froze. He did not know how to reply; his blood was pulsing loud and hot in his ears. He waited a moment for it to pass and when it did not he said, 'No.'

He looked down at the top of the dark head bent over and felt tight with fear, and a powerful sensory memory of having felt a fear like this in just this way, pricking cold at the nape of his neck, many months before. It was not hard to touch it, when he chose to, nor to touch the despair that had followed. But he did not choose to, any more. He had set it aside.

'You know she's going to marry Marshall Bruce?' Rachel asked suddenly.

'Ziva told me. Do you think she really will?'

'Yes. I think so.' She paused. 'I hope she does.'

Adam remained silent, willing her to change the subject. Instead she continued.

'You know, I was just so horrified by everything about him back then, when it all first came out. But being judgemental doesn't really get you anywhere, does it? It's not real life. She's always defended him, always. And of course Ellie is unconventional but she still needs . . . you know, I know that's a funny way to see it, but he's sort of taken care of her in a way. And she needs taking care of.' She did not look at him.

Adam swallowed. 'Well,' he said, evenly, 'she went through a lot when she was younger. Loss . . .'

'Yes. But it's more than that, I mean. Because she came home and then . . .' Rachel paused, '. . . she lost other things.' She stood up and met his eye unsmiling, but without challenge. 'Other people.'

'Rach—'

'Ads, shush. Not – no, please. I just, I'm just – I think he'll take care of her.' She still held his gaze, direct and urgent. 'I want to know that someone's taking care of her. She deserves someone to do that.'

He watched her take a breath. She moved with a deliberate, slow grace; her shoulders rose and fell, her chest rose and fell. She raised her chin, tipping her face towards the sun in defiance of threatening tears. He said the only words he had.

'I think you are magnificent.'

She exhaled a quiet laugh. 'Silly.'

From the open doors the sound of voices reached them. A proud Linda Pearl could be heard admonishing Jasper with ostentatious volume, sounding scandalised by her treasured son-in-law and thereby securing him the attention she believed he deserved. Jaffa called for Ziva to sit down already, what did she think she was doing carrying that heavy teapot? Ziva's reply was inaudible and then Jasper's voice rose and there was laughter from all of them, at what was probably a circumcision joke, or one about Jewish mothers.

Rachel began to smooth the creases from her dress. 'Anyway, enough now. We should take him in. The sooner we take him in the sooner it's over with.'

'But it's all going to be fine, *he's* going to be fine.' He said this as much to reassure himself. They had said it, alternately, to one another.

'Yes, of course. He's fine. He's here. I can't quite believe it, I think. Do you ever just think – do you ever just think how lucky we are?' Her eyes were still too bright; her throat was flushed.

They stood, silently, side by side. Adam reached for her hand. For a moment both thought the same thought, quietly, about a little girl who had almost been. Seven weeks is barely a baby, barely a life; only hospital analysis had told them that there had once been a daughter. During an ultrasound one morning they had heard a healthy heartbeat, whistling and throbbing like dolphin calls, and the first blood had been that night. Adam had known about the pregnancy for six days.

It had taken strength he hadn't known he had, love he hadn't known he'd felt, to make her turn back to him. It was only the force of Adam's will; his sudden clear and urgent longing that had convinced her. And they were lucky, the obstetrician told them. It had been early; it had been swift and clean. Six weeks later was the beginning of their son.

In his carrycot the baby startled, inexplicably, shocking himself into a fleeting moment of wakeful fear that passed almost instantly into placid curiosity and then a look of utter exhaustion, a brief kaleidoscope of feeling. He yawned, gummy and hippo-wide. One eye opened, deep sapphire blue. A tiny fist shook as if in protest. They laughed.

'Kobi,' Rachel whispered. 'We have to take you in now, little one. It's going to be horrible but then it'll be over, I promise.'

She was tired, Adam could see, not simply the exhaustion of this first week's motherhood but a deeper weariness. She had a pallor in her cheeks and dark, bruise-purple shadows beneath dark eyes now often clouded with anxiety. In these last months she had begun to look older. In the sunlight there were fine lines visible on her face, tracing new worries. She had lost the innocence that had been so long preserved. He wondered if she knew that it had gone. Her lack of awareness had enraged him once yet now, sometimes, Adam found himself pitying her that lost simplicity. Life had taught her suffering. Maybe he himself had taught her suffering – he could not bring himself to pursue that line of thought. But with the sacrifice of her innocence, it was undeniable, she had bought her strength. To Adam, she had never been more beautiful.

Already in his *tallit* Lawrence stood in the doorway, squinting at the dials of the camera that hung on a fraying leather strap around his neck, where it had been for almost every hour of the last eight days. Adam had increased the resolution on all the cameras in the family so that these first portraits could be reproduced in brilliant detail, metres wide. Clear enough to preserve every nuance, every moment, every cell. Frowning in concentration Lawrence cupped his hand over the screen, anxious to be prepared. As Rachel and Adam approached, hand in hand, he looked up and Adam caught his eye. Lawrence smiled.